The Secret Society

MIKELL DAVIS

Christopher Scott Publishing Group

Published by

CHRISTOPHER SCOTT PUBLISHING GROUP
25 Fullerton Street
Boothbay Harbor, Maine 04538

www.cspublishing.com

cspublish@aol.com

Copyright   1997

Printed in the United States by

Patterson Printing
Benton Harbor, Michigan

1st Printing   1997

Edied by Victoria Lynn Scott

ISBN#   1-889149-09-8

MIKELL DAVIS

ONE

JANUARY 1980

Christopher walked into the grocery store. He was wearing a long dirty over coat, a raggedy blue scull cap, and some old worn down military combat boot's. It was the second day of January, and it had been snowing since the day after Christmas. It never snowed on Christmas but when it did snow it snowed hard.

Every outer garment that Christopher was wearing was covered with snow. As soon as he walked threw the door, he stamped the snow off of his feet, he brushed his overcoat off, then he removed his hat and shook the snow off of it. The hat was drenching but he shook the snow off and replaced it on his head. He was also wearing some raggedy gloves that he had hidden in his house. He took them off, and place them in his overcoat pocket. When he took his gloves off his hands were ice cold, and he blew them to keep them warm. It wasn't his breathe that heated his hands, as much as it was the heat in the store. His hand's were bright red from being so cold.

The grocery store's security booth was right next to the first aisle so the only way that he could shop was if he walked past them, and when he walked past he caught the security guards attention. When Christopher saw him staring he just ignored him and continued to walk. He cut a left into the first aisle and placed a few item's into the little cart he was carrying. Every time that he paused and looked down the aisle he could see the security guard following him, watching him, or walking past. It pissed him off but he tried his best to look at it as if the security guard was only doing his job. He couldn't help but wonder if the guard had followed him if he wasn't dress so shabbily.

Christopher walked down the aisle, picked up item's, and read the back to check the ingredients. Then if it was acceptable, he would place it in his cart. When he glanced down the aisle, he noticed that the guard wasn't following him. He placed a couple of item's in his jacket or pant's pockets, which ever it fit into.

This was his trick of stealing from a grocery store. Some of the items he would buy, and even use a coupon, the other's he would steal. It didn't mean anything . Grocery stores of this size made thousands of dollars a day. Him taking a little wasn't hurting anybody.

Christopher walked down to the meat aisle, and he slipped a couple of steaks down his pants. Now he had enough. His cart was full, and he had hidden as much as he possibly could in his clothing.

As soon as Christopher started heading for the register the security guard that had followed him appeared at the end of the aisle. He had done this many times before but the security guard scared him popping up at the end of the aisle.

Christopher paused, and picked up a item and acted like he was reading the ingredients like he had done to so much of the other merchandise.

The security guard laughed, and chuckled to himself. Every time someone got caught shop lifting they did something stupid. Something that made them look suspicious. The security guard just shook his head. He could walked down the aisle and approach the guy, or he could just wait down at the end of the aisle, and put the guy threw tormented hell of not knowing if he's going to be searched or not. It was a little to late to play tonight, the store was closing in a couple of minutes. The cashiers were counting their registers down, and last of the customers were in one line if their were anymore customers left.

The store was large but they only used one security guard a shift. The manager was at the door letting the last of the customers out. Once they walked out he would lock down behind them.

"Excuse me sir! The store is closing. Could you please bring your items to the front of the register?" The guard yelled.

Christopher glanced down the aisle and ignored him. After picking up a couple more items he started heading down to the register.

The security guard started walking up the aisle to where

Christopher was standing. They met close to the end of the aisle. Christopher noticed that there were only about four customers left in the store. All of the cash register's were closed except one. The cashiers at the other registers were counting their money down.

The guard grabbed Christopher's cart, and his shoulder. Christopher snatched his arm away. It seem like the guard was trying to get a grip on him.

It was late and the guard was tired. "Look man, I watched you put items in your clothing. It's late and I'm tired. I don't want to call the..."

Christopher stepped back. "I don't have anything on me ."

The guard just shook his head. They never learn do they. He was really to tired for the shit. He grabbed his walkie talkie and pressed the talk button . "Brad to the base. Please send a couple of guy's to aisle two. See what you made me do. Now, my boss is a cracker. He's gonna call the police. See, I tried to save your black ass."

Christopher stepped back a couple of feet. "Okay...Okay.... Here take this nasty ass shit." Christopher reached into his pocket, and pulled out a couple of items.

The security guard just shook his head . "Come on.... You took more shit then that. I watched you."

By the time Christopher started pulling the other shit out of his pocket, another guy showed up. He was young, about the same age as Christopher. In his last years of high school, or his first year in college. Early twenty's Christopher estimated.

"Brad's what's up? " He had the expression on his face, and the excitement in his voice where Chris could tell he was the kind that loved to ruff somebody up. Even as he was asking the question he was approaching Christopher.

"Everything is cool. He's leaving."

"Nah fuck that. I'm tired of these mother fucker's coming in here stealing." He grabbed Christopher by the arm, and started pushing him towards the door.

"Yo... You ain't got to push me. I'm leaving."

The young boy looked at Brad. "Did you search him?"

"Nah."

"Well let's take him to the back and strip search him."

Brad didn't really want to but he agreed.

"Yo man I gave ya'll everything." Christopher was pleading.

"Fuck that.... Shut up..." The young boy was not trying to hear it.

Both of them grabbed one of Christopher's arms, and they realized he wasn't as small as he appeared in the big clothing. It did'nt bother the young boy. He knew Christopher was intimidated by the way he was acting. He pushed Christopher threw the doors that lead to the meat department and the freezer. They had fucked so many people up back here that it wasn't funny.

Christopher flew threw the door and fell on his hands. When stood up and turned around to face them, he was carrying a silver snub nose 38. As soon as the young boy saw the gun his jaw dropped open. His voice didn't allow it but he mumbled. "Oh shit." Out of his mouth.

He looked Christopher in the face, and tried to conceal his fear.

Christopher looked at him. "Shut the fuck up before I shoot you in the mouth. " Christopher reached in his pocket. He was carrying a roll of electrical tape. "Brad take this tape, and tie big mouth's hands and feet up, and then place some tape of his mouth, and if you don't tie him up good, I'm gonna put a bullet in your head."

Christopher threw Brad the tape, and he went to work. Christopher placed his gun to the back of the security guards head while he tied the young cashier up. This made the security guard uneasy. He was afraid that Christopher might make a mistake, and misfire the gun.

"Why you got to place that shit at the back of my head?"

"It's in the back of your head in case one of ya'll act stupid, and I have to blast your ass."

Christopher watched as the guard tied the cashier's legs, and hands.

"Now flip him over, and wrap some of that tape over his big fucking mouth." The security guard did every thing that he was instructed to do.

"Now we're going to walk to the front, and your going to open the front door. If you even budge... I'm going to blow so many hole threw you.... You will leak for the rest of your life."

Christopher grabbed him by the arm and walk him back in the shopping area. They walked directly past the cashiers who were busy counting their registers down. None of them even looked up from what they were doing. Once the manager saw that all of the customers were gone he retreated into the managers office to finish off the necessary paper work for closing.

Christopher, and the security guard turned the corner to the entrance. When they got to the door he noticed that four men were standing outside of the door wearing mask. He unlocked the door, and the others rushed inside. The guns that they were carrying were so big it was enough to frighten security into listening.

"A, I want you to hit the managers desk with me. Bee, and Cee you guy's can hit the registers. I want this shit done fast. We only have a couple of minutes. Dee I want you to tie everybody up..... Brad will help you."

Corty gave Christopher the craziest look in the world, and then he asked the question.

"Who the fuck is Brad?"

"He is!" Christopher pointed to the security guard. Corty placed his gun in his waist band, and extended his hand out to Brad. "Nice to meet you Brad."

The others broke into laughter. Corty pulled his pistol back out of his waist band. Grabbed Brad by the arm, and walked him around the corner with the others.

The manager's booth was a small booth that separated the entrance and the exit of the supermarket. Christopher walked up to the cage where the manager was in a chair working on a machine that looked like a calculator. Punching buttons, and writing on pieces of papers that looked like receipts.

He didn't look up from his work until Christopher was dead on him. By this time Christopher had pulled his mask down, and had his gun pointed directly at the manager's face.

It took seconds for the manager to realize what was going on.

"Listen, I know you probably got some kind of button back their that can alert the police. You probably have your foot on it right now. But this is the deal. If the police come here because you alarmed them then you'll be leaving in a body bag because I don't have the time or the patience for jail."

The manager was scared to death. Christopher could see his chest heaving up and down. It wasn't until he had the managers attention that he made the announcement.

"Okay.... Everybody freeze, this is a stick up." By this time, Corty and the security guard already had all the cashiers on the floor, and was in the process of tieing them up.

Martin and Lyn were at the front of the store emptying the cash registers.

Lyn looked at Martin. "We can't use these food stamps. Should we take them?"

"Hell yeah! Didn't Zee say take every fucking thing? It's quicker... We'll sort threw the rest of this shit later."

Corty was standing next to Christopher, " A hit the door." With out another command given, Corty walked over to the door and shot the knob off. His gun let off a loud explosion sound, and several of the female cashiers started screaming. They didn't calm down until they heard the shots stop. Christopher shielded his face away from the debris. He walked over to the door, and kicked it open.

The manager was still sitting in his chair. He didn't move one inch. Christopher walked into the manager's booth. He glanced around, and saw the paper work on the desk. Then he glanced at the floor. Their was a bunch of money lying in a safe.

A was standing directly behind Christopher. Without even turning around he gave the command . "A, go get two paper bags, and tell Bee, and Cee if they're finished to get the fuck out of here. Tell Dee to come in here, and tie this mother fucker up. I want you to come back and help me fill up one of these bags, and then I want you to leave too.... You got it?"

Corty didn't even wait around to answer he was gone.

Christopher forced the manager to lie down on the floor, and then Corty came in the booth, and tied him up. It wasn't really enough room for all of them, so once Christopher stacked one of the bags, and passed it to Corty he stepped on the managers back. "Sorry."

After the others stepped out, Christopher lifted the last bag. He glanced over to the surveillance camera system in the office, and shot it. The manager jumped. They had him lying face down, and he didn't know if he was being shot at or not.

Christopher saw the light switch panel, and clicked all of the buttons the opposite way that they were going, and the lights switched off. He placed the gun in his waist band, and walked out into the shopping area of the store. The lights were not completely off. They were dim. He glanced around. Every where he looked, their was somebody tied up and stuffed some where. He smiled.

Christopher walked to the exit of the store. He was carrying the large brown paper bag. When he got outside Charlie was standing next to the phone booth pretending to be using it. He was the look out.

As soon as Christopher walked out he hung the phone up, and walked with Christopher to the get away car. He was the driver.

They jumped in the car, and pulled off. Christopher looked at his watch. "Let's get the fuck outta here. Their is a delivery truck that comes in about fifteen minutes."

"Do you still want me to make the call?"

"Yeah go ahead, fuck it."

Charles pulled over and went to a corner phone booth. He dial 9-1-1.

"Hello. Emergency dispatcher. May I help you?"

The voice on the other end was so pleasant. He often wondered who these people were. Did they look as good as they sounded. Or were they just a bunch of old hags that sounded good only on the telephone.

"Yes...... I just saw a couple of guys with masks run into the supermarket on Absecon Boulevard."

She was about to ask another question, but Chuck hung up. He jumped back into the car, and sped off. By the time they got a couple of blocks away they saw police cars with their sirens on headed towards the supermarket.

The hardest thing for Christopher to get was a safe place for them to meet. They never did find a place that they considered safe but they did find a place where they could have privacy.

Charles pulled the car up to David's pool hall. David's pool hall was located several blocks away from Pacific Avenue, and Pacific Avenue is only a block away from the boardwalk. Almost every single casino in Atlantic City was located on the board walk.

Christopher chose David's pool hall because Marc's sister dealt with David, and he hooked her up with an apartment above the pool hall. David's pool hall wasn't the safest place to meet but it had privacy, and they needed a place where they would not be interrupted. The pool hall was in an old business district. There wasn't too many stores that still operated on the block. There were two other bars on each corner that did fairly good business.

A lot of young hustler's use to sell speed, heroin, and marijuana from the pool hall but the police shut it down, and the hustlers either moved down to one of the bars on the corner, or to another location.

Now that the other dealers were gone things got pretty quiet in the area. At least at the pool hall. For years it was a gambling joint that got raided occasionally, but once the dealers started using it the police closed the pool room down.

David ran numbers, the gambling spot, sold a little bit of speed and heroin along with the other dealers that came to his establishment. He was in the process of reestablishing the gambling spot.

Chuck parked the car next to the pool hall. Christopher knocked on the door. "Chuck I want you to run up stairs get the key's, and run these cars to the projects with Marc."

Chuck hated doing the little odd jobs but he was getting paid for it, who gave a fuck. Christopher had to knock several times before the door came open. Shit there was a peep hole. Why don't these stupid mother fucker's look threw it. A few seconds after the second string of knocks, the door came open.

It was Mister David, and he had a pissed look on his face. "What the fuck is going on. You stupid young mother fuckers. Y'all got to stop running in and out of my shit."

David dressed like a bum. He had on a nasty unclean tee shirt, a dress shirt over top of that, and some seedy polyester type slacks that really didn't fit. They said in his day he was sharp, but his day must of been long ago because he never dressed nice as long as Chris could remember.

He did drive a nice car, and kept a gorgeous looking young lady. Marc's sister use to be good looking, but now she was getting fat and out of shape. She would get pregnant, and never lose the baby weight.

When her children 's father came home she did good. But this time instead of making money, he started sniffing speed, sold most of his possession which were old and out of style anyway. This time he went to jail, and left Marc's sister with nothing.

Christopher walked threw the pool hall, the smoke in the room hit him in the face. He didn't know that David had reopened the gambling spot. Their were all these older people sitting around tables playing cards. Thing's that looked like casino chips were on the table.

Mr. David grabbed Christopher 's arm. "Listen, ... If you leave, and go out of the front... Come back in the front way. Plus tell Marc to get the fuck down here.

The jukebox was in the background blaring. Christopher could barely hear him, but he understand every single word he said. He just shook his head yes. He had things to do, and business to take care of so he pulled away.

Marc's sister's apartment was up stairs at the very top of the building. The building was in terrible shape. It was late, and Christopher could hardly see up the steps.

"Damn, this looks like a good place to kill a mother Fucker." Christopher laughed. Chuck was thinking the same thing.

" This s is a fucking rat hole. No kids shouldn't have to live in this shit."

They got to the top of the steps, and knocked on the door. When the door flung open. The other guy's were already there.

Without even saying a word the group burst into laughter.

Corty shook up two bottles of champagne, and popped the corks. "Yeah". He kept screaming. "It's on."

Christopher sat his bag on the table. One of them came up to him, and place a joint in his mouth, and lit it for him. He took a deep pull, and inhaled. The weed was decent. He had better, but at least it helped him relax. He couldn't believe it either though. They had pulled it off.

Christopher picked up the bags and dumped them on the table. It was money, food stamps, and all kinds of receipts all over the table.

Christopher had to admire it himself. Their was a lot of money on the table.

"Marc did you get the rubber bands that I asked you to get?"

Marc looked at him in a sarcastic way. "Of course I did. What do you think I am a dummy?" He followed it with a smile. A trait in the future he would be known for using.

Christopher stacked the money in denominations. Then he took the money, and made one thousand dollar stacks. "Take the receipts, and the checks, and throw them in a trash can far from here Chuck."

Charles was sitting on the arm of the chair that was in front of the television. He was sipping on a bottle of wine, and pulling from a joint. He just looked up, and nodded his head yes.

It only took Christopher a couple of minutes to count the money and stack it in thousand dollar stacks. After he stacked the money up he pushed it to the side. The only thing left was a bunch of single dollar bills. He stacked them into a paper bag, and rolled the paper bag up.

Occasionally Marc's sister would come out of the room, fix herself something to drink, ask them to be quiet, and then retire back into her room. The children were asleep. She knew she should not have let her brother have his get togethers here. He was to damn disrespectful, and never listened, or did what he said he was going to do. He said a quiet little football game. She was going to curse him out when his friends left. If she could wait. If not, fuck it. He would just have to get cursed out then.

Christopher stood from the table. His neck was killing him. He started counting the stacks. A smile crossed his face. Thirty-nine thousand. He knew they were doing right by hitting the store the day after the first. Everybody in the room counted as he counted, but they didn't start to scream until he made the announcement. "Thirty-nine thousand."

Marc came over with another bottle of champagne, and popped the cork. This time instead of passing it around to drink, he poured it on Christopher, and everybody attacked Christopher with embraces, and yells of victory.

Marc's sister came out from the back. Enough was enough. "Look ya'll mother fucker's......"

Before she could start cursing. Christopher stood up , and passed her the bag full of singles. "This is for letting us have our party here."

Marc's sister opened the bag, and almost fainted, and then she looked at the table and saw all that money stacked. The first thing she thought was drugs, but the next day she learned better. The supermarket robbery was all over the paper and the news. The next morning she regretted speaking over the phone with her girlfriends, telling them about the money her little brother gave her for allowing him to have a party. Now they were calling her telling her they think he robbed that supermarket. She would just dismiss them as crazy. The singles turned out to be almost two thousand dollars.

After seeing the news she got scared. She even tried to offer half of the money back to her brother. A day later she felt a little better when the police announced that nobody was seriously hurt in the robbery. The third day she felt excellent. The police announced that they had no leads.

Christopher, Corty, Corey, Martin, Lyn, Marc, and Chuck divided the thirty nine thousand. It came out to five thousand, five hundred, and seventy dollars apiece. The only money that they had to cough up was two hundred and fifty dollars a piece. They owed that to Little Aaron for the guns. Two hundred, and fifty dollars is a lot of money for some used guns, but what are you going to do when you need it and don't have a 9 A.M. connection.

The Secret Society

Christopher and Little Aaron met at the bar that Little Aaron's father owned. Christopher and Little Aaron were the same age. They had been friends since they were children. Christopher had grown up in the project's. A nice clean one, and Little Aaron grew up in a house that the children on the block called the mini-mansion. Even though his father was a criminal he owned a lot of property in the city, and other small business. He ran Atlantic City for the Philadelphia black mafia, and they ran Atlantic City for the Italian mafia.

Every since Christopher could remember, Little Aaron had everything his little heart desired. He could be selfish, and ignorant sometimes but on a whole, he was okay. He got a long with Christopher because he thought he could boss Christopher around. He didn't know Christopher was only using him to play with his toys. A role they would play with each other for years. So when Christopher needed guns for the robbery, he stepped to Little Aaron, his best friend who had gun connections.

In the day time Little Aaron help run his fathers legal business, and at night he helped him operate his illegal businesses.

Little Aaron's father was into all kind of rackets. Anything illegal that made money. He sold heroin, speed, Marij uana , and cocaine. Every since junior high, Little Aaron was trying to convince Christopher to start selling   weed for him. Christopher thought about it but he didn't want to owe Little Aaron anything. Especially after how he acted sometimes. Forget that. It could be murderous. Big Aaron not only sold drugs, he extorted other dealers, and legal businesses. He ran numbers, operated several small illegal casino's under the protection of the Atlantic City police department. He had several of their officers on his payroll. But thing's changed after the legal gambling operations started. His crumbled. Only the lottery, and numbers operation survived. A lot of the people that use to come to his gambling joints stopped coming after the casinos came. Why risk getting caught in a gambling spot raid when you could go to the casino, and get better treatment, and not go to jail if you're caught there. After the casino's a large majority of Big Aaron 's business was narcotics.

He became filthy rich from selling heroin and speed. The cocaine business was growing but no where as strong as speed. It's white counterpart.

When Christopher walked into the bar he was surprised to find Lyn and Marc sitting at a table together. They were really close, and had hung out together since child hood. All of them were close because they grew up in the same neighborhood, or close to the same neighborhood.

They were sitting at a table with Big Aaron, and Crazy Rodney, Big Aaron's partner. They were both legends in the streets of Atlantic City. Especially Crazy Rodney. He was known for hurting people.

Christopher had the money for the guns in his pocket in an envelope. He didn't want to pass it to Little Aaron in front of his father, in case Big Aaron didn't know what was going on.

When Christopher glanced over towards Big Aaron he motioned his hand for Christopher to come over and sit. "Christopher. I saved this seat for you." Christopher wasn't scared, just a little confused. But he took the seat anyway. Little Aaron came over and sat next to him.

"Did my son tell you I wanted to talk to you?" Big Aaron asked.

Little Aaron looked at Christopher, and prayed he told him the truth.

"No..... I had to speak to him anyway, and he said he could see me today... I didn't even know you were here. I can leave, and come back if your busy......"

"Nonsense... I want to speak with you."

"Christopher you know me..... " He didn't explain himself, but Christopher understood.

"Yes . . . "

"You know what I do right.....?" He asked again.

"Yes . . "

"Well listen, and get this straight . . . . I don' t fuck with kids. You hear me? You ain't nothing but a baby to me..... My son sold you some guns right . . . . . ?" He didn't let Christopher answer. He continued.

"He sold you some guns that didn't even belong to him.....
and he didn't have my permission.... I'm going to tell you this one
time.... I know everybody, and everybody knows me... People are
talking about ya '11 robbing that fucking supermarket. If my name
comes up in this shit. I'm going to kill you... you, and you...." He
pointed to Lyn, Marc, and Christopher.

"I do not do business with children, and if you get picked up,
my name better not come up in it. Is that understood?"

Christopher never felt so uneasy in his life. If Mr, Aaron
wanted to, he could kill all of them. Christopher promised himself
he would never do business again with out carrying protection.
Even if it's with a friend.

"Where's the money for the gun's?" Christopher reached
in his inside coat pocket, and Crazy Rodney jumped. He was
about to reach for his gun when Christopher pulled out the
envelope. He laid it on the table.

Mr. Gaston picked it up. Opened the envelope, and
counted the money. "Seventeen hundred dollars. How much
money did ya'll take from the supermarket?"

Christopher was about to lie but decided against it. "Thirty
nine thousand."

Mr. Gaston showed a smile of approval. "That was good...
But the next time you come to me. If your getting something from
me. You know he doesn't own any guns don't you? "

Christopher nodded his head yes.

"Okay then, come to me next time. Because technically
you owe me. If some of those punks you did this shit with implicate
my son, do you think his lawyer is only going to want seventeen
hundred dollars?" He didn't wait for Christopher to answer.

"If one of your boys get caught and my name comes up.
I want nineteen-five for my lawyer fees." He picked the seventeen
hundred up and hit his son in the face with it. "Not including this.
Hear.. Punk thanks for risking my life with out telling me."

Christopher felt embarrassed for Little Aaron.

"You know what! My stupid ass son let you guy's cheat
me." Now they were really scared. More confused then scared.
Christopher was only worried because he was wondering what

kind of bullshit Mr. Gaston was going to come up with now.

"You guys divided up the thirty nine thousand evenly. But you used my guns. That means I was a silent partner. Where is my silent partner cut? "He paused, and started staring into the air. He was trying to figure out his cut.

"It was seven of ya'll. If you add me in, my cut comes to forty-eight and some change..... Here's what I'm going to do. You guy's really didn't know, so I'm going to let you slide. But the next time, I want in, and I want a partners cut. If I find out you did something, and didn't let me in, then I want my forty-eight hundred. . ." He looked and directed most of his conversation towards Christopher, letting him know that he knew he was the ring leader.

"Chris your a good kid but your playing with the big boy's now, and you have to pay big boy dues."

When Christopher left he did'nt know whether to feel confused, or betrayed. All the other guys sold drugs for Little Aaron. Maybe Little Aaron ran his mouth to his father with out bad intentions, and once his father learned how good they did with the robbery he got greedy, and wanted a cut. It didn't matter.

Christopher was new to this. He did'nt know if he would have given up a cut , or not. He just would have handled it how ever it rolled.

In the years to come he would learn that the small discretion was a blessing in disguise. He would need Mr. Gaston's assistance in a lot of things, and that little meeting turned out to be the beginning of their business relationship.

A relationship that would make Christopher powerful, and rich.

Two weeks after Christopher had the meeting with M. Gaston and Crazy Rodney, Little Aaron contacted him again, informing him that his father wanted to see him.

Christopher set the meeting back for another week. Now he devoted a lot of his time trying to figure out how he was going to commit his next string of robberies.

Mr. Gaston requested that the meeting would be in the morning because he usually didn't open the bar until three o'clock in the afternoon.

The Secret Society

When Christopher came this time he brought Corty, and they were both carrying pistols which their jackets consealed.

This time instead of remaining seated when he entered the room, Mr. Gaston jumped to his feet, walked over and embraced Christopher. A sign of respect.

Christopher took his seat. "Corty sit over there. I want to respect Mr. Gaston's privacy."

The statement brought a smile to Rodney and Big Aaron's face. They were impressed.

Mr. Gaston opened the meeting. "How is business going?" He already knew the answer. He had been in the robbery business when he was younger.

Christopher waved his hand in an unsteady line. "It's going okay."

Big Aaron just smiled. "I know. Christopher there's no real money in the robbery business. Plus, I watch you." He pointed his finger at Christopher. "You're too talented for the robbery business."

Christopher did not say a word. He just listened. Mr. Gaston was right.

"I want you to come over and start conducting business for me."

Christopher was still silent. He did shift in his chair. He gave Mr. Gaston his undivided attention.

"Christopher this shit I'm involved in...This shit is big, you just don't know it because that's the way I want it to be. That's the way it's got to be because of the god damned snitches. I'm a powerful man, and I want you to come over and work with me. In the beginning you can do little things. I need somebody to collect my money from these lazy ass mother fuckers. Plus, I got a group of young boys out of Philly on their way down. We're going to start extorting any hustle that's not down with me. Impose a street tax. My family is making a killing off of that in Philly. This drug shit is getting crazy, and when I turn everything over to Little Aaron, he's going to need his own family. Out of the knuckle heads he runs with, you're the only one that impresses me. You come work with me and I'll guarantee that you're going to love it. I mean I got some old heads, butnow we're too old for this drug shit. The guys I ran with got destroyed when Jersey got the lottery and casinos. Drugs are the future, and I want you down with me. If you don't want to get dirty and distribute, that's fine with me. There are a lot of other things you can do for me. It's steady pay."

Christopher didn't know if Big Aaron knew his financial situation or not, but he could not refuse the proposition based on his financial situation along. He needed the steady income.

"Mr. Gaston, ever since I got in this buisiness, my goal was to work with you and assist your son and your family. I would never disrespect you or refuse the offer."

Mr. Gaston stood up, then Christopher stood up. Christopher knew what to do without ever being told. He walked towards Mr. Gaston and embraced him.

The two me then walked towards the bar to make a toast.

TWO

Christopher took the fifty-six hundred dollars that he made, and spent it in a couple of weeks. He gave his mother a thousand dollars to pay her bills and do whatever she needed. Then he gave her another thousand dollars to put in her bank account.

When he gave her the money she complained she knew he was doing something illegal, but she also knew that he was a grown man, and their was nothing that she could really say to him that would make him stop. She felt bad accepting the money because she didn't want him to think she condoned what he was doing.

"Listen. I didn't do anything illegal. I won a couple of thousand dollars in the casino." He was so convincing that she started to believe him, or maybe she just wanted too.

"I don 't know Chris. If I find out you did anything wrong then I'm going to give you this money back."

Christopher knew the argument was a no win situation, so he just kissed her on the cheek, and left.

He took another thousand dollars. Put a down payment on a apartment, moved his things from his mothers house, and bought some little house hold items. He still had about twenty-five hundred left. He bought some clothing, and kept the rest mainly to pay bills, or to relax a little. The money gave him the opportunity to have a little fun while he planned his next robbery.

The other guys blew their money as soon as they made it. Martin and Corty went   and put down payments on two brand new cars. Corey already had a car so he put a nice system in it. He bought his mother some things, and bought himself a nice living room set.

Marc, Lyn, and Charles bought drug packages from Little Aaron. All of them sold drugs for Big Aaron except Christopher. He would have started selling eventually, but decided against it because he lived with his mother. One time a couple of years earlier when he was in high school he bought a drug package and his mother found it, and threw it in the trash. That was 'nt the part that really scared him. What scared him was that he thought she was going to put him out, but she didn't. Instead she called the police to the house, and told them what he was doing. They tried to lock him up, and put him in a drug program. Since she threw the drugs out, the only thing they could do was put him in one of the out patient drug programs and try to get him help. It was crazy. He was his mothers only child, and she could be over protective. That was his only brush with the law, but it was enough to keep him straight threw his high school years.

The robbery business is a very profitable business, but the work is not very steady, and Christopher learned this very quickly. Atlantic City was a growing industry and the opportunities seemed limitless, but everything that Christopher wanted to do was to dangerous. So instead of taking extremely risky risk he purchased six pounds of marijuana from Little Aaron.

Big Aaron had been selling drugs so long that eventually like every other dealer, the police got onto him. For several years he went threw the pattern of trying his best to change his method. He let his partners do all of the work. That worked for a while but eventually they would either fuck up by stealing, or get caught because they became hot.

The older, and wealthier Big Aaron became the farther he pushed himself away from street activity. The best thing he could do to keep his strong hold on the street was to recruit younger people and control them as much as possible. This worked, but by the time he learned this he was so much older than the crowd that was controlling the streets. It wasn't until his son reached his high school years that he was able to reestablish himself in the street. That was where his son came in. His son did all of the little business and he conducted all of the serious business. They didn't make money like when he did it himself, but they made enough for him to consider it a successful return.

Junior, the name that people close to Little Aaron called him, ran his fathers speed heroin, and marijuana business. Before the casino. His father controlled the largest black numbers operation in the area. His father owned bars and other types of property. He had connections with the black mafia organization that operated in Philadelphia. Besides drugs, his father made a lot of money by loan sharking. Most of his loan sharking customers were guys that wanted to buy drug packages. If they did'nt pay, then he would contact some people from Philly and have them come down to hurt the people that owed. Just recently he started using the guys that worked for his son. What good were they working for him if they couldn't help him out in more ways then one.

Junior sold Christopher a pound of marijuana for two hundred and fifty dollars a piece. Christopher took the weed to his new apartment and dumped it out of the one pound zip lock bags that they came in. He dumped all the weed on the table. After opening two pounds, and spreading it across the table their was no more space.

He took some scissors. Went to the local hardware store, and purchased several packs of small manilla envelopes. The envelopes we usually used to place things like nails, and stuff inside. But the dealers bought them and packaged weed in them. They sold the packet for five dollars a piece.

Christopher took the scissors, slowly picking up buds that he thought was to big to place in the manilla envelopes. He broke all of the big buds into small one's, and stuffed them into the bag. Once the two pounds were bagged up, he took a break and rolled himself several joints.

Junior came to the apartment to help him but instead of helping he jumped on the telephone, and started running his mouth. Plus he was busy. He was constantly getting calls on his voice pager. Some kind of messages where he had to return a call. He rolled a couple of the joints, and lit them while Christopher bagged the rest of the weed.

Junior told Christopher. "My father wants to talk to you. Have you ever stole a car before?" Christopher just smiled.

"No I ain't never stole a car before. Why?" He smiled to himself. Maybe they thought of him as just a petty thief.

"Cause my father's partners runs a chop shop up in Philly and he needs people to steal cars from the casino parking lot. Then run them up to Philly. You can get a couple of hundred dollars for each car. All you have to do is make my father partners."

Christopher smiled again. He thought about it. Big Aaron had go on Martin, Lyn, Corey, and Marc about doing robberies with Christopher. Even though they dealt with Junior they still were really working for Big Aaron. He never really talked to them. He usually let Junior rely the message. This time he pulled them all together.

"Why, and the fuck are ya 'll going around committing robbery's? You can't go around selling drugs, and robbing motherfuckers, it just don't mix. Keep on, and your going to end up in fucking jail." It was a warning, and advice. But Big Aaron's advice was like the law because he was a legend, and anything he said to them they considered good as gold. The only fucked up thing was, the robbery was the first time that they had seen a chunk of money that large at one time.

Christopher had earned his respect amongst them. They knew that he was going to be a future money maker.

Christopher and Lyn sat in the grey truck he purchased from a Philadelphia chop shop. The van was a plain steel colored grey cargo with nothing in the back. Not even chairs to sit on. Big Aaron had introduced Chris to the chop shop people. They wanted

Christopher to start going into the casino parking lots. Steal nice luxury cars, drive them all the way to the chop shops in Philly so that the chop shop people could change the numbers, break the car down and resell them at a extremely cheap price.

It was a tremendous money making business, and Christo pher did it. He did'nt do it for long because he could never find dependable people. Big Aaron hooked him up with a bunch of junkies. They were expert car thief's, but that was about it. Christopher treated them like babies. Which was exactly what they acted like. They would go on a casino parking lot and argue about who wanted to steal which car. Sometimes Christopher would just stare in utter disbelief. How could grown men? Grown criminals conduct business like this? Now he learned why so many criminals landed in jail. Half of the time when they were suppose to make a run Christopher couldn't find them. He would complain to Big Aaron, but Big Aaron would just brush the complaint off. Christopher did'nt know that half of the men were junkie's that owed Big Aaron a favor. They were allowed to keep half of the money that they made off of the cars, but they were also expected to pay off some of the debt they owed to Big Aaron. It could be a debt several years old. Big Aaron never forgot.

Once when Christopher went to the chop shop, Smash the short black guy that ran the place asked him why didn't he come that much.

"I can 't work with these guy's. Number one, their a bunch of junkies and number two, they don't listen."

Smash, the owner of the chop shop dismissed the junkie reference. He had been shooting heroin and speed all his life. Well most of his adult life and he still knew how to make money.

He placed his hands over Christopher's shoulders. "Listen kid. I can hook you up with some stone cold killers."It was a word that Philly people used to represent anybody that did illegal work, and did it seriously.

"I mean these boys pick pocket. Anything. Break in cars. Anything. They'll take your fucking watch off of your hand in front of your eyes, and you won't even know it. I'll talk to Will for you, and see how he feels about it."

The Secret Society

It was weird hearing him say that. Christopher had seen Big Will go down to the bar to visit Big Aaron. Big Will ran the Philadelphia black mafia. Christopher had seen his pictures in Philadelphia news papers, read articles on him, and every thing. He was a legend in the street of Philadelphia, and South Jersey. He was allegedly connected to the Italian Mafia. He was powerful. Period.

Christopher and Lyn parked the car at the back entrance of Charleston's Liquor Company, Inc. Charleston's Liquor Company was located about six miles from Atlantic City in a city called Pleasantville.

Just like Atlantic City, until the casino's came the Pleasantville was dead and void of business life. Now that the casino's came a lot of businesses that were operating in Atlantic City had moved to the Pleasantville area to build larger facilities. When they started construction on the first casino in Atlantic City, Charlestons Liquor was just a small liquor company working out of a small building in Atlantic City. With the rewards of contracts and the
casino industry constantly growing it expanded to a larger facility in Pleasantville.

With prosperity comes adversity. The owner's were under investigation for having ties with organized crime. In fact the man that owned it was alleged to be a member of the Philadelphia mafia.

The liquor company was located right off a main street nestled in the woods. Pleasantville had a lot of area's that still were not developed yet. A lot of casino's had come to the area, and build storage houses, and other facilities. Then their were other types of businesses. Like a couple of liquor plants. A couple of repair shops, but they were all hidden in the woods. The only way that you could really tell that a business was in the area was because the I was usually a sign at the beginning of the road that let you know a business was located there.

Lyn drove the truck down the end of the road. After driving a couple of seconds he saw the enormous security gate that surround Charleston liquor. Besides the facility, their were nothing but trees. Lyn pulled up as close as he could to the gate and then he backed the van up into the woods.

They had outside security camera 's on the outside of the building. He doubted that they had security camera's near the gates. Their was no need for it. Anything valuable was sitting yards away, next to the facility.

The property was enormous but that was mainly for the trucks. When Christopher took a glance he realized how many truck's they owned, he gave a whistle. He was impressed with the size of the company. The little money they were going to take now would not hurt one bit.

There was a security booth at the beginning of the gate, but it was empty. Christopher bought a small pair of binoculars and glanced threw them. Nobody in the security booth. Cool. It was stark winter, and obviously to cold for someone to be constantly standing out in the booth. That meant two things. Either they had a serious camera system, or they only used outside security when it was day light business hours.

Christopher had come a couple of days earlier just to case the place, and saw all types of luxury cars parked on the inside of the gates. Obviously the owners.

Christopher pressed the lever on the side of his seat and reclined his chair. Lyn pressed the lighter button in, and lit a joint. He was glad Christopher had started selling weed. Now he could get high for free sometimes. He was tired of spending twenty, forty, sometimes fifty dollars a day on nickels. He smoked so much sometimes, he did'nt think it even affected him anymore. He did feel funny when he wasn't high though.

Christopher and Lyn waited in the woods for a half an hour then a truck came to the gate. A few minutes after the truck came to the gate a security guard wearing a regular uniform appeared.

Tha t's why they don't stand in the booth. It was to cold for the clothing they wore. The security guard came out of the facility carrying a clip board, and a cup of coffee in the other hand. He sipped the coffee as he walked towards the booth. The security guard walked to the cab of the truck, and passed the driver the clip board. The driver must have signed it, and passed it back. The security guard walked into a booth, and punched a couple of buttons. The security gates slid open.

Christopher glanced down at his watch. It was one thirty p.m. Things were going right on schedule.

It took a couple of minutes for the security gate to open.

The liquor truck turned on it's lights, and started down the dirt path. Christopher, and Lyn ducked at the same time.

"Oh shit. I pray to God they don't see us." Christopher reclined his seat more. Lyn was about to start the truck as soon as they passed but Christopher grabbed his hand, and prevented him from putting the keys in the ignition.

"Wait one second.... We'll catch them." They both glanced over to the security booth. The guard had not left the area yet. He was walking over into the dark area as they were watching. He disappeared.

"Okay.. Now let's get the fuck outta here." Christopher took another pull off of the joint, and passed it to Lyn.

The truck drove down the Absecon Boulevard straight threw Pleasantville into Atlantic City. Christopher, and Lyn quietly tailed it.

Pleasantville is only six miles away from Atlantic City. It would have taken the truck about ten minutes to get to the city, but there was snow on the ground, and they had to drive cautiously so it took them twenty minutes. Every time the driver of the truck went to put on brakes, the truck slid a little bit. The truck went down the Boulevard and then made a left into Thelma Donaldson Bar, and Grill.

The two delivery boys pulled the delivery truck onto the bar's property. Corey and the others were sitting in front of the bar in front of an abandoned gas station that had been out of operation for several years now. They were in a white Caprice Classic that was camouflaged because of the snow.

When the delivery truck pulled up they jumped out of the sedan dressed in white winter coats that camouflaged them as well. They even had on white masks. The only way that you would notice them was the large black guns they were carrying.

They surrounded the truck and the delivery boys. The boys were so busy jumping out of the cam that they didn't even notice them until they were on the ground.

The largest one named Rocco jumped out of the driver's side. Young Italians were crazy. It was damn near zero degrees out, and the only thing Rocco and his cousin Vinnie were wearing were thin company jackets. They figured that a couple of jobs per night, the would be running in and out of bars. They were quick.

As soon as Rocco jumped out of the cam, he was greeted by Corey who was standing and pointing a sawed off double barrel shot gun in his face.

To Rocco's surprise, "Oh shit."

"That's right, put your fucking hands up."

Foolishly Rocco tried to bluff Corey.

"Fuck you."

Corey flipped the double barrel gun in the air like he was at a rodeo displaying a trick. The barrel of the gun was in his hand. He swung the gun at Rocco like he was carrying a baseball bat. The handle smashed Rocco in the mouth. His jaw cracked as he slammed to the ground.

Just as this was going down, Christopher and Lyn pulled up in the white van. Vinnie just obeyed the orders that were commanded.

Martin led Vinnie over to the door of the bar. He knocked and a man that looked exactly like a stone cold alcoholic answered the door. He didn't see Martin standing beside Vinnie.

Once the alcoholic opened the door, Martin and the others forced their way in. Christopher and Lyn immediately ran to the back. They knew there was an office there. They checked to see if anyone was hiding back there.

Mr. Davis and another alcoholic were standing behind the bar counting the register down. The only reason that Mrs. Davis let the alcoholics work for her was because they were old friends of her husbands. Micheal Donaldson Davis at one time was the man that headed the Philadelphia and South Jersey black Mafia. Before he died, he was highly respected. If he were alive today, whoever did what was happening now would have wound up dead.

Everybody in the city wondered why she was the only person to have the stupidity to put her entire name on her bar and grill. It wasn't her vanity. It was the vanity of her late husband. He was a big time number runners since the thirties. By the late sixties he was a millionaire. But he was old. Big Aaron's father use to work for him. He was the reason that Big Aaron got into the Philadelphia Black mafia. He took all of his money, and invested it into property. He had just died in the mid-seventies, at the age of seventy. His friends called him Donald. When he first came to Jersey. He was a cab driver.

Now his wife ran the liquor store. She was getting old and in her mid-sixties. But she didn't act like a liquor store owner. She acted like a sweet grandmother. Her wealth had taken care of her, she was still in shape, and she dressed very nice. She would help anybody that she thought sincerely needed it,

Everybody wondered why she still worked late hours. Why did'nt she get somebody to run the bar for her. It was because she just didn't trust anybody. She had four girls, and one boy for micheal Davis Donaldson, and they were grown living in other cities. One had moved back to Philadelphia with his family up there, and became a junkie, but the rest were doing excellent.

When the liquor truck pulled onto the bar and grill property, Lyn, and Christopher pulled up beside it. Martin, and a couple of the other guy's pulled up on it's other side.

Christopher held the meeting to divide the robbery proceeds at his apartment. His girl had moved in with him. She was pregnant and expecting their second baby. She spent most of her time in school at the local community college. Then she would go to the Shore mall. A small shopping center that was located in Egg Harbor Township. Egg Harbor Township was the city that was connected border to Pleasantville. She use to work full time but once school rolled around and the pregnancy, Christopher didn't want her working at all.

Mrs. Donaldson had seven thousand dollars in cash in the back room. Plus they got another three hundred, and some change out of the cash register.

Christopher wonder what she was doing with that type of money in the bar. It couldn't have been the receipts from one day of business. Maybe she kept the money in a safe, and didn't remove it until it accumulated to a certain amount of money.

Big Aaron had gotten the vans for them from the chop shop, and he was the one that rented the storage house in Pleasantville. For this little bit of work he would be cut in as a partner.

"What ever cash ya'll get I want half."

Christopher looked at Big Aaron like he was crazy. He was about to say it but he caught his self.

"What do you mean half?" Christopher asked. He didn't understand. Big Aaron was robbing them, and that was'nt fair. Christopher would feel like a fool asking them to cough up half of the proceeds.

"I mean if you make a dollar. I want fifty cents."

Christopher shook his head in disbelief. At first when they started doing business. Christopher was afraid to voice his opinion. After he realized that he was considered one of the top money makers, he started to voice how he felt.

"Mr. Gaston.. I can 't tell the fella's that. I mean that's not fair, and ain't nobody going to go for it. We might not even make no real money off of it."

"So what do I get then?" Mr. Gaston asked.

"A even piece of the pie."

"A even piece of the pie. What the fuck is a even piece of the pie?"

"We'll split everything in half. It's six of us not counting you. That makes seven. So off of every dollar we get we'll split it by seven."

Christopher was sitting at the table. They had already popped the bottle of champagne. He sat in front of them, and counted the money out. It was seven thousand, three hundred and twenty four dollars. Their was change in the register, but Christopher told them when they did a job forget the change. Unless it was wrapped up, and a large amount. Who the fuck wanted to rob a place, and get five hundred dollars in quarters.

After Christopher counted the money out. He bought it to everybody's attention. "See seven thousand." He picked up one of the stacks of money, and placed it in a envelope. He licked the envelope shut and placed it in his coat pocket. He didn't even have to tell anybody what it was for, they knew it was Big Aaron's cut of the profit.

" Chris." Corey threw Christopher a bunch of papers. Christopher picked them up.

"What the fuck is this?"

"I think it's the ordering sheet. It has all the prices of the boxes on it."

Christopher could do nothing but smile. "Good job."

Every single one of them were making money selling drugs, but this extra side money that they were making doing stick up's was coming in handy. The other bars were starting to make more money than King Tut's. They were getting a lot of complains on the quality of the speed. The heroin was going fine, and the marijuana mainly because it was so scarce. Whenever Christopher got competition it usually disappeared because the competition could'nt keep it. In some places cocaine powder was popping up. It didn't take a strong grasp mainly because it was to expensive. A kilo gram was about forty to fifty thousand in New York. A lot of people liked cocaine because it gave a stronger hit than speed, but the high didn't last as long as speed which was good, because most of the cocaine customers were casino employee's, and they didn't want to be at their jobs looking like space cadets. Some guy was purchasing cocaine and cutting it several times just to bring the price down. But unlike speed it couldn't take so many hit's of cut, and if you cut it too much it became garbage. So everyone stuck to selling speed.

Christopher, and a couple of the fellas went to the warehouse the next morning after the robbery. The storage house was one of those complex's where business would rent storage space. Family's would rent storage space. Their were even some people that rented space and put their second car in storage.

The storage space that Big Aaron rented for Christopher was just big enough to drive the vans in. Christopher didn't tell Big

Aaron, but he had his girlfriend rent another plot in the same establishment. The night after the robbery they went to the storage house, switched the liquor to a different plot. It was too late. Mr. Gaston had already been their, and removed a couple of the boxes.

"See that's why I don't like that greedy mother fucker. Now how and the fuck are we suppose to make money if this fat pig is drinking all the fucking liquor? He's a fucking ass hole." Marc was crazy, he always spoke his mind. The other's just laughed. They were not afraid, but they just didn't speak their mind.

"That 's cool when I see him to pay him his money. I'll tell him he has to deduct that."

Marc gave Christopher a doubting look. "I hope you do to. This mother fucker got to learn." Marc was pissed. Mr. Gaston was making money hand over foot just because he had a little connection.

Christopher and Mr. Gaston met at Mr. Gaston's bar and grill.

Christopher walked in, and their was the regular crowd. Some dealer's that Big Aaron let work out of the place. Which were a few. Two thing's would make it possible for you to work out of his bar. One, if you really knew how to make money, and two, if you were really close to Big Aaron he would let you hustle in the establishment. Occasionally if you owed him money, and he wanted to keep a tab on you then you could hustle there. Christopher had proven himself from the door. Big Aaron always told him.

"King Tut's too fucking hot. You need to come over here and start selling your weed. Don't be no dummy, and think you can make money in one place."

Christopher and Big Moe walked in. Big Aaron's partner was in their chastising some old head. They spoke and Christopher walked past straight to the office.

Big Aaron's office was straight to the back. It was the place he conducted most of his legal business if he was in the bar. Christopher knocked on the door.

"Come in." The voice inside the office said.

Christopher walked in, and Mr. Gaston was looking over the paper's from one of his apartment's.

"What's up?"

"Nothing." Christopher replied.

"We got seven thousand from the bar." Christopher reached in his pocket and passed him the envelope. "Here's your share. One thousand."

"Cool." Big Aaron had gotten the beat up van's for five hundred a piece. Now all he had to do was resell them, and everything he did was profit, The store house was about one hundred a month. He took several boxes from the van. The liquor in those boxes alone were worth a couple of hundred. He was making money with these young boy's. It was starting to seem like the good old days.

"How much is the liquor worth?"

"About a hundred grand whole sale. If we sell it half price and you tell us which bars are safe to approach we can make about fifty thousand just by cutting the price in half."

"Well I got a couple of bars in Philly that have put thousands of dollars worth of orders in already."

"Well, all you have to do is give me the word. Cause for a thousand or more we deliver." Christopher smiled.

The police might be hot on those vans. Don't use them until I check with my man down town."

Christopher didn't even mention the boxes Big Aaron took. He thought fuck it. Why argue. I'll just short him a cut of his money.

Big Aaron contacted all the bar owner's he knew on the streets. It only took two weeks and a half to distribute all the liquor. They sold liquor to almost every bar in Atlantic City except Mrs. Donaldson. More than half of the liquor was sold to bars in Philadelphia. It was a hassle but Christopher wouldn't bend. They would go to a bar in Philly that Big Aaron had contacted and the owner's would beg.

"Come on this shit is hot, and you want me to pay half of the market price. You must be fucking crazy. Fuck."

Christopher would just turn, and walk away.

Then the bar owner's would try different approaches.

"Come on fella's. I'm best friends with Will. He's going to be pissed the fuck off that you guy's charged me this much."

"We're not working with Big Will. We're with Mr. Gaston."

"I know Aaron. Is this his shit? Cause if it is, he, I, me." When that didn't work they went further. "Look why don't you guy's leave it here, and pick the money up later."

Christopher would just shake his head. "Sorry cash on delivery."

Some of the bar owners went as far as trying to stall them, or get them to come back so that they could rob them. By the end of the two weeks the liquor was gone with an overwhelming demand for it's return. Once it was gone, bar owners were calling and talking more reasonable prices.

When the two weeks were over they had divided a little under fifty-thousand dollars. Their was a future in high jacking, but it was extremely too hot in a small town like Atlantic City. Everybody was talking about the high jacking, and the police were getting tighter and tighter.

Christopher had made enough money off of the robbery that he wouldn't have to do anymore robbery's if he didn't want to. The robbery business was exciting, and very profitable, but it was also extremely risky. The word on the streets was that the police were looking for them for the robbery.

Mr. Gaston checked into it, and found out that the police didn't have any real leads. They just had some people that they wanted to question.

Christopher, Marc, Junior, Martin, and Derrick Rose were in the King Tut 's bar playing pool. This is where Christopher, and the other's conducted their business. The other bars were busy but it was pretty slow because it was winter. The Atlantic City drug flow is controlled by the casino's. Most of the drug user's worked in the casino. So if casino business was slow then street business was slow. Then you had the hard core junkie's that had to get high no matter what, but a large majority of the business was casino employee's. Winters in Atlantic City was slow for the casino's business wise, and that slowness crawled right onto the streets.

The only time that there was really business was late night

after the employee's got off of work, or the early hour right before they went to work. The weekends were always very busy.

Christopher, and the other's were at the pool table in the back playing pool. If the police were coming in then somebody at the front would usually try to give a signal. The only way that Christopher could protect himself was to stash the weed in a brown paper bag in the trash can. Once he started doing it the other guy's started doing it too. Sometimes they would confuse packages and get into arguments. Christopher came up with the suggestion that they start using different colored bags. It worked. His package never got confused because he was usually the only one with weed.

Casino employee's would come into the bar. Come straight to the back and approach Christopher. Weed was so scarce that after a couple of week's he was known as the weed man. They would come in get his attention, and just stated the number they wanted. "Give me four. Give me five."

Casino employee's always spent money. Then their were his regulars that came in, and purchased weight. Everybody complimented him on how big his nickels were. They would always ask him if he could get them quarter's and half ounces of weed. He realized that their was a lot of money in the marijuana business.

Winter was almost over, and every single day Christopher's business was picking up. He went from making five hundred a day to fifteen hundred, and this was with out spending time in bars. He needed help, and he needed it bad. By the time that March rolled around he would hire Corty just to watch his back and be a look out. Then he would eventually hire a couple other guy's that could work the day shift for him. He liked dealing from four o'clock in the afternoon until twelve at night.

Christopher and Derrick were in the back playing pool. Christopher was the only one selling weed. Everybody else was selling heroin, or speed. It was one of those night's that it was slow for everybody else but Christopher. Customer's were approaching him left and right. They would come, Derrick would give a yell out to one of the one's in the front, and they would scream back whether the coast was clear or not. Then Christopher would run to the trash can, and handle the transaction. The other guy's were at the front having drink's.

Lyn pulled up in his brand new 318i BMW. Christopher had tried to talk him out of doing it, but he couldn't. They didn't have anything better to do with their money. He traded his old car in and bought a brand new Bimmer. Lyn wasn't stupid though. He let is girl drive most of the time. The only time he had it was when the crew was going to the movie's, a concert, or some kind of event. He spent most of the money he had made off of the high jacking. He already had money from selling speed and heroin. It was known that once Lyn got on a money mission he would spend hours upon hours in the bar making money. Sometimes he even went to the park because he was cool with the older guy's that dealt in the park. The older guy's wouldn't really let anybody come in the park. One park was strictly heroin, and the other was strictly speed. Cocaine was fighting it's way onto the street corners with little success. The cheaper it became, the more that it seemed to pop up.

Lyn pulled up in front of the bar. His girlfriend, and a couple of her friends were in the car with him. He had his system blaring. Foreign cars had very load systems. His car was dark blue and he was having it customized. He had his name printed in small letter's under the door handler and he had his name printed on the leather seat's. A lot of the older guy's were into Cadillacs and Lincolns. Big American luxury cars but the foreign cars were much more sporty. Lyn had a stick shift, and he raced threw the city when ever he had his car. After he got his car the others wanted to get foreign cars.

Lyn ran straight to the back of the bar and bought four nickels of weed off of Christopher. This was light for him. He usually smoked more. His girl and all of her friends loved to smoke weed. So if he wasn't smoking he was buying some for his girlfriend.

He also had some business to conduct. His cousin Peanut was selling in the bar for him. He walked over to Lyn, and they had a few words. Lyn was just nodding his head to the music.

There were a couple of girls in the place that he was knocking off occasionally. He kissed a couple of them on the cheek. Careful not to stay too long. His girl was crazy. She was a fighter. His cousin passed him a wad of money as discreetly as possible. Lyn took his money and he bought nine ounces of speed. He decide to sell most of it in weight. Which was the street word for wholesale. He got his money, and stepped out of the bar.

As soon as Lyn stepped out of the bar he noticed the undercover detective car speed around the corner. Shit. He might be right in the middle of a drug raid on the bar. Shit. He continued to walk to his car just to play it off. Before he could get into his car, the detectives slammed on their brakes. The car slid a little and almost hit his legs. Fuck it. He ran.

The police officers that were in the first car jumped out and surrounded his brand new Bimmer. They drew their guns. "Get the fuck outta the car."

Lyn did' nt look back, but he could hear the girls screaming. Lyn cut the first corner. Then he thought about the weed and started reaching into his pocket so that he could throw it away. By the time he started reaching in his pocket, two of the officers that were chasing him jumped on his back.

Their weight slammed him into a car. He hit his head hard, and he was dizzy. The officer's started kicking and punching on him, but they had to stop because a crowd was forming.

"Get the fuck up you coward." Both of them were exhausted. This mother fucker could run.

The officer's picked Lyn up and placed handcuff's on him. They walked him back threw the small crowd towards his car. One of Lyn's eyes were black but nobody had punched him in it. He looked at his girlfriend. They had emptied her and her girlfriends bags. They dropped the content's on the hood of the car and were searching. He didn't worry about them. They would be fine. His girl had a driver license.

The officer's shoved Lyn in the back seat of one of the detective's cars. The police headed down to the police station.

"Yo what the fuck are you taking me down town for Sergeant?" Lyn did'nt know the officers ranking. He just called all of them that or detective.

The cop was just a regular detective, but he liked the title. "We're taking you down for being in a drug area."

Lyn just smirked, and got comfortable in his seat. It was going to be a long night he could tell. Hopefully they didn't get the rest of the crew.

The station was only fifteen minutes away from the bar, but they got there in five because the officer put the light on top of the car, and sped the entire way.

'Asshole's.' Lyn thought. 'These stupid mother fucker's were probably the cause of a dozen accident's'. When they got to the precinct they opened the back door and one of the officers pulled Lyn out. He fell to the ground.

"Ah my fucking leg's. I think their broke."

The officer that was pulling him paused. Walked back and stepped on his leg. "Naw it's not broke. You would have screamed louder." The other officers broke into laughter.

They took Lyn into one of those rooms that you see on television. A room with the two way mirrors. One of the detectives pulled his chair right next to the one they sat Lyn in.

"You know why your here?" The officer asked.

Lyn just looked at him. He was a young punk. "NO."

"Your here cause we're trying to help you. We got evidence on you for robbing that liquor store. We went threw all the guy's that did it with you, and we picked you to get the deal."

Lyn was confused and shocked. How the fuck did they find out. Somebody snitched.

"The deal.. Fuck you. I don't want no deal. I want my fucking lawyer."

"Listen, you been locked up before right."

"Yeah, and ?"

"And we want to help you." It was the rookie again. Lyn couldn't respect him because he looked so young. He couldn't have been older than twenty-five.

"Look, all you have to do is..." The interrogation door flew open. All of the officers were a little startled.

An elderly man walked into the room. He was wearing a

tweed vest, and nice rimless glasses, balding in the middle, but foolishly he tried to cover it by growing his hair, and tossing it over his bald scalp.

"Hi gentlemen. My name is David Briggs. I"m Mr. Lamp's attorney. I have been informed that Mr. Lamp was arrested, but when I called down here on behalf of his family I was told he hasn't been issued a bail. So I assumed. Only assuming gentlemen that he might be getting interrogated, and I'm here to inform you that I am his attorney. Lyn, as your attorney I advise you not to say another word without me present."

Lyn smiled. The attorney looked at the other officers. "Could one of you kindly retrieve me a chair. I'm old, and my back is giving out on me. It's my young girlfriend. At first I thought she wanted me only for the money." He grabbed his back, and forced himself in the chair. "I was wrong . Well gentlemen what do we have here? Are you charging my client?"

The officers looked around dumbfounded. One of them got up and stepped out of the room.

"Well. Cause if not his mother and father are on there way down here. They took off from work."

The telephone rang interrupting the lawyer. A rookie picked it up. "Yes... Okay. Cause his lawyer's here. Good I'll tell him."

Mr. Briggs looked at the officer. "Yes."

"That was the computer room. The finger print's came back negative. You're client is free."

The lawyer stood up and put his papers back into his brief case. The officers uncuffed Lyn.

Mr. Briggs noticed Lyn's eye. "Are you okay?" He grabbed Lyn face like he was a father inspecting a son's football injury.

"You sure?"

"Yeah I'm fine."

"Gentlemen if you don't mind me asking. Was this conversation recorded?"

The rookie lost his cool."Fuck you! Ask your client. We don't cooperate with lawyer's. Were not snitches."

The lawyer reached in his pocket and pulled out a card.

"Well, the next time you want to speak to my client. Here's my card call me little man." The lawyer laughed to himself.

The day after the incident the lawyer was sitting in his office. His intercom broke with his receptionist's voice.

Christopher walked threw the door. He was dressed in dress slacks and a dress shirt. He never got dressed up unless it was important. He had a meeting with Mr. Gaston. An important meeting. He walked in the office, and extended his hand.

"Are you Mr. Davis?" He asked.

The lawyer reclined in his seat. He was tired. He needed the break. So he would hold a little conversation. He grabbed his neck, and stretched.

"Yes may I help you?" He removed his glasses and cleaned them.

"How much do you charge for retainer's?"

The lawyer placed the ends of his glasses in his mouth. "A thousand dollars."

Christopher reached in his pocket and pulled out a list of people. It had ten names on it.

"Here, this is a list of people that want to retain you."

The lawyer looked over the list, and smiled until Christopher reached into his pocket and pulled out a envelope. He dropped it on the la lawyer's desk. "Here 's ten thousand. My name's the first one on the list."

The lawyer grabbed the list, and looked it over again. Then he pressed the intercom. "Betty. I'm going to need you to come in here count this money. Put it in the safe, and write this young man some receipts."

"Fine Sir. I'll be there in a second."

The lawyer was impressed. "Who referred you?" A good lawyer always wanted to know who referred his clients.

"Lennard Lamp."

"Oh Mr. Lamp. Can I fix you some coffee while your waiting for your receipts?"

Christopher looked at his watch. "Sorry, but I'm gonna have to pass. I have an appointment. Can you just send the receipt to my house. My numbers on the paper. Call my wife, and send the receipts by mail." Christopher extended his hand, and they shook, Then he got up and left. The attorney walked him to the door. Christopher walked out to Martin's car, he had just purchased a brand new eighty-one Lincoln Continental. He stood outside while Christopher went to talk to the lawyer. He looked like a bodyguard.

Mr. Davis would have laughed at them, but he looked at the envelope in his hand, and he knew. These young men were serious.

Christopher and Martin drove down the block. They did'nt have anything to do today beside the two meetings. They were on their way to the first meeting. After the police had picked Lyn up the fellas had gotten together, and decided it was time for them to get lawyers. Plus, they were going to have a meeting to see how they could better organize the bar. Things were getting sloppy over there, and they had decided maybe it was time that they all started working together.

Christopher, Martin, and Corty left the meeting together. They had gotten together in a small restaurant in Ventnor. Ventnor was the city that bordered Atlantic City on the shore side. It shared a boardwalk with Atlantic City. It didn't have business on the Ventnor side of the boardwalk. It did have beaches. Not that many blacks went to the Ventnor boardwalk. The only thing to do on that end was the beachs and blacks did'nt go to that end of the beach. They stayed in Atlantic City.

Ventnor was too small, and the police acted prejudice. They did have nice children's clothing down their, and a few small businesses. Plus they had a couple of small restaurants. Christopher, and the rest of the crew went down their and had their meeting.

Christopher asked Corty to come with him to the meeting with Big Aaron. Some how the Italian's had found out that Christopher had something to do with that high jacking. Mr. Gaston told Christopher that they wanted to talk to him.

" Christopher don't be scared. They don't know shit. They just got word on the streets that you had something to do with it. They found out that you might have had something to do with it. I told them you were with me, and you didn't have anything to do with it. So please don't go in here, and fess up. They don't know shit. Don't tell them shit." The last thing Christopher was was afraid.

When Christopher pulled up to the bar he notice Mr. Gaston's car, Crazy Moe's, Mr. Johnson's car, and two brand new Eldorado Cadillac's. It must of been the Italians. They loved Cadillacs. They were status symbols to them as well. He would have bought a gun but Mr. Gaston assured him that he didn't need one, and the Italian might feel disrespected if he bought one. Mr. Gaston told him that if he bought one please leave it in the car.

"Plus I know your not going to need one. I'm going to be there, and Big Will." The reassurance made Christopher feel safe.

Their were usually some hustler's standing out side of the bar. But Mr. Gaston must have cleared them to prevent any police scrutiny.

They parked the car directly in front of the bar. When they walked inside of the bar their was a young Italian standing guard at the door. He was wearing a blood red shirt and black slacks with some leather boot shoe's. He also had on a leather suit jacket. They were really popular with them. His gun was bulging threw his coat. He was assigned to guard the door. He frisked them as soon as they entered.

Mr. Gaston, Crazy Moe, Mr. Johnson, and one of his young bodyguards were sitting at the table. Mr. Johnson's bodyguard was wearing a lot of jewelry, and he looked very young. Their was a middle aged Italian man with a bodyguard that looked a couple of years younger than his boss. Christopher felt like a baby compared to these men, and he was correct. Compared to these men he was a baby in age, and power. But not in business. He was constantly growing. In a few years he would be just as powerful, or more powerful than these men, and they knew it. Their was another Italian standing near the exit. He was even bigger than the one at the entrance. They looked like twins.

Their was only one other seat at the table. Christopher took it. Their was a open bottle of wine at the table. Mr. Gaston introduced the two. Then the Italian reached for the bottle, and pour Christopher a glass of wine.

Christopher just looked at it. For some reason he didn't

trust it until he saw the Italian pour some of the wine in his cup and start to drink. Then he pick his up and swallowed some.

"Christopher it's a pleasure to meet you. " Even the friendly greeting rubbed Christopher wrong. Something was amiss. Now he truly regretted not bringing any protection. The Italian extended his hand again, and they shook.

"Do you know who I am?" Christopher glanced at him. He did look familiar. He looked like one of the mobsters he had seen in the paper. The man looked Christopher in the face.

Before Christopher could even answer he continued. "Well I'm family. This man here told me your like a son to him. That means your like his family. Well this man. " He pointed to Mr. Johnson. "He 's like a brother to me. He tell's me that Mr. Gaston's like a brother to him. So if he's like a brother to him, and he's's like a brother to me, and your like a son to him, we're family. Get it."

Christopher was'nt going to reply but he did. " Yes I understand."

"Listen, the word on the street is that you hit my beer truck, made off with all that liquor. That beer truck belonged to me, and some very important people. We all lost a lot of fucking money over that truck. My people were so pissed off we decided who ever did it we were going to kill. Then we got the word it was you and before we decided to take any action I decided to check up on you, and see if you were with anybody.. Big Will say 's you're his family 's son. Well that's what saved your life. You sold that wine for half it's whole sale value. Cool. That's not what pissed me the fuck off. What pissed me off was that I didn't get my cut of profit."

Christopher could have saved himself but he didn't. Mr. Gaston had told the truth. They didn't know he got a cut. That means he didn't tell them he thought that he did it, or they would be asking Big Aaron for their cut.

"Where the fuck is our money? Where's my fucking cut?"

Christopher stayed relaxed. He took a sip out of his drink. "I don't know who told you I stole that liquor but it's untrue. I don't have anything that belong's to you. If I could help you I would. Especially since where family." This was the first time that Big Aaron heard Christopher lie, and he was convincing.

"The truck that got robbed wasn't it legal. Wasn't it covered by insurance. The police will catch the guy's."

"Listen." Christopher could see the anger in his face. He looked around the room, and stopped at Mr. Johnson. "Does he understand this shit? It does'nt matter if the shit was legal, or illegal. When somebody scores big in this town we get our share. I got word from reliable people that you had something to do with it. Your lucky I got in touch with your people to see if you were somebody of importance. Cause if it was up to me. I would just split your fucking head wide open. But these people here tell me you are a good kid. But if you keep fucking me around. I'm going to fuck you up. I heard you made fifty-thousand. I'll take five grand, and we're even."

Christopher finished his liquor. "I told you, I didn't have nothing to do with it."

Before Christopher could say another word Mr. Tracco jumped over the table, and landed on him. To be a older man Mr. Tracco was strong, but Christopher was strong also, and they wrestled for a couple of seconds. Martin and Corty jumped on him because they saw the bodyguards approaching. Mr. Johnson's bodyguard jumped to his feet, and Mr. Johnson grabbed his coat. He sat back down.

They each had a grip on each other. Both of the Italian bodyguards pulled there pistols out. They placed them to back of Corty's and Martin's head. Neither budged.

"Tell this mother fucker's to back off."

Christopher looked up and signaled them to back away. They both got up and raised their hands in the air. Mr. Tracco released his grip. He was exhausted, but he didn't want to let it show.

"Listen punk. You better send one of these mother fucker's to get my money, or their not going to see you alive again. I don't want five thousand now. I want ten for the hassle.

Big Aaron walked over, and he was going to pull Mr. Tracco off of Christopher, but the Italian bodyguard pointed his gun at him.

Mr. Tracco looked up. "Mind your fucking business." He lifted Christopher to his feet. "Look, send one of these mother fucker's to get my money, and then I'll release you." He had his gun drawn. "Sally I want you to tell Paulie to bring the car around the side. Carmine stay here with him. When he brings the money, then you call me, and I'll let this young punk go."

Salvatore did'nt even respond, he rushed out of the door.

"Tell your friends to relax, and sit tight until we leave. When we leave they better haul ass, and go get my money. Once Paulie get's the money your free. But if he doesn't get it. Then I'm gonna have to teach you a lesson about street etiquette."

Christopher was embarrassed. "You heard the man. Go get the fucking money."

Anthony Tracco place the gun to Christopher's back. He pushed Christopher to the side door, and they exited. Anthony pushed the side door open, and the Cadillac was in the alley where it was suppose to be.

When the door closed. Anthony felt the double barrel place to the back of his head. He was surprised, and then he looked in the car. Where the fuck were his men.

"Drop it."

"Fuck you." Anthony replied.

"Mr. Tracco. Please. You have a gun to my back. He has a gun to the back of your head. I'M not a fool. I wouldn't kill you unless you made me. If I killed you the whole mob would be after me. Over a couple of thousand. Listen, you don't have to drop your gun. Just step away from me and I'll step away from you."

Mr. Tracco let his hand drop to his side. He was surrounded. There were cars on both ends of the alley. Christopher walked down the alley with the guy that had the gun to the back of Mr. Tracco's head. He made sure Christopher got into the car. Then he jumped in and they pulled off.

When they got a little distance Corey asked. "Why didn't yu let me kill him?"

"Cause I didn't want to cause a war. I just wanted them to know we're not fucking punks. I want everybody to know that as a family we're not nothing to fuck with. Once you drop me off. I want you to drive back, and let them know we didn't have anything to do with the robbery. But if we can help them we will."

"Do you think their going to try and retaliate?"

"Retaliate! Why we didn't do anything."

"Do you think that Big Aaron set you up?"

"NO. Hell no." It was a lie. Christopher really didn't know what to think. The only people that could have told the Italians were the bar owner's in Philly, but they really didn't know him. He didn't think that Big Aaron said anything because they could have just as easily went to him, and asked him to collect the street tax for them.

THREE

The families heroin business exploded. Big Aaron never made it official but Christopher was put in charge of the entire operation. All of the other members had say so, but what ever Christopher decided was the final word. Big Aaron had made this decision because he didn't want any conflict amongst them. He was the one that made the decision.

"Christopher's in charge of this thing. If you have any problems with him come to me. If you have any problem with anything else go to Junior, or Christopher. I do not want to be caught in the middle. Don't bother me with any nonsense."

The family set the bar up with two distribution shifts. They put four dealers in the bar for actual distribution, and then they put two look out's at the back room exit, and two look out's at the entrance. That was for the morning shift.

This new heroin was so addictive that it made the customers sick. Every morning the bar was swarming with customer's. The afternoon and the night shift were busy, but not as busy. On the night shift their were three distributors inside of the bar. One look out in the back, and one look out in the front.

The police could not break the system. As soon as a look out noticed a regular police car he alerted the other's. The other's thought that to be to cautious, but Christopher wanted it that way. He told them.

"Sometimes they'll send a regular patrol in just to see if it's busy. If it looks busy then they send the vice units." It sounded crazy, but it obviously worked because nobody ever got arrested.

The only thing that Christopher really had a hard time convincing them to do was let other hustler's come into the establishment to distribute. It was such an important issue that they had a meeting over the topic. They had the meeting in Mr. Gaston's business office at his bar.

Andre was snapping. "You mean to tell me I risk my fucking life to clean that bar out, and you want to make it open house. Your a crazy mother fucker. In Philly we kill motherfucker's for that."

"First of all, this city's ten times smaller then Philly so it's ten times hotter. The only reason I want to make the bar open house is because the police keep coming but their not making any arrest. That's why occasionally they'll put a patrol outside for hours. If they can't get us they start fucking with the customer's. Their locking customer's up."

"Fuck those junkies! So what, a junkie get's caught with a five dollar bag. He ain't gone do nothing but sit in jail, and get clean. Then want the shit even more." He laughed with his statement.

Christopher interrupted his laughter. "Or become a snitch."

"So what are they going to do put a wire on a junkie, and set one of us up for making a five dollar bag sell?"

"Listen, it's winter and we're making about ten to fifteen thousand dollars a day on the morning shift. Night shift can make anywhere between five to ten thousand dollars a night. Together that's about twenty, twenty-five thousand dollars a day. How long do you think the police are going to allow us to make money like this before they start applying direct pressure? At least if we let other dealers come, and work out of the bar. The police will have somebody else to lock up. Their going to get tired of coming to our bar making no arrest. If we corner the market then who the fuck are the police going to lock up? Right now we're making all of the money but what's going to happen if they get enough time to pick up our pattern?"

Christopher was right. If they completely cornered the market then they would be the only police target left. Which would only assure their eventual arrest.

"I'm confused. I know you ain't talking about setting nobody the fuck up."

"Aaron don't ever disrespect me like that again in your life. Coward's set people up. I have never, and I will never in my life harm another man unless he try's to harm me. If snitching is his way of harming me. I'm not going to snitch on him. I'm going to kill him." The other's just stared. It was rare to see Christopher upset.

"The only thing I'm saying is let other's distribute from the bar so that we don't catch all the heat,"

"What about the look out's? Everybody know's when they whistle that means the police is coming."

"We'll just change the code to something nobody but us understands. The other dealers will come at their own risk. We can't keep making all the money. We have to share."

When Christopher finished speaking they all looked towards Big Aaron, he had the final say so.

"Christopher is right. We got to let other people make money."

Andre wouldn't give up. "What about the other bars. Fuck that. They could go to the other bars, and make money." Christopher answered again. "The only problem with them going to other bar's is that were the strongest family." Big Aaron never made it official. Them being a family. But now that they were working together they had started using the term on their own. "And it will be nothing for them to close the other bar's down. It's all a bunch of independents The most organized place besides our bar is the park, and the only reason their organized is because of Jughead." Jughead was an older dealer that dealt from the park. He knew how to make money, and had been making money off of selling drugs for years, but he was always getting locked up for something stupid. He would come home for a year. Sometimes two, and then the police would knock him off again. Plus most of his worker's were junkies, and they were always messing up. Even Jughead got high. People on the street's were saying that he was using the new heroin, and starting to do bad. He wasn't working as many day's as he use too.

"We could just close the night shift down. That might save

us." It was just a suggestion,

"Naw, fuck that." Big Aaron was finally speaking. He was going to settle it right now. "We'll try what Christopher said first. The bar is open to any distributors, just make sure they don't benefit off of the look out, and then their dealing at their own risk. If it cut's down some of the heat, and stop's the police from putting cop's outside of the bar. Then cool."

Andre was still pissed. "Fuck that I'm telling you. Your wrong! One of them mother fucker's might get strong, and come against us."

"If the open bar doesn't work then we'll enforce a street tax. If the street tax don't work then we'll clear the bar out again, and start over again. We have the man power."

Christopher and Little Aaron were lost. Little Aaron asked the question.

"What's a street tax?"

His father answered. "A street tax is when you make some body pay you for dealing."

"Why, and the fuck will they pay us for selling."

Andre answered. "Because they will be selling in our bar. So they have to pay us."

"What if they refuse to pay?" Christopher asked.

"Then we smash them out,"

Big Aaron interrupted. "But we won't use the street tax unless we absolutely have too. The last time we did that we had a bunch of fucking snitches running around. That's the last option."

The meeting was almost over. They had to discuss a trip they were making to New York to buy some marijuana. Big Aaron's marijuana connection got messed up. Little Aaron and Christopher dealt with a guy that had connections in New York, and they were about to go check the connection out.

Big Aaron had let Mr. Johnson in on the heroin connections he had in New York. Mr. Johnson was already dealing with the Italians for the pure heroin. The only thing he needed was somebody to show him how to cut the product. Once he had that he would prevent the other's from buying from the Spanish boys.

He didn't mind that they were doing their own thing as long as he got his cut. He couldn't believe the money that they were making from the new heroin cut with morphine. Andre told him sometimes he would come, and their would be lines of customer's outside of the bar waiting to be served.

The drug scene was changing again. By the time that the New Year rolled around the speed business was starting to die. Cocaine was getting bigger every month. By the time that eighty one rolled around more, and more people started selling powdered cocaine. It didn't completely destroy the speed business like morphine heroin did to scrambled heroin, but it was running neck to neck now in distribution.

Bacause Christopher was never initiated into the family, by early eighty he was allowed to conduct side business. Besides the activity that he did for Big Aaron and Mr. Johnson.

Mr. Johnson was impressed with Christopher so much that he offered him the opportunity to do hits in Philadelphia. Christopher contemplated it for a while and promised him if it was absolutely necessary, he would do it. It was a promise that he would regret. Mr. Johnson immediately put him to work. Unfortunatly for Christopher he did not need the money. He had to many other promising opportunities.

Martin, the right hand man had a cousin named Francis Goode, he had connections with some young boys in the Bronx who sold the new heroin. It was cut with morpnine base. The new heroin cut with morphine was ten times more addictive. If you did not have the heroin after a certain amount of time, you had physical withdrawals.

The speed business was quickly being replaced by cocaine. The high from speed lasted too long. The cocaine high was stronger and it didn't last as long, it was excellent for casino emplyees who did not want their fellow emplyees knowing when they were high.

Doing hits for Mr. Johnson did have one small advantage. Christopher and Mr. Johnson established a direct relationship. Christopher convinced Mr. Johnson and Big Aaron to invest in his heroin connections. In exchange, Christopher received complete control over the other distributors. Christopher was in charge of the distribution and running daily operations. For their investments, Mr. Johnson and Mr. Gaston would become Christopher's partners, splitting whatever profits that he made.

Mr. Johnson was so impressed with Christopher, he asked him to join the family. Christopher drove to Philadelphia to see him once a week without Aaron Gaston in attendance.

Christopher and Mr. Johnson were walking in Mr. Johnson's back yard. Mr. Johnson lived in a mansion in a very exclusive neighborhood. All of his neighbors were multi-millionaires.

"Christopher, you join this family and I will let you run everything. Mr. Gaston and Moe will retire and you can run everything."

Christopher was surprised. He knew that Big Aaron would disapprove of that. After the incident with the Italians he did not trust either one of them.

"I don't know Mr. Johnson. What about Junior?" Chrisopherasked.

"Fuck Junior. This is business. You must know who the fuck I am. I run this shit."

Christopher stopped him before it went any further. "It's not that Mr. Johnson. I just don't want to make that kind of commitment yet."

"Well, don't wait too long, one of these days I'm going to ask you to join, and I'm not going to take no for an answer."

"What about Michael and Andre?" Christopher asked.

"Michael's good. He's a good kid, he listens. He knows his place. He's going to be under Aaron until he retires. Andre is a fuck up, and if his father wasn't a Lieutenant, I would have him killed tomorrow. But you and Michael, I would make Lieutenants and you could run the entire shit."

The meeting was over. Mr. Johnson was going to be busy preparing for his daughter's wedding. He told Christopher about it. "Do you believe this shit? This mother fucker asked Wilamina to marry him, but sets a fucking two year wedding date. I swear to God. I don't understand you kids."

Christopher just smiled as they walked away from the crowd of bodyguards.

FOUR

Christopher, Martin, Little Aaron, and Franklin drove in Christopher's brand new Mercedes Benz. Christopher treated himself to a brand new Mercedes Bent. The largest series they had out in eight-one. The car was beautiful. It was black with silver trimming, and black leather interior. It was brand new. He put the car in his mother's name who had excellent credit. It was so expensive that they gave her a hassle when she tried to purchase it.

He realized that he was going to have to get some kind of business so that he would have a legitimate excuse for all of this money he was making. They were building a brand new mall on the beach in front of one of the casino's. The family decided to go in it together. It would be cheaper, and cost less.

Little Aaron already had a brand new 325i BMW, and he was in the process of buying a house with his finance in Absecon, New Jersey. A small city that was about ten to fifteen miles outside of Atlantic City. The house was being build from the ground. It would be completed by June and he had intentions of getting married in June. So as soon as the house was completed he would be ready to move in with his brand new wife. His family was excited. Beside the new year arriving Junior's wedding was going to be the biggest event for the family.

All this talk of marriage had Christopher's fiance pressuring him into a date. She didn't know that he was going to set the date for July. A month after Junior's. He just didn't want their wedding's to be too close, and one to over shadow the other.

Big Aaron Gaston's marijuana connection had just gotten locked up a month earlier. Christopher told Junior to step to Franklin because Franklin was connected with some Rastafarian that operated out of New York city. If they didn't have anything, a lot of times Franklin would come to Christopher, and Christopher would take the money to Junior so that Franklin could get a deal. The price of marijuana went up, and down. For a couple of months it would be one price then a drought or something would happen, and the price would skyrocket. Or a big shipment would come in, and the price would drop. It was an up, and down business but it was profitable enough to consider the instability worth it.

The family was making so much money off of heroin that Christopher decided to step back from the weed. He turned control of the operations over to Corty. Corty was young, and quiet. Christopher turned everything over to him because the rest of the family was selling heroin, and speed.

Their was good money to be made in marijuana, but heroin, speed, and even cocaine was much more profitable. When you dealt with the other's you saw a larger profit, and the product moved about ten times faster. Especially heroin. Nothing moved faster on the streets than heroin. It was probably because of it's physical addiction. When a customer used heroin, after a couple of try's his body became physically addicted so the customer actually needed the product. That was why the morning shift was so busy. Every morning junkies were in the bar searching for their daily medicine. That night before they were probably shooting, and snorting the entire night away.

Heroin customer's were different from any other kind of customer's. Because the drug made them sick they acted crazy if they couldn't get it, or if it was bad. The customers were almost uncontrollable.

The speed customer's were similar. When they were high off of speed they acted irrational. They could not be controlled. They would be so hyped up that they did crazy things. A speed, and a heroin customer would approach you even if a cop was standing outside of your establishment.

Some morning's Christopher would come to the bar and see lines of customer's standing outside waiting for it to open. Sometimes those lines never died done, and that was why the bar was so hot. Heroin bought a lot of business especially if you were operating properly, and the way that Christopher, and the family was operating was perfect.

When Christopher passed the marijuana operations over to Corty they decided that it would be better if they moved to another bar. A bar with less police scrutiny. Keep the operations separate.

The marijuana business was completely different. Corty was able to sell a majority of the weed wholesale. Then he broke the rest down in nickel bag's. That made the most money but the wholesale went faster, and the demanded for wholesale had to be met.

Christopher would always tell him when he complained about losing profit from wholesaling.

"You have to satisfy your customer. If they want weight." The other word they used for wholesale. "Then you have to sell them weight. Plus it's much safer. You don't have to be out there as much."

Christopher, Franklin, and Junior pulled up in front of the store where the Rastafarian conducted their business. When Christopher found out that they worked out of store front's he was impressed, and he contemplated if the same thing could be done with heroin. Probably not. Heroin was much busier than marijuana traffic. The police would catch on to it.

Corty, Martin, and one of Franklin's partner's pulled up in front of the store front a couple of seconds later. Franklin agreed to turn over his connection, and in return he would be allowed to place some distributor's in the new bar that Corty was working. Christopher agreed to help him distribute some wholesale if need be. It was a business proposition that any dealer in his right mind couldn't refuse. It would stabilize his distribution, and if it didn't make him rich, he stood to make a decent amount of money.

When Christopher, and the rest of the fellas walked threw the store there were Rastafarian all over the place. There was a group of them sitting next to a large refrigerator that held beverages, and their were a couple more sitting in chairs behind a wooden, and plexi-glass counter in the back.

Franklin walked to the large metal door that separated the front and back of the store. He knocked on the door, and we heard a voice on the other end.

"Who!"

"It's me. Frankie." The rasta opened the door, and he noticed the other's standing behind Frankie.

"Who the fuck is dem?"

"These my brother's." Frankie turned around and looked back as if he was checking to make sure nobody jumped in the crowd that wasn't suppose to be there.

"Okay come in." The Rastafarian opened the door. When they walked in the back it was like another city. A cloud of smoke rushed out, and hit them in the face.

The Rastafarian gave Franklin a hug. "What's up dred?" They always called Frankie Dred, even though he wasn't Rastafarian. It was a way of showing their affections.

"I'm chilling. Where is Gad?" Gad was a name taken from one of the twelve tribes of Israel . Rastafarian believe that they are descendants of the twelve tribes of Israel; They believe that Rastafari Haile Salasie the last emperor of Ethiopia is Jesus Christ in the second coming. So once they adopt the religion they change their first names, and take a name from one of the twelve tribes. You receive your name by the month of your birth. Every month represents a tribe. Franklin didn't know Gad's birth name, he just knew he was born in the month that represented that tribe. He had been conducting business with them for a couple of years, and now they treated him like a brother.

"I ain't no where, Gad is, but me gone beep him for you." The rasta replied. Then he added. "You want a spliff?"

When he thought about it he wondered why he even asked. He knew that Franklin loved weed. Franklin introduced everybody.

The rasta that let them in walked over to the stereo. The system was playing some music by a Jamaican artist none of the guy's had ever heard before. He turned it up, and the girls that were in the back of the store constantly visiting started singing. One of them got up with the rasta guys and started dancing. Their were always people in the back of the store. Singing, dancing, and smoking.

The rasta that let them in went over to a cabinet, and

opened a cabinet draw. He pulled out a large zip lock bag. It was filled with small packet's of weed. He reached in the bag, and pulled out a little bag.

"Here. Take this bag of tie stick." As soon as he said tie stick every bodies eye's lit up. You couldn't even find tie stick in Jersey. It was rare.

Christopher reached in his pocket. "Rasta. Let me buy a couple of bags of that. Is it good."

The Rastafarian looked at him like he was crazy. "Is it good. It's excellent."

Christopher pulled one hundred dollars out of his pocket, and threw it on the table.

The Rastafarian broke out into a broad grin. Especially after the other's started reaching into their pocket's and pulled out more money.

Reuben walked into the store, he was Gad's right hand man. When ever Gad was busy, and could not make an appointment he handled the business. He was also the person that Cad trusted the most. When Reuben walked in he was with four guy's that looked like bodyguards. They were all dress in either suit's or dress clothing. Casual cloths at the least. As soon as he walked threw the door the guy's that were sitting at the tables playing cards jumped to their feet.

"What the fuck going on? You lazy mother fucker's can't find nothing better to do. Jeremiah." He screamed the name, and the young brother that was at the register immediately dropped what he was doing, and walked over to Reuben.

"What the fuck dem girls in here doing?"

Jeremiah had the dumbest look on his face. "I don't know. Dem here with Paul." He looked at Reuben, he did not want to have anything to do with it.

Reuben looked at his little brother Paul. This was just the reason he did not like to hire family. They took advantage. He stuck his finger out, and motioned Paul over.

When they got close enough to each other to whisper he spoke. "Paul what the fuck wrong with you?" His little brother felt bad about doing something he was told not to do. He looked away.

"Listen. Ain't I tell you. You fuck with she, and they burn you. Dem girls fuck with stick up boys, and they going to burn you. The next time I see them here I'm going to snap. Get them the fuck outta here."

Paul whispered something to the girls, and they put their jackets on, and left. He probably made up some kind of excuse.

Franklin waited for Reuben to finish talking, and then he approached them. When he approached them they hugged.

"What's up Rasta?"

Reuben replied. "Nothing dred." They called anybody dred. It was just a figure of speech with them.

"Where are your people?" Franklin pointed to everybody that had come with him. By this time they were sitting at tables playing cards, or smoking weed looking at the television that was set up in the back.

"Gad waiting for us. You driving?"

"Yeah we're driving."

"Come on then. We gone hold the meeting at the apartment."

Reuben, and the four guy's that were with him. Franklin, and the rest of the family walked out of the store. Reuben walked over to his car. It was a eighty silver gray jaguar. He had silver factory rims put on it, and one of those top of the line stereo systems inside. The car was beautiful. Silver was his favorite color. He was going to keep the car for a year, and then trade it in for something new. He would never keep a car for more than a year, or two. The window's were tinted, and you could not see the interior.

Reuben looked at Franklin. "Frank you drive with me, and will let them follow." They both jumped into the car but they did not pull off until he knew that everyone was ready to move.

"So what's up brother?" Reuben asked. He had been doing business with Franklin for years, and he had their absolute trust.

"Ah just chilling."

"How is Jersey treating you?"

"It's treating me good but it can always be better."

"What's up with these guy's?"

"Who? The guy's with me? They good people. They get money. Plus their straight up. I wouldn't bring them if their were not straight up."

Reuben looked at him. He misunderstood the question. He did not mean were they straight up. He was just being nosy, and wanted to know if they were spending any real money.

"They got money?"

"Hell yeah! There coming to spend dough."

Reuben just listened. That's all he wanted to know. He pressed the lighter in his car in, and lit a joint. He passed the joint to Franklin but he warned him first.

"Be careful. That shit is strong." He pulled on the joint one more time before he passed it to Franklin.

They rode down 125 St. past the Apollo, and the shopping center directly to West Side High way. They took that all the way to the exit on forty-second street, and then they turned off one of those street's, and went to Cad's apartment. He lived directly off of the street next to Central Park. He lived in one of those fancy apartment's with door men, and valet's.

When Reuben pulled in front of the apartment building one of the valet's ran towards the car. He turned towards Franklin.

"You better tell your friends not to leave any valuables in the car. These mother fucker's will rob you blind." He reached in his pocket, and passed the valet a dollar. He saw the shocked look on Franklin's face.

"Only a dollar."

"Look some of dese white people don't give them shit." The valet was standing right there, he obviously over heard the conversation. "Oh no this is fine sir. Thank you."

Reuben had another joint in his mouth that he was about to light. He gave it to the valet. If Gad was their he would have snapped out. He always told them not to do anything with the valet's. He didn't want them to know that they were involved with anything illegal. This was not that kind of neighborhood.

Their were only two valets that worked in the building. So when the second one came out. He left one of the cars parked, and pulled off in the second car. He was going to park them one at a time.

Christopher looked at the building. He was impressed. The building was white stone instead of brown stone. A few yards from the ground the first apartment window started. Even though they were listed as apartments they were actually condominiums.

When they walked to the entrance the door was pushed open by a door man. He was an elderly white gentlemen. Kind of plump. He was wearing a uniform that looked like a security uniform, but it was only a door man uniform.

He put on a smile, and treated all of the tenants with respect. "How are you gentlemen doing today?"

They almost replied in unison. "Fine."

"We're fine."

Some said. "We're doing okay."

"Do you need any help with your bags?" He was talking to Christopher because he was the only one carrying a bag.

"No but thank you sir." Christopher's finance had gone shopping, and purchased him some Coach luggage. Christopher was carrying a enormous black leather Coach duffel bag. Full of money.

They walked threw the apartment building, and it was furnished like it was an exclusive hotel. Everything was quality. The front desk, and the security desk were made out of marble. Their were pictures set in wooden frames.

When they got on the elevator, Christopher was surprised at how spacious it was. He glanced around. Everything was in excellent condition.

They rode all the way to the sixteenth floor. It was the floor with the penthouses. When they came off Christopher noticed to marble floor. It was beautiful. He walked passed several door. There were no numbers on the doors. He wondered how the visitors found what ever residence they were visiting. Then it hit him. You were not coming to visit anybody in this building unless you knew where you were going.

Reuben lead them down the hallway. He watched all of them as they admired the building. They were impressed the same way he was impressed when he came over to the country. They had come a long way from the small apartments in Harlem.

Gad's girlfriend was sitting on the living-room sofa watching television. When the door bell rang the television automatically switched over to the security system.

She was sitting in between Gad's legs. They both looked at the television at the same time. Just to see who it was. It was Reuben.

Gad pushed the security lock on the door. The lock automatically clicked.

When Reuben heard the door click he turned the knob. When they walked into the apartment it was beautifully decorated. There were all kinds of Afrocentric painting hanging from the wall. You could tell that whoever lived in the apartment had money, and was use to it. The quality of the furniture let you know that this family had money for years.

Reuben headed them down the hall way into the living-room. The living-room was completely furnished. Their were more Afrocentric pictures hanging on the wall. The smell of marijuana filled the air. The white carpet was so thick that they really did not want to step on. It was that beautiful.

When they entered the living-room, Gad jumped to his feet to greet them. He walked over to Franklin, and hugged him. Then his girlfriend spoke by waving her hands. They must have just woke up because it was early. They were both completely dressed though.

"Elle." Gad screamed out the maids name.

The maid walked from the bathroom. She had a bunch of towels in her hand.

"Can you please bring some coffee for these gentlemen, and Reuben get some chairs from out of the dining-room."

The apartment was enormous. It had a sunken living-room. A fish tank that went across one side of wall. He had a black television in the living-room. A nice stereo system too.

The maid bought the cup's of coffee in some beautiful china. She placed the coffee pot on the living-room table, and placed a kitchen mat under it so she would not stain the furniture.

"If anybody wants any more coffee or needs anything else we'll be in the kitchen. Please excuse me."

Gad smiled. She was professional. He like the fact that she impressed his company. She excused herself, and walked into the kitchen. She was making lunch for them. She was a student at N.Y.U, and in her spare time she did maid service for a house keeping agency. If the customer's like you then they pay a fee, and request that you become permanent if you chose to. Gad liked her so much he advised her to quit her job, and told her he would pay her double what the agency was paying her, and she did.

"Gad I want to buy about a hundred pounds, but I'm going in with my partner's here, and we're looking for some kind of deal. If I get one-hundred pounds, how much are you going to charge me?"

It took Gad a couple of seconds. He had to figure it out in his head,

"Look Frank you've been dealing with me for years. You no I don't cheat nobody. If you get one-hundred pounds of the ses I can give it to you for three-fifty a pound. That's good because I sell the pounds up here for five hundred. I know you can go to Jersey, and get about seven. If you get the tie that's seven fifty, and I can't go no lower because I'm buying that from somebody else. They won't give me a play. Even thought that shit is expensive you should get it. It's got people running around like their smoking cocaine. That shit is good."

They all smiled. He lit a joint of the tie stick, and passed it around. His family grew weed in Trinidad so he could give cheap prices, but the tie stick came from another connection, and he could not afford to give any breaks. The quality alone was a deal.

Franklin, Little Aaron, and Corty glanced over towards Christopher. It was really his decision that needed his advice.

"Well what should we do?" Franklin asked.

"Let's just get fifty pounds of the tie stick, and get the rest in ses. We can sell the tie stick as dimes, and the ses as nickels and weight."

"We're going to sell that ses overnight." Corty added. "I

know you don't want to come back in a couple of day's. The tie-stick is going to take a little longer because it's much more expensive. Maybe we can do the tie in dimes, and the ses as all weight."

Christopher looked at him. "It doesn't matter whatever you and Frank figure as best. I need a calculator though. I can't figure all this shit out in my head."

Christopher and the rest of the family had taken their jacket's off. Every single one of them were carrying guns except Franklin.

When he got the chance he whispered to Christopher. "I told you we wouldn't need any guns." Franklin had told him they would not need guns the rasta's could be trusted.

Christopher had long stopped believing in trust. There was really no such thing as trust. Only business, and safety was a part of business. He told Franklin he was bringing his gun, and that he should let the rasta's know so that they would not be alarmed.

One of Gad's bodyguard was sitting in one of the chairs behind him on the sofa.

Gad looked in his direction. "Go get me a calculator."

The bodyguard ran in the kitchen and returned with a calculator. He handed Christopher the calculator.

Christopher started punching buttons on the calculator. He talked as loud as he punched the key's. "Seven hundred, and fifty times fifty pounds is..... Thirty-seven thousand, and five hundred dollars." He pause for a second. He was trying.

"That leaves us with twelve-five. Twelve-five divided by three fifty is...,thirty-five, and seven ounces. You might as well make it thirty-six since we're spending fifty grand with you."

Gad smiled. "No problem." He preferred to do big transactions anyway.

"I have to count the money first, and then one of my brother's will go, and get the weed. Don't worry. The money stay's in your possession until the deal is done."

Christopher picked up his duffel bag, and walked it over to Gad. He opened the bag, and counted the stacks of money. It was fifty stacks. He placed the money back in the bag, and passed it to one of his bodyguards.

The bodyguard grabbed the bag, and walked towards the kitchen.

"He's going to take this in the kitchen, and count it. You can go in their if you want."

Christopher would have gone, but he decided against it. He wanted a show a little bit of trust. Just a little.

The maid walked out of the kitchen. "Gad. Lunch is ready."

Gad's girlfriend must have heard her yell because she came from out of the bedroom as soon as the maid yelled lunch.

Gad's girlfriend looked more like his sister. They both had reddish dred's with a reddish complexion. Their similarities really made them an even more beautiful couple. Gad kept his girlfriend with the nicest clothing. Anything that she wanted.

Gad walked them into the dining-room. The maid had set up the dishes, and set a couple of bottle of wine on the table. They walked into dining-room, and took seats where ever they wanted too.

A few minutes later Gad's bodyguard returned, and took a seat. "It's all there."

Gad nodded his head in approval. They ate lunch, and made small talk. When they finished lunch Gad and his girlfriend gave them a tour of the apartment.

When they came back into the living-room there were a bunch of boxes on the floor.

Gad looked at the boxes. "Pick those boxes up, and take them into the dining-room.

They placed the boxes on the dining-room table. Gad walked over, and split one of the boxes open. They opened the boxes, and the tie-stick were in plastic pound bags. The ses was wrapped up in Christmas wrapping.

Gad pulled a pocket knife out. Ran a knife down the pack. This was the first time that Christopher had seen the weed packaged like this. It was packaged like this it came from a factory.

Gad dug his hand into one of the packets. He pulled out a hand full of weed.

"All of the packages are over weight. This one should still

be five pounds."

He threw the weed on the table, and started rolling it up. They lit the weed. The smell lit the entire apartment. That as the perfume smell he smelled when he entered the apartment.

Christopher placed his nose to the bags. The smell was serious. He could tell by the way it smelled, and the way that it looked that it was good.

FIVE

The family switched the marijuana operations over to another bar. Franklin did not care. Christopher had him cut in like he was one of the family. He had never made so much money in his life. It was after seeing the families operations in effect that Franklin realized how serious things were. He had to be a part of this. But like most dealers. Once he was exposed to the money you could make off of heroin and speed. Marijuana did not matter.

In the beginning Christopher let Franklin put workers in the bar, but they could not compete with Corty and his crew. So after a couple of months Franklin gave up his force, and worked out a partnership with Corty, Christopher, and Little Aaron. He would distribute as much wholesale marijuana that he possibly could, and Corty would handle the small distribution. If he invested his money then he would receive a cut of the profit. This was less money for him, but it was also less risk and hassle. He could sit back, and still make thousands.

One of the main reason's that Franklin slowed down was because he wanted a piece of that heroin money. The only thing with that was if he wanted a piece of that action he was going to have to put in some physical work. Franklin did not like it. It seemed too risky. He did it for a while just to make some serious money.

The only problem the family was having with the product, was sometimes it would drop. If the product dropped. Then they would have to cut deals.

Christopher and Junior sat with Pedro. The Spanish guy that was their heroin connection. They were bringing this man about fifty to a hundred thousand dollars a week. They would bring so much money to him it became to dangerous to meet him at the spot. So he had to let them come to one of his apartments for business. They were definitely his biggest customers.

Pedro, Christopher, and Little Aaron had become tight after a time. Pedro would come to the casino and lose thousands of dollars. They would show him the city, and he loved the quiet area. Mainly because the casino's were their, and it was still quiet. That was what impressed a lot of people about Atlantic City. It was building beautiful casinos constantly, yet it was still a quiet place to live. Pedro was born and raised in the Bronx so he was not use to anything like this. He loved it.

It was Christopher and Little Aaron that made him start spending all that money he was making. They did not know it though. When he saw Little Aaron's house he decided to buy one in upstate New York. He did not spend a lot of time in it because it was too far a way. He did move his wife and children into a nice condominium in lower Manhattan around the Spanish area. The condo was not enormous like the one that Cad lived in; in downtown Manhattan but it sat on the Riverside Drive, you could see the water, and New Jersey's beautifully lit skyline from one of his windows. He let his wife furnish the apartment. Sometimes he would bring her, and a couple of her girlfriends to Atlantic City. Little Aaron's wife and Christopher's fiancé would take them to Philadelphia, Cherry Hill New Jersey, and the near by city's to shop. Things were changing for everybody.

Little Aaron's wedding took place in June, and it was spectacular. Mr. Johnson, and his entire family came to the wedding. The legal ones, and the illegal ones. It gave Little Aaron an opportunity to see how large the organization was.

It was the night of that wedding that Christopher and his finance set a wedding date. They decided they would get married in August. It would be a short notice for everybody but it would also give everybody enough time to recuperate from Little Aaron's wedding.

Little Aaron held a reception at one of the fancy restaurants located a couple of miles outside of Atlantic City. At one of those exclusive golf courses. His picture was put in the Jet magazine, and the local news paper courtesy of his father. His new bride was pregnant, and expecting again. So things were looking up. The only thing messed up was this heroin problem.

Christopher, Little Aaron, Pedro, and a couple of his bodyguards were sitting in the living-room of one of the apartments that Pedro used for business. Christopher and Little Aaron had brought bodyguards, but not for protection. They knew that Pedro would never hurt them useless it was business. They just brought them because it was safe to travel with them. A safety precaution.

"Pedro listen. Poppy." Christopher did most of the talking. He was the one that really ran everything. "It's not that were not happy, and were not saying that your doing anything to the product. It's just that we need to get it pure. We need to get it where we can cut it ourselves. The product keeps falling. Their is nothing wrong with the quality. The customers love it. But it will only stay strong for a couple of days, and we're tired of traveling back and forth spending fifty thousand. One-hundred thousand every couple of weeks. It's crazy. Now if you give it to us pure, and show us how to cut it. We can come, and spend five-hundred thousand. Maybe a million dollars. But we have to get it pure. So if we leave it sitting some where it won't get weak."

A lot of times. Especially if he was getting complaints. Pedro would act as if he had difficulty understanding English and he would have somebody translate. But that was bullshit. He was Puerto Rican. He was born in America, and understood it perfectly. When he first met Christopher and Little Aaron he acted like he did not understand English well. But that was a lie. He had been in there presence at the casino too much not to understand English

"Chris I understand. But I can cut it for you. If you want to buy a key of heroin pure, it costs you quarter million. But if I cut it for you, I give it to you half price."

Christopher shook his head. Little Aaron did not understand, so he was about to agree.

"Christopher that sounds good to me. We can make a

million bundles out of that."

Christopher just smiled. Sometimes he could get a little irritated when they did not understand.

"Listen, he was going to explain it one more time. "If you cut the heroin for us it does not make a difference. Then I might as well come and buy it in bags. Everybody knows that it's the cut that gets weaker everyday, and the weaker that it gets the weaker the products potency becomes. We need it pure. Then sell us the morphine base, and teach us how to properly cut it, and we'll cut it as we sell it. Then we'll eliminate the problem of the product falling. We can buy more product, and give better deals because of the deals we're getting. If you teach us we can cut it ourselves. If you cut it, then we can't spend the money we want to spend because the cut is going to get weaker everyday, and the products going to end up garbage by the time we get to the end. Give it to us pure, and we won't cut it all. We'll cut it in portions. Only portions of distribution, I know you won't make a lot of money wholeselling, but our business is growing, and if you want to keep us as customers you have to grow with us, or we'll just have to find somebody that can handle us. Don't tell me our connection can't handle us no more."

Pedro looked at Christopher. Christopher could tell his words had gotten the point across.

When Pedro got mad he spoke with an accent. "Christopher don't ever disrespect me...... I love you guy's business. I ain't letting you take your business no where. Give me a couple of days, and I gone make good price for you. Okay?"

"Okay. "

Pedro jumped to his feet, and extended his hand. He promised Christopher and Little Aaron when they came that he would take them to this nice sports bar and restaurant in the Bronx to eat dinner.

Pedro had been in the heroin business with his family for years, and he was never impressed with anyone the way that he was impressed with Christopher. He admired the man. He was a young business genius.

Christopher sent one of the bodyguards down to the car to

get a present he had bought for Pedro. The bodyguard went to get it, and bought the present back upstairs.

"Pedro. I bought you this present."

Pedro looked at the beautifully wrapped paper, and shook the box. He placed it to his ear.

"You not mad at me are you? This no bomb."

They all burst into laughter.

"It might be. Open it."

Pedro took the box and unwrapped it. When he opened the box it was a pound of marijuana. His favorite.

This was the biggest deal that Christopher had ever done. It didn't take money. It only took thought, and that was one of the things that made powerful men powerful. You can not run an operation on physical skills alone. You have to have brain power. A lot of men that operated the streets did not know this. They used intimidation to rule their criminal empire. That was the easy part. The hard part was using your brain to it's full capacity. It saved a lot of bloodshed, and police scrutiny.

Big Will would have problems in Philadelphia, and gun fire would settle it. But gun fire was not always the best way to settle a street dispute.

When Christopher and Little Aaron returned home they held a meeting with Big Aaron, and told him the details of the deal. He in turned went to Philadelphia, and had a meeting with Big Will. If everything fell threw with Pedro then Big Will could reestablish his strong hold on the heroin business in the black community. The Spanish were slowly taking heroin distribution over like the Chinese were taking it from the Italians. Big Will had learned years ago, whenever you got in a business, and the business did excellent, take as much as you possibly could because it wouldn't last. So when the scramble business got shook up, he understood. Now he was getting another opportunity to establish a strong hold with the Pedro connection.

It did not matter though. By early eighty-two he had become a millionaire from selling heroin alone. Even though he lost his strong hold on the heroin business in Philadelphia, a new drug was popping on the scene, Cocaine. Cocaine had been around for years but now it was hitting the streets, and hitting the streets in a strong way.

The family purchased a store in the Ocean One Mall. The mall was located on the beach in front of one of the casinos. They did it just so that they could have something legitimate to cover the money that they were making. They were also looking at other things they could invest in independently.

Big Aaron would always tell them. "If you put your money in something legitimate then you'll always have something. As long as you don't own it entirely yourself. Then once you retire you transfer everything legally back into your name."

There were other dealers selling heroin in Atlantic City, but the family's bar was the strongest distribution point. It was never really slow. Christopher kept it freelance. Anyone could come and sell from the bar as long as they did not act stupid, or did not cause any kind of commotion.

Once that the family started getting the heroin pure they were able to cut it, and start selling whole sale. Instead of people coming just to buy bags they could come, and buy bundles at a discount price. Then they could take those same bundles, and sell the bags at the same price that Christopher and the family was selling for. It would be the same quality. Christopher explained to Big Aaron that, yes they would make a little less but it would push the family to a larger scale, and a safer position.

They already had people coming from other cities buying bags. There were other cities in the area that were selling five dollar bags for ten dollars. Once the family started wholeselling they would be able to sell the bundles for twenty-five dollars which came out to two dollars, and fifty cents a bag. Then the customer could in turn resell the bag for five dollars, or more. The profit did not seem big, but if you spent a couple of hundred dollars, you could double your money in a short period of time. Why waist the time of going to New York. Christopher knew there were other dealers that would still travel to New York regardless of how cheap his prices were, but it did'nt matter because the smaller customers he had the more competition it created for the other dealers.

He decided the only way that they could make the move to wholesale was to move to another location. The bar would remain the main distribution point, but if somebody wanted to buy a bundle they would have to beep him. Little Aaron, or one of the workers.

Christopher put his share of the family business in his mother, and fiances name. Then he had himself listed as an employee. This way he would be able to establish some legitimate credit for himself, and do little things like open bank accounts, and get credit cards. He knew acquiring a legal front was extremely important to his future.

Business was going so well that Christopher moved his stash house to a city called Pleasantville. He did not want to live in the same city that he stashed his product. Once he got married he had intentions of buying a house in Atlantic City, or one of those little cities in the Atlantic City area. Gad was in the process of helping him find a condominium in New York. He wanted a condominium in the same place that Gad lived, but they did not have any units available.

The family was making so much money selling heroin that sometimes it would scare Christopher. If they did not make twenty thousand dollars a day between the two shifts then it was slow. If it was a good day they would make sometimes double that. Christopher was hearing all kinds of rumors. The police were upset because they knew that they were dealing from the bar, but they could not catch them.

Four o'clock until six o'clock was a shift change for the family. Christopher worked with the morning first shift because it was the busiest, and he liked to stay on top of everything. He liked working the second shift better because it was more relaxed, and the dealers that worked that shift made their money in spurts. They could sit in the bar and play pool, or just kick it with the girls.

Christopher collected the money from the morning shift. He went to the back of the bar were Mr. Beck stored his alcohol and other little things. He counted the money. They had made a little over twenty-thousand. After he counted, and rubber banded the money, he would give it to Mr. Beck. He would hold it in his safe. Then Christopher would get one of the young ladies to carry the money to the car. He would drive her around the corner, take the money, and let her out. There was always some young lady in the bar that was willing to make a hundred dollars. The family gave Mr. Beck a couple of hundred a week for not complaining.

Christopher did not bring his car this morning. He arrived late. He went to the dealership with Corey to buy a brand new car. Corey had dropped him off. He worked on the night shift so he promised Christopher he would pick him up, and take him home once he beeped him. Christopher beeped him, and he called back. He said he would be there in fifteen minutes.

Christopher sat at the bar and ordered a drink. He had a joint in his pocket. He pulled the joint out, and lit it. He did not want the police to walk in and search him. By the time that Corey pulled up he was finished smoking his joint. He called Debra. She was home, and she came right over.

Mr. Beck was tending the bar. Christopher waited for him to finish serving his drinks, and when he got his attention, he spoke to him.

"I need that bag."

Mr. Beck stepped to the back, and when he came out he was carrying a brown paper bag. He discreetly handed it to Christopher. Christopher passed it to Debra. She was sitting right next to him. She placed it in her pocket book.

Christopher glanced over at two of the workers that were on the morning shift, and playing pool.

"Chuck. I need you and Berry to make sure that she gets to the cab stand safely."

"Is she ready now? Cause we got money on this game."

Christopher gave him the most serious look he had ever seen. They did not have to ask what the look meant. It meant business comes first.

Christopher walked to the front of the bar. Corey was outside in his brand new Corvette. It still had a temporary tag on the car.

When Christopher walked out of the bar, he saw the undercover cars approaching. Damn he was leaving just as they were about to raid. He was glad now that he gave Debra the money to carry. Hopefully they made it around the corner. He did not want to look in their direction.

Corey had the music in his car blasting. The sirens drowned the sound of the music out. A group of undercover officers ran in the bar, and another group surrounded Corey's brand new car. They all had their guns drawn.

A television news van pulled up and a crew of reporters jumped out. They ran towards the bar as bravely as the vice officers did.

One of the vice officers walked over towards Christopher and Corey. He held his badge out, and walked over to Christopher and Corey. He was followed by another officer.

"What's up with these two." The superior officer asked

"Yeah this is two of them." The officer had his gun drawn, and told them. "Put your hands in the air. Your under arrest."

A shocked look crossed Christopher's face. "Under arrest. Under arrest for what?"

The officer was patting their pockets and searching them. "Your under arrest for possession of heroin, speed, and marijuana with the intent to distribute."

Christopher was still shocked and pissed off. He glanced into the pool room, and to his surprise the police were bringing other dealers out. Once the realization hit him, he looked around. The street's were covered with police.

There were undercover cars, a couple of police vans, and some regular cop cars. Their were the news reporters running around snapping pictures. He could not believe it. He was praying they did not know about his stash house in Pleasantville. He had a half of kilo-gram of pure heroin stashed there. He knew just to keep his mouth shut until he found out what was going on.

The police took them down to the station. After they loaded the van, and the reporters from the news stations got a chance to take their pictures.

While they were being walked to the police van, Corey looked over at his brand new car.

"Hey officer. What's up with my mothers car?"

"Oh she can come get it. If she's got a job."

They loaded the van, and Corey watched as one of the officers jumped in the car. A crowd of officers surrounded the car. They were saying amongst themselves they hoped one of the dealers had the car in their names. Then they could go to the auction and buy the car dirt cheap.

It took a couple of hours of sitting down town. Then the dealers were informed that they were apart of a six month undercover investigation. Some of them had either sold to an undercover, or helped another dealer make a transaction which was conspiracy.

Christopher was confused. They might have had something on him, or they might not. That confusion was put to rest when he saw some of the new rookies undercover walking around down in the station approaching people.

They would walk over to dealers, and say. "Remember me. My names Bob the junkie that bought all that dope off of you."

Christopher was really shocked when he saw Little Aaron bought down in handcuffs, and a couple of other people in the family. Then they bought Corty down. Damn they must have even made weed buy's.

Christopher did not know it but his lawyer was down at the precinct an hour or two after the arrest. Everybody in the family was bailed before the county bus arrived.

After everyone was processed the news reporters waited outside of the station so that they could get one good shot of everybody locked up in the raid. A lot of the dealers covered their faces when they walked outside to load the bus.

Christopher, and the rest of the family were sitting in his living-room watching the eleven o'clock news.

A pretty Afro-American news reporter came across the television.

"Today police put a dent in Atlantic City's drug market after rounding up the suspects in a six month undercover drug investigation. The police seized all kinds of drugs and money off of small time dealer's operating in the city. The operation was called operation gram, and targeted small time dealers that operated out of homes, parks, projects, and bars. Here we flash back to an earlier scene at the Atlantic City police department. Where officer Michael Clark head of the narcotics unit and made a statement."

Officer Clark was standing behind a wooden desk that had several microphones sitting next to it. News reporters were asking him all kinds of questions.

"Today we put a serious dent in the drug business. We focused mainly on small time dealers. Fortunately the city does not have any major distributors yet, and with raids like this we should be able to prevent that from happening.

Marc burst out into laughter. He was drinking from a beer bottle. "Those stupid mother fuckers. We was making thousands out the bar, and them mother fuckers did'nt even know it." He just shook his head in disbelief.

The other made comments too. Corey's mother went down to the station, and picked the Corvette up.

"Yo, I told you them mother fuckers don't have nothing but small sales on us."

"I told you don't trust that junkie." Martin was talking about the undercover that kept trying to buy large quantities. "Where in the fuck is a junkie going to get big money to spend constantly."

"That's it, that's the key. From now on if your not a dealer you can't keep coming speeding big money. I see now the only way they can get us is threw small sales. If they think you're really getting money then they try to buy big from you, but if their not a dealer, and they don't know anybody that can back them up as being one then don't sell anything big to them. Junior what's up with your Dad?"

Little Aaron shook his head. "He pissed the fuck off." Was the only thing he could reply. "But you know what really got him pissed. The police are still asking questions about him. He's pissed."

The police really scared Mr. Beck. They told him they thought that he was connected with the dealers, and if they found out they were going to take his license. He beeped Christopher a million times but the police confiscated all of their beepers.

Mr. Beck did calm down until he spoke with Christopher.

"Now Christopher you know I respect y'all, and I like y'all, but I can't let you make me loose my license for selling drugs. You guys are going to have to find another place."

"Mr. Beck your from the old school. Don't let them pussies fool you. If they had anything on you, you would be. They don't know nothing. Only what you tell them, and you only deal with me and you know I ain't telling them shit. So don't worry. In fact, if they keep fucking with you here's my lawyers card. Tell them to call him, and I'll pay for it." That was the only thing that relaxed Mr. Beck.

Big Aaron, Little Aaron, Crazy Moe, Christopher, and Martin were sitting in Christopher's attorney's office. He did not stop using the lawyer that Big Aaron used but he did get another lawyer. Big Aaron always told him. "Establish a relationship with your lawyer. Make sure that you become close. You don't want him to look at you as his client. You want him to look at you as his friend. When they think of you as friends then they take your case personal. They stop looking at you as a crook, and more as a businessman."

That's the one thing that Christopher never denied Big Aaron. Big Aaron had taught him a lot of things. He would have never known some of the things that he knew now if it were not for Mr. Gaston. He owed him a lot of respect.

Christopher's attorneys name was Norman Wright. He had a dark complexion with a receding hair line, but he kept him self so well manicured that he appeared handsome.

His hair was always trimmed, and neatly combed. He had beautiful teeth. His nails were always manicured, and he wore quality expensive clothing, and beautiful colored ties. His shoes were always top notch leather, or some kind of animal skin. He had just started practicing a couple of years earlier, but he had already done good for himself. He was married, and expecting his second child. He had purchased a house, and was in the process of finding something bigger. He was born, and raised in Atlantic City so when he finished law school at Howard University, he returned with the desire of at least trying to serve his people at affordable rates.

These were some of the characteristics that attracted Christopher. What attracted Christopher the most was that he was young, black, intelligent, and soon to be very wealthy. These were the things that made Christopher trust him. He wanted to deal with somebody that he thought would understand his reasons in life.

Christopher took Mr. Gaston's advice, and built a relationship with his attorney. He invited him to dinners. Found out that he played golf, and introduced him to Mr. Gaston who was an serious golf lover. He tried to do things with him, and introduced him to any legal business opportunities that he came across. He also let it be known that if his attorney needed any personal favors he was there for him. Any business that Christopher had that required a attorney he bought to his lawyer first. Even if his lawyer did not have expertise in that particular field. Even though Christopher knew that it was only business. He also learned that Mr. Gaston was right. Having that real relationship paid off. Norman would call Christopher at home, and discuss his case.

Christopher called him when he got locked up, and it was Mr. Wright that handled his bail and everything. Now they were sitting in his law office.

Norman was sitting behind his desk. He told Christopher he did not want to discuss the case until he had the discovery.

Norman's office was small but it was furnished beautifully. He was making money off of Christopher, and the rest of the family, but most of his money came from suing people in accidents. For a lawyer it was the best kind of business. Because the cases were usually settled out of court, and the lawyer had always received a chunk of the money for representing the case. Mr. Wright did not have a lot of white clients because once they found out that he was black, they did not even want him representing their case. He did not worry about it. Afro-Americans were moving up in society, and offering a lot of work. He was praying that eventually he would receive some of those minority contracts the casino's were giving out, and some of those city contracts. If he got a couple of those he would be able to hire some other attorneys, and become a small firm. For now business was going good. He was making an extremely comfortable living and really could not ask for more.

When they came in his office he had already sat seats out for them. They each jumped into a chair. They came in, and shook hands. The telephone rang.

Mr. Wright picked it up. "Hello.... Yes.... Yes." He placed the phone to his chest. "Excuse me fellas this is only going to take a minute." He removed the phone from his chest, and returned to the telephone. "Listen I'm in here having a meeting with some pretty important clients. If your can leave the information with my secretary I'll get back with you immediately. Yes. Yes... I understand Mr. Kranz please.... Leave the information with my secretary. Okay. Thank you." He hung the phone up.

Mr. Wright was sitting behind his desk. He had a small table set next to his desk that had a china set. Then he had another table set up near his window with a brewing coffee pot.   It was rare that Christopher dressed up unless it was   important business. He consider seeing his lawyer important business. He had a meeting with Mr. Johnson that afternoon. Everyone was dressed to the tees.

They were all dressed so nice that it looked like a legal business meeting between some powerful lawyers. They were all wearing nice suits.

The suit Christopher was wearing was nice but it was also conservative. It was navy blue single breasted wool pinstriped suit. He was wearing crocodile boot shoes, and a crocodile belt. He never wore jewelry, but now that he was engaged he wore a princess cut diamond band. He never wore bracelets. He owned a gold name tag with a Cuban link, but he rarely wore it. Sometimes he wore a eighteen karat gold Rolex watch.

Mr. Wright had a folder in his hand. He opened it, and browsed threw the papers. He placed his reading glasses on his face. They made him look older. More intelligent.

"Christopher I talked to the prosecutor on the case, and I talked to the Judge. They don't have shit, and they know it. The only thing they were trying to do was make a street sweep. The prosecutor is kind of pissed. He told me some informants said that you, and Aaron run this shit. I don't know what their going to do, but I think their going to come at you again, but this time in a more serious way. So you better be careful."

Mr. Wright had received the discovery. The discovery was a list of the documented evidence that the state has against a witness. Every person charged with a crime receives one.

"I looked over the discovery, and they have you both on a couple of sales, and mainly conspiracy. That's the worst part. They have it listed in the discovery." Mr, Wright flipped threw the pages, and found the page that he wanted. He passed the piece of paper to Christopher. "They have listed here that you two might be the ring leaders because you never really deal with the customers with hand to hand distribution. That's all bullshit. I told the prosecutor to shove it up his ass. I ran down the list of my clients, and told him if he can't come with some probation to go fuck himself."

They all broke into laughter. That's what they liked the best about him. He was straight forward, and he did not take any bullshit.

"I figured I'd get everybody six months probation, and a thousand dollar fine. You can stay out of trouble for six months can't you?"

Christopher did not even look up. He replied with a sly smile.

Little Aaron was the first one to comment. "If their offering probation maybe they don't have anything. Maybe we can take it to trial, and beat it."

"They don't really have anything. I mean they have enough to charge you, but not send you to jail. If we take it to trial then you guys might be hit. You'd be facing cops. Who do you think a jury is going to believe. You, a bunch of young black men accused of selling drugs, or a bunch of white guys that protect, and serve. That's not counting the evidence. They might have some heavy evidence, but I think the only thing stopping them is that they could not buy anything serious enough from you guys. The way you set it up they really did'nt know if you guys are united or not. They don't know at what level your dealing on. Every single sale they made was a small sale. They assume you guys were making money because the place was constantly busy. But then they figure on those dumb blacks don't know how to save. If you guys want to go to trial we can do it. But to me, it's a waste of money, and the Judge is going to send you to jail for wasting taxpayers money."

Little Aaron still wasn't satisfied. He did not want a record. He did not want probation. He did not want to be labeled.

"I see what your saying, but good lawyers beat cases."

"Yeah cases that can be beat. But if the case can't be beat then they get you a hell of a deal, and believe me I got you a hell of a deal. Plus, if you pay your probation fine then your six months is chopped in half. Provided you stay out of trouble."

"What about my father? Did they mention my fathers name?" It was the question that had brought Mr. Gaston to the room. He had to know if they were running his name.

"No he did'nt mention your father's name. But that does'nt mean that they don't think your father has anything to do with it."

The answer put a smile on Big Aaron's face. The most important thing was that he remained protected. He was old. He had paid his dues. Now it was Christopher and Little Aaron's obligation to protect him. They knew it and understood it. Nobody wanted him to have to retire early. There were too many things that had to be done, and they knew they needed his guidance.

Christopher had already moved his stash houses, and now he was in the market for purchasing his own house. He did not marry his fiance in August. They decided to wait until June of eighty-three, and that was only a few months away.

Ever since the raids the police started harassing him. It did not matter. The family had moved up to whole sale heroin. They were mainly selling bundles off a beeper. They were operating out of the bar but at a slower pace. Business resumed a couple of days after the raid.

Christopher had another argument with Andre.

"See I told you. Them mother fuckers locked us up because we were letting too many people deal from the bar. If we would have cut shit down we would have been straight."

Christopher was his superior. He had long learned that he

did not have to watch his tongue. "You stupid mother fucker. If we would not have let the other dealers in the bar, they would have came and locked us all the fuck up."

"No they would'nt have. We were doing shit so smooth that they would have over looked the bar."

"Your crazy. You see they raided Lucy's." Lucy's was a small bar on the Westside. If any dealers came there it was only once in a blue moon.

"I'm glad it was other guys there. It takes some of the heat."

Christopher was right. Martin was there. He was carrying his gun. If Andre would have moved he would have filled him with bullet holes.

Mr. Wright reclined back in his chair. "So what are you guys going to do? If you take the probation, I can make a call today. Arrange the next court date available, and we can have this thing done in a months time."

Big Aaron whispered something to Little Aaron. "Okay will take it"

They looked at Christopher, "Let me think about it."

They stood up, and shook hands with the lawyer. They walked to the car. The car was parked in front. Crazy Moe, Big Aaron, Little Aaron, Christopher, and Martin piled in Mr. Gaston's Bentley. It was brand new. Sterling white with white leather interior. Big Aaron rarely drove it unless he was going out of town.

When they got into the car and pulled off, Big Aaron opened the conversation. "Listen, those mother fuckers are pissed off, and they're going to come at us again. I want y'all to either slow up, find another place to deal, or just break up, and go separate places."

"I don't know, what ever you say Dad."

Christopher looked at it differently. "Mr. Gaston this is no disrespect. But them pussies can't fuck with us. This is the game. People got to go to jail. You can't deal, and not get locked up. As long as they keep catching us like this, we don't have shit to worry about. Shit, a couple more years we'll all fuck around and be millionaires. I say we keep moving, and just make sure that all of our big customers are legit because that's how they're gonna come and try to hit us. We have to screen the customers that buy weight. Shit, this is business."

Once again Christopher was right.

"I don't give a fuck what y'all do. I just want you to be safe. Extra safe. I don't want anything to happen to y'all. Who's going to run this shit when me and Moe are gone?"

Moe drove the car to Big Aaron's house. They covered a little more business in the car. When they got to his house, Christopher's brand new Mercedes Benz was parked outside.

Martin and Christopher jumped in the car and pulled off. Whenever Christopher went to do business he brought Martin along as his bodyguard.

Plus Christopher was about to have another important meeting with Franklin because he ahd met some boys that knew some Dominicans in New York who were selling crack, and fish scale cocaine. The price of cocaine had dropped from forty thousand doolars a kilogram to twenty-five and thirty thousand. Depending on the availability. By the time that eighty-two rolled around speed had all but sidappeared.

Franklin was the one who could have become a millionaire with all the connections that he had, but he did not have the business, or the organizing genius that Christopher had. None of them did. Christopher was a criminal genius, and he did not even know it.

Franklin had completely turned over his marijuana business, took his crew and concentrated on his heroin operations. He was having problems with Andre and Michael's men. They were running around trying to extort people who were not a part of their organization.

Michael aned Andre worked independently of Christopher, but they were still under William Johnson and Aaron Gaston's command.

Christopher knew that they were there to strengthen Mr. Johnson's stronghold on the area. After Christopher went to New York and established his cocaine connections, he presented Mr. Johnson and Aaron Gaston with another proposition. They would become his partners by investing, and just like the heroin profits, would be split down the middle. Of course, they could not refuse. They had already mades hundreds of thousands of dollars with Christopher.

One of the lieutenants in the Italian Mafia was selling cocaine wholesale. He was dealing with some Colombians, and giving a large majority of the cocaine to Mr. Johnson, and he was giving it to his lieutenants. Surprisingly, the Italians were cheaper than the Dominicans, but they could never keep the cocaine on a consistant basis, and the cocaine was an exploding business. Especially with the introduction of crack and freebase.

SIX

In early eighty-three Gad rented his condominium to Reuben, his right hand man in Harlem. He couldn't really sell the condominium to Reuben because he didn't own it. He couldn't sell it because legally his family's realty company in Trinidad owned the condominium and several other residence in the building.

Gad gave the condominium up mainly because it was too expensive to use as a meeting place. He promised his wife that once they got married he would move her into a house.

Gad, and his fiancé got married in Trinidad at his families estate, Christopher and the entire family attended. Gad's family was one of the wealthiest, if not the wealthiest family in Trinidad. They had all kinds of real-estate. Small companies. They were extremely powerful in Trinidad. He had family in government, but a majority of them were just plain wealthy businessmen.

Gad purchased a house in Nyack. It was in upstate New York. Once you get outside of the five boroughs, and your headed North, it's considered upstate. His residence was only thirty minutes outside of the city. He could not move too far. He had to go to Manhattan, and conduct his business every day.

Gad purchased the house in an exclusive area. He wanted to keep his new family as far away from his business as possible. His wife loved it. The house was beautiful, and it still was far from the city. So she could still do the things that she used to do. Invite her friends and family over. Everybody that lived in the neighborhood was a millionaire. The properties starting prices were a quarter million dollars, and up.

As soon as Gad moved into the area he had the property surrounded by a fence. Then he had a security system set up on the inside and outside of the house. Video security cameras, and some other forms of surveillance. He was about to get some security dogs, but his wife asked him not too. She did not want any animals around the baby until she got older.

Gad still had his other apartments in Harlem where he conducted his business, but he used them for business purposes only or whenever he wanted to take one of his female friends somewhere.

He always had to be careful because his wife did nothing all day but ride around the city shopping for the baby or hanging out with her friends. She use to work for a computer company in Manhattan, but Gad asked her to take a leave of absence at least until the baby turned one year old.

It was five thirty in the morning when the enormous black truck pulled up in front of Gad's house. Then two more black trucks pulled up. Instead of parking in front of the gates entrance like the first black truck. The other cargo vans pulled up on opposite sides of the gate. It seemed like as soon as the vans came to a stop all of the side doors slid open simultaneously. At least ten men came out of each truck. They were all wearing black clothing. With black jackets, and black skull caps. Some of them had pulled the scull caps over their faces, and they turned out to be black ski mask. Every single one of them was carrying a rifle with a laser on the scope. They all took positions. The first van that arrived was parked outside of Gad entrance gate. It's lights were off, and the engine was so quiet you could hardly hear it running. Within minutes the other agents that had pulled up on the side of the house, had jumped over the gate, and surrounded the house. They surrounded the back and front. Some of them had D.E.A printed on the back of their jackets, and the others had FBI, or A.T.F on the back of their jackets.

When they had the house surrounded which only took

seconds one of the officers looked in the corner of the front door. He tapped his superior on the shoulder, and pointed towards the security camera. "Look sir."

The superior looked up at the camera, and picked up his walkie talkie. "Back door, There's a camera."

"Ten four." Was the response.

The superior looked at his watch. Everything was set up in one minutes intervals. He waited for his second hand to hit the twelve, and then he picked up his walkie talkie again. "Were ready."

The truck that was in the entrance turned it's lights on. The men jumped out of the van. Five lined up on one side, and the other five line up on the other side. The van slid into reverse, and backed up a little bit. Then it went forward, and burst threw Gad's fence. His silent security alarm went off. The alarm went to a security system, and then the security system sent it to the police. The police were informed that once they received the call from the security company they should send back up cars to the house.

Gad, and his wife heard the first explosion, and then the second explosion was the door getting kicked in by the agents. The house was completely dark so the agents turned on their scopes. The agents formed teams of two, and kicked every single door in.

After Gad heard the door explode. He jumped from the bed, and ran to his dresser draw. He pulled out his brand new ASTRA A-75 9mm. It was all black. His wife jumped out of her bed when she heard the explosion. After Cad grabbed his gun he told his wife to sit over there in the corner. Then he jumped on the opposite side of the bed against the wall. If anybody came threw the door he wanted to have a perfect shot. He was mad that he didn't take that machine gun that Reuben tried to leave at the house. He could hear the police screaming out 'police,' but he wasn't sure, and he wasn't putting down his gun until he saw who it was.

His security system flashed threw his head. If it was a robbery the police would be outside of his house in seconds.

He glanced over at his wife. She was crunched up in the

corner. Covering herself. She had picked the baby up out of it's bassinet as soon as she jumped to her feet. The baby had started crying. By now it had stopped. She was scared to death. The only thing that calmed her was that she heard the doors flying open, and the men were screaming police.

The bedroom door flew open, and a dozen or more agents were in the room within seconds with there guns drawn.

Gad was standing in the corner with his gun drawn. Once the agents got him into focus, they started screaming obscenities

"You rasta man. Drop the gun. Drop the fucking gun."

"Drop the gun or your fucking dead."

"Drop the gun. You got a couple of seconds." Every single one of them were screaming a command. It was absolute chaos.

For a few minutes Gad's wife got scared because she didn't know if her husband was going to drop the gun or start shooting. She covered the baby who was screaming at the top of her lugs now.

Gad laid the gun down, and the officers rushed him to the ground. It seemed like seconds, and they had him penned with handcuffs on.

The officers that had his wife surrounded with guns took them off of her. One of them walked over to her. "Your going to have to come into the living-room with us Mrs.. We have a search warrant." He pulled the papers from his back pocket.

They walked Gad into the living-room. It was enormous. It had a fireplace, and the opposite side of the room had a small water fall that slid down a flat brick wall. They had just finished furnishing the living-room with white leather, and white carpet. Their favorite. There were small wooden animals sitting in the living-room. All kinds of plants. A big screen television.

They walked Gad over to the living-room couch, and made him take a seat. Then they bought his wife out, and sat her on the couch. There were agents all over the place. Walking all threw the house.

Gad was handcuffed, but they didn't handcuff his wife. Gad was acting civilized so they did not want to start any commotion.

Gad heard the officers let out a loud scream. They found the money. It did not matter, there was nothing that he could do about it.

One of the officers started checking the dresser drawers on the other side of the room. When he opened the bottom drawer both sides were filled with money. He called the other officers in the room, and they started stuffing money in their pants, and there coat pockets. Everywhere they could hide money.

One of the officers walked into the living-room, and started asking questions. "I don't have nothing to say. Speak to my lawyer." Gad was confused. He did not know why they raided, but he would wait and hear from his lawyer. They read him his rights.

"We don't have a warrant for your wife. She is free to go as she pleases, but she can 't touch anything until we leave."

"Can she use the phone?" Gad asked.

"Yes, but she has to get permission."

His wife asked. "What do you want me to do?"

"Go to your mothers house, and call my parents."

The officers continued to stuff money in there pockets until their superior walked into the bed-room.

"That's enough. Shit, we got to leave enough money to put in the fucking papers." He looked over to the officer that was in his division. "Applewhite did you get any money?"

"Sure did sir."

"Okay that's enough. The papers are outside already. I'm going to let them, and evidence in. Okay." He turned around, and walked outside of the house.

The officers picked Gad up and walked him outside of the house. They placed him in a patrol car. The car pulled off. Gad looked at his house, and his destroyed gate for the last time. When they road through the gate, the police had set up a barricade. The police car pushed it's way past the other officers, and the news reporters who were snapping pictures. When the car pulled up near the reporters they started snapping pictures. Gad turned his face away from the cameras, but he didn't try to cover it.

The drug enforcement agencies raided several of Gad's businesses. They found several pounds of marijuana, but not as much as they thought they were going to. They found a few guns. The only place they found a large amount of money was in Gad's house. They locked up several of his associates, and the entire incident was on the news and in the papers. It didn't make front page, but it was a nice size article.

The officers tried to bring a bunch of reporters in the house, but Gad's wife met them at the door. "I don't want anybody in the house unless they're with the police or have a warrant. The first person she called was her lawyer. When the police left a couple of hours later she placed a call to Gad's family in Trinidad, but that was a couple of hours after the raid when the police left. By the time she called they had already gotten the news, and his mother was already on a private jet. She flew into Florida, and then she flew another private jet to Upstate New York.

She was met in Upstate by some family and friends that she had in New York, so by the time that Gad's wife was making phone calls, she got in touch with her at her mothers, and asked her to meet her in one of the condominiums she owned in downtown Manhattan.

Gad's mothers private jet landed in an airport in Upstate New York. When the jet landed it was met by three car entourage. Two brand new black Range Rovers, and a brand new black four door 850 Volvo. All of them had tinted windows. They would have brought just the trucks, but they decided they better bring the car in case she felt uncomfortable in the trucks and wanted to drive to the city in one of the cars.

The Cessna landed at a commercial airport that dealt with private service also. She would have caught a regular flight, but they took too long, and when there was an emergency she would use her family's private jets which were usually reserved for business.

That morning when she got the word, she rounded up the family she was taking with her, and they caught a private jet to Florida, and then another jet to Upstate New York. That was another reason she didn't use a commercial jet, because she brought two million dollars over in cash, and she didn't want the hassle of dealing with customs trying to get the money over. The legal way would be money transfers, and sometimes that could take days with an amount of money this large. So instead she flew over on a private jet herself.

The pilots were also the crew. They were the men who assisted her off the plane. Gad's mother Mrs. Ebbie brought two of her daughters with her. Two daughter in-laws, and her youngest sons girlfriend. She was going to need their support, and to help her conduct some legal business.

The pilots opened the hatch, and the ladies walked out. They were all wearing fur coats, and carrying at least a bag a piece. The girls had the opportunity to pack. The only thing that she did was gather two million dollars in cash, and stuffed it in her suit case.

The bodyguards walked over to the airplane. They greeted Gad's mother, and his sisters. One of the bodyguards tried to grab her bag. She pulled the bag away.

"That's okay. I have this one."

He immediately realized that it must have money, or some important documents in it. He walked them to the Range Rover, and opened the back. They placed their luggage in the back. He walked them to the back of the truck, and opened the doors. Gad's mother, and his eldest sister jumped in the back. The other ladies got into the Volvo, and the other Range Rover.

The trucks pulled off. It was snowing. It usually took about an hour to get to the city, but with the snow falling it was going to take a little while longer.

As soon as the vehicles pulled away Gad's mother reached into her coat, and pulled out a cellular phone. She glanced over at her daughter.

"Find Shirley's mother's telephone number for me."

The eldest daughter was carrying an expensive brief case, and she pulled out a large leather address book. She read the number off to her.

Gad's mother dialed the number, and Shirley picked the phone up. "Hello. May I speak to Shirley."

"Yes. Hello. Momma." Everybody called her Momma. Even her daughter in-laws.

"I've been trying to call you. Did you hear what happen?"

"Yes. I have. I'm about an hour away from the city. I want you to meet me at the condominium on Riverside. Have you ever been there?"

She hesitated for a second. "No I've never been there."

"Okay then. When I get to the city. I will call you, and have one of the bodyguards pick you up from your mothers house,"

They hung the phone up. She looked back at her eldest daughter. "Find the lawyer's number in that phone book. Tomorrow I want you to give him a call, and let him know we need to see him. "

She nodded her head.

"I want Shirley and the baby to stay with us until this thing blows over, and then she can decide if she going back to Trinidad with us, or if she is going stay in the states."

It was amazing how much Gad and his mother looked a like. They were a really nice looking family. She had the sandy hair that he had, but her's had turned grayish and the mixture of the two colors was beautiful.

She was slim and she still had a nice shape for her age. She looked like a she was a twenty year old with silver hair. She was still in shape, and she wore beautiful expensive clothing. She was gonna have to go to the village, Macy's, Bloomingdales, Lord, and Taylor to buy some clothing while she stayed over here handling her son's business. She had some clothing at the condominium, but it might not be winter attire.

"When we get to the condominium I'm going to rest. So you guy's can take a bodyguard and get whatever the house needs."

"Momma we don't need no bodyguard."

"Girl don't argue with me. I'm tired. I said you need a bodyguard, and I don't want you going anywhere without one. If you do just catch a flight out of here, and go home tomorrow.

Gad's mother went to the condominium on Riverside drive. She didn't know whether the police were following her or not, and she really didn't care. The only thing that she would be dealing with is cash.

The condominium was smaller than the ones that they owned downtown, but besides size, they were just as nice. They had owned this one for years. She remembered coming to this condominium as a child. When the neighborhood was majority white. It was in a high rise building. It's picture window over looked the river, and the tree's that lined the Riverside Drive. It was really a beautiful scene. The people that lived in the building now had money, but it wasn't as exclusive as it use to be.

When Gad's mother went to the condominium she checked the safe, and Gad had a little over a million dollars in cash in the safe. She organized that, and sent it back to Trinidad on a private plane with her eldest daughter. That was probably the main reason that she brought them. Their husbands would be running the business one day, and they would have to learn how to handle things like this. Unfortunately, the inevitable.

Gad's mother, her second daughter, and a bodyguard drove to the law offices of Alfred Sherinwitz.

Alfred Sherinwitz had represented her family ever since the early seventies when one of her brothers had caught a charge. He was a young promising attorney then. Not very handsome, and not a very sharp dresser, but he listened. That was important for a client/lawyer relationship. The lawyer must understand that he worked for the client.

Visiting for the federal holding facility was only at a certain time, so Mr. Sherinwitz and Gad's mother had to hold there meeting in the Range Rover.

Mr. Sherinwitz agreed to drive to the airport, and see Mrs. Ebbie off. Then the body guard would drive him back to the city, and turn around again to pick up Mrs. Ebbie. This was easy work for the bodyguard so he didn't complain.

They picked Mr. Sherinwitz up at his law office in downtown Manhattan. He took a couple of minutes to come down to the car. They parked in front of the building so that he would be able to find them.

When he walked out of the building he was only wearing a suit jacket.

Mrs. Ebbie looked at him. Some of these lawyers were

fools. They had money. They made money. But they wouldn't spend anything on themselves. It was crazy.

The bodyguard opened the back door for him, and he got in. He placed his hands to his mouth to stop the chill that was running threw his body. He was carrying a brief case. They shook hands. They had been friends for years.

As soon as they got into the truck the bodyguard pulled off into traffic.

"So what are we facing?" She was straight forward, and to business. He didn't have time, and she didn't have time.

"It looks bad but it's not really bad. First of all the case is a federal case. Now that's bad because the government is not like the regular police. They want a conviction. If they don't get a conviction they're not going to stop until they get one. They raided the house, and they found a couple hundred thousand dollars. That's gone. They want the house and the three cars that were parked outside."

When the police raided the house Gad's Mercedes Benz, a Toyota Four Runner, and a 318i BMW that was his wife car, and they took that. They were going to keep it because she didn't make enough legally to afford it.

Gad's mother wasn't worried about it. The only thing that pissed her off was that they got the money. She was glad they didn't know anything about the other condominium. Then they would have gotten the other money. "Does Gad know who set him up?"

"I received the government's evidence sheet, and your son sold a couple of hundred pounds to a government informer."

"A government informer. Who is a government informer. A cop?"

"No, he's not a cop. He's somebody that works with the police or the government."

"A snitch."

"Yes a snitch. But he brought a police officer with him on some of the transactions, so they have it just like Gad sold to the police. Plus they got a couple of guns outside of the stores, and his residence. I talked to investigators, and they want your son to become an informer."

"An informer."

The lawyer interrupted her before she could add it. "Yes a snitch."

"That's not possible."

"I don't know, I think I should talk to your son first. They think your son knows people. He won't have to set up the people that he buy's from. He can't set up some of the people that buy from him."

"Let me tell you one thing. This is business. None of my sons are cowards. Cowards snitch. You can not be in any business, and be coward. If I find out you even tell my son he can become snitch then I'm gonna fire you. You understand me." She was pissed off. If her father could hear this he would be rolling around in his grave.

"If he is convicted how much time is he facing?"

"He's facing ten to five years with the weed conviction. The guns are bad but since they don't have him committing any violent acts, he's pretty safe on that part. I can get all the time ran together. I say at the most were looking at a little over five years. Federal time."

Now she was really pissed. This man wanted her to destroy other people over five years. That's why Caucasians did not last in this business. Because they were cowards.

"It might take us a couple of months cause they really want to pressure your son into becoming a snitch. That's how the fed's get most of their cases. From dealers snitching on other dealers. I can get it down it's just going to take a little time.

"Now the other guys. As long as they don't start snitching they'll get the same amount of time or less. Most of them are only facing weapons charges."

That's good. She was glad to hear that. That meant less legal money.

"How much is it going to cost for each defendant?"

"Well your son's case we're going to need at least fifty thousand dollars to start, and the other guys will be about twenty-five thousand cash a piece because they have lesser charges. Now if we have to go to trial then the price tag doubles. Cash with no payment plans."

"You'll have your start up money tomorrow."

"The only thing that really scares me is they might try to hit your son with tax evasion. That means more plea bargaining, and more cash."

She gave him an evil look. She hated lawyers. If the police did not break you then they sure would.

The conversation that Mrs. Ebbie had with the lawyer made her trip to the private airport in Upstate quicker. They were at the airport in no time. By the time that she arrived her private jet was fueled, and waiting for her. They went over a couple of things, and then she exited with her daughter to visit her son.

It took them a little over an hour to get to the federal holding cell that they kept Gad in. Then they went threw a army of security. Then it took another hour before they could even locate Gad, and bring him down.

When he came down he looked rested. In fact, he looked like he had been woke up out of his sleep. As soon as his mother saw him her heart started racing. This was the hardest part of the business. Seeing your love ones locked away.

Gad took his seat, and they greeted each other. She asked him how was he feeling. He told her things were good. He was only worrying about his wife and the baby.

"They're fine."

Good, he was satisfied.

They discussed a little business.

"I'm going to sell all of the store fronts. I'm putting them up for sale tomorrow."

"I don't know if their going to let you do that."

"How can they stop me? You were only leasing the stores from your parents realty company. They can confiscate any of that property. They're lucky they got that house and those cars. They're not getting anything else. Now these devils might get evil, and give you no bail. So I'm going to need you to write me, and send me the list of the names of the people I can trust, and the people I can't. I don't want you to worry. I'm gonna handle everything. I put a couple of thousand on your books, but if you need anything else you let me know. Shirley and the baby are going home with us for at least a month. But I'll send her back once a week to visit. Okay?"

Gad could only smile. His mother would never change. When she was a child her father had taught him these things, and now she had to go threw them with her. Finally she was letting his sisters handle everything. It was about time. She needed the rest. She had been doing this for years.

SEVEN

When the word reached the family that Gad had been arrested and charged with a federal crime they were not only upset, they were sadden. With out the connection that they had threw Gad the family would lose thousands of dollars in income. For the first month things were smooth because Corty had just made a move, and purchased a large amount. They didn't know the details of the arrest so Christopher told Corty to lay low just to be on the safe side.

The marijuana spots were doing excellent. Business was steady and good. Corty and Franklin handled most of that. The only thing that Christopher had to do was make the initial transaction in New York, and get the product back.

He didn't know if the feds were onto him so he disappeared for a couple of days just until he found out if they were looking for him, or not. He had been in touch with Gad's mother, and she asked him to lay low until she found out the details. She came all the way down to the city to tell him this. She stayed for a couple of days with his wife, and her daughters. Then she went shopping and did a little gambling. The ladies didn't really like gambling. They preferred to shop, and attend the shows at the casino.

When Christopher returned to the area, Corty picked him up from the airport. It was a medium size airport that was located in a city called Pomona, New Jersey. It catered to commercial and private flights,

Corty drove a eighty-three Acura Integra, and his wife drove a Acura Integra coupe. They were much too small. So when

91

he went to pick Christopher up from the airport he drove in a rented Buick Century. He hated the car but he had to have something to pick Christopher up in. The only other person to accompany him was Lionel. One of his workers and bodyguards.

They pulled up in front of the airport entrance, and Christopher was standing their with a bunch of luggage. Corty knew that he went on vacation to one of the island, but he didn't know which one. His wife would fly out and meet him on weekends.

The bodyguard pulled up to where Christopher was standing, Corty jumped out, and they embraced.

"How was your trip?"

"It would have been better if my wife could have stayed with me."

"You didn't meet any bitches over there?"

"I meet a couple of girls, but I really didn't fuck around."

They put the luggage in the trunk, and pulled off.

Once Christopher got into the car he let out a deep breathe. Even though Chris had his vacation Corty could tell that he was still tired.

"What's up? You okay?"

Christopher rubbed his head as if he had a headache. "I'm fine. I'm just a little fucked up over this Gad thing. I can't believe they knocked him the fuck off."

"Who set him up?"

"I'm not really sure. But I know they got an idea."

"Well don't let that shit bother you. We'll handle it. I promise." Corty smiled. Not having marijuana was kind of killing him. He use to sell speed occasionally when he first started dealing drugs, and he would have switched back but everybody had switched to using cocaine. So instead he purchased heroin. Christopher told him to take it easy, and be careful. He did.

"What's Gad and his people going to do?"

"I'm not really sure what they're going to do, but his mother said she was going to get in touch with me this week, and I guess will have a meeting. They got everybody. I don't know if they're going to jet, or if their going to set something else up, "

"I hope they set something up quick because my customers are starving."

"How about you?"

"Oh I'm fine. I don't give a fuck how long it takes. I'm really just worried about my customers. Did you hear that Andre beat this mother fucker up at the bar, and the police are looking for him. Plus, he fucked some of Mr. Gaston's and Mr. Johnson's money up at the casino. Nobody has been able to catch him. I know where he is at. He's in a room with one of those chicken head bitches. I bet you. That's not even the bad part. The bad part is that the police are going to Jokers houses looking for him. The guy he fucked up is on a respirator."

"Why'd he fuck the guy up?"

"He fucked the guy up for fucking with Sandra."

"For fucking with Sandra. Everybody's fucking Sandra."

"I think he just don't like the mother fucker. It really doesn't matter now because the mother fucker's almost dead. The police have been sitting in the bar for hours."

"What?"

"How's everybody making money?"

"They not making money, and now they're trying to come to my bar, and fucking make money. You know my bars too small."

Christopher shook his head. He left, and got a little relaxation. The bar was entirely to hot. They were going to have to leave and find another location now. Definitely.

Andre really pissed him off because Andre had been doing stupid things ever since he came. Nobody could touch him because he was one of the family. Christopher was hoping that now maybe if he fucked up some money, Mr. Johnson would make him stay in Philadelphia.

By the time that early eighty-three rolled around the speed business in Atlantic City, and the South Jersey area had completely disappeared. Cocaine was taking over in a strong way. It was starting to pop up all over New York. The thing that was really making the cocaine business explode was free basing. Free basing was when a person cooked the cocaine to it's purest form, and smoked it. Either in a glass pipe, cigarette, or marijuana. It was spreading like a craze. Young dealers were using it and the customers really loved it. It was spreading in the casino industry. The only thing that casino employee's did was sniff. Christopher wanted a piece of that cocaine money.

Mr. Johnson, and his family in Philadelphia were already selling cocaine and getting rich. Christopher had become a millionaire from selling heroin. He knew that the rest of the family had made thousands from selling heroin too. The family was becoming rich, and powerful.

He knew that Big Aaron, Crazy Moe, and Mr. Johnson were sitting back and making thousands of dollars a week just as partners. They made a couple of thousand a week from getting a percentage of the family's heroin profits.

Christopher wanted to enter the business, and organize it. Michael, one of Mr. Johnson's lieutenants, was already coming down and selling powdered cocaine in the bar. He was doing excellent. Mainly because nobody really had it.

He would purchase the cocaine, and cut it several times. Then he would bottle it and distribute it with some other guy's he brought down from Philadelphia. There was already a market for whole selling. The other dealers wanted ounces, quarter ounces, and more.

Corty did not know it but Christopher flew to Trinidad for a private meeting with Gad's family. In return for promising he would make an attempt on the life of the informant who turned Gad in, Gad's family was going to give Christopher special favors.

After that he flew to New York where he was met by William Johnson and Aaron Gaston. There they met with the Dominicans who were selling kilograms of cocaine fro twenty-five thousand dolars each. They purchased fifty for twenty thousand dollars each. That was a million dollars. Christopher was going to didtribute all of it and split the profit with Mr. Johnson and Mr. Gaston.

In addition, Mr. Johnson bought another fifty so he could supply his lieutenants. It was official now. They were leaving the speed business completely. They had no other choice. Crack cocaine had already reached Philidelphia and it was spreading in epidemic proportions.

EIGHT

It took a little over a month but Christopher moved his entire operation to the projects. He picked one of the projects that was relatively quiet. It was only temporary. He was going to make a move uptown to one of the streets that was loaded with heroin, cocaine, and marijuana houses so his customers flow would blend in with the traffic at everybody else's spot. This way he would not have to worry about the police.

If things really went smooth, since the only people he took was family he could just set up an elaborate look out system. They can take the risk of getting raided as long as they had enough time to dump the product. Things were changing.

Another option was to move locations every couple of months. That would be good. After Christopher moved the location, and moved up to selling bundles only, business slowed down a little bit. He had found out a couple of months after the raid that the police knew that he controlled everything. Now whenever they caught somebody with heroin they would ask questions about him. It had become annoying. Dealers he hardly knew would come to him, and warn him.

"They're on you bad boy. They want you." He was tired of hearing it."

Christopher figured the only way that he could still supply Martin, Corey, Lyn, and Marc was if he made them partners. He would give them about a kilogram. Four and a half ounces of heroin already cut, and prepared for distribution. They would in turn sell it powder form, but the largest majority of it they bagged into bundles, and then customers would come, and buy bundles or bags from one of their spots (distribution points).

Junior, Big Aaron, Crazy Moe, and Mr. Johnson still got their cut of the profit threw Christopher, so they were happy the profit wasn't as big because of the new form of distribution, but it was good enough.

The Secret Society

Little Aaron's business suffered because now that they all broke apart he actually had to form his own crew, continue heroin distribution. At first he did bad but Mr. Johnson sent a couple of guys down to help him, and he start doing pretty good. He became partners with Michael from Mr. Johnson's crew.

Christopher and Little Aaron already invested their money together. That was partners enough. So Christopher cut him out, and started taking the partnership money directly to Big Aaron. Mr. Gaston had money invested in his son and Chris, so the new form of distribution didn't really affect his cut that much. Mr. Johnson received his cut of the profit out of Big Aaron's cut.

Christopher held a meeting so that they could handle all of this. At first everybody was a little scared to make the move mainly because they thought if they broke apart things would fall apart. They were really scared to change. They had all become rich together, and now they were separating.

Christopher held important meetings at his house. He purchased a split level house in a predominately middle class neighborhood. Their were doctors and lawyers that lived in the neighborhood, but it was still middle class. He didn't buy something too extravagant because of the police scrutiny. They didn't bother him, and he liked it that way.

Atlantic City was predominately black. Most of the whites had moved to the outskirts of the city. To cities like Ventnor, Margate, or Longport.

For some reason Christopher loved the city. Since he knew that nothing was in his house he stayed in the City. Every body else advised him to move. He was too big for the city. The police would eventually try their best to destroy him, and staying in the city would make him an easy target.

Christopher had remodel his house. The interior and the exterior. It was beautiful. In the down stairs of his house was a bed-room. A small storage room. The entrance of the garage was in the storage-room. A laundry-room. A bath-room, and a den. His den was exactly like his living-room upstairs. He used his down stairs room as an office, and he placed another desk, and a pool table in the den. It was furnished nicely. His own private business office.

The only time his wife came down stairs was to wash clothing, and get something out of the storage room. She always checked first to make sure he was home because if he was home she didn't want to interrupt him, so she wouldn't make a single step downstairs.

Mr. Gaston was the last to arrive. He brought Crazy Moe over as his bodyguard. Christopher had several chairs brought down stairs so when he held a meeting his people would have a place to sit.

"I don't know if you really know why I called you here, but I have talked with each and everyone of you a couple of times. At one time or another everybody in here has talked to me about it. When I left a couple of weeks ago for that one month vacation all hell broke lose. Nobody worked together. In a way it was kind of good. But I see now we're going to have to have some kind of organization. We're going to have positions so if anything ever happen the family will know how to move. If not, this shit is going to crumble as soon as something happens to one of us. But if we organize then we can at least have some kind of command base, and know where we'll be moving. I'm a millionaire, and I know if the rest of you don't have hundreds of thousands then something is wrong. What we need to do is organize, and carry titles. Just like Mr. Johnson's family, and just like the Italians. I have thought about this for a couple of months. I didn't prepare anybody because I didn't want any hassle. If anybody has any objections they better speak now. If we don't change now, we're going to lose everything. Now nobody has to join this thing. You're free to leave right now. But if you stay after the meeting I'm going to need Your answer. If anybody doesn't agree they better speak now or forever hold their peace. This is the time now. The time to speak."

"I'm in." Martin was the first to raise his hands, and the others started raising their hands.

Christopher shook his head. "No... No.. Wait I have to explain everything. I'm going to take the position of head of the family." Christopher glanced over towards Big Aaron. He showed no emotion. Maybe he didn't object. Christopher would explain the details to him later.

"I would have made Big Aaron the boss, but he has obligations to Big Will, and I didn't want to start any conflict. Little Aaron will be my counselor. My right hand man. He will advise me on all decisions.. He will be my partner. He will be the second head of the family. If anything ever happens to me, he takes over. Then Martin. He'll be my underboss. My left hand. If he will be under Little Aaron succession wise. But he will hold the same authority. He's next in line. Now I hope that none you take this personal. I picked them mainly from seniority. I have been on the streets with Martin and Little Aaron since I was a baby. They have taught me all that I know, and they have watched my back. Both of them can easily refuse this position right now with no hard feelings. I will understand. Corty, Lyn, Corey, and Marc will be lieutenants. They will be aloud to form crews, but nobody will be aloud to join the family with out the permission of the family. Everything will be elected by vote. If one of you has any problems. Then that problem will be solved by vote. If something happens to one of the boss, counselor, or the underboss then the family must have a vote on which lieutenant takes a higher position. I hope this seems fair to everyone. If you have any objections speak now. Another thing is all this fighting. There will be no fighting amongst family members. If you have a disagreement bring it to the table. Nobody in the family can bring harm to anybody without the family's permission. This will put an end to all this foolishness."

Everyone knew that he was referring to Andre. The police were still coming to King Tut's looking for him. It was crazy. The young man he hit had died. The last that Christopher heard he was back in Philadelphia working for Mr. Johnson who was pissed at the fact that he lost almost two hundred thousand dollars of his money gambling.

"What's up with Mr. Johnson?" Big Aaron asked. This was important, he had to know. If Big Will got cut out it could start a war.

"I'm going to receive a cut out of all the profits and out of that cut I will give you, and Big Will a cut. Organizing is going to secure everybody's money. Period. Nothing will really change. I just wanted to do this so things can run smoother. That's my only reason. Plus I want to protect myself, and make sure we have a strong unit. I want to surround myself with loyalty."

"What about Michael? Why didn't you cut him in?"

"I would have loved to cut Michael in, but he's obligated to Big Will I thought. We still can do business with him. I know they were sent here to help you and Junior out. If Little Aaron agrees we can make them partners with the family, and you can talk to Mr. Johnson to see if he will let them operate freely, and just give him a cut of the profit."

"He's not going to do that. He makes more with them distributing for him."

"Well, their part of the family too. They can do their own thing under our protection. I know Michael's a businessman, and he's not going to do anything stupid. We can have a meeting with Mr. Johnson, and arrange everything."

Corty who was the weakest lieutenant because he sold marijuana, and he spoke. "Excuse me, this really has nothing to do with the meeting. I just don't want you to forget. We have that meeting with Gad's family in Trinidad. I need to get with you and make arrangements. I don't know who's going or what. Can I speak to you tonight."

"Of course." Christopher reclined in his chair. They all had drinks sitting in front of them. His wife knocked hard on the den door, and pushed it open.

"Dinner's ready."

Christopher smiled at her, "Okay honey." She turned out to be a good wife. He was happy that he married her.

"Well that covers everything I wanted to say. If you have any questions, we can get together later, and roll over the ruff edges. I want everybody's answer within a week. If I don't have your answers by then I'll just move ahead with the people that want to move with me."

What happen next Christopher didn't expect. Martin raised his glass. "To the family." The other's picked up their glasses, and they crashed in a toast.

Then Christopher was shocked again. Corty stood up and walked over to Christopher. He kissed both of his cheeks, and then he kissed his hands. He embraced him with the brotherly love he truly felt for Christopher.

"I pledge my eternal loyalty." Christopher embraced him back. The other's lined up and embraced him, and pledged their loyalty also.

Then Big Aaron stood up, and embraced him. "Congratulations."

Then Crazy Moe stood up, and patted him on his back, "Congratulations."

After this meeting, they were officially a family.

NINE

It took months for Michael to get the word to Andre that he had covered the debt that he owed to Mr. Johnson. Andre was entirely too smart. So instead of immediately popping back on the scene, he went to visit Michael. They had a long discussion. He spent a couple of weeks with Michael, and then he returned to Philadelphia.

They came to the agreement that he would work things out with Mr. Johnson, and then he would hire a lawyer, and return to Atlantic City. Once that he got there he would turn himself in to the authorities. The lawyer promised him he could get the murder charge brought down to involuntary manslaughter.

He would end up doing a couple of years, but not life. He would probably end up with something like fifteen years with a five year stipulation. This lawyer was good.

Before Andre could do any of this he had to return to Philadelphia and visit Mr. Johnson. Disappearing for long periods of time like that was enough to make anyone suspicious. If somebody disappeared the family assumed he was locked up or working with the police. Dead and missing, or running for their life because they crossed the family. When this happen usually they wouldn't run for long. It was easier just to become an informant, and live under police protection.

Andre had disappeared for three months. Everybody

knew that he had fucked up a quarter of million dollars, and feared for his life. So instead of trying to explain he went to his father, and told him his intentions. His father gave him a couple of thousand, and told him to disappear. He traveled to a couple of other places, but he always seemed to end up back in Jersey at the casino.

He would go down south open up a powder, and crack operation. This worked a lot of times, but it had the tendency to be risky. He found it was easier to gain the dealers trust and then rob them. It worked for a while. The only time that it foiled was when the other dealers would catch on to what he was doing to them.

Andre got a couple of thousand dollars together, and got the heart to see Mr. Johnson. Michael had started letting him come back to the city, and he was making a little money. When he came back to Atlantic City he met Michael at one of the bars that he operated out of now. It was early eighty-three, and everybody was switching over to selling powdered cocaine. It wasn't as profitable as heroin, but it made money. It was easier to acquire, and it was just as steady.

Michael had put it to him straight. "You is a stupid mother fucker. Look at this." He pulled a wad of money out. "Were making all this fucking money, and you want to run around here with hoe's gambling. Stupid shit. You beat mother fuckers up over girls that don't deserve it. Fuck them hoe's. I talked to Big Will. I told him I fucked up some of the money, and that we were working together to pay him back. I gave him about fifty thousand so far. He wants that money but he's not really to worried about it. It was all tax money I had saved up for a couple of months when he was going threw that trial."

Mr. Johnson had gotten locked up on a conspiracy to murder trial, and a stipulation of his bail was that he be put on a monitoring system. Once they put him on the bracelet he stopped all business. He let it be known that the only thing that he would be doing was commands. It would be the lieutenants responsibility to account, and protect the money. The trail only lasted for about a couple of months so that's how the tax money accumulated to that amount.

Any money that Mr. Johnson received a cut of with out

investing any of his own money was considered tax money. It was really all profit. A lot of the lieutenants could make money anyway that they wanted to as long as they gave Mr. Johnson a cut of the profits. That was why it was called a street tax.

Once Christopher joined the family, and they started making serious money in Atlantic City again. Mr. Johnson realized that it was better to keep the lieutenants directly working with him. It was about the same amount of money, but more important it was more control.

With the cocaine Mr. Johnson would give Michael and Christopher a couple of kilo grams of cocaine. They would take it back to the city. Whatever profit they made Mr. Johnson received half. Mr. Johnson let his intentions be known. As far as he was concerned Christopher was Big Aaron's successor, Michael would be his right hand man in Jersey. When Christopher and the rest of the family became organized it hurt Mr. Johnson. He had a better business proposition for Christopher. One that would make them richer, and more importantly more powerful.

Mr. Johnson would learn over, and over again. Power was more important than wealth. Mr. Johnson was wealthier than Christopher, but Christopher was more powerful in Atlantic City. Eventually he would be much more powerful and wealthier.

Andre and Mr. Johnson met at one of the apartment's he kept in North Philadelphia, Andre was informed to come alone, Mr. Johnson didn't have anytime for childish games. Only business.

Andre pulled up in a Buick Regal. He hated the car. He was used to driving around in Mercedes Benz's, Jaguars, Porsche's, nice foreign cars. This would do, it was for free. It was a girl's car he had met a couple of months ago. Her family had money, and she had a good job working at a bank. It was her car, but he took it over. At first she would let him hold it while she went to work. Then eventually he would take it anytime he needed it. Sometimes he would not even pick her up for work. Sometimes he would not come home for days. He did not care. If she complained then he would fuck her up. He knew that eventually she would get tired of him, and stop beeping him. He told her the last time that he spoke to her. No matter what, the last thing she better do was call the police, and she was too afraid to. She knew that he drove around with pistols, and everything. She didn't want to get him in trouble.

Andre pulled up to the apartment in North Philadelphia. It was a quiet section. He had been there a couple of times before when he was in good grace.

Mr. Johnson controlled a large part of North Philadelphia, he had a bunch of young men who were selling heroin, speed, and crack in the area for him. They called him "Godfather." They gave him the title of pimp because he had a lot of young lady friends. It was the money.

Andre pulled up in front of the building. Mr. Johnson owned a Bentley, but he never drove it unless he was going somewhere important. When he was running around the city conducting business he usually drove around in his fully loaded Acura Legend. It was an ugly champagne color, his wife loved it. It was suppose to be one of her cars. He himself preferred his Cadillac Eldorado.

Andre pulled up to the apartment. The Acura Legend was parked outside. The one thing he had to hand Mr. Johnson was that he was very disciplined. He woke up early in the morning, and went around the city conducting legal, and illegal business.

There was a time that he could go around the city without always having a bodyguard, but once drugs became the strongest way to make an illegal living a lot of things changed. Mainly violence. Philadelphia's underworld became more violent with the drug explosion.

Andre parked the car. He was carrying a gun. He knew better than to carry the gun to a meeting with Mr. Johnson unless his intentions were to kill him.

Andre pulled the gun from his waist, and placed it under the front seat. There was a bunch of trash in the car so he didn't worry about leaving it there, and somebody breaking into it. It was to junkie. Car thieves like to steal cars that are appealing. Who wants to joy ride around in a lemon.

Andre got out of the car and rang the door bell. It took a couple of minutes before the buzzer went off. Andre pushed the door open. Went into the lobby of the apartment building, and caught the elevator to the floor of Mr. Johnson's apartment. The security guard at the desk spoke to him. He must have remembered him from the past.

Clifton, Mr. Johnson's bodyguard opened the door. Big Cliff had been working for Mr. Johnson for over twenty years. He had murdered for his boss. Did some time for his boss. They were inseparable. Cliff was one of the few people that Mr. Johnson truly knew he could trust. Cliff wasn't in the business for the money only anymore. He had long ago became wealthy. Not as wealthy as he could have been, but wealthy enough to be happy.

He owned a couple of pieces of property, and a small grocery store in West Philadelphia. All thanks to Mr. Johnson. Cliff was short, but he was solid. He always dressed up. He was wearing a sports coat, dress slacks, and some decent loafers. When they were running around in the fifties, sixties, and even late seventies they were into clothes. But now they just dressed in business attire because the young generation was into different types of clothing. They didn't wear suits, and dress clothing like the gangsters of old. Instead they ran around with jeans and sneakers on. The only time they dressed up was if they attended an event.

Big Cliff looked threw the peep hole and opened the door. He peeped threw with the chain lock still attached to the door. Andre was pissed. He just looked down so he wouldn't have to stare in his face, and be even more disappointed.

The door swung open. Big Cliff was standing there puffing on a cigar. He had a gun in his waist band. As soon as Andre entered the apartment Cliff stopped him by placing his hands on his chest.

"Lift your hands," he still had the cigar in his mouth, and the smoke was bothering his eyes. He patted Andre down, Andre was a little frighten. They might have used all of this as a set up. He felt a little trapped.

He was a little at ease because Mr. Johnson conducted business here, and it wouldn't be wise for them to kill him here.

Cliff searched him and walked away leaving him standing there. The television was on. Shanice, Big Will's girlfriend, was in the kitchen making dinner. He could see her from the kitchen. She had a black eye.

He would later find out that Big Will blacked her eye because he found out she was cheating on him. Andre just laughed. What did he expect? These young ladies are not going to sit around and wait for some old man.

When Big Will came from the back he was pulling on a cigar. He walked over to Andre, and they hugged. "What's up boy?" He patted Andre on his back. "Come into the office."

Big Will owned apartments all over Philadelphia, and in every single apartment he set up some kind of office. This office he had a desk, a telephone, and a few other little things. His offices looked like the office a business man would set up in his home.

Big Will sat in the chair and folded his hands. Andre could see the disappointment on his face.

"What happen?"

It took Andre a couple of minutes to get the words out. "Them fucking casino's."

Big Will interrupted him. "Not that I mean where the fuck you been? Michael explained the money situation to me. Where the fuck you been? You know what's the first thing I'm thinking when you disappear? I'm thinking either you got killed or the police got you trying to make you a snitch. I knew you weren't locked up cause of my boy's in the precinct. I know you ain't dead because we keep hearing you're here and there. Are you getting high? Cause if you need help we'll send you to a drug rehab. I was pissed. I need you in Atlantic City, and your running around here getting high, and chasing bitches."

Andre was relieved. Mr Johnson was more worried about him than anything else.

"I swear to God. I ain't been getting high. I just got scared because I owed you that money."

"Michael told me ya'll messed it up gambling in the casino. I was pissed. But I was young once. I'll tell you this. If you're ever disrespectful enough to fuck my money up again, I will kill you. I was more hurt that you guy's were ditching me. We're a family. I love you guys like family so don't treat me like shit."

Andre was hurt, and embarrassed now. "I swear to God it

will never happen again."

"You guy's are running around doing stupid shit while Christopher is running around bringing me money. I sent you guy's down there to help him. We're trying to put something strong together. I need everybody. I have to help you with this case, and lose you for a couple of years. That could fuck up my plans. I was going to clean Atlantic City out then you, Christopher, Michael, and Little Aaron could run shit. I didn't want to start a war without you here. Christopher and them are babies. They don't know how to handle them selves."

"So what do you want me to do?"

"I want you to stay up here with me and your father. Your going to become my bodyguard, and my personal watch dog over Atlantic City. Your going to collect my money. Your going to settle a couple of little problems I'm having down there, but I don't want you down there all the time. Your going to stick with me up here, and bodyguard me. The only time you go to Atlantic City is when I command you to go."

Big Will smiled after the comment. Andre was about to say something but he didn't. He took the gesture with affection.

"Plus if I see you anywhere near the casino's I'm putting my foot square dead in your ass. I want you right here on my side, you hear me?"

Andre smiled, he was proud.

"Do you need any money?"

"No, I got thirty grand for you.

"That's what the fuck what I'm talking about. Business."

Big Will got up walked over to him, and they embraced. Andre really felt like he was Big Will's son, and not a lot of lieutenants got this type of treatment.

"You know what else saved you two silly mother fuckers, right?"

"No. What?"

"Your father gave me all my fucking money. I couldn't even take it from him. I gave it back. But you two, your going to pay me every dime. I should have charged you interest."

Andre was overwhelmed. He knew his father would

intercede. He also felt bad. He remember telling his father what he did. They argued, and his father told him. "Your costing me more than your worth. I wish that you never got involved in this shit. Or you would have stuck with me, but no your hard headed. Let's see if your smarts save your life." His father gave him twenty-five grand. He took half of it to the casino, and lost it in a day. He was praying the God's were going to let him win, and save his life, but they didn't.

"When do I report to work?"

"I want you at my house nine o'clock in the morning sharp. You hear me?"

"Yes sir." He smiled.

TEN

Republic of Trinidad, and Tabago Port of Spain

Gad's family owned businesses all over Trinidad, and Tobago the small island that was located twenty miles northeast of Trinidad. His family owned a majority stock in a Government Private Petroleum refinery. They owned their own small Petroleum refineries, a petrochemical plant, a steel mill, and a company that produce fertilizer. They also owned factories that processed foods, beverages, textiles, electronics equipment, and plastic goods.

That did not included their real-estate portfolio that included thousands of undeveloped acres, hotels, condominiums, and apartment complexes. Gad's mother was legally worth more than two-hundred million dollars.

Her family was the richest and most powerful family in the Republic of Trinidad, and Tobago. They influenced politics. Everything. In Trinidad they were treated, and lived like royalty.

Ever since the island was discovered by Spanish explorers marijuana had been widely used. The Arawak, and Carib Indians that lived on the island used it for medicine purposes. Once the explorers came in contact with it, and found out it's potency they used it for pleasure. The Trinidadian people did not know the true worth of it until the late eighteen hundreds when tourist started visiting the country, and purchasing the herb. By the early nineteen hundreds the islanders realized they had a profitable business, and start profiting off of it. The islanders would set up small businesses near the tourist attractions. In those businesses they would sell marijuana. Most of the tourist were Americans. They would come over to the tourist area, and purchase pounds. Then take them back to their country, and sell them. They made a lot of money, but the competition was ridiculous. A few of them had decided to go to America themselves, and start distributing themselves.

By the early nineteen tens, Gad's grandfather on his mother's side had opened a small novelty store in the tourist section of town. He was in business for a couple of years, and built a clientele of tourist that would come, and purchase pounds. They would take these pounds back to the countries that they were from.

It was a couple of years after he started his business that he met a group of young black gentlemen who owned bars, and grocery stores. All kinds of businesses in America. They told him about the unlimited opportunities that America had for a young black business man, such as himself. They explained that if he could get the product to America, then they could take the merchandise to New York, Chicago, Atlanta, Philadelphia, Washington D.C. and all over the east coast where there was a growing demand for marijuana. The black men that Gad's grandfather had met ran all kinds of illegal rackets. But the biggest money maker for these men were speak-easies. The illegal bars and liquor houses they had set up. You could sell anything there. Club owners had to go all the way to California to purchase marijuana, or sometimes as far as Mexico. If not they waited for what ever West Indians lived on the east coast to head down south, and get them marijuana.

Gad's grandfather was making money, but he did not start making serious money until he started transporting marijuana to America. It only took him a couple of years to become a millionaire, and by the time that the thirties and the forties rolled around everybody was shipping marijuana to America. With the hippie explosion things only got better.

Once Gad's grandfather became a millionaire he purchased all kinds of property in Trinidad. He mainly invested his money in up and coming businesses. He purchased a house in Miami, Florida, Dallas Texas, and New York City. After a couple of years he made so much money that he would spend his summers in Trinidad, or another island. Where he owned several more houses. He taught his entire family the business. His son's did most of the physical operations.

Gad's grandfather never retired from the marijuana business. He had a stroke in the early seventies, and died a couple of days after that. But by the time that he was dead he had amassed an enormous legal empire. He owned several restaurants in Trinidad. Large amounts of shares in refineries. Real-Estate in Trinidad, and New York city. He was worth more than fifty million, and growing. Legally, he did not have to distribute marijuana any more.

He had pushed his family into Trinidadian politics. Like most powerful businessmen he wanted his family involved in politics like Joseph Kennedy had done with his family. One of the men that he really admired.

Gad's grandfather was highly respected in America and New York. Eventually because of his influence in Trinidadian politics he became highly respected. His loved ones called him the General. When in all actuality he should have been called genius.

Gad's grandfather even owned share's in British West Indian Airways. This allowed him to purchase some private planes. He established his own private airline, and was able to transport his own product to America instead of hiring someone to do the work for him.

When he passed away he divided his legitimate businesses amongst his children. His empire divided was not as strong but it still provided his children with legal wealth beyond their dreams.

The Secret Society

Gad's grandfather owned a private boat company. His family was loved, and treated like royalty in Trinidad. Christpher, Little Aaron, Corty Franklin, and two bodyguards flew to Miami, Florida to meet Gad's brother, and some of his bodyguards. They stayed at Gad's family houses in Plantation Florida for a day. Then the next morning they caught a private jet to Trinidad.

The moved very fast because they had important business to take care of in Trinidad. Plus Christopher and the rest of the family was traveling with over one million dollars in cash. They loaded the plane with the money, and flew over to Trinidad. Martin was left behind to conduct business, and run the family.

His father had tried to persuade him to flee the country, but Gad was against it. This was his opportunity to make his own money.

"Dad look. My lawyer says I'm facing a couple of years. Now I can flee, and never return to the country. Then we have to find somebody else to operate the business. Or I can go to jail for a couple of years, return to America, and still conduct business if I choose too."

His father could not disagree. His son was a grown man.

Gad's family met them at the British West Indian Airways. Then the plane refueled and flew to a private airport. When they got to the airport they were met by Gad's family. His father Isachar was there, his younger brother Naptali was there as well. He was the splitting image of Gad, but he had dark colored hair. When they came they arrived with a couple of bodyguards. They picked them up in four fully loaded Jeep Grand Cherokee's.

When they walked over to the truck they all embraced. Even though they did not all know each other it was a form of respect. Isachar looked at one of the bodyguards. "Bring all their luggage with me, and we'll go straight to the compound."

Most of the bodyguards were carrying weapons. This was normal for Trinidad with all the kidnaping and other commotion. The airport was in Port of Spain, but the estate that Gad's family lived on was located on the outskirts of a city called Tunapuna. Gad's mother had grown up on the estate, and after her father died it was willed to her. It was only natural. Her other sisters had married wealthy men, and she was closest to her father. Every one knew she was going to get the main estate. They loaded the luggage onto the truck, and then they drove to the compound. It was a little less than an hour away.

Trinidad is tropical and mountainous. The scenery was beautiful. It looked like a picture straight out of the jungle. Some area's were surprisingly still undeveloped. When they were driving they were passing small huts. There were children playing in front of huts and near the roads. Occasionally they would see some old women sitting on the porch of a house playing cards, or drinking rum. Every one waved when they drove past, and screamed their names. They were celebrities.

When Christopher came to the country for a month with his wife, he learned the country. It was beautiful. He loved it.

The only reason that they were in the country was for a business meeting. They had to iron out the details on how they were going to operate the business. Especially since Gad was facing time.

The compound was beautiful. It was a large stone white building made in a sort of Egyptian style. It looked so modern that Christopher was surprised when he found out that Mrs. Ebbie was raised in the house. The last time that he came to hide out for a month he stayed at one of the condominiums Gad's family owned in the capital. The more he did business with Gad and his family, the more he realized how powerful they were. They had so much property that it was amazing.

Now that he was seeing the compound that he had heard them talk about several times, he was impressed. The trucks pulled up to the front of the compound. There were several men standing in front of the entrance at a security booth. They were all carrying automatic machine guns, and assault weapons. When the truck approached the gate, one of the security guards walked over with his gun drawn, and approached the truck.

Isachar rolled his window down. The security guard peeped threw the car. No matter who was in the car he would not let it pass unless the occupants gave the pass word.

"Is everything cool?" The security guard had a deep voice.

The Secret Society

"Sin everything is Iry." The security guard waved his hand, and the gate came open. In Trinidad a lot of people made money off of kidnaping, so the security guard had to check every single car, and make sure that everything was okay.

The actual compound was about a half a mile away from the gate. The long road that lead to the house was surrounded by trees. Gad's family had imported all kinds of animals over to the estate, and some of the animals were running around freely.

When the trucks came to the main grounds of the compound their were several expensive cars parked in front. Their was a small stable on the side of the house with several horses. A heliport for helicopters, and something that looked like a small airplane landing strip.

When the trucks pulled up a bodyguard walked up to the trucks, and opened the doors. He escorted them to the entrance of the estate.

When they entered the mansion they were greeted by four maids dress in the short maid uniforms. One of the things that impressed them the most was how physically attractive most of the maids were.

"You can leave your bags here, and the maids will show you to your rooms. If ou're not tired we can have lunch now, and you can freshen up later." He glanced at his watch. They had enough time.

Two gentlemen dressed like butler's came from the back, picked up their bags, and walked with them while the maids escorted them to their rooms.

The maid walked Christopher to his room. It was beautiful. It was decorated in Indian motif. The room had a picturesque window that showed a view of the mountains. Directly under the window was a swimming pool, but you could not see it unless you walked onto the balcony. All of the rooms had fire places that were lit even though it was already warm. They were all nicely furnished. They even had Jacuzzi's. They had little dining areas in them. The bedrooms looked like apartments.

The maid and the butler walked to the bedroom door. "I will check back with you in a half an hour when lunch is ready. Do you want anything particular, or whatever the chef has on the menu?"

"I don't care what it is as long as it's not pork. I don't eat pork."

The maid just smiled and walked out of the bedroom.

Christopher walked over to the balcony, and looked over the edge. It was beautiful. He saw a bunch of women standing over by the pool playing with some children. They were wearing jewelry, and just relaxing. The pool was on the lower ground of the estate. The entire house was cut into a small mountain.

Christopher took a bath and changed into some comfortable clothing. It seemed like only a couple of minutes passed, and the maid was knocking on the door.

Christopher opened the door. She was beautiful. He never really cheated on his wife. Occasionally he would pick up a girl, but not very often. He was too busy. Plus his conscience would always bother him if he did. So he never did.

The maid was Trinidadian, but she did not have any dred's.

"Mr. Goines will be ready for the lunch meeting in five minutes. I will escort you when you're ready. I'm outside of the door."

She went to close the door, and he stopped her.

"No... You can sit right here until I'm ready." He picked the remote control to the television up and turned it on.

Five minutes later she walked him to the office where they would be holding the meeting. They walked threw the office and onto the balcony.

When Christopher walked onto the balcony the others were already sitting at the table conversing "I didn't hold any-thing up did I?"

"No brother, we were just sitting here chatting. How is your room? If you need anything. Just let one of the servants know, and we'll bring it to you. The telephones, and everything work."

One of the men dress in a butler uniform walked over and took their orders for breakfast. Rastifarians are very health conscience people. They usually only eat natural foods. Most of them don't even eat meat.

"Christopher, I have been discussing it for weeks now with

my son, and we have decided to pull out of New York all together. Now I don't know what we'll do in a couple of months, but for right now that's the decision we're going to stick with. We don't know what the feds know, and we don't want to find out." Gad was released on a quarter million dollar bail. One of the restrictions of his bail was that he not leave the country, or New York State. He had to report to a probation officer at least once a week. The first week that Gad came home he violated that. He had much to important business. The feds had put a permanent tail on him, but once he was able to ditch it he went to Trinidad. His family decided that it would be much to dangerous for him to keep taking risks moving around so they set him up in a house in Miami, Florida. The only time that he would go to New York was to visit his probation officer, and then he would have to ditch the fed's, and leave town again. Now that the trail was in process he was thinking about moving back to one of the condominiums that his family owned.

"My wife does have family working in Miami, and Texas that I could turn you onto, but their her brothers, and business wise we have no connections. We want to keep our business relationship. If you can bring your money to New York we'll fly it down to Trinidad for you. But New York is a little too hot, and we don't really want to do any business there."

They were really scared.

"We need you to bring the cash to Texas, or Florida. Preferably Florida. From there we can take it to Trinidad, and instead of you paying seven hundred, fifty dollars a pound we will only charge you two hundred dollars a pound. That's a hell of a savings."

"What about the money? What if something happens to the money?"

Gad jumped in on the conversation. "If you can get your money down to Florida we can guarantee it's safety to Trinidad. That's no problem. Plus, let's say you come and buy a thousand pounds. We want to front you a thousand pounds. So everything you get we double. At two hundred dollars a pound."

"So how and the hell are we suppose to get two thousand pounds out of Florida, and you got those cops going crazy down there over that cocaine shit?"

Gad looked at his father with the 'I told you so.' look.

"We can fly the weed to Texas where it's less heat. You can drive anything out of Texas. As long as your not coming out of Mexico. Now, the only problem that we have with coming out of Mexico is that it's going to cost us money to fly that shit over to Mexico, or Florida. Now that I'm gone we're trying to get all the big customers to bring their money to us. We'll cut back, and only do transporting. Once I come home from prison maybe we'll set something back up. But this time my uncle Asher, and Naptali will run everything."

"Why don't you send them over now?"

"We wanted to, but we don't know what the fucking pig seen." Isachar was pissed. He still had federal warrants in the United States. That's why he left the country. So he understood why his son would rather do his time in America then run, and never really be able to return comfortably. It was also the reason he was a little hesitant on sending his youngest son over there. He did not want anything to happen to him.

"Another reason we want to pull out is because we think that the feds might try to bring my mothers real company into this. I don't know, it's crazy. My family thinks it's better to move back, and survey everything before we try to make a move."

Just as they were talking a helicopter flew over their heads. They all followed it with their eyes. It was flying low. This compound was busy. It was where they conducted all of their business. Christopher did not see Gad's mother yet.

"So how is the delivery money going to affect us?"

"Where ever we deliver it's going to cost you a hundred more a pound. You still pay ten times cheaper than if you were buying it in New York. You can save a lot of money. We could have gave you a higher price, and then add the flying fee, but we want to be completely honest. The way that were operating now we need every single customer."

"Corty, how long will it take us to move about a thousand pounds?"

Corty paused for a couple of seconds, and contemplated

"I figure about a month. Give or take a couple of weeks. Depending on if we catch the first of the month."

"That's the soonest I would be able to have your money Gad. We don't have the clientele for two thousand pounds, but if you give us a little time we could move it."

"With a four hundred dollar savings. If you drop your price you'll have no problem."

One of the bodyguards walked over to the table. "Lunch is ready." Then he bent over and whispered something in his boss' ear.

Isachar looked over at his son. "Sacha is here." Then he looked over at the bodyguard. "Set up some more chairs. Their going to eat with us."

Fifteen minutes after the helicopter landed some bodyguards escort Antonio Sacha and his bodyguards to the breakfast table.

Christopher and the other didn't know it, but at the time Sacha was one of the most powerful cocaine lords in Columbia. He had started out a regular thief and then in the late sixties he switched with his family to the marijuana business. By the late seventies cocaine was getting more profitable each year. He sat and watched his friends make millions and millions of dollars until he entered the cocaine business. Now only a couple years later he was the most powerful cocaine baron. He made millions of dollars in profit a day.

He walked over to the table and shook everybody's hand. When he got to Isachar, Isachar stood up and they embraced. They had been doing business for years together.

Whenever Isachar's crops were messed up he would go to the Colombians and buy marijuana. Mrs. Ebbie's father used to do the same thing once the business picked up, but his connection died, and eventually they started doing business with Sacha.

They did not talk business while they had lunch. They finished eating, and then went on the estate and rode horses. Isachar wanted to show them the property.

Sacha's bodyguards followed every move he made. Once

he almost fell off the horse, and before he could fall one of the bodyguards was on the ground next to him waiting to catch him.

Isachar rode the horses a couple of miles past the estate, and they approached a couple of factories. The factories looked like legitimate factories, but once they got inside Christopher realized that they were only storage houses. There were thousands of barrels of marijuana.

The business was getting so advanced that now they were sending the marijuana over in a factory seals. When the family purchased pounds they were already wrapped in plastic.

In every single factory that Gad's family owned there was a living quarter, and eating area. When they arrived lunch and everything was already prepared. They went into a private room. It was furnished like an executive office in a building off of Wall Street. It looked like a conference-room. After they entered the room a bodyguard stood outside to watch guard.

Levi, Gad's uncle on his mother's side, was second in command of the operations in Trinidad. He was actually more powerful than all of them in the room, but he played a less important roll. In Trinidad he was powerful, but he held no influence over business in America like his sister's children did. When he first entered the business he was responsible for over seeing Trinidad operations, and never really left that position. His father wanted him to over see his legitimate holding, he never did. Instead, he would go to the Florida estate, and waste his time dealing with women. His father hated men who put women in front of business. So they fell off and had a weak relationship.

When they walked into the conference-room one of the bodyguards walked in, and whispered something into his ears. He turned around to Levi, and whispered in his ear.

"The boys from Texas are here, I want you to entertain them until I finish conducting my business."

When Levi walked away he closed the doors.

Once the doors were closed Isachar started the meeting.

"Antonio these are my partner's from America. Chris, Corty, and Franklin. They came with a million dollars, and they want to buy some pounds. They're going to spend a million, and

I want to spend a million. How much are you going to charge us for the pounds?"

Christopher didn't know why the Colombian was so upset, but he could tell something was wrong. "Marijuana." He smiled, and let out a little smirk. The smirk that someone would do when they were frustrated.

"Char." He always called him by his nick name. "Why do you always do this to me? The reefer is for the kids. I want you to help me make some real money. I tired of the weed. You know who sell the weed. My son for school money. I tell him ship the weed to make a little million. If you help me I give you the weed. I swear to Jesus." He raised his hands in the air to swear by his testimony. Colombians were very devout Catholics, and they took their religion serious.

Isachar was a little upset. Every time they did business they went threw this. "Antonio you know I can't do this. I told you my wife."

"Your wife. Your wife. You listen to me. I can package the product. I can fly it to you. All you can do is guard it for me. Store it for me. Then I get my people to fly it out. I even send my guards to protect it. I pay for everything."

The argument was useless. They went threw it all the time. "I give you. Thousand dollar a key. Just for storage. You make easy million. Couple million a week."

"Antonio I swear if it was mine I would do it. But my wife she is scared."

Isachar did not know it, but Antonio had lost a lot of respect for him when he let his wife make his business decisions.

"I glad when your wife retire." They all laughed.

Christopher leaned towards Gad. "What are they talking about?"

"Senior Sacha wants my father to store cocaine for him, and he's telling him he'll give him one thousand a key just to store it."

Christopher shook his head in complete amazement. "Why won't your father do it?"

"My father would do it, but my mother won't give him

permission."

Christopher spoke up. "Excuse my ignorance. Do you mind if I speak?" He looked towards Isachar, and he nodded Christopher on.

"Why don't you just buy your own storage house here?"

One of the bodyguards that were with Senior Sacha translated for him. Sacha understood English, but he could get lost if you spoke to fast.

When he replied he replied in Spanish, and the bodyguard translated. "I would but this fucking government. It won't work with me. If I open storage house here. It will be raided in months."

Isachar interrupted, "I would open the storage house for him but my wife will kill me. She thinks if we fuck with cocaine that the American government will come, and take everything we got. You know our government works with the American government. Really, our government does not give a fuck but sometimes they have to make arrest. My wife family control the politicians over here but if we get into cocaine we might lose them."

"What if we become partners, and we invest in our own property? Then we could conduct business on our own."

Gad's younger brother Naptali spoke. He was quiet the entire trip. "We could become partners, and invest in property together but we could never let them use us as a storage house. Sacha says right now if he sends key's here he will provide his own protection but the only thing is if anything ever happens to that product. He'll blame us, and start a war. There is one thing we could do. We could start buying our own cocaine. Fly it to the states, and sell it. Now I'm with that."

"How much is Mr. Sacha going to sell us the keys for?"

The translator was listening to the conversation, and he translated as they were speaking.

Sacha spoke but he spoke in Spanish, and the translator had to translate for him.

"The keys are five thousand in Colombian depending on the circumstances. If I have to fly them over I must charge one thousand, two thousand extra."

"What if we fly them over ourselves."

"Then you pay five-thousand."

Christopher was completely amazed. Five thousand dollars a kilo was amazing. He was paying twenty thousand dollars a piece from his Dominican connection. If he came over with a couple of hundred thousand then he would make a fortune. He had already formulated a plan.

"Mr. Sacha I have some other important business here, and I want to handle that first. Then I'm going need a way to contact you so we can go over the details."

The translator translated everything to Mr. Sacha in Spanish. When he replied he spoke threw the translator. It was easier.

"That's good then. When you finish with your business here you can come back, and we'll handle our business in Colombia. Isachar will handle everything. But I also want you to get in touch with my people in Florida until you can make it back to me. Okay?"

Christopher nodded his head yes that he understood. The meeting was over that quick. They went over a few minor details with the weed thing, and then they returned to the main compound When they went back they did not ride back on horses. It would take too much time. They flew two helicopter's back.

Christopher, and the other's stayed in Trinidad for one more day, and then they flew back to Miami. They spent another day there, and then they took a commercial flight back to Atlantic City Airport in Pomona, New Jersey.

When they arrived at the airport there were six bodyguards waiting patiently for them. As instructed. The bodyguard received their instructions at the last minute so that no police, or enemies would have any idea.

"Martin and Aaron, I want you to ride with me. We have some business to discuss. Just tell your ride to follow us to my house."

They both went and gave their bodyguards their instructions.

Once they were all in the car, Christopher opened the meeting. "So what do you think? What should we do?" These were his two right hand men. They helped him make all his decisions, or at least gave him the affirmative that he did the right thing. This made them the two most powerful men in command next to Christopher.

"I don't know Chris. Why did you buy all that fucking weed?" Martin never really knew of Christopher to make a big mistake. But this time maybe he invested too much money in something they needed.

"Fuck the weed. We're going to make a killing off that cocaine at five-thousand dollars a key. Even after you add the transporting expenses. Shit with a price like that we'll be able to distribute in any city in America, and make a profit. Were making money with the Dominicans now. We're about to make millions off of the cocaine."

"What are we going to do about Big Will?" Little Aaron asked.

"He can get a cut. I want you to make reservations for Florida, and then next week were going back to Trinidad. From Trinidad we'll fly to Colombia. Right now that's the most important thing. Setting this thing up with the cocaine."

"What about all that weed?" Martin asked.

"I want Corty to leave that little bit of cocaine he's fucking around with alone. Tell him to concentrate on the weed. He's going to be handling that until I get my head on straight."

"Aaron you can arrange a meeting with your father and Big Will. We'll give them the opportunity to become partners. Who could beat a deal like this. We can all make millions. I'm telling you, Cocaine is going to make this family even richer."

It seemed like it took no time to reach Christopher's house. All of his cars were parked in the driveway.

"Maritn. Tell Corty I don't want him associating with Gad to much. He's out on bail, and I know the feds know he's sneaking down to Florida. They're probably trying to set something up. I want him to conduct his business with Naptali. Don't forget that . That's important for safety."

Christopher exited the car. A bodyguard escorted him inside.

ELEVEN

Atlantic City, New Jersey

As soon as Christopher got back to America the family started working on their plans for the cocaine business. It was Christopher that directed the operations. He already knew where he wanted to go. The family's heroin trade was going strong, but sometimes it would get to hot. Christopher wanted the family to start concentrating on cocaine more. Cocaine spots did not receive as much police scrutiny as heroin. The profit's were not as strong, but comparing them they came as quick.

Christopher opened a small real-estate company, and every single titled member in the family owned a share in the company. Once he came home from over sea's he decided to use the real-estate company to expand his cocaine business.

Christopher took the family's money, and invested a large majority of it in cocaine, and real-estate. Threw the small real-estate company he went to Miami, Florida, and purchased several residence. So that when he went down to Florida to conduct business he would have a base He purchased a couple of house's in Plantation, Florida so that when the rest of the family came down to conduct business they would have a place to stay. All of this was going to cost hundred of thousands of dollars at least. Christopher estimated that it might cost between two and three million. He made sure that he spent his own money. Who ever was the boss of the family would have to have a stronger position than any other member in the family on all business affairs. It was just common sense.

Then he took the family's real-estate company. Off the Shore Realty, and purchased some property. Land tracts in Trinidad. This was all with approval from the family first, of course.

Christopher, Little Aaron, Corty, and two bodyguards flew down to Miami to have a meeting with Sacha's lieutenants. The family only spent a half a million dollars the first time, They purchased fifty kilo's at ten thousand dollars a piece.

Christopher decided the best way for him to distribute would be to geive each lieutenant a couple of kilo's at ten thousand a piece, and split all profit's. It was a matter of trust. The family sold fifty kilo's in two weeks. It only took that long because they had to wait on people that owned money.

The family set up distribution points in apartment buildings. The customer's would come to the apartment. Pay for what ever amount of cocaine they wanted. Then one of the soldiers would run to another apartment in the building, and bring back the material. This gave the family a lot of strong points. First, a person would have to complain to the police about drug trafficking, and then the police would have to investigate. They could not set up surveillance in the building without being detected. They would have to send in undercovers, and pray that they found out where the stash apartment was located. it would take months for the law enforcement to make arrests, unless somebody started running their mouths. That was why Christopher made it a rule that what ever soldiers operated in the spots be carefully picked. The family sold the cocaine by the gram. They sold the grams for twenty dollars a piece. The only way that the grams would be cheaper was if you came and purchased large quantities. A gram cost twenty dollars, but if you came and purchased a kilo you only had to pay eighteen or nineteen dollars a gram.

The quality was so good, and the price so cheap that the family forced all of it's competition out of business. Michael, Mr. Gaston, and Mr. Johnson started suffering until they made a business arrangement with the family.

Christopher and Mr. Johnson held a meeting in Philadelphia. Christopher agreed that they would get Mr. Johnson's family kilo's for the same price that they were paying as long as they were paid transporting fees. The Italians that Mr. Johnson was dealing with were charging him fifteen-thousand dollars a kilogram, but Christopher was only charging him ten-thousand, and one thousand dollars a kilo gram to get them out of Florida. Mr. Johnson made a fortune on what he saved alone.

He could afford to give the kilo's to his lieutenants for fifteen thousand a piece. They could sell them for twenty-thousand, or sometimes as much as twenty-three thousand dollars a key. Not counting the fact they made even more money by cutting the material.

Christopher's family operated completely different. He made it a rule that anybody caught cutting his material would be killed. He gave the lieutenants partnership rights. He covered the transportation fees. They were giving the kilo's for ten thousand a piece. What ever profit they made they divided equally. If they made ten-thousand off of every kilo then they would give Christopher five-thousand. He would split the five thousand dollars with Martin and Little Aaron. The lieutenants would split their five thousand with the soldiers that operated in the spot. Every single week they were meeting customer's from other parts of New Jersey, that wanted to buy large quantities. It only took a couple of weeks for the family to have strong distribution points over the entire New Jersey. Christopher realized there was no limitation to how enormous distribution could go.

He was meeting with people in the North Jersey area constantly. He would work out deals with them, if they came and purchased five or ten kilo's on a regular basis then he would give them five or ten on consignment, and let them pay the family the money when they sold the material. Christopher did not have to give them anything because the cocaine was selling faster and faster each week. He only gave them over so that they would not take their business to the Dominicans in New York.

He talked with Little Aaron about expanding the family to North Jersey, but he decided he did not want to. He did not know the guy's from that area well enough to talk about expansion. They were already making money there. Why did they have to establish roots there? Christopher explained that would only be unnecessary trouble.

Within a couple of months the family went from distributing a hundred key's a week to distributing about two hundred and fifty a week. The family was making so much money that Marc and Corey were the only ones allowed to distribute heroin, and they sold weight only.

Mikell Davis

The family's cocaine business grew so strong that Michael had to keep moving his operations. It was not until Mr. Johnson and Christopher worked out a business deal that Michael could even compete.

Michael was not foolish, so he cut a side business deal with Christopher. Christopher would front him five to ten kilo's apiece for fifteen thousand a piece. The quality was so good, and the price was so cheap that Michael was able to establish a little clientele of his own in Philadelphia. Mr. Johnson was fronting him a couple of kilo's for the same price. The only thing with Mr. Johnson was that he could not keep the product enough.

Christopher's family was buying so much cocaine after a couple of months that it took them weeks sometimes to sell it. If Mr. Johnson did not get with Christopher then he would have to go up to twenty-thousand a kilo which did not hurt because you could easily sell a kilo in South Jersey for twenty-five thousand. The only problem was the Christopher's family had the South Jersey area wholesale market cornered. You could hardly make any money unless you worked with them. Christopher's prices were so cheap that he destroy all of his competition.

Michael and four of his soldiers were in his apartment preparing money that they owed Christopher's family. Christopher came and gave Michael twenty kilo grams of cocaine for ten thousand dollars a piece.

Michael still distributed in Atlantic City. But he eventually expanded to a city called Millville, and Bridgeton. It would only take him two weeks to sell the kilo's that Christopher gave him. Most of the time he would cut the product. If Christopher gave him twenty kilo's by the time he finished cutting them they would be thirty. He would have to stop cutting all together because Christopher's lieutenant Lyn had opened a spot up in Vineland, and Ocean City. They were too close to his cities, and he knew that if he continued to cut the product he would lose his customers because all of Christopher's lieutenants sold high grade cocaine, and they were making ton's of money.

So much money was coming in that his lieutenants ended up sharing customers. What Christopher did was give them territories. Each lieutenant had to find his own city so that they would not keep running into conflict over who's customer was who's.

Michael was sitting in the dining-room of a condominium that he owned in Ocean City. Even though he operated spots in Bridgeton, Millville, and Atlantic City he resided in Ocean City because it was a quiet neighborhood, and he did not want anybody knowing where he stayed just in case somebody tried to snitch, or rob him. He was using it as sort of a precaution.

Michael was sitting at his dining-room table, he had the two hundred thousand dollars that he owed Christopher spread across the table. First, he and his soldiers placed the money in denominations. After they got the money denominated he ran it threw the money machine. After he ran it threw the money machine, and saw that it was two hundred thousand. He counted it to one-thousand dollars stacks, and rubber banded them together. Michael had four of his soldiers with him while he was organizing the money.

Ten of the kilo grams that Christopher had given him he took to friends in Philadelphia. They would buy two or three, and he would give them two or three for seventeen, or ninteen a piece. He would have charged them more but Christopher suggested that he shouldn't.

One of his soldiers was in the kitchen cooking dinner. They usually had girls over at the apartment, making dinner, or just relaxing. It was a three bedroom condominium, and two of his soldiers lived with him. Now that they were making so much money he was going to look for a different condominium. He did not want to hustle with them, and live with them. It was too risky. When he wanted to relax with a girl or something they got in the way.

After Michael finished putting the money in rubber bands he placed the money in two large paper bags. Christopher would take the money out of the bag, and count it when he got home. Their entire system was based on trust. Michael had miscounted before, and Christopher told him to make sure that he double checked. He never wanted Michael to feel as though he had tried to cheat him because he never would.

Michael loved dealing with Christopher because all that money he made with Christopher he never gave Mr. Johnson a cut.

Christopher and his bodyguard pulled up to Michael's condominium. Ocean City was such a quiet area that Christopher did not like it. Later, he found out that their were only about ten police officers on the entire force. Including the day and night shift he did not mind. He was contemplating buying a place here himself.

When Christopher finished a package, and knew that he would be running around collecting money that was owed to him he would get a rental. The city cop's sometimes harassed him when he drove his car. So a lot of times he would just rent a car to throw them off. The city was too small to hide from them.

Christopher and his bodyguard parked in Michael's condominium and entered the house. They exited the car. One of Michael's soldiers answered the door. They loved Christopher. Everybody loved Christopher.

Christopher and his bodyguard walked into the apartment. Michael was sitting at the table with two brown grocery bags. He stood up and walked over to Christopher, and embraced him.

"What's up?"

"Nothing? Did your man from Philly ever call you?"

"Yeah he called me. He said he's going to need five key's, but I told him we're freezing right now. How long do you think it's going to take before you're situated again? I know he's going to wait because they love that shit you got."

Christopher just smiled. "I told you. Quality and price. That's the only thing that counts. So how many are you going to need?"

Michael paused to think for a second. "Well I'm gonna have enough money to buy at least ten of my own. If you give me fifteen plus the ten, I'll buy. I'll give them ten, and as soon as I make a hundred fifty thousand you'll get your money off the top."

"If they're buying five, and your buying ten. Then I might as well give you thirty. That way, you give them five. Plus, by the time...." Christopher broke his own speech. "No your right we better move slow. I can't afford to lose, or wait for any money. This property is killing me."

"Mr. Johnson's killing me. If I was not working with him I could work with you, and probably go straight back to Philly, and get rich."

"I told you what to do. Ask Mr. Johnson could you break off, and just pay him commission. If you give him half of your profit he wouldn't mind."

Michael gave Christopher the craziest look in the world. "You must be crazy. This is not sweet ass Atlantic City. This shit is real with Mr. Johnson. If I told him I wanted to break off he would have me killed in a minute."

One of the bodyguards that was sitting in the back. Shook his head in approval. Mr. Johnson had hand picked them, and sent them down personally. At first Christopher would not discuss business with them. But after Michael let Christopher know they were all unhappy, Christopher loosened up around them.

"Big Will know's I' m doing something now, and he scared to death. I trust a couple of the lieutenants, but I haven't been home in so long. I don't know if I could trust them. I want to turn them on to you because I know they could make millions."

"I'm already making millions." Christopher added.

Michael just smiled. "Nah... I meant millions more."

They talked about a couple other little things, and then Christopher picked up the bag, and left with his bodyguard.

"Do you want Cleo to walk you outside?" Michael asked.

"Nah were cool." He tucked the bag under his arm, and walked behind his bodyguard out of the door.

Christopher and the bodyguard walked to the trunk of the car. The bodyguard had the keys. He opened the trunk of the car, and Christopher placed the brown paper bags in the trunk. The bodyguard closed the trunk. The entire time he was glancing around. He did not want anybody to be able to come behind him, or the police to be watching because sometimes they would follow Christopher around, and Christopher told him to always look out, and be mindful of the police.

They placed the bags in the trunk. The bodyguard walked over to the passenger side of the car, and let Christopher inside. As soon as he closed the door, he saw a guy approaching the front of the car with his hands in his pockets.

The bodyguard reached in his waist band, and pulled his gun out.

Christopher was sitting in the car. When he saw the guy approaching the car reaching for a gun, he turned his face towards the locks of the car, and reached to pull them open. The only time he carried a gun was times like this. He went to push the door open.

He did not see the other two guy's who were hiding around the trash can. They both came out. One of the guys lifted his gun, and placed it near the window before Christopher could push the door. The gunman pulled the trigger. The bullet went threw the window, and went into Christopher's head. His body slammed against the steering wheel.

Christopher's bodyguard heard the shot, and pulled the trigger. His gun was aimed at the assailant approaching the car. He did not see the guys standing behind him.

The other man that was standing behind him pulled the trigger, and shot the bodyguard in the back. The impact from the bullet pushed the bodyguard against the wall.

The gunmen that was firing at Christopher walked up even closer to the car. He stuck his hand threw the window, and fired several more times. Every hit made Christopher's body shake. He was dead after the first shot.

Christopher's bodyguard tired to raise his gun. The gunman that was approaching him, stood over him and fired a couple of more shot's into his chest.

The gunmen that killed Christopher looked into the car. The front window was smeared with blood. He looked at the other gunmen.

"I don't see it."

"I think they put it in the trunk." The gunman who shot the bodyguard replied.

The one who killed Christopher walked back to the trunk,

and fired several shots at the trunks lock. The trunk popped open. He lifted it and reached in, and grabbed the bag with the two-hundred thousand in it.

They jumped into a get away car, and sped off.

It only took minutes before the nearest cop arrived on the scene. A few minutes later there was an ambulance and a crowd of people that lived in the condominiums. A forensic truck, and news reporters from the Atlantic City Press. Ocean City was so small that it did not even have it's own paper.

Christopher and the bodyguard were killed at five o'clock in the evening. Within a hour the news had reached the city. The police department was one of the first to know. The head detective that headed the vice unit held a brief meeting. This was the four to twelve shift which was the busiest. "I don't know if any of you had your scanners on at home, but they killed Christopher Larkin, the one we were investigating. I'm not sure as to what's going on, but I want to set up some special surveillance team so we can find out what the fuck is going on. I'm pretty sure the feds are going to find out if they don't already know."

The night shift meeting was as simple as that. It was over.

Corty was one of the first to receive the news. He had a cop that was close to him on the force that kept him informed with all of the latest events. When the cop got the words to him, he was not sure.

"Listen don't go flying off the handle. I think your boy just got killed in Ocean City. I'm not sure."

"Who?" Corey replied. "Which one of my boys?"

"I think his name is Christopher Larkin, but I'm not sure because one of the vice units had to go over there, and identify the body. Another guy was shot up bad too, but he might not be dead..." There was a pause over the telephone, "Hello are you there?"

Corey just hung up the phone. He was in total disbelief. Two of his soldiers were sitting in his house playing cards with him. They had things to do.

He looked at one of them. "Listen I want you to take my car, and tell Lyn to meet me at Christopher's house. You hear me?"

"What's wrong. You alright?" The bodyguard sensed something wrong because of the way Corey's demeanor changed.

Corey ran into the bed-room and picked up his gun. He never really carried a gun. Their was no need too.

"Rock, I want you to come with me. I think one of our people got killed. Just keep you mouth shut, and find Lyn." His wife was sitting in the bed-room breast feeding his daughter. She heard the conversation, and got scared.

Corey and Rock his bodyguard/soldier drove over to Christopher's house. On the way there Corey kept getting beeped. He was kind of scared. He never got beeped like this. The only thing that relaxed him was that when he pulled up in Christopher's drive way, all of Christopher's car were there except the ones he kept in storage.

Corey and the bodyguard buzzed the alarm on the gate. Christopher still lived in the modest house that he purchased when he first got married to Anita. His wife was constantly renovating it, and it was the prettiest house in the neighborhood. But they could have afforded better. Christopher promised her he would buy her a new house, but she refused. She had grown up in Atlantic City, and loved the house, and the neighborhood it was built in.

Christopher's mother buzzed the alarm. "Who is it?"

"It's me Mrs. Larkin. It's Corr."

The alarm buzzed again, and they entered the property. They walked to the porch, and the door opened. Everybody was crying. Christopher's wife, his mother, and the children.

Christopher's wife walked over to him, and embraced him. It sounded foolish, but he had to ask the question. "What's wrong?"

"The police called. Christopher's dead." The words hit him again, and surprisingly his legs got weak. He never thought he would react like this in a situation. He always thought he would be more stable. It was his love and respect for Chris that was making him weak.

"Did you go and identify the body yet?"

"I can't go, and Momma's scared to go."

"Damn." A couple of tears started to stream from his eye's. "Call down there, I'll handle that. Rock call one of our people, and then call my wife. They're going to stay at my house. Is that okay, Anita?" She shook her head yes.

Rock went into the kitchen, and made the phone call. It took him a couple of minutes. As soon as he came out of the kitchen the door alarm rang. It was Lyn. They buzzed him in. When he came threw the front door he had tears in his eye's. He could not hold it back, especially after seeing tears in the family's eyes.

He blurted out. "Christopher's dead."

Christopher's mother, children, and wife started crying again. His wife was in the bed-room, and they all heard her outburst.

Lyn and Corey embraced. "What's up? What do we do now?"

"I'm going to have Rock wait, and take them home to my house, and then we're going down to the hospital to identify the body. Did you bring a bodyguard?"

"Yeah, but fuck a bodyguard?" He opened his jacket. He was known for carrying big guns. Corey would have chastised him for doing that in front of Christopher's family, but he understood and forgave him.

"Come on lets get the fuck outta here. Rock you make sure they get to my house safe, and then you meet me at the hospital. Keep your mouth shut okay?"

Rock nodded his head yes.

Lyn, two of his bodyguards, and Corey drove to the hospital. Lyn had a cellular phone, and everybody was calling him. Between Corey, and Lyn they used the car phone at least twenty times.

Corey would told him when he got on the phone. "Don't tell them anything. Don't tell them were going to the hospital. We don't know who's behind this shit. One of them could be behind it." He pointed to Lyn's bodyguards, and they looked at him like he was crazy. But they understood the point.

It only took ten minutes to get to the hospital. Then they

explained the situation. It took another hour, and some phone calls before they got permission to identify the body.

Lyn and Corey bearded the elevator with two hospital employee's. The hospital seemed gray, and dull. The smell alone made them sick. They walked into a private room.

When they walked into the room there were a bunch of steel doors. They walked over to the door labeled Christopher Larkin. Seeing Christopher's name on the door made both of them sick to their stomachs.

The hospital worker slid the door open, and Christopher was lying on a metal slab. The doctor pulled the slide out. The eeriest thing about seeing Christopher's body was that it looked peaceful. He had two bullet holes threw his head. His eyes were closed, but it looked like he was sleeping.

Tears streamed down both of their eyes.

"Is this him?"

Lyn answered. "Yes...."

The doctor slid the slide back, and Christopher's body would never see light again until it was picked up, and taken to the morgue.

When Little Aaron received word of Christopher's death he rushed to Christopher's house. One of Lyn's bodyguards was there letting important people in. He called an emergency meeting.

All of the lieutenants and soldiers gathered at Christopher's house. When they came to the house there was a group of undercover officers parked on the block taking pictures of everyone that entered the house.

Lyn, Corey, and the two bodyguards were approaching the hospital exit. Corey had just got off of the phone calling his house. He informed Anita that she would have to get with her lawyer's, and let them handle Christopher's legal business. She asked him if it were true, and he told her yes, but he wanted to lie and say no, He would have, but he knew she would never forgive him once she found out the truth.

"I gave your bodyguard the keys to my house."

"I want you and Ms. Larkin to stay with us until the funeral."

He could hear Ms. Larkin in the background asking whether it was true or not. She must have said yes because he heard her scream.

When they got to the exit of the hospital, two vice officers approached him. " Can we speak to you for a minute?"

"Yeah. What do you want?"

"We want to talk." Corey just looked at him. He was a young rookie punk.

"We just want to talk."

"Nah, talk to my lawyer." He brushed past them.

Lyn, Corey, and the bodyguards drove back over to Christopher's house. There were dozens of cars parked in front of the house. Lyn and Corey saw a bunch of undercover at the end of the block.

Lyn was upset. When he saw the undercover parked at the end of the block he put his middle finger up at them, and they flicked their high beams.

Corey and the two bodyguards laughed.

When they entered the house they received a warm reception. Marc and Cory walked over. They embraced. "At first I thought you guy's were hurt, but your bodyguard told me you were at the hospital. Was it him?"

Corey shook his head yes. Tears came to both of their eyes.

Little Aaron had two bodyguards set up at the gate at Christopher's house, and they turned the security system off. A reporter from the Atlantic City press, and some reporters from News Channel Forty were at the house gate asking questions, and snapping pictures. When they approached the gate, and asked questions the bodyguard answered.

"This is private property. If you set one foot on this property, I will be forced to call the police."

A young reporter that worked for the news paper gave a sarcastic remark. "The police are right down there. I'll call them for you." The remark made everybody laugh.

They held the meeting in Christopher's business office, It was newly renovated, and expanded. The pool table no longer took up most of the room.

Little Aaron did not know how to open the meeting. "Listen, Christopher's dead, Corr and Lyn identified the body. But I don't want anybody to make a move until we find out who's at the bottom of this."

Martin was slightly crying. He was probably the closest to Christopher. "Find out who the fuck is down with this. Michael has a place in Ocean City, and I talked to Christopher right before he went there. Michael and Big Will's behind this. Ask your father to find out what's the deal, and get ready for war. Period."

Everyone was shocked to hear Martin speak like this because he was never violent. He was the peaceful one.

Corty was shocked. "Michael killed Chris? He's dead. Fuck that, it's on."

"Calm down. We won't make a move until we find out the details. Where was Christopher's bodyguard?"

"He's in the hospital." Lyn answered.

"Who was it?" Little Aaron asked.

"Franklin."

"Is he hurt bad." Aaron asked.

"I'm not sure. We'll find out later. I didn't know Christopher was coming from Mike's! Mike's dead! We don't need any more proof."

"Listen I don't want anybody touched until I hear from Big Will. I don't want anybody touched without my permission. Is that understood here?" He did not wait for a response. "I'm the fucking boss here!"

Big Aaron came in and broke the meeting. He walked over, and embraced all of them. Then he took a seat next to his son.

"Dad can you get in touch with Mr. Johnson?"

"I've been calling him since I got the message. As soon as I find out, we'll see." Even though Big Aaron worked for Mr. Johnson he was still considered part of the family, and very much trusted.

That was enough for everybody. "I want everybody to be safe until we find out who's at the bottom of this. Watch out for the police. You see them at the corner? Shits going to be hot. From this point on the meetings will be held at my house. Martin I want you to get with our lawyer, and make sure that Anita conducts all the legal business." He continued

"Are you going to take the position of head of the family?"

"Yeah, if the family will accept me. I'm ready when ever the family gives me the word. I don't want to rush anything."

"I don't think we should do it now, Martin."

The meeting was over. Before Martin left, Little Aaron grabbed his hand to hold him back. "Remember I don't want anybody to make a move without my permission, and be careful because the police are out like crazy. This is the last meeting here. The meeting tomorrow is at six, and at my house. If you find out anything important get with me tonight, or tomorrow at the meeting. Martin I need you to stay with me for a little while. Tell your bodyguard to sit tight."

The rest of the lieutenants got up, and exited the room. Big Aaron, Little Aaron, Martin, and Crazy Moe were sitting in Christopher's business office.

Christopher had a minibar set up in the office, and they were drinking Hennessy. Martin usually never drank, but he needed a drink tonight.

"Martin tell Corty to get in touch with the Colombians, and the Rastas. Let them know what's going on. They might want to come to the funeral, but that might not be cool until things cool down." He walked over and glanced out of the business room window. The undercover cop car was still sitting outside of the house. "I wonder if that's regular police, or the feds?" Who gives a fuck is what he was really thinking.

"Mr. Gaston you're going to have to find out if Big Will had something to do with this because somebody's gonna have to provide some answers. Everybody's pissed, and I don't want ridiculous bloodshed."

"Honestly, I don't think Mr. Johnson had anything to do with it. He would have told me. But I'm going to see him first thing in the morning, or maybe tonight. I called his house, and his wife will relay the message. It's important."

David Murray, the head of the local drug enforcement

agency, Alfred Mintz the head of the Prosecutors office, and Michael Moore, the head of the Atlantic City vice unit were sitting in the Prosecutor's office discussing the murder.

David dropped a ton of pictures on the table in front of the both of the men. There were pictures of Christopher, and almost everybody else in the family. Then he opened the envelope of pictures that his agents had taken the day of the homicide.

"Look at this. They held a meeting at his house. All of these guys are working together. I'm telling you. They're organized. If they're not organized they will be soon. Look at this!" He started placing the pictures with the faces on the other pictures.

"What's this homicide going to do to our investigation?" Mr. Moore asked.

"Truthfully, I don't know. It might hurt it, or it might help if they go to war. If they go to war they have to surface, and we'll be right there recording every single thing. We just have to stay on our toes. Write to the Governor, and try to get some more men recruited because we can't watch them by ourselves. There's not enough of us. We have to find out who's the enemy, and watch them. Then find out who's the leader, and watch him."

"I thought you said you had some informants?"

"I do have informants, but we haven't penetrated the actual organization as of yet. We're still working on it. If they are an organization. For now, we have to relay on surveillance, and pray this Judge grants us phone taps."

Michael lifted the pictures. "He will. Cause surveillance ain't shit. How are five or ten men going to follow fifty?"

The meeting was brief. They went over a few more things, and then the meeting was over.

TWELVE

North Philadelphia

Michael's death was a powerful blow in the war, and it sent across a heavy message. It took a couple of days before Big Will would confirm that the meeting would go on as scheduled but being the businessman that he was he held the appointment.

Big Will divided Philadelphia in four sections. Then every single section was divided by North, South, East, and West. So all together, Big Will had twelve lieutenants. Not counting their soldiers. His counselor, and underboss. He had his connections with the Italian Mob, and people that did business with him, but were not in his family. They were considered associates.

Big Will's had control over the Philadelphia underworld before heroin really got big in the mid seventies.

In the late sixties and very early seventies. With the permission of the Italian Mafia, Big Will took over Philadelphia. His first step was to build allegiance with all of the number runners, pimps, and petty criminals. He did this with the assistance of the Italian Mafia. So by the time that the drug business got big in the mid-seventies, half of the people dealing were either coming to him for protection or loans. He also had control over all of the loan sharking, and gambling house's in Philadelphia. Eventually he had enough lieutenants and soldiers, so he did not have to depend on the Italians for physical power.

The Italians also had control over Atlantic City's underworld so when Big Will took over for them, he was introduced to Big Aaron which he had already been doing business with. Big Will's father, and Big Aaron's father used to do business together. Big Will's father could have started his own family, but he was not strong enough or intelligent enough.

When Big Will organized his family we would have named Big Aaron his counselor, or second in command, but he already had a counselor and an underboss. They did establish an understanding that if anything happen he was the next lieutenant to get a controlling position in the family.

Unfortunately for Big Aaron neither the counselor or the underboss ever died. They all grew into old age, and millions together.

Aaron's organization was relatively small until the heroin explosion. Then his organization grew a little bit in size, and wealth.

Big Will balanced his power with his lieutenants. If one lieutenant was disobedient then he would use the other lieutenants to discipline him, and discipline was usually murder.

As long as he kept his lieutenants from organizing he was fine. If he even suspected them of organizing behind his back he would have them killed.

Big Will had helped Big Aaron get established in Atlantic City. Together they removed all of his competition, and established his numbers business and his gambling houses. They also established a loan sharking operation. These operations alone bought in millions a year. So when drugs came, they really got rich. The only thing that the Italians wanted was a percentage of the profits, and they were happy.

Big Will had a lieutenant that owned a famous restaurant in North Philadelphia called Albert's. Albert's restaurant became so famous in the early seventies that you could find all kinds of famous celebrities dining there. Whenever a Afro-American star came to Philadelphia, and they knew somebody, he would come to Albert's restaurant, and club. Albert's was also a jazz club, and some of the most famous black jazz musicians would come drop by the club, and play for free.

Albert's was so famous that white people would come just to see it. It was becoming a Philadelphia landmark. Politicians and gangsters would mix on the regular.

Mr. Johnson decided to hold the meeting at Albert's. It was famous, and it was not unusual to see a bunch of luxury cars parked outside. Plus if the police saw his car at the restaurant they would assume that he was eating dinner.

Fat Al, the lieutenant that operated a section of North Philadelphia for Mr. Johnson and his family, was big. Big in weight and size. He mainly ran numbers and gambling houses for the family, but once drugs got big he got into loan sharking, and financing drug dealers. Like most of Mr. Johnson's older lieutenants, he would never actually get involved in the distribution of narcotics. Instead, he would just finance and stay in the back round. Drugs were too dangerous. Why try to distribute drugs when you could just finance the other guys, and not have to worry about the police.

When the seventies came and drugs rolled around in Philadelphia heavy, he was already rich, and the owner of a famous North Philadelphia restaurant. Big Albert was one of Mr. Johnson's most powerful lieutenants because the dealers that operated in North Philadelphia made millions of dollars selling heroin, and cocaine. At first he would just finance them, but collecting money owed to him became too much of a hassle. Instead, he found out if you made them soldiers they acted better, and showed more loyalty. Just like Mr. Johnson, he pitted his soldiers against each other. If one of the soldiers messed up, he would get another soldier to murder him.

Little Aaron told them the proposition that Mr. Johnson sent through his father. He also told them. "It's your decision on what we do. I could never make a decision like that on my own without your permission. That decision affects the entire family."

Marc was the first lieutenant to speak up. "So what do you think we should do?"

"I don't know. I have been thinking about it, and business wise it's like two powerful casino's merging. Plus, he guaranteed that my lieutenants would keep the same power that they always kept. He's planning to retire in ninety, or ninety-five. Five to ten years, regardless of what we do he's promising peace, and he wants to have another meeting. I saw his family united last night, and if they really wanted to go to war they could crush us. They're two times our size."

Corty, the new found renegade, spoke up. "They're two times our size, and they have two times the trouble. Our wealth alone is our strength. We have stronger cocaine connections. I bet you he wants our connection. No matter how strong he is, he won't ever be able to compete against us because of our connections."

"Corty, don't be so closed minded. This is business. Eventually our family's will probably unite. We can't keep going on warring. We have to make money, and the only way we're going to make money is to make peace."

Corty could no longer be quiet. His opinion had to be heard.

"That's exactly my point. He said we can have peace. You tell him we don't want to join his family. The only thing that we want is peace. If he does not make a move in a couple of weeks then we'll know it's peace, and we can resume business. All of our customers are waiting. Jeremiah has taken over Michael's operations. But they can't compete with us on the wholesale prices. Plus our quality. That's the most important thing, quality and price."

"Corty, how did you know that Jeremiah took over Michael's operation? I asked you to lay back didn't I? Wasn't that the command?"

"Yes, I obeyed your orders. I wasn't going to hit him, or anything. I was just keeping a watchful eye on him so if they try anything funny then I will be able to roast his ass immediately."

"Well, this is the second command. Don't lift a finger against these boys without my permission. Okay. You got it?"

"I got it. I got it."

"Now, what's the vote on joining forces with Mr. Johnson's family. I want you all to think about it, then I'll give him the answer in two weeks."

"I'll tell you now. Fuck him."

"Lyn?"

"I'm with Corty. I'm against it."

"Marc?"

"L.A., I think Corty's right. We should wait. I don't like Big Will, and it seems like were turning our backs on Christopher."

"But this is business. Open your minds."

"Robert?"

Robert was the newest lieutenant. "I don't know, honestly. I know we definitely don't need him, I'm not trying to mind anybody's business, but I'm assuming all of the other lieutenants are millionaires. Were doing fine."

Little Aaron was upset, but not angry. He could not believe how closed minded the lieutenants were. "It's not about money. It's about power."

"Martin and Corey. What do you think?"

"I'm with the rest of the family." Martin said.

"Maybe in a couple of years. The only thing I see bad about it is we'll be obligated to him. That's heat, and everything. I don't know. We're doing excellent, and were strong regardless of the merger."

"Okay that's the vote then. I'll wait for a couple of weeks, and then I'll tell my father to tell Big Will, no."

He held up his glass of liquor in a toast. They raised their glasses. "To the family."

Their glasses clashed, and they replied. "To the family."In unison. The meeting was over.

THIRTEEN

Plantation, Florida

Michael's murder got news coverage in the Atlantic City press, and other local news papers. All of the news stations that operated in Philadelphia showed coverage. Even the news papers in Philadelphia ran small articles.

The article in the Atlantic City press ran. "AUTHORITIES FEAR MOB WAR BETWEEN TWO BLACK ORGANIZED CRIME FAMILY'S"

Mr. Johnson could not stand it. All of this publicity brought on heat from the police, and he could not afford heat from the police. The things that upset him more than that was when the papers ran articles naming him as boss of Philadelphia's Black mob. They even made mention of Albert's restaurant, and claimed Albert was an associate.

Little Aaron and the family decided that they would wait for at least three weeks before they resumed business. This way if the police were following them then they would be able to confuse them.

Martin suggested that they all go on vacation for a couple of days to different places, so if the police were following them it would be hard for them to keep a tail. He also told them when they returned, try to lay low so that nobody knew that they were home.

Little Aaron, Martin, and Corey were down at the home that Little Aaron owned in Florida. He sold the house that he owned when he was the counselor in the family. Once he became the boss he moved into the house that Christopher lived in when he came to Florida. The area was nice. It was mainly populated by people that had money. The homes in Florida are not big in size, but they are spacious length wise.

The house that Aaron moved into was spacious. It had a small indoor pool. A nice living room, and it was three bed rooms, and his wife loved it. She would take his children to the beach, and just shop all day. Occasionally, they would fly to the Bahamas to gamble, or have an extended vacation.

Little Aaron, Martin, Corey, and three bodyguards were sitting at the table. After they finished eating Little Aaron asked the bodyguards to excuse them, they had some important business to discuss.

Little Aaron was dressed in some casual summer clothing. If things went as planned he would be spending half of his time in Florida, and Maryland conducting business. The house in Trinidad was completed, and now they were waiting on the small warehouse they made to be completed.

Big Aaron and Crazy Moe walked in the kitchen. They had just arrived that morning, and Little Aaron did not want to discuss business until they came. Anytime they came into a meeting, they all stood and embraced each other.

"Corey. What's up? Have you been keeping an eye on Corty like I asked you to?"

"Of course. You know when you tell me to do something I jump on it immediately."

"So what has he been up to lately?"

"Robert said he's doing the usual. Going to dinner, and riding with his soldiers."

"Do you think he's been following Jeremiah?"

"I don't think he's following him, but I do think he's keeping an eye on him."

Little Aaron just shook his head. "Corty's too hard headed. I'm going to get rid of him. He's got one more time to make a mistake, and he's history. If we make peace and conduct business with Big Will, he's going to give me any problems?"

Corey was caught a little off guard. "Corty's a good kid. I just think he's a little upset. He'll calm down."

"What if he doesn't calm down. Will he be easy to hit?"

Corey put a surprised look on his own face. "What are you asking me? Can he be hit?"

"Yeah. Find out if Robert thinks it can be done."

"Okay. "

"Listen you don't even have to use Robert. We can use my men. Since he's following Jeremiah, let Miah set him up." Big Aaron knew that his men were capable.

Martin corrected them. "No, we couldn't involve Miah because if the other lieutenants find out then they might think we betrayed them and start another war. If we do the hit on Corty, we have to use our own men."

The family had not conducted any business since Christopher's death. Martin suggested to them that when they were about to transport, that they should not let the word out to anyone. Their were to many snitches on the streets right now, and the last thing they needed was police scrutiny.

The family's real-estate company rented out some storage spaces to a dummy company that it owned.

Little Aaron, Martin, Corey, Big Aaron, Crazy Moe and a couple of bodyguards were in one of the ware houses. Martin, Corey, and Little Aaron brought a million dollars a piece. Plus, Lyn, Marc, Robert and Corty brought a million a piece. Big Aaron, and Crazy Moe brought four million a piece. The family knew that a large majority of the money belonged to Big Will. Crazy Moe was a millionaire, but he did not have a million dollars to invest in cocaine.

All of the lieutenants counted their money, and sealed them in boxes. Little Aaron was sitting behind a money machine breaking every single box open. Then he would recount the money to make sure the correct amount was there.

In all, there was eleven million dollars sitting on a table. They were going to fly the money to Trinidad to a private or commercial airport. From there, the plane would be met by some Government official they had paid off. Then it would be flown by private airplane directly to one of Sacha's estates.

Sacha was charging them five thousand dollars a key, so they would be able to buy two thousand, and two hundred keys. Sacha was going to charge them one thousand dollars a key for it to be flown into Trinidad. Then from their they were on their own.

Corty had worked out a deal where they would be able to pay him his two million, and two hundred thousand dollar transporting fee later. The kilo's would be stored until night fall. Then they would be broken into eight two hundred, and fifty kilo shipments, and raced to Florida by speed boat. The family's real-estate company was in the process of trying to purchase a dock to load, and unload boats. From there, the kilo's would be loaded into vehicles, and driven to warehouses. The next night the vehicles would be fixed, or changed, and the product would be driven out of Florida to Maryland. Drivers were permitted to stop, but they had to make it to Maryland that same day, and they could never lose contact with base. They were ordered to contact base once every hour. Base would be a hotel room. Once they got to Maryland they went to a ware house. The warehouse had indoor parking. In Maryland a new set of drivers would remove the merchandise, and drive to New Jersey. Once they were there a soldier from the family would take the product to a stash house. The family purchased fourteen hundred kilo's, and they would be sold in about two weeks, if that.

They already had customers in North Jersey alone that wanted to buy ten, and twenty kilo's. If those customers were trusted they would get extra as long as they knew to pay their debt as soon as they got the money. The system was simple, but it worked. It never failed, surprisingly. When the family got back they would start distribution. They would always make sure they were home before the product got home.

Then they would take the material and start distribution. The kilo's that L.A., Corey, and Martin brought had to be distributed first. Once they were paid their money, the lieutenants were expected to split their profit with the family. Everyone was expected to at least double their money. If the lieutenant paid six-thousand for a kilo-gram he could come back to the North, and sell that same kilo-gram for at least twenty-thousand dollars. A profit of fourteen thousand. They were expected to give the family half of the fourteen. Each lieutenant purchased about one hundred, and sixty six kilo-grams. The profit on that was two million, and three hundred thousand. The family's cut of that was half. Off of one shipment alone. Little Aaron, Martin, and Corey would make millions in profits, and it would only take the family about two weeks. Almost every single lieutenant had major customers in Newark, Patterson, Camden, Bridgeton, Vineland, and other city's in New Jersey. Some of them had customers in Maryland, Atlanta, New York, Philadelphia, and city's all over the east coast. Business seemed to be growing every single day.

It took the family a little more than two weeks to distribute the cocaine.

Big Will sent Andre down to Atlantic City as one of Big Aaron's soldiers. Even Jeremiah was considered a soldier. But instead of answering to Big Aaron he answered directly to Big Will. He had the title of a soldier, but the power of a lieutenant. When Big Aaron and Crazy Moe retired he would assume their power and title. Big Aaron did not hold anymore street power. The only way that he made his money was threw Jeremiah, and the other soldiers that Mr. Johnson sent down. The heroin, and cocaine that he brought, they would distribute. In return for this, he split his profit with Mr. Johnson, and the soldiers that worked under him. He made a decent living still. It did not matter, he had become a millionaire several years ago.

Mr. Johnson sent Andre down so that he could protect Jeremiah. He did not have anymore intentions on a hit, but he also knew that Jeremiah needed somebody strong down there in case he needed protection. He did not want to send Andre because he was wanted on a murder charge, but he had no other choice. Now, they would have to get back in touch with his lawyers, and renegotiate his arrest. When the lawyers did get in touch with the judicial system, they did not want to hear it. The ultimatum was, he turn his self in, and do the twenty years with the five year stipulation, or he get arrested on a warrant, and face trail. The family decided it would be wiser that he just turn himself in, and he would be home in five years. Another stipulation on his plea agreement was when he was released, he get his parole transferred to Pennsylvania.

Little Aaron, Martin, Corey, Big Aaron, Crazy Moe, Jeremiah, and one of his bodyguards were sitting in a restaurant that Big Aaron, Big Will, and Michael's family owned. They had just purchased the restaurant a couple of weeks before Michael had gotten killed. For a couple of weeks the police had undercover surveillanced the place, but that eventually died down. Once in a while undercover cops would ride past to check, and see if any familiar cars were around.

Little Aaron and Jeremiah had been meeting secretly for weeks, and none of the family really knew. But now that the peace was made, they openly showed their friendship, but only to a certain extent. Before this meeting, Little Aaron, Corey, Martin, and Robert were at Little Aaron's house having a meeting. Things were finally smoothing over, but they had to make arrangements for Little Aaron's new plans.

It took Little Aaron a little while to have confidence in his leadership role, but once he realized his power it seemed more and more each day he was exercising it.

Robert paused. He had been following Corty around for a couple of weeks, the only time that he stopped was when they got the cocaine shipment, and they had to start distributing. That was first, and he could not let watching Corty interfere with him making a living.

"I think my men can do it. It would be easier if we had a definite place."

"What do you mean, a definite place?"

"I mean, if you could get him to come to a meeting or anything then we could follow him the entire day, and hit him after the meeting, or before."

Corey put in his input. "It would have to be after."

Little Aaron asked him. "Why?"

"It would have to be after, because the only person Corty

is going to have a meeting with is you, me, or Martin. Nobody else is going to budge him. If we have this meeting, we're going to have to make sure that he's hit after the meeting for get away purposes. I mean, I would hate to be at a hit, and the police come harassing me with questions. If he meets, then the hit will have to be after. If not, it's too risky."

"How would you get him to wait behind?" Little Aaron questioned.

"You could tell him that the police is outside, and it's better to leave separate. Anything. I don't think he will be expecting anything. Now that I think about it, I think that it would be better to just follow him, and knock him off. But if we fail, the other lieutenants might think it's a war, and retaliate."

"That's important too. We don't want any of the lieutenants flying off of the handle. I want some men on Lyn too, because he's the only lieutenant that I could see acting crazy. If we get a tail on him, and a tail on Corty then we're straight. I talked to my father and Jeremiah has some guys that could do the work."

Martin butted in, "That's not a good idea. If the other lieutenants found out you used Jeremiah to set Corty or Lyn up, and let them do the hit, they might come against you thinking you had something to do with Christopher. Corty and Lyn are ours. Let us handle them. We can handle them. I'll talk to Marc, and I'll let him in. He's about business. He understands. I'll just tell him Lyn's doing some tricky side business, and then once Corty's gone if Lyn acts up, Marc's men will hit him. It's as simple as that."

Later that evening Little Aaron, Martin, Corey, Jeremiah, Big Aaron, and Crazy Moe had that meeting at Michael's family's restaurant. They picked a table in the corner, and the entire section was sectioned off. The other customers in the restaurant were several yards away. All the tables that were in talking distance of the family's were empty.

Little Aaron had not filled in Martin or Corey on the details of the private deal he made with Big Will. Now was the time for the details.

"I talked with Big Will, and he said if we decided to join with his family. First, we have a meeting, and straighten it out with the lieutenants. Then we make Jeremiah a lieutenant. You know Big Will's going to want insurances. Then my father, and Moe retire. They get a piece of the real-estate company. My father and Moe will retire so they will help operate the company. We have to introduce Big Will to the Colombians and Jamaicans. He's expecting to have a hard time with the Italians once he starts purchasing his own material. If something jumps off, we promise our support. Their going to be mad when he starts paying a street tax because they know he's not going to give them a fair share of his profits. It was better when he was moving their material. But us on the other hand, we might have a problem with Lyn, and that's why I want a tail on him. We get to keep our power structure if we merge, and nobody from his organization will be able to ever control our family. Only the boss. Who ever is the boss of our family answer to only the boss. Plus, we'll be able to take positions in their family. Like counselor, underboss, or maybe even boss."

When Martin and Corey heard the proposition they realized why Little Aaron was anxious to make the merger. His power and opportunities would increase ten times. Business wise it was like the biggest drug distributors uniting. With Mr. Johnson being the larger promising his smaller competition a future of completely running the company. Genius.

"If we merge. Big Will promised to retire in five years, and completely relinquish his power. The only promise that he wants is that the family guarantees him protection from anyone that might want to harm him for something in the past." They were all impressed. "But I can't do this with out your full loyalty and cooperation."

"You have my loyalty." Martin was always eager to show his loyalty.

Then Corey raised his hands. "You know you have my loyalty."

"Now this Lyn kid. I'm telling you my men can handle him. Just turn me on him." Jeremiah was eager to get things moving.

"If we use his men, Corty, and Lyn's soldiers are not going to follow us when we want peace. Somebody is going to have to take over their crews. One of their soldier or will lose all of their business."

"You're right Corey. What do you suggest?"

"L. A. we can't use Miah's men for the hit. Marc has to do the work. Once we got the tail on Lyn if we have to hit him then we'll let Jeremiah's men be back up. We have to settle this ourselves. I'm going to start trying to talk some sense into Lyn. Maybe we won't have to do a hit on him."

"Did you arrange the meeting with Corty?" Little Aaron asked.

"Yeah, I set it up for a week. By the time that the next shipment is in, and we're back from Trinidad, it will be time for the meeting."

"Good. Then... That's it." The meeting was over.

FOURTEEN

Atlantic City, New Jersey

Little Aaron arranged the meeting with Corty before they made the trip to Colombia. He did not want to conduct business before they did the hit because after they killed Corty it might be hot to operate. Plus, they might have to kill Lyn so he knew the police would put on the heat.

Little Aaron decided that they would hold the meeting at night time under Corey's suggestion. If they were going to do a hit then it should be done at night. That would help the hit men, and the get away drivers escape.

Earlier that morning Robert, Corey, and his soldiers blueprinted the place, and found out where would be the best place for the hit men to wait. It would be easy. Especially since Corty did not know what was going to happen. The element of surprise was murder.

Little Aaron and one of his bodyguards were the first to arrive at the meeting. They chose his sneaker store because their was no other place they could meet, and Corty not suspect something suspicious.

A lot of people ate at a restaurant across the street, and if the police hassled him he could say he was there. Martin, Robert, Corey and one of Robert's soldiers that was always body guarding Corey, arrived. The bodyguard would have to stay up front. This was too important of a meeting.

Corty and one of his soldiers that was his bodyguard arrived at the meeting.

A couple of minutes after him Jeremiah and two of his bodyguards arrived. It was time to hold the meeting. Big Aaron and Crazy Moe were sitting in the bar watching television. They had their police scanners on praying when the hit went down they would here the reaction on the air.

Corey had advised them to stick together most of the day. He wanted everybody to be at the meeting after the hit. Big Aaron and Crazy Moe had a couple young ladies there at the bar.

When they all got in the sneaker store, they had seats. Little Aaron introduce them, Corty did not want to shake Jeremiah's hand. But he shook it out of respect for Little Aaron.

"Corty, the only reason that I'm calling you here is so that I can get some support from you on this move I want to make. I know how you feel about Christopher, and this Mr. Johnson thing. But I have talked to Martin and Corey, and I know they have your respect. We think it's the future to join families. We're not going to jump into any serious moves, but we're already thinking about doing business with Jeremiah. But you know we can not do this with out you. The Colombians are not going to deal with anyone beside you. Neither will the Jamaicans. We need you. This is business, and we need you. If we keep going at this rate we'll be filthy rich, and able to retire in a few years."

"Corty, I don't know you but this is big business. Nobody can do it without you. If our family's combine, that means with your family's connections we could expand, and cover the entire Philadelphia. Not counting the other city's threw out Pennsylvania. We know your already expanding to other parts of New Jersey, and right now you can't keep enough cocaine. But if we expand like this your talking millions. Eventually billions. The cartels will beg to do business with us. We'll be unstoppable. Think about it.

Hundreds of millions of dollars. Not to mention the street power."

Corty just smiled. "Listen to this, and don't take this as disrespect." He saw the expression on Jeremiah face change as soon as he said it. "But we can do all of this without uniting as one. It's just like the street tax law, and I learned this from Christopher. We can go around and collect a street tax, but for what? We already have the majority of the business. We have already expanded to other parts of the east coast, and might make it to the west. The more territories we try to expand on the more police scrutiny, and cases. This shit is not going to last for ever. I know I can't quit the family. But I have a couple of million now. I don't want to be sixty making cocaine shipments. By ninety-five I should have at least two-hundred, and fifty million saved. I don't want to run around here like a Colombian kingpin trapped in business for life. After a couple of years I want to retire, and run the family's legal businesses. If L.A. says we're going to merge, I have no other choice, he's the boss. But I hope that in a couple of years I'll be able to retire, and operate the family's legal business. That was Christopher's goal. Make enough money to go completely legit. The way the police is on us now we won't be able to retire if we keep running. Let's quit before they make us quit. We can set up some reliable lieutenants, and make money for a couple of more years. But we don't want to keep our hands in the cookie jar forever."

"Christopher was right, but this is the life we choose, and we have to stick with it. Of course we all want to retire, but we also have to grow. If Christopher knew how to grow he would be here now. Do I have your support?"

"Of course you have my loyalty and support. I love you like a brother. You're my boss. What ever you say goes."

He stood up, walked over to Aaron, and embraced him. Then he lifted his hands and kissed them. The ultimate sign of respect.

"That's it then. Let's move on with out plans. Jeremiah, if you don't have anything else you want to cover I need to speak with my family in private. I'll have a bodyguard escort you to the door."

Jeremiah stood up and embraced Little Aaron. Then he

embraced everyone else in the room.

Once he left, Little Aaron spoke. "The meeting's over. I just wanted us to leave at separate times for police reasons. Corty, I need you, and I'm glad I have your support. I will be in touch with you to go over the details, but if you have any questions then feel free to contact me." Now the meeting was officially over.

"Aaron we should leave first, and then let Corty leave." Martin added in.

Little Aaron just shook his head okay.

Little Aaron, his bodyguard, Corey, and Martin left. The bodyguard had parked the car in front of the store once they told him they were ready. When they were walking out of the store Corey stepped in front of Little Aaron and protected him like a bodyguard.

When they came out of the entrance, the car was right in front.

Little Aaron looked up the block. He saw a car, and he knew it was Robert and his men sitting in it. Corty was dead. The bodyguard put Little Aaron and Corey in the back seat. Martin sat in the front seat on the passengers side.

Once the driver got in the car, he turned the ignition on.

Corey raised his gun with the silencer on it. He shot the driver in the back of the head, and then he turned the gun on Little Aaron, and shoot him in the head three times. It was the weirdest feeling in the world. Seeing the look of surprise and fear cover Little Aaron's face when he got hit. The bodyguard was slumped over the front of the wheel, and Little Aaron was pushed against the door in the back seat on the drivers side.

Robert pulled up in a getaway car. Before Corey jumped out of the car he looked at Little Aaron dead for the last time. For Christopher, he thought to himself. For Christopher, and the family.

Corty and his bodyguard left the store threw the back door. When they got outside, the back door lead to an alley. They walked threw the alley, and jumped into there car, and pulled off.

It took a little more than an half an hour for the words to come over the scanner. A lady had walked past the car in front of the store, and noticed all the blood smeared on the window in the back seat. Then she looked at the drivers window, and saw Little Aaron's bodyguard slouched over the steering wheel. She ran down to the end of the block, and called the police. By the time that the word came over the scanner the police announced. "Two men found shot on the fourteen hundred block of Atlantic Avenue."

Big Aaron was puzzled. Who else died. He beeped his son and he beeped Jeremiah. Fifteen minutes later they announced they had a positive identification. A couple of minutes after that the telephone rang. It was Little Aaron's wife on the telephone. She was crying. "My husbands dead. My husband's dead." Big Aaron tried to calm her down. "Are your sure?"

A detective picked up the telephone. "Hello. Who's this?"

"Who's this?"

"It's detective Neil Gram from homicide. Who is this?"

"It's Aaron Gaston."

"Oh hello Mr. Gaston. Your son might have been killed tonight, we might need you to come and positively identify his body."

Mr. Gaston's head started spinning. "I'll be there." He hung up the telephone.

Crazy Moe had left a couple of hours ago to eat dinner.

He told him if he needed him, call him at the house. They were both happy that they would be able to retire. They hated losing the money, but now they would help run Christopher's old construction and realty company. They could spend some time traveling with their wives and girlfriends.

The first person that Big Aaron thought about was his wife. She would be destroyed. He had drove his 300 Mercedes Bent to the bar. Now that it was his son that might be dead, he was a little afraid to leave the bar. It was closed. He exited the bar, and their were a couple of men standing outside drinking liquor straight out of the bottles. It was the guys that sat outside of the bar constantly begging for money.

Big Aaron walked over to his car, and closed the door. He kept a small gun under the seat. He reached for it, and placed it on the passengers seat. When he stuck his keys in the ignition and turned the car on, it exploded.

Corty and rest of the lieutenants in the family held a meeting at his house. The Atlantic City Police Department had set up a surveillance team for him, but somehow every day he lost them, or they either got pulled away when it seemed like a slow day. The police considered him a low level member of the organization so they never really watched him for long periods of time.

The head of the homicide and the vice unit were outside of the bar. Big Aaron's car was blown to pieces. When they arrived his body was still in the car burnt beyond recognition. The detectives from homicide were upset.

"A fucking car bombing, and a double homicide execution style all in one day, and every single one of them were suppose to be under surveillance. I can't believe this shit." He was wearing plastic gloves. He bent down, and picked up one of the pieces from Big Aaron's car.

The detective from vice spoke. "You can't keep watching them all day."

Corey lived in Pomona on one of those dark roads surrounded by woods. He had long moved from the city. Number one, it was to hard to find a nice house, but most importantly he wanted to leave so that the police would not be able to easily surveillance him. If a undercover sat out on this road then they would stick out like a sore thumb. The house that he lived in was middle class. Any hard working couple with good jobs, and not that many children could have afforded it. That was when he bought it. Now he had renovated it, and build an in-ground pool, and some other things. The day that Christopher died he had a high tech security gate set up, and a surveillance system. Plus, he had patrol dogs, and whenever he came home he had at least one of his soldiers follow him home. When he found out the plot about him being murdered he really did not come out. He knew that Little Aaron and Jeremiah were meeting secretly, and he did not want to get hit by the element of surprise. All of it was business though. He thought to himself, he had never dreamed when they started out five years ago that they would all be millionaires, organized, and that he would be head of the family. Christopher would be dead, or that he would be a murderer. Life changes. It was strange how some things happen.

Corty had a lot of property, so all of the lieutenants were able to park inside of his gate. He had set up a group of bodyguards to guard his gate, and another group were driving around the block like sentries looking out for the police. Corty was never the type of man that dwelled on power, but he could feel the new power, and control that he had. This time when he came home, and his men greeted him he could feel their awe, and admiration. He was the head of the family now. He was completely in control.

Corty came home and washed his face. He kicked off his shoes, and went into his den where he would be holding his meeting. The first person to arrive to the meeting was Martin and a bodyguard. Martin walked into the den, and when he saw Corty he embraced him. Then grabbed both of his hands and kissed them. The ultimate sign of respect, Then Corey, Lyn, Robert, and Marc came to the house with their bodyguards, and when they came in they embraced him, and kissed his hands the same way that Martin had done it. Once all of the lieutenant were in the den they closed the den doors so they could have privacy.

Corty really did not know how to start the meeting. "First thing I want to state is I respect, and appreciate everybody's loyalty that are here with me tonight. The moves that I made were not personal. They were business. I love each and everyone of you, and I consider you my brothers. Now it's time for us to conduct business like we care for each other. Business like Christopher would have conducted it. L. A. and Big Aaron are dead. I'm assuming the position of head of the family. But I can not assume this position with out your blessings. If anyone disagrees, I'm going to ask them to speak now or forever hold your peace." He paused for a second. He wanted to make absolutely sure that nobody objected. "Being that I'm taking the position of boss I have always been satisfied with Martin being the counselor, and Corey being the underboss, and it is my intention to keep it that way. If you have any objections you should speak now. I will pick a soldier to take the position of lieutenant from my crew. I don't know what the reaction from Big Will is going to be, but we're trying to get in touch with Jeremiah and Crazy Moe to make the peace. Hopefully things will go as planned. Corey did you hear from your people yet?"

"They didn't beep me yet, but I'm sure they will. Probably to night. They usually call me at night."

"I want everybody to be careful and safe. I want all of you to move around like we're at war unless you get the word from me. Plus, don't go out to much because the police will be on alert after tonight. Just move with ease. Next week we make our move to the bottom, and resume business. Besides that, the meeting is over."

Marc stood up. "I want to make a toast." He waited until they filled their glasses. "This is a toast to Christopher, L.A., and to Big Aaron, and to the family. May they rest in peace."

They sat for a few minutes discussing business amongst themselves and then they embraced Corty before they left. Some undercovers were parked outside of the house, but it was not a surprise because the sentries had seen them as soon as they came.

Corey and one of his bodyguard drove to Galloway Township to a small park that Galloway Township had built in the community under the community beautification program. He had been meeting officer Donahue here since they started doing business in eighty. They went to school together, and when Corey was in high school he sold marijuana for Donahue. Corey was surprised when Hose became a cop on the police force but it really worked out for the best because once they got together, Donahue started helping Corey. Donahue started giving Corey information on police tactics. What they knew, and what they were planning on doing.

Corey's bodyguard pulled the car up in front of the parking lot. When Donahue drove up he drove in his own car instead of the police issued car that he worked in.

"Did you here about the three guys they found. Two in a car and one blown to pieces?"

"I heard."

"Did you know them?" Officer Hose asked.

"No, not really. I don't know them.."

"Well vice and the feds are setting up surveillance teams.

I won't be able to meet you for a couple of weeks. All you have to do is beep me, and if I can meet you I will call you back. If I hear anything important then I'll call you immediately."

"Do they have any leads on who did those boys?"

"Hell no. You watch the movies. You know the cops don't know shit until the police get a snitch. You got my money."

"Has there ever been a time that I met you, and didn't."

They both smiled. Donahue was a little nervous. Especially since he knew the department was looking for leads on that murder. If they ever found out that he was taking money from gangsters, and providing information against the police they would have his shield, and try their best to send him to federal prison.

FIFTEEN

The family attended the double funeral services of Little Aaron and Big Aaron. Their wives were destroyed. Mrs. Gaston moved in temporarily with Lisa, Little Aaron's wife, to help watch the children, and to give each other emotional support. They were both confused, and did not know who to turn to. Lisa convinced her mother-in-law that Mr. Johnson had something to do with their murders. When Lisa got the chance she got in touch with Corey. He was always over at her house, and she thought that she could trust him. She begged him to avenge her husbands and father in-laws murder.

"Listen to me Lisa, and this is the only thing that I can tell you. We know who had something to do with your husband, and father-in-law... and we're going to handle it. I promise."

"Who was it? Maybe I can help."

Corey smiled. "Listen to you. You know I can't tell you anything like that. Plus, if I opened my mouth your husband would be rolling over in his grave. We're men, and this is a man thing. I promise you we'll handle it. In fact, one of the men that was there is some where buried on side of a road right now."

A couple of weeks after the funeral they got back in touch

with Lisa. Corey was the one that they used to approach her. Obviously she trusted him.

"Lisa you know the kind of business we're in, right? And you know that we need most of our legal businesses to help us out?"

Lisa did not say a thing. She just nodded her head yes.

Corey explained to Lisa that the family was going to need her to sell her percentage of the realty company to the family. She would makes millions off the sale alone. She agreed.

Christopher's wife, and his mother just sat on the millions that they had acquired from the sale of their property. She always kept in touch with the family if she needed little things. Like if one of the construction workers had tried to beat her out of money, or charged her too much. The only reason she even kept Larkin Construction and Realty open was so that Christopher's former employee's would have an income. Unfortunately, she just did not have the interest. She was in the process of selling the company's equipment, and leaving the business alone.

At first Big Will was going to retaliate, but he decided that it would not be a wise move. Even though Big Aaron did not hold any street strength, he was a globe of information. Jeremiah really did not know the city, and with Andre gone things were a little hard for him distribution wise. He would have to conduct business and war tactics. It would be too hard. He really did not care about L. A., or Big Aaron. Their death was business. He had to make sure that Jeremiah and his business interest were safe. Since they did not have any tactical moves at the time, he sent down ten soldiers as a security. A week after the murder his worries were put to rest. Corty sent Martin and Corey to have a meeting with Jeremiah. They assured him that they had no hard feelings for him. That L.A., and Big Aaron were killed because the family figured out that they had set Christopher up. Plus they agreed to have a peace meeting if Big Will felt it necessary. They gave Jeremiah the avenues to get in contact with them. The only guarantee that they wanted was for people in their family, and their associates be able to operate freely with out any form of harassment from Big Will's people. Big Will had no other choice but to agree.

The Secret Society

It took a couple of weeks for Corty's lawyers, and Lisa's lawyers to handle the sale of Lisa percentage in the realty company, but as soon as it was finished, Corty and his family took a vacation to the main house in Trinidad. Lisa had got in touch with Corey and Corty to let them know the FBI had approached her about wearing wires, and finding out any information that she could on Corty, and in return if she had any problems with the IRS they would make sure she did not do any time.

When she came to Corty's office and told him, he broke out in laughter. "Those crackers are crazy. Your husband leaves you a real-estate portfolio, and they're telling you you're going to get in trouble. They're crazy. Every single piece of property is legit. Tell them to kiss your ass, and go to hell. I want you to get with my lawyer, and if they come to visit you again then I want you to get a restraining order placed on them, and tell them to stop harassing you. Then get a financial lawyer because you haven't done anything wrong. If you need any documentation from me. Get in touch with me, and I'll have my lawyer get in touch with your lawyer." The next time that the agents came to her house she called the police, and tried to have them arrested. The police could not lock them up, but since they did not have a warrant they were forced to leave.

Corty had a small business office added onto his house. Hampton Realty Company. He conducted a large majority of his business from that office. The family's legal business was expanding just as much as it's illegal business. Corty, Corey, Martin, Lyn, Marc, and Robert all had their own small private contracting companies. These companies combined were what Off The Shore Realty was. Their company was buying property in the South Jersey area, but not heavily. Instead, in South Jersey it made it's own money contracting for commercial and private use. The casino provided it with a lot of business. Which it did not need because in Maryland and Florida the construction business was doing a lot of it's own work. Corty remembered when Christopher first approached the family with opening a construction company. He explained if nobody hired them to do work then they could purchased their own property, and build real-estate themselves.

Now only a little over five years later, and the company was already worth several million dollars, and constantly growing at an alarming rate. When Corty sat and thought about it, he knew why Christopher died. He died because he was before his time. The entire time he existed, his enemies must have felt at though he needed to die because he was too much of a threat. Alive, he would destroy their business future. Dead, they would destroy their own. Which to them seemed better because it would take longer, or never happen.

Being head of the family, Corty would spend a lot of time traveling now. Especially when it was time for new shipments.

The house that Corty owned in Trinidad was copied off of Egyptian style. It had only been built a couple of years earlier, and was worth half a million dollars. In America the same house would have been worth millions. Sometimes Corty would come to Trinidad, and have to stay for a couple of weeks. His wife had to stay home and watch the children. But every single Friday that he was there she would catch a commercial flight and stay until the children would have to return on Monday. It was not hard on their relationship because she trusted him, and when she came he made sure their was no evidence of another woman, if their was one.

The family's real-estate company in Trinidad was expanding. They also owned a small construction company that did a lot of work on the tourist section of Trinidadian cities. Those contracts were worth millions. The only problem they had was that the Government had it's hands in everything that went down in Trinidad.

The family was still sending private planes to Colombia purchasing thousands of kilo-grams of cocaine. It was easy flying the product into Trinidad. The hard part was speed boating the product into Florida. They purchased a private, and commercial dock so that at night they could secretly ship the product into Florida. But they did not feel absolutely safe with this, so instead they opened small dummy companies in Texas, Louisiana, and California. They wanted to get more product, but they did not feel safe the way they were shipping. That was one of the reason's the family kept investing it's money into different companies. When the lieutenants would complain, Corty would explain that assets were money too. In fact, it would be harder for the police to confiscate their assets. Plus as long as the assets made legal money they could not lose. Sacha showed them how to put their money in Swiss bank accounts, and Island bank accounts.

He would joke. "You might have to kill one of these bastards for stealing from you twenty years from now when your retired, but for now it's good." Even though it was a joke Corty took it serious, and he always kept a constant check on his money.

The family owned small fruit factories in Trinidad, and they mainly used them for storage houses. Places to store the product. They were also building small apartment complexes in the capital, and using the penthouses in the building as storage houses. The only people they really had to worry about were the government soldiers. They would come shoot a place up and steal every thing in site. Then sell it back to you at a ridiculously cheap price, or sell it to somebody else.

Corty, Martin, Corey, Naptali, and some government official were sitting around the business table in Corty's office. He had an office built into all of his properties. He did not want to leave his house, unless it was for extremely important business. If he was not in the house he was at the factories offices conducting illegal, and legal business. He did all this in an eight hour working time frame. He would always tell Naptali who ran around like a chicken with his head cut off.

"I've got to many millions to be running around here chasing money. It you rush when you slip up you fall on you face. If you move slow when you trip you might be able to catch your balance without ripping your face a part."

Corty walked over to the enormous business table that he had set up in his business office. The house was majority glass windows. Corty wanted to see the beauty of Trinidad while he sat in the house. The rest of the men in the room followed him to the table. He was carrying a bunch of blue prints. Sacha and some of his lieutenant were there. The closest they would come to America was one of the islands.

Corty laid the blue prints across the table. He was about to speak when Robert walked into the room. Excellent. He needed to be interrupted.

"Excuse me gentlemen. I have some very important business. It will only take me a minute. Lunch will be ready in a couple of minutes. I will meet you in the dining-room.

"Naptali, Martin, and Corey I need you with me. Mr. Jouby. I'm ready." The men that were dressed in military outfits walked into the room. Robert was carrying a brief case. He laid it on the table. Corty grabbed it, and opened it. He popped it open, and pushed it over towards the General.

"There it is. Two million dollars." Two months protection money. A million dollars a month seems like a lot for protection, but it was not as costly as it seemed because the lieutenant split the cost. Plus the military protection guaranteed them protection on some of their legal businesses. In Trinidad, the military was like the mob. They wanted a piece of everything illegal. It did not bother Corty. To him it was business. He did not mind paying anybody off as long as he could see where his money was benefiting the family's business.

The General smiled. "This is no money. You make this in a day." He was always trying to pry into the family's business to see if he could squeeze them for a little more.

"General, if I was making this a day. Then you wouldn't see me. I would be retired." He stood up, and shook the generals hand. "Robert see them to the door for me. Thank you."

The General was a fat obese man. "Oh. See me to the door. I can't eat? I want to stay for lunch too."

"Sorry General. The lunch is a business meeting, and I would let you stay but I have to respect their rights to wanting privacy. If you want to, you can eat in the kitchen."

Corty got up, and shook the General's hand. Robert escorted the general, and his men to the kitchen where the servants ate.

Corty walked back over to the enormous table where the blue prints to the new factory was lying. The only reason that the meeting was called, so that Corty could show the family the blue prints for the new factory. Corty walked over to the table. He opened the blue prints and spread them across the table.

Corty placed his finger on the blue prints. "This spot over here is the factory. It's small because it will only be used for delivery, exporting, and storage. We don't want to build large facility's because if they ever got raided then we lose money, possibly on the product, and money on actual business lost. Our goal is to build as many of these as possible so that once one is raided, we already have one built to move to. I don't trust the General. I feel safer with the product stored here then in America, mainly because our government is not as cooperative as you government, Naptali. Your government understands business."

Corty did not let them know that he would be building his own private ware house with underground storage houses. He was also going to build some in America, and the only people that were going to know would be the lieutenants.

Corty had suggested to Naptali in privacy that he build his own warehouses. Anytime you shared something, it resulted in unnecessary conflict.

He returned to the blue prints. "Were going to have our security system set up here. We won't have to worry about intruders because the building is private property, and secluded."

Naptali and the others were studying the blue prints intently. He pointed to a spot on the blue prints. "What's that right there?"

"That's the airplane hanger, and the small line over here is the airport strip. This small box looking building is the airplanes control center."

"Impressive." The Colombians were smiling. "This is impressive. You mean business"

Corty had a landing strip on his estate property, but he could not be to directly involved in business. Once he had this first factory open he was moving all of the business to the factories. This was the first one. He had intentions of building several more. At the cost of one million, or a million and a half. One shipment would pay for that cost. The family was making millions, but a lot of it was being put into legitimate businesses.

"This place right here is all business offices. We all have our own business offices."

Building the property would not be hard because the family already owned a small construction company, and that construction company was quickly becoming one of the biggest black owned businesses in Trinidad. The General was helping the family get all kinds of government contracts.

"So this is it." He walked to the end of the table. There was a large blue print rolled up and rubber banded. He rolled it and handed it to Naptali. "This is yours. Give it to your architect, and if you want to make any changes get with me immediately."

After they finished in the business room they went threw the other doors. This looked more like a living-room. It was furnished in all white. The only way that you could enter the room was threw a locked door in the business-room. The other room was an addition. When they walked into the room, Corty had thirty-five million dollars in cash sitting on a table. Everyone had sent over five million dollars a piece. They were going to fly over to Colombia, and purchase seven thousand kilo-grams. Sacha was going to fly the product over for a thousand dollars a kilogram. Which was going to cost the family an extra seven million. Corty had worked out a deal where his own planes would pick the product up from Colombia, and ship them to Trinidad themselves. A seven million dollar savings is a seven million dollar profit. Business for the family was excellent. The family's business went as far New York, Pennsylvania, Virginia, Maryland, and other east coast cities. Most of the time when they met the customers, they were small customers. Customers who only purchased five and ten kilo-grams a piece. Christopher had set up a different system. If a customer purchased five or ten kilo-grams, but could distribute more in a decent amount of time then Christopher would give it to them. The family's distribution was twenty times bigger than when Christopher was alive. Every single week they were meeting more customers. Then Corty realized it was safer to make a customer bigger than try to actually find new customers. The houses that they operated in South Jersey did not even count for ten percent of the family's income. The houses had small customers, and that was good when business was slow, but the only time that business was really slow was near the end of the month. The customers from out of state picked their product up, or had it delivered. Delivery was free of charge no matter where you lived as long as the customers were purchasing a large enough amount.

Corty, Naptali, and the men in his family would fly to Colombia and test every single kilo-gram that they purchased. Corty refused to take kilo-gram if it was not white fish scale cocaine. It was considered the absolute best. He did not know until he flew to one of Sacha's factories that the cocaine came in powder form. Then at the factory it was transformed into bricks of cocaine, and wrapped. All of the product that passed Corty's inspection was wrapped in factory plastic, and stamped with T.S.S. For the secret society. A logo that the family used when they were just a street gang robbing grocery stores, and stealing cars.

Once they got into the living-room Corty closed the doors behind them for more privacy. There was a little kitchen, and bar fully stocked in the corner of the room.

Sacha never hesitated when it came to business. "How much is this?" The money was spread across the table.

"Thirty five million." Corty replied.

"Thirty-five million. How many keys is that? A couple of thousand. Right?"

"At five thousand dollars a key it's seven thousand keys."

"You come and get seven thousand keys, and it's gone in two, three, weeks. But if you let me give you seven thousand more, then you don't have to come back. Plus you help me. I got about one hundred thousand keys buried right now, and my factories produce at least a thousand keys a day easy. I have all this product, and not enough outlet. I need your help."

"Poppa, I could come and buy fourteen thousand keys if I wanted to, but there no where for me to store them. That's the only problem. I don't mind sitting on material. But do you know what the American Government would do to me if they even knew I was transporting seven thousand keys a month. They would charge me with treason. The President is already trying to make it where drug traffickers get life, or the death penalty. Plus, where am I going to store fourteen thousand keys. If I ship that many keys, and break them into small shipments it would take me days, and a lot of risk to get them things into Florida. I'm trying my best of get ports in other places, but most of the other city ports are too quiet, and if I'm not careful the police are going to catch on to me."

Poppa interrupted him. "I can handle that. Hernandez tell them."

Poppa had introduce them to Hernandez before. He was a kingpin from Mexico. The family did not know it but he was probably the most powerful kingpin in Mexico. He had government officials. Everything. He shipped himself personally at least one hundred thousand kilo grams threw Mexico every two weeks. He, and Sacha had been billionaires for years now. They had so much money and cocaine, the only thing they could do was sit around and try to figure new ways to distribute it.

"You can start shipping threw Mexico, but I'm not supervising no seven thousand keys of cocaine. You have to send more than that. But you can definitely use Mexico. Of course we will have to set a fee, but it will be worth it, and any shipment that I ship I guarantee,"

They were impressed. But the organization was not at that point yet. It was not needed.

"Okay. I'll talk with my lieutenants, and I'll let you give me an extra seven thousand keys. But I'm telling you now. If there is a time limit my answer is no cause if I'm going to be shipping like that then I'll have to take my time. Period."

"Corty you know that's no problem. The only thing I want is my money, and my money at a decent time."

"I forgot to add in Naptali's money. If he's going to do something you'll have to talk to him."

Poppa looked at Naptali. "I already talked to him." They all smiled. Especially Poppa. He had just made a seventy million dollar deal with half of the money guaranteed.

"Corty from now on. If I give you extra. I guarantee it to Trinidad."

Corty smiled. "Thank you Poppa. That's what I need."

The business meeting had carried over into lunch time, and a few minutes after the meeting a maid knocked on the door. A bodyguard carrying a gun opened the door. "Excuse me sir. Are you gentlemen ready to eat?"

"Yes. You can take our orders."

She walked over to the table, and ignored the money sitting around. She was dressed in a maids uniform, and she was beautiful. When she walked past Poppa he pinched her behind. He loved Trinidadian women. She took their orders, and left.

It took another twenty minutes for the maids to return with lunch. They ate lunch, and watched tapes from America. After lunch Corty escorted them outside of the estate to the cars.

Corty's estate was filled with all terrain trucks. He had two Range Rovers parked outside. Two Nissan Pathfinders, and two Toyota Four Runners. He walked Poppa and his entourage to the trucks. The trucks would take them to the airport or they might stay overnight at one of the condominiums that Poppa and his family owned.

Poppa walked over and admired the Range Rovers. He loved them. It was a brand new eighty-six even though eighty-seven had not arrived yet. They always released cars a year before the actual year, and every time a new one came out Corty got it by trading his in. He knew Poppa wanted a truck.

"Poppa you like this?"

Poppa just smiled. "I love this."

"Here take it then. Take it to the airport, and fly it in. It's a present from me." Poppa just smiled. He never refused a gift. It was ignorant, and against his belief. He walked over to Corty and kissed his cheek. "Thank you."

It took a couple of days to arranged for the fourteen thousand kilo-grams to be shipped over from Colombia. First, Sacha had them delivered to his factory from storage. Then Corty, Naptali, and some of their lieutenants checked every single kilo-gram. Some of them would pull seven grams out of the package, and cook it. If the product came back rock form then it was good enough. That's what took the longest. Then the cocaine was

shipped to Trinidad, and stored in warehouses. Naptali had to fly back because he was buying five thousand
kilo-grams of his own. From Trinidad the family had the cocaine shipped to ports in Pensacola, Panama City, and St. Petersburg Florida. They tried their best not to go to Miami, it was too hot. They also shipped to Biloxi and Gulfport, Mississippi. They were presently in the process of trying to purchase ports in Louisiana. Since they had five different shipment points, the shipment was broken into five packages. Each port was sent twenty-eight hundred keys. From each port a lieutenant, and a group of soldiers would drive the kilo-grams all the way to Maryland warehouses. From there the product would be shipped to other warehouses in South Jersey by different drivers. Corty would come and split the cocaine in half. He would store half of the material and give the other half to the lieutenants. The only rules they had were that the material not be cut, and that they have the same prices.

Henry Ingram was Corty's most trusted lieutenant, and the one that Corty choose to elevate to the position of lieutenant. He was one of the hit men with Corty and Corey when they hit Michael. Besides being Corty's most trusted soldier he was his first soldier. So when Corty announced that he would be the one to take over the position of lieutenant, and head his old crew. It came to the surprise of no one.

Corty, Corey, Martin, Lyn, Marc, Robert, and Henry were sitting in Corty's dining room. Business was put on hold so that they could have this meeting. It was important. Once Christopher organized the family they never really had an initiation until Robert joined. Henry would be their second initiation.

"Henry to do you know why you're here?"

Henry was relatively quiet. The other men knew him in the room, but Corty was the closest to him. He responded. "Yes."

"Your here to be initiated into the family, and pledge your undying loyalty. Once you join the family you can not quit. It's permanent. You will be allowed to retire. With permission from the family, but that is something we will go into later. If you don't want to join the family you have to let us know now. But if you join, then every man in this room is your family, and you become a part of this family. You have to have undying loyalty to this family. Are you ready for that commitment?"

Henry looked at him solemnly. "Yes."

"Okay then. You may pledge your loyalty."

Henry stood up walked over to Corty first, and embraced him. Then he kissed his face and his hands. "I pledge my undying loyalty."

He walked to the other men, and did the same thing. The meeting was over.

Six months after the peace was made, the William Johnson crime family suffered another terrible blow. William Johnson was cleared of attempted murder, but he was convicted of possession of deadly weapon for illegal purposes. The conviction carried a two year sentance and two years probation.

His lawyer tried to get the judge to continue bail until the appeals process was satisfied, but he denied the motion.

James Clark became the acting boss and Thomas McCant became the acting counselor. None of the lieutenants were elevated in rank, because Mr. Johnson did not think they would like the demotion after he came home. He also did not want to offend any of the other lieutenants by picking among them.

SIXTEEN

Ninteen Eighty-Seven

BOOK TWO

By the time that nineteen eighty-seven rolled around Mr. Johnson's family was changing again. Change in the criminal world was inevitable. It's just the way legal and illegal business is, by the time that eighty-seven had rolled around Big Will's family still had strong holds over cocaine and heroin, but only in black neighborhoods, and even in those neighborhoods they had to fight to keep control. There was always some tough guy popping up trying to establish his own business, or do business without paying a street tax. Collecting money from dealers that operated in your neighborhood was not the only purpose of the street tax. The street tax gave the family the know how of what was going on in the streets. If you collected a street tax it provided the family with information on who was trying to muscle in on territory. Other dealers were not going to pay a street tax then sit, watch competition come, and operate without paying. So whenever some competition moved onto a block that Big Will's family controlled he was informed, Big Will was never really bothered with these things. The lieutenants would bring it to his attention. He would order a hit. Most of the time he would get another lieutenant from another area to handle the hit so the lieutenant working the area of the competition would not catch any heat. This format worked perfectly. The family experienced the same thing with cocaine. They had a strong hold in the black community where the product ended up, but the Spanish and Dominicans were making a small fortune selling wholesale. The only people that really bought whole sale were the people that lived in small areas near by.

The down end of the narcotics trade was that every time Big Will looked around, a soldier, or lieutenant was getting locked up on a drug charge, or somebody had made an attempt on one of their lives. Sometimes things got so wild Mr. Johnson would just let them run wild. A bad thing about the street tax was not all of the family's competition wanted to fight back. Instead, a lot of them went to the police because they were already informants. The people that Mr. Johnson had down at city hall were constantly telling him his name came up in some transcripts, or over a wire tap, or that some young boys were running around in this area saying they worked for Big Will, and that they were taking over in his name. All of this made the FBI extremely interested. Even with all of this, Big Will's family was the second largest criminal organization in Philadelphia. He was the second most powerful crime lord in Philadelphia. The head of the Italian Mafia was more powerful then Will, but none of his lieutenants. The best thing about Mr. Johnson was that the authorities did not really know anything about him.

Occasionally Big Will's lieutenants would give him problems, but he never forgot his tactic of using one lieutenant to eliminate another lieutenant, and it worked. He knew that the lieutenants were doing a lot of side business. Some of them had even tried to break off. He quickly eliminated that. He did not need another war. The little war they had in Jersey was enough. Plus he planned on retiring in a couple of years. He wanted to live his last few active years in the family collecting a couple of more million. He knew his time was coming to an end. The drug business was the most profitable enterprise, but it was also the most risky. He did not see the odds of someone ever completely controlling it for long periods of time. If the police did not get him, then hit men would. One thing he could depend on was his alliance with Corty's family. Plus he had his alliance with the Italians, but they were slowing going off to jail on federal charges, or fighting amongst each other for control of the organization. That was another reason that Big Will was considering retiring. One of the Italian Capo's had mentioned his name in a trail, or just plain snitched on him, and since then the FBI kept picking him up drilling him for information. The only way they stopped harassing him was after he purchased this high price lawyer and pressed harassment charges against them. Then their superior put out the word that they were going to have to leave him alone for a while.

A couple of months after Mr. Johnson and Corty's family made the peace, Jeremiah stepped to Corty complaining about how he really could not make any money working with Big Will. His quality was not good, the price was not fair. If he wanted to cut the cocaine he could not cut it, and resell it. Customers would complain. He wanted quality good enough to cut.

"First of all your only paying ten thousand a key from me. That same key goes for twenty thousand wholesale. Why do you cut it. Ten gee's profit ain't enough?"

"That's when I deal with you. Will charges me fifteen thousand a key. Sometimes I can get twenty five. Twenty three but believe me he's cutting it, and it's garbage if I cut it."

"Your dumb too because when you cut it, it slows up the profit. I can't front you anything if your going to take all year with the money." Corty did not mind giving extra to help a person out, but he did not need to. He could not even supply his customers demand. They wanted more each time.

"Plus, I have all of these other guys that want to spend money. The other lieutenants are willing to spend millions. Threw me you could make a lot of money in Philly."

"Okay. We'll see. But I hope you're not trying to set me up. Because if you are, look at these men. One of these men will be the last people you see. Because if something happens to me. They're going to kill you." Corty stood up from his seat, extended his hand, and they shook hands.

Jeremiah eventually turned him on to several other lieutenants in the family. But Black was the strongest lieutenant that belonged to Mr. Johnson's family. He was young, but unlike the others he was wise enough to get into other rackets, and sell drugs. He loan sharked, ran numbers, and a couple of gambling spots. Gambling started dying once the casino's in Atlantic City started growing. A gambling house on the streets of Philadelphia did not provide the same atmosphere, or safety as a Atlantic City casino did. You could win money from one of the gambling house in Philadelphia, and then the same people that operated that house could have you robbed. It was common. But now a lot of the high rollers were young dealers, and they did not have the time, or the patience to deal with the streets after spending days on the streets making a living. When they went to the casino, if they were classified as high rollers, they were given suites, and complimentary rooms. Everything. Their girls, and family could walk the boardwalk, visit the malls, beaches, and clubs, then do some shopping.

Frog who was Black's right hand man, Crazy Eddie a lieutenant in Big Will's family, Corty, Martin, Corey, and Jeremiah were sitting in Black's suite at one of the casino's. Police surveillance was nothing to the family anymore. There was always some kind of cop following them around. But the undercover would not follow them into the casino's, and by the time they set surveillance up the meeting would be over. They used rent-a-cars so the cops could not label their cars. The authorities from Pennsylvania and Jersey started working together, and sharing information. They even got in touch with the casino control commission. The commission controlled the casino's. It was like the casino's judiciary system. It was regulated to keep crime, and criminal elements out of the casino. If a person was any way involved or associated with organized crime they would ban you from the casino. They would not even let your legal businesses benefit from the casinos, if it was proven that you were involved in crime in any fashion.

Each of them brought bodyguards, but there was no need because they knew they could trust each other. There was really no particular reason for the meeting. Every time that Black came down to the city to gamble he got in touch with Corty. Most of the time he had come so they could conduct business. Then Black would spend a couple of days in the casino gambling.

Black had spent a million dollars with Corty, and he charged him ten thousand dollars a key. He got one hundred kilograms. They had been dealing together for a while now, and Black had Corty's complete trust.

"How is everything going?" Corty asked.

"Honestly Corr. I need more. I'm finishing those hundred keys in less than a week. I need more. But Big Will has my money tied up. I really want to just deal with you and the Mexicans but I'm going to have to wait. If everything goes right at this meeting with Big Will then I'll be straight."

"I told you if there's anything that I can do, just let me know."

"The only thing I need Corr is that extra material."

"That's no problem. If you buy one hundred then I give you one hundred." Corty decided to give him extra mainly because his profits were so strong, if he took a loss it was usually a profit loss only. So it gave him the flexibility to give out cocaine without customers having the money up front. Occasionally, he would lose money, but most of the time his people came threw.

Mr. Johnson's family was naturally divided. The younger lieutenants were more heavily involved in the distribution of narcotics, and the older lieutenants were still involved in the old rackets like numbers, loan sharking, gambling, and sometimes extortion. The older lieutenants were established businessmen in their communities. They were not as respected on the streets as the younger lieutenants, but wealth and comfortability made up for it. The younger lieutenants were always getting into trouble with the law. The older lieutenants rarely got into trouble. They were involved in drugs but mainly from the investment end. They would lend their soldiers money to buy drugs, and get a cut. Or they would get narcotics from Big Will, and give it to their soldiers. They never got directly involved with distribution like the younger lieutenants did. It was too risky.

Andrew Stewart ran a large majority of the numbers business, gambling houses, betting, and loan sharking in North Philadelphia. He was probably Big Will's strongest lieutenant out of the older ones. He had operated in his community for years, and had the respect of the entire area. He had been a millionaire for years. He owned property, a small flower shop that was where he got the nick name "Andy Rose," from Will. Most of the members in the family had nicknames because they shared the same first name as another member, or they used it to disguise their true identity. A lot of times if they were on the telephone, they used nick names. To disguise their identities in case the phone was tapped, Rose had strong influence in North Philadelphia, his soldiers sold tons of cocaine and heroin for him, and they were loyal to him. If they ever got into a jam he helped bail them, paid for their lawyers. Everything. He was loved and respected in North Philadelphia. He had so much money he did not have to commit another crime if he did not want too. The only reason that he still operated was because he was obligated to the family. He did not mind. This was his way of life. This was the way he choose, and he did not complain. In fact, he was happy. That was why he gave his soldiers a lot of freedom. Mainly because he did not need all that money. He could be greedy and try to make much more, but why? When dealers paid him just for letting them operate in his neighborhood, he did not want to get too involved, then the police could tie him into drug activity.

Black, Crazy Ed, and two bodyguards walked into Andy Rose's flower shop. Nobody really came in to by flowers that much. The other side of the store was changed into a grocery store, and Big Andy spent most of his time working in the grocery store. Occasionally, Andy would come over to the flower shop side and sit around. His daughter ran the flower shop for him.

When they walked into the flower shop Andy's daughter pointed them to the back. Andy and a couple of his buddies from the neighborhood were sitting in the back playing cards.

Black walked into the back. Andrew was not playing cards with the others. He was sitting at a desk writing number receipts.

Black, Crazy Ed, and the bodyguards walked into the back room. As soon as Andy noticed them he jumped to his feet. He walked over, shook their hands, and they embraced. Andy was alarmed by the visit. The only time he usually saw them was at meetings that Big Will called. Or if Crazy Ed needed some of Andy's soldiers to help settle a disagreement.

"Mr. Drew." Crazy Ed was always respectful. He titled him "Mr." Because Andy was old enough to be his father. "I need to speak with you."

Andy looked over at the men that were playing cards. "Excuse me gentlemen, but the game is over." He did not have to say anymore. They understood. Important business was at hand. They dropped what they were doing and left.

"Andy, we're not happy with the way things are going with the family, and we want to sit down and have a meeting with Mr. Johnson."

"Why are you coming to me? You should be talking to Clark?" Clark was second in command.

"First of all you know Big Will don't use no beeper, and he never answers his phone. The only time we hear from him is when he's ready to drop off a package, or he's picking up money. We don't even see him then because he sends a soldier."

"Well I could talk to him for you, but I don't know. I have to wait like everybody else. What's the problem? You didn't mess up any money or anything?"

"No." Crazy Ed replied. "We just want to have a little meeting." He wrote down his beeper number and home phone number on a piece of paper and passed it to Andy.

Black was going to keep the information back, but he could not hold it. "We have a business proposition, and we wanted to present it to him."

"I think you better talk to Clark. I can't arrange no meeting."

"You can at least try." Black asked.

"I can try, but I'm not making no promises." Andy added in.

Andre, his lawyer, the head of the organized crime task force of New Jersey, and the head of Pennsylvania's organized crime task force were at the state prison that Andre was incarcerated at, in one of those private rooms usually reserved for private lawyer and client conferences. Andre's lawyer was a elderly Jewish man who was licensed to work in New Jersey and Pennsylvania. He represented his case. He also represented his appeal.

The head drug enforcement agent in Pennsylvania opened the conversation. "Mr. Robinson, my name is Timothy Trilli I worked for the Pennsylvania drug enforcement agency. I came here to help you, but you also got to help me."

"How can you help me?" Andre's lawyers had been talking to him for weeks telling him that the police wanted to talk to him and see if he would cooperate.

"We need someone smart enough to help bring William Johnson down."

"William Johnson. I don't know anybody named William Johnson."

The agent reached into his brief case and pulled out a bunch of surveillance pictures of William and some of the lieutenants.

Andre picked up the pictures and looked at them. He was not in any of them. Thank God.

"Look, I don't even know him."

The agent smiled. "Mr. Robinson we have a confidential informant outside right now that says he got a command from his lieutenant to knock you off, but then Mr. Johnson had some trouble in South Jersey, and you helped settle it so he let you live for a little while."

Andre was a little shocked but the words sounded made

up, and the officer could see the doubt in his face. So he added.

"Plus, you messed up some money down in Jersey. The new word did not come out yet, but we think when you come home, your history will. I'll be back in a couple of days with some statements said about you by your boss, and some recorded conversation. I'll talk to the prosecutors in Philadelphia, and they're about to hit you with another indictment." The agent pulled out another series of pictures. This time it was a picture of a man at the crime scene, his face was destroyed by bullets. "You're being charged with his murder, and we have an informant willing to testify."

By this time half of Andre's physical strength left him. "Now we can hold this indictment back. Talk to the judge, and keep you out of jail for life if you work for us. But we have some questions, and we need some answers now."

William Johnson his counselor, and right hand man James Clark, Andy Rose, Black, and Crazy Ed were sitting in Carla's a restaurant that was located in Andy Rose's neighborhood. Carla's was a soul food restaurant that was almost a famous as Albert's, but since it was in a North Philadelphia neighborhood it did not get as much business as the other famous soul food restaurants. When it first opened in the early sixties a brother that was in the Nation of Islam under the Honorable Elijah Muhammad opened it, and the food was delicious. By the time the mid seventies came the family that owned it converted to another form of Islam, and the food changed. They started selling hala meats only. That's meat that was slaughtered by Muslims. The meat was delicious, fresh, and tender. Halal meats were so good, word soon spread about how good the food tasted, and Carla's business expanded even more. The restaurant was nicely furnished.

Even though the neighborhood was not that quiet the restaurant was posh. The waiters and the waitresses dressed in uniform. The waiters wore tuxedos, and the waitresses wore long black dresses.

Andy Rose arranged the meeting. He was the only one that Big Will and Black both trusted. Unfortunately, Black was foolish enough to believe that Andy Rose who was a close and trusted lieutenant to William Johnson probably before he was born was going to betray him. They did not really know the details of the meeting, but if Black acted up then Big Will was going to put a hit out on him, and Andy Rose promised that he would personally handle it. Andy handled security. He had soldiers sitting in the restaurant eating, and he had the building surrounded by soldiers sitting outside of the restaurant in parked cars just in case anything went down. All of this was mixed in with the regular breakfast clientele of the restaurant.

Andre Robinson walked threw prison reception. He had gone to court that morning, and the judge granted him the appeal just like the agents said. He got in touch with Mr. Johnson, and asked him to send somebody to pick him up, but Mr. Johnson said to him that might not be safe because the police were watching him, and he did not want Andre caught up in surveillance as soon as he came home. Especially since he had some special jobs for him to do. Instead, he got someone to give Andre's son's mother some money to rent a car, and drive down to the shore to attend his appeal, and then pick him up if he was released. Andre did not even deal with his babies mother.

When Andre got all of his possessions together, he changed back into the clothing his girl had sent him to come home in. She was the one that was suppose to pick him up, but when Big Will sent somebody to her with the money and a rent-a-car, she was know where to be found. Andre's first stop was to a hotel, and then his second stop was to his girlfriends house. He was going to kick her ass. How dare she mess around on him before he came home. Andre was carrying all his possessions in a big plastic bag. He walked threw the hall way of the building. When he noticed the open door a smile crossed his face. The only way he was going to stay out of here was if he contacted that F.B.I. agent. He walked threw the door, and he saw his sons mother. With her hair done and make up on she did not look bad. She always had a nice body. She was not in shape like she use to be. She still had the weight and the thickness, but it was not tight anymore. When she took her clothes off. It fell a little bit. Andre walked over to her, and they embraced. She was wearing some kind of cheap perfume. He was upset already.

"Did they give you any money?" he asked.

"Yeah." A smile crossed her face. "They gave me a thousand dollars, and this rental car for a couple of days. The guy that brought the money told me to tell you to get with Big Ray when you come home." She smiled. They could use the money.

"Give me the money." She reached in her pockets and pulled it out.

He snatched it away from her. "I had to spend some of it on tolls and gas."

He grabbed the wad and counted it. Then she passed him the car keys. He jumped in the driving seat. He turned on the car so fast that she thought that if she did not jump in the car when she did he would have pulled off without her. At first Andre was not going to do it. But after riding he calmed down, drove to Philadelphia to a nice hotel room.

Big Will, Clark, Black, Crazy Ed, and Andrew were sitting in the restaurant ordering breakfast. It took them a while to agree on which place to eat, but Andy felt more comfortable here in his neighborhood where he could guarantee security.

"Mr. Johnson." Black had never addressed him like that before, his greeting lacked warmth. He usually called him Big Will. "You know I don't have anything against you. This is business. I don't have anything against how you run the family. The thing that I want is to work out a deal where I no longer have to get my product from you. I have connections, and I want to use them. Of course you will still get your cut. I just think me and my crew could make more if you let us generate our own money. I know you guys have made millions. You should step back and let us make a little bit now. If you go into semi-retirement then we could move the way we want to move. You will still get your share."

"I could never retire and still expect a cut. I don't want to be affiliated with the family like that if I retire. As long as I'm getting a cut the government can still hit me with conspiracy. Plus, when I retire I don't want nobody coming up to me asking me to interfere between disagreements with the family, or involving me in anything where I might have to take sides. But yes, to tell you the truth. I'm ready to retire. I'm ready to leave this family. The only responsibilities I want is to operate the legal business. Another thing is I can't speak for the other family members. I don't know if they are going to want to retire or not. We can hold another meeting. I know that I can't retire over night. It's going to take me weeks.... Maybe months for me to get things in order. I could go into a semiretirement early though. But first, I would need some guarantee's from the family. I mean like in a couple of years I don't want somebody putting a hit on me over some petty bullshit. I will need permanent bodyguards. Everything. There are a lot of details we have to go over."

"It's not really that anybody's not happy. All of the younger lieutenants are going to jail, and that's okay because this is business. But the more we're united the more were limited. If he separated a little bit it would be harder for the police to concentrate on us." Most of the lieutenants had current drug cases, or some other kinds of charges.

"Honestly Black. I don't think that is true. I don't even think the police know we're united. It's just this drug shit. It's to risky. Eventually they'll get on to you."

"That's it." Black added. "We're not afraid, and if you gave us some freedom we could make some serious moves." The conversation was interrupted by the waitress bringing breakfast. The waitress quietly sat all of their plates on the table.

Once the waitress left Clarkie spoke. He was upset. He looked at Black with hatred in his eyes. A hatred in this business you were not suppose to reveal. Especially to an enemy.

"You young guys don't understand anything do you. Were a family. That's why we lasted this long. The minute we break a part they're going to destroy us. Things are perfect. You guys have to learn loyalty. I mean your suppose to be loyal to this man. He gave you a start. You were a bum in South fucking Philly when we found you. Getting high and shit. This is how you come to me.... Us. What happen to your loyalty? We helped clean South Philly out for you. You're fucking crazy. You don't know loyalty."

Black felt disrespected, but he kept his composure. "I got

loyalty. I came here in peace. I only made a suggestion. A suggestion that me and half of the other lieutenants feel is right. An opinion that I will stick by. But If Mr. Johnson says fuck retirement. Then he has my undying loyalty. I would kill the men that suggested the meeting. But then again they're right. You guys have made millions legally, and illegally. What more do you need now. Give us a chance. You're greedy, and your greed is sending us to jail while you sit back and grow older. You worked for yours, now let us earn ours."

"You're rich. You're a millionaire, aren't you?" Clark asked the question, and he knew the answer.

Big Will interrupted. "Lower your voices." The other patrons in the restaurant were so close they might be able to hear.

The waitress returned to the table. "Would you gentlemen like anything else?" She could look at them and tell they were gangsters so she tried to act her best. Gangster left nice tips. Every single one of them were dressed nicely. They even had on nice clothing. They also wore very expensive jewelry. If they were not gangster they must be wealthy businessmen.

"Yes. Could you bring us some coffee." Black called the meeting so he would be expected to pay for the check when it came.

"Yeah, I am rich. But you're filthy rich, and you don't have to do anything else."

"Well, here's my answer now. If I retire it will only be on Will's orders. If not. I'm sticking around at least for a couple more years." That was the same as declaring war. The meeting was fine in the beginning, but things were starting to get a little out of hand now.

"What we need to do is call a meeting with all the lieutenants, and see who shares this idea with you." Clark was really upset now.

"Clark enough." Big Will did not want him to start an argument. The last thing you wanted to do was let him know you considered him an enemy. Then he would be on guard. Nothing was harder than doing a hit on somebody that knew they had a hit on them. It was much easier if the person did not expect it.

"Clark you need to learn to listen. We have been talking about retiring for years, and we all know it's time. I really think this is a blessing. We have discussed it in private many times, but honestly Black we did not think the lieutenants were ready for us to retire. We thought if we retired they would think we abandoned the family, or something else tricky. If you guarantee our permanent safety. Then we can sit down and arrange the retirement of every single older member that wants to retire. Of course it's going to take years. But in about ten years you have the position that you want, and everybody else will be happy. In fact I could have the counselor and underboss out of here in five years. Two and a half years a piece as boss." The bosses word was the only word that counted. That could be more problems. What if when Clark got the chance to be boss he put a hit out on them. Black made his decision early. If Clark took over they were going to hit him to protect their own lives.

Black did not realize that Mr. Johnson was only acting civilized at this meeting. As soon as he left he was going to call an all out war.

The waiter returned with the coffee in china cups on a tray. They sold soul food, but the restaurant was still elegant. The waitress sat and asked them what kind of coffee they ordered. None of them really paid attention to the animal walking towards them carrying a semi-automatic weapon with a silencer on it. The gunman lifted the gun and pointed it towards Big Will's face, and pulled the trigger. The force of the bullet pushed him out of his seat. When he got pushed out of his seat his feet hit the table, and it flipped. The noise got the entire restaurants attention, and everyone went into hysterics. The gun man pushed the chair aside, and he was about to hit Big Will in the face again, but Clark jumped up and started to run. The trigger man had been doing hits since he was a teenager. He pulled the trigger and shot Clark in his back while he was running. Clark's legs froze on him. The gun walked over to Clark who was laying on his back. Clark tried to cover his face, but the trigger man pulled the trigger and emptied his clip in Clark's face. The diners were running all over the place. The gun man ran to the back where the kitchen was located. He ran threw the kitchen and out the back door into a get away car. By the time he got to the back door their were people running out of the restaurants front door.

Word of Big William death spread quicker than a message over a telephone line. Before Black even ordered the hit he made sure he had the support of most of the young lieutenants. He still decided to lay low. Even though the older lieutenants did not have the street influence that they use to have they were still dangerous, and not to be taken lightly. They were the same ones in the seventies and late sixties who cleaned out the streets for Big Will, and they were still capable of those same deeds.

Philadelphia had several news stations, and all of them were out at the crime scene by the time the police had arrived.

Black, a couple of lieutenants, and a couple of soldiers were sitting around the television watching the news. The handsome black news caster that always told the news came on the scene.

"We're live at Carla's famous restaurant. The restaurant that is known threw out Philly for it's delicious cuisine. But tonight Carla's became famous for another reason. Now it will be famous for it's mob scene. Today authorities reported that two gentlemen who were shot here this morning while eating breakfast, might have been the victims of a mob hit. A black mafia hit." A picture of Big Will and Clark came across the screen. A lady's voice told the rest of the story. Black stood up and turned the television off.

Andre had been in the hotel room for two days by the time that Big Will and Clark were killed. The night that it came on the news he beeped Ray. The lieutenant that had provided him with the rent-a-car and thousand dollars. He was sitting on the bed watching the news when the incident came on the screen. He was in total disbelief and shock. He always thought that Big Will was too strong for anyone to ever challenge him. He had only been gone for two years. Could things had changed that quickly. He picked up the phone and beeped Ray. It took Ray a little over an hour to call back.

The telephone rang. "Hello. What the fuck is going on man?" Andre did not even wait for Ray to identify himself. Nobody knew he was in the hotel except the owners.

Ray was on the other end of the line. "Man this shit is crazy out here. W'ere going to need you."

"Who, and the fuck did it?" He tried his best to sound concerned.

"I don't know. I mean I know, but I can't talk right now.

"These phones are burning baby."

Andre immediately got the message. The phones might be tapped. Don't say anything further. Plus Ray was an old timer, and old timers always thought the phones were tapped. It was a precaution that they never took lightly.

"Listen, I'm going to need you to sit tight until tomorrow morning, and then I'm going to call you early so be ready. I got things for you to do."

"How are you going to catch me. I don't have no ride unless I keep the rental for a couple of more days."

"Don't even worry about that. When I call you tomorrow meet me at my store. You remember where my store is don't you?"

It took him a couple of minutes to think about it, but he remembered. "Yeah I remember. But if I don't, and I get lost. I'LL call you from my girls house." That put a smile across her face. She was praying they were going to stay together.

The next day after the hits Black and Frog were sitting in Blacks kitchen eating breakfast. Black had only been living in the house for six months. He lived there with his girlfriend of nine years, but they were soon to be married. He bought her a hair salon that did well, and almost everything he owned valuable was in her name in case he ever got into trouble. He would hate for the police to confiscate his valuables. His house was beautiful. It sat in an exclusive suburb of Philadelphia. It was not as big as a mansion, but it was large. A place he dreamed of, not like where he grew up. He could come here and get away. Black owned a 740i BMW, Jaguar XJ6, and his fiancé drove a 9000 CDE Saab. Every single car was a eighty-seven "Spanking brand new." He said. Every thing but the Saab was parked outside of the house. In the morning his girl woke up, took the kids to the babysitter, and then went to work. She did this faithfully every single morning. Frog bought a house, but when things settled and he got promoted to lieutenant he was moving into one of the vacant houses he saw in Black's neighborhood. Frog dropped the paper on the table with the articles of Big Will and Clark. "Did you read this shit?"

He looked nervous. "They know shit. Did you talk to the other lieutenants yet? What's up?"

"I haven't talked to anyone yet. I'm going to have another meeting with the young guys, and then I'll try to have a meeting with Ray and them, but if they don't want to meet, it's war or peace. I don't give a fuck. It's too late to turn back now. It's on." Black picked up the paper and read the article. The police seem to know more than he thought. "We're just going to have to be very careful."

The head of Pennsylvania's organized crime task force knew a lot of things about Big Will, and they were expecting a war. They were right.

"Guess what?"

"What?" Black was irritated. Sometimes Frog could get on his nerves.

"Andre's home."

"What?"

"Yeah he's calling that girl. I think he's in a room or something. But he already called Charlene and threaten her."

"Why?"

"You know she a ho, and she fucking all these different guys."

"We need to get in touch with him."

"For what?" Frog never liked Andre. "He's a fiend." That was the slang word for drug abuser.

"He's a fiend, but he's not a fiend when he comes home. We need to get with him. You know that boys known for putting in work. He's a stone cold killer."

"Fuck that, we don't need him. If I see him I'll knock him the fuck off for you. He's no real threat."

Black just laughed. Sometimes Frog could be narrow minded. It must have come from growing up so hard. "Listen. You did good with Will and Clark. But no hit unless you get permission from me. Hit's cause heat."

Frog was upset. But he had to give his chain of command respect. "Yes sir."

Black patted his back.

The telephone must have rung the first thing in the morning. Andre was up having sex all night, but when it rang even though he was tired. He jumped up and answered it.

"Hello."

"Hello. It's me." Ray never really identified himself over the telephone. That was incriminating.

"Yeah what's up?"

"What's up. I need to see you."

"When?"

"Now."

"Okay. I'll meet you at the store in twenty minutes."

Ray was impatient. "Twenty minutes. You can't make it ten."

"Ten minutes. You're a half an hour away."

"I know, but this is important."

"Okay. I'll be there in five minutes."

"Good that's the shit I like to hear. Your one of my boys now." The line went dead.

Andre shoved his girl up. Then he brushed his teeth. He still had the clothes he had worn from prison on. As soon as he got some money he was going shopping. Then he was going to Charlene's, and beat up who ever she was fucking, and move his clothing in her house. "Fuck that. She's not going to fuck up on me." His girl was still laying in the bed. He smacked her right in the face. "Get up bitch. I got business to do."

She jumped up slipped her clothes on, and tried to brush her teeth, but he was rushing her. It took her five minutes to get together, and then they were out the door, and onto the elevator. They jumped on, and rushed down to the floor."Fuck leaving a tip, and fuck paying the phone bill." Andre told her."These people can kiss my ass." He was excited.

Ray and one of his most trusted soldier were waiting down stairs for them when the elevator came. The elevator door opened, and Ray pulled out his semi-automatic pistol. Andre noticed him, and was in complete shock. Before he could move,. Ray had pulled the trigger and shot him in the face. He grabbed Andre's girl, and threw her out of the elevator against the wall. She hit the wall so hard she fainted. The soldier that was with him was carrying a machine gun. Once Andre's girl hit the wall, the soldier with Ray took a couple of steps into the elevator, and sprayed Andre's body full of bullets.

They ran outside and got into the get away car. The soldier asked his lieutenant, "I heard Andre was a crazy mother fucker. We could have used him in case we war against Black, why did we have to kill him?"

Ray was loved and respected by all his soldiers. That was the only reason he even tried to explain. He never wanted them to feel as though they could not come to him. If they were intimidated by him then they did not trust him. How could he trust somebody he felt did not trust him. He kept all of his soldiers close to him. In a lot of ways it benefited him. His soldiers truly loved him. The disadvantage was; one time a little petty drug war broke out and the competition shot him up. If he laid back like the other lieutenants his enemies would have never known that he even played a role in narcotics.

"Big Will had given me the command before all this shit broke lose. Andre was a serious soldier. But he was untrustworthy, and I can't have untrustworthy people around me at a time like this. You see what trusting somebody too much can get you. Look at Will and Clark. That's why Clark's gone now. For trusting somebody too much."

When Will got in touch with Ray, and told him about the meeting. Ray asked him if he wanted to use his men for security.

"No. That's okay. Andy's going to handle security."

"You sure?" Ray asked. "They might pull something."

"No not Andy."

SEVENTEEN

Andre's homicide did not shock the divided family, and neither did the other things that were occurring. What really shocked the family was the fact that Big Will did not die. It took a couple of days before the newspapers, or the general public got the story, but on the day of Clark's funeral all the local newspapers ran articles that William Johnson, the head of the Black Mafia in Philadelphia, and South Jersey was alive, and recuperating in a Philadelphia hospital under guarded protection. It took days before Black would be able to get the details from his police connections. Mr. Johnson was shot in the head, but instead of the bullet going straight threw it, exited from the top of his scull removing a small piece of his scull. He had not fully recovered yet. He was having difficulty speaking and comprehending, but he would live. He was also functioning without the support of a life support system,

Mr. Clark's funeral was held three days after the shooting. His family was praying that Will would be able to attend, but he had disappeared, and nobody knew how to go about contacting him. Mr. Clark was having a closed casket funeral. When the hit men shot him in the back of his head it came out the front and destroyed his face. He left his ex-wife with the responsibility of handling his funeral even though they were divorced. It was the bond. He left a will. His ex-wife, children, and grandchildren got a majority of the estate. His insurance would cover the cost of burial. His family decided to hold the services at the funeral home in the neighborhood he grew up in with Big Will. They had been friends since he was a child. Their fathers ran numbers together. His family used the same funeral home that had buried his mother and his father. This was his neighborhood. The neighborhood where he had met his wife, and raised his children until he became wealthy. When his wife divorced him she returned to the same neighborhood. Just a nicer section. Clark bought her and the children a beautiful home. He was loved, respected, and feared in this neighborhood so when he died his neighbors and friends came out to pay their last respect ten fold. Most of them knew he was involved in crime, but none of them knew to what extent. Know one knew that he was second in command of the Black Mafia until they saw the articles in the paper. All the lieutenants in the family attended. The young ones and the old ones. Corty and his lieutenants came. The funeral was so crowded everyone could not fit inside to pay their respects. When the preacher saw the crowd he made his eulogy as short as possible. This would have to be taken to the grave site. He made the announcement to the family, and then apologized to everyone who missed viewing the body. They should have come earlier to the first viewing.

The family members did not see them when they entered the funeral home, but after everyone started leaving there were at least four different news vans parked outside, attacking the mourners with questions as soon as they came out. Some of the news reporters noticed members of the family coming out and heading towards their cars, they rushed them and started badgering them with questions. Some of them started snapping pictures. When Black came walking out with his bodyguards they covered his face to prevent the reports from snapping any pictures. The other lieutenants and family members had to do the same thing to conceal their identity. The older ones let the reporters snap pictures. They just ignored them. The funeral home was so crowded that some people had parked several blocks away because their were not enough parking spaces.

Animal entered the hospital. He was wearing a tailor made blue suit with some matching alligator skin shoes. He walked to the front desk and asked the receptionist where the gift shop was located. Then he purchased a bouquet of flowers. Several balloons that said. "Congratulations on the baby," and "Congratulations on your new born girl." After he purchased the flowers and balloons he took his time, he scribbled a couple of words on the card just in case something went wrong and he got stopped. His handwriting was terrible. Animal walked to the elevator. A couple of people that walked past him said congratulations. His plan was obviously working. He pushed the button for the floor that he was told Big Will might be on.

A heavy set white lady stepped on the elevator. She pushed eighth floor for the maternity ward. She noticed the button for tenth floor was pushed. The floor for the terminally ill.

She looked at the balloons before she spoke, "Excuse me

sir are you going to the maternity ward? Did your wife, or family just have a baby?"

"Yes." He looked at the fat white lady. She was dressed in a white nurse's uniform. "Yes. I'm going to maternity."

"You pushed the wrong floor." She was pleasant.

"Oh my father is dying also. I have to check on him."

The nurse was embarrassed that she asked the question. It was rare, but it did happen. Sometimes people had family expecting babies, and at the same time another family member, or friend expecting death.

It took a lot of connections and a little bit of money, but Black got the information on where Big Will was located. The only thing that he needed was the right hit man. It took him a little while, but he had the perfect person. He had a soldier named Animal, and he was rightfully titled. He was an Animal. He had been killing all his life. He just did not care. One time in a shoot out in the park he told his friends he started aiming at the kids because they kept getting in his way.

Usually, Animal worked with Steven and his younger brother Joseph. They were a three men hit team with a completely successful record. Every single hit they did they were a success. Steven was in the family. He was actually a soldier. Animal was an associate to the family, and so was his little brother. But once this war was settled Crazy Ed planned on initiating them.

Animal walked down the corridor to room eighteen twenty. He was praying that the information was correct, but once he saw that their was no police officer sitting outside of the door it might be wrong. If this was his room, and he was not under guarded protection then the police had under estimated the strength of the family. When he came he brought his best automatic weapon. The one with the silencer on it. "It's larger and it can blow a hole threw a steel door. Imagine what it's done to some of my enemies head." He would always laugh after he bragged about it. Before Animal did a difficult hit he did a test run. If it was a difficult hit he wanted to check out the area, and see how hard it would be to do the hit. Usually his hits were so easy that no test run was needed. On some of his test runs he would get lucky, and be able to do the hit. That's why when he went he always carried his gun. Animal got to the door, and there still was not any cops in sight. If their was only one cop in the room he was going to shoot him, and pump as many bullets in Big Will's face as possible. He did not believe in chest shots. They were too unreliable as far as making the hit successful. He wanted to hit all of his victims in the face if possible. He loved the reputation that he got in leaving his victims unidentifiable.

Animal entered the room. He saw Mr. Johnson lying in bed with all of these tubes sticking out of his nose and chest. His head was turned so Animal could not tell if he was conscious or not. He might have been talking to somebody. Oh well, he hoped it was not his wife because he had never killed an elderly woman before, but he would. He had no problem with it. He took a few steps before he pulled his weapon out. He wanted to make sure he had an aim on whoever else was sitting in the room. He wanted to hit the able people in the room first. His motto was always; "Hit your target first, but if target has a bodyguard, or someone who could return fire, identify them, and hit them second if possible." He never wanted to do a hit, turn around to run and get shot in his back. Animal did not see the officer sitting down in the seat watching the football game on television.

The officer jumped to his feet. There were no visitors to the room unless they called from the nurses desk. He immediately placed his hand on his gun. They were face to face.

"Excuse me, sir, may I help you?"

"Yes. Is this Denise Claiborne's room?" Animal asked. He looked stupid asking. But the flowers and balloons made it a valid mistake. If Animal would have known he was there he would have whipped his gun out and shot him. He still wanted to do it, but the cop had his hand on his gun already, and he was not that fast.

"This is a private room. You'll have to ask the nurse at the station for the maternity ward. The baby floor." Animal was not even really looking at the officer when he spoke. He was looking at the room and Big Will laying helplessly and unconscious. He wanted to pull his gun out and just pump a couple of bullets into the side of his head, but he could not with the cop standing there.

"I'm sorry officer."

"That's okay. Mistakes happen. Congratulation on your kid." Animal turned around and walked out of the door. His plans were to turn around start blasting, but he did not know if the cop was directly behind him watching or not. He started walking away just in case, and he was glad that he did because by the time he got a few steps away he noticed the officer running down the hallway towards him. Everything went into slow motion. If the cop reached for his gun he was going to hit him with the bouquet and the balloons, and then reach for his gun and start blasting.

The officer was getting closer and closer.

"He's okay. He's okay." The officer down the hall screamed out. "He's here for a newborn." The officer running towards Animal started slowing his pace. "He's looking for his newborn."

When they came face to face the officer did not even offer apologies or speak. Instead, he got a good look, and kept walking past.

Animal did not ask the receptionist for the maternity ward or anything. He headed for the elevator, and took it down to the next floor. Then he hit the stairwell. If he stayed on the elevator there could be somebody waiting for him, like another police officer. That could be dangerous. Suppose the nurse told the officers he knew what floor he was on, and they started to chase him. He always thought of things like this. If that was the way the police were guarding Big Will, he was dead. The day after the Clark's funeral the news papers ran big articles on the family. They had several different articles in the paper. One of the articles read, "WHO WILL HEAD PHILADELPHIA BLACK MOB." It ran pictures of almost all the lieutenants, and gave it's opinions of who was the most powerful, or who was the one that might have ordered the hit on the boss. All this bad publicity was making everybody crazy. There were pictures of the lieutenants, pictures of Big Will, and Clark laying on the floor dead. They even had pictures of different lieutenants entering the funeral home. War was too hot, and it had to stop. Differences had to be settle immediately. They even ran a little article about the war in South Jersey two years earlier, and how they believed that both organizations were some how connected. They did have several leads on who was at the restaurant at the meeting, but if any body had information on the homicide they should get in touch with the authorities immediately, and they were promised that their information would be held confidentially.

Ray Guns, the lieutenant that ran West Philadelphia, Big Cliff, William's bodyguard that was ordered by his boss to stay home that night, Big Albert, the one that owned the famous restaurant in South Philly, Phillip Bones controlled East Philadelphia, and Thomas McCant the family's underboss were sitting in Al's restaurant eating dinner, and really holding the first official meeting since Big William's, and Harry Clark's incident. The only older lieutenant that was not invited was Andrew Stewart, mainly because he was no longer trusted. He was the one that had set Big Will and Clark up for the murder attempt. All of them were upset. They had all been arrested before and charged with crimes, but they never had attention brought to them at this level. Fat Albert was really upset. When he first started out some dirty cops that he was paying off framed him in a numbers case, but besides that he was charge free. All of his sons were doing well. One was a cop, and another was a firemen. His daughters were married to doctors, and his other son-in-laws helped him operate his family business, the restaurant. It was getting more famous by the day. This war was pissing him off. He was not afraid to battle. He had been in the Korean War as a kid. He had killed people before when commanded by Will, and he had killed to protect his illicit business before. The thing that scared him most was that his wealth and businesses were in jeopardy. He had come too far for this. He was ready for any solution. He wanted peace, at whatever cost. Be it a hit, or just make the peace. By the time they called their own meeting they already knew the details of the meeting that Big Will had with Black. The only people that knew he had survived the attempt on his life were his most trusted lieutenants. He had never thought in his wildest dreams that Andrew would set him up to be murdered. Big Cliff, his most trusted bodyguard rolled him into the restaurant in a wheel chair. He could not walk well. They removed the chair that sat at the head of the table so that his wheel chair could be pushed there. His doctors told him that he would have to stay, and receive therapy, but he left anyway. He could hire a private therapist to help him recuperate. His underboss arranged for him to come home. Plus, his underboss arranged for all of his security. His wife and grandchildren were moved from the house. They moved in with his underboss, Thomas McCant. They loved it at his house. It was not like the small mansion that Mr. Johnson owned, but it was nice. When Cliff pushed him threw the doors he looked a little tired, and he had lost a lot of weight. Recovering from a bullet to the head could take a lot from you. He had a large hospital patch placed over his head. The doctors said that the bullet removed a large chunk of his scull. He was hurt and upset when he saw it, but his family reminded him they just wanted him alive. If he would have died maybe his family would have made peace, but now he lived, and it was war. Nobody new exactly what his commands would be, but they naturally assumed it would be to fight.

"Ray have you heard anything from Rose yet?" It was kind of hard for Big Will to speak. He was weak from medication.

"I haven't really heard from him yet, but I know he's going to try and get in touch with me."

"What about you Tommy? Have you talked to Corty or any of his people yet?"

"Yeah, I spoke with him. He said he had nothing to do with it, and he refuses to take sides. He said if we need anything, and he can help us he will."

"Do you believe him?" William asked.

"I believe him, but I don't trust him. It does not matter anyway. The only thing we need is for him to mind his business."

"I'm not going to draw this meeting out. I don't know if Thomas informed anybody, but Rose guaranteed my safety at the meeting. He's a traitor. These men, they are so foolish. I was going to retire. The only thing they have done is fucked everything up. I'm not sure which of the younger lieutenants are on our side, and I don't care. We have to settle this thing ourselves. But I'm not going to go to war if I don't have your support. I was going to retire anyway. But I could not retire without the approval of all of the lieutenants. That would be disrespect. We could just let them break off and go about their business. The police are going to destroy them anyway. The only thing they know is violence."

Ray was upset. "We can make the peace, but Rose has got to pay. Or what if we try to make the peace and Black doesn't want to because he thinks were a bunch of pussies. We don't know what his plans are. Things were going excellent, and he goes starting something like this. I don't give a fuck what nobody says. He's never going to be my boss. I have been on the streets entirely too long to let some punk who's made a couple of million selling drugs be my boss. He doesn't know anything about respect. I don't trust them. If he wants to make the peace then he better come with some good conditions. Your the boss. You have been the head of this family for years. If you want to retire you can retire. We'll give you permanent protection. A soldier from each of our crews."

"I agree with that. As long as the rest of the family agrees. But I'm not going to retire until this mess is settled. Then I'll retire officially, and Thomas will be made head of the family unless you come to a different agreement."

The meeting was over. William really felt he could trust the other lieutenants. After he woke up in the hospital and got his senses back, his family told him that Clark was dead. It broke his heart to lose his closes friend. Then the realization that Rose had set him up for the young boys nearly destroyed him. It was Albert and his men that formed a private security team, took his family to shelter and it was Albert's house that he let the hospital people set his equipment in. He called the meeting, and all the people that he thought he could trust came. Albert's men took his wife home so that she could get the house ready. Then William had a couple of his bodyguards take him past the cemetery. He had a brand new eighty-seven four door Jaguar XJ6. Four bodyguards escorted him to the car when the meeting was over. Big Cliff was the driver. They drove over to the cemetery. When they got there, Big Cliff opened the door and let William out. He had to walk with a cane until his balance came back. Big Cliff grabbed his arm and pulled him out of the car. The cold wind was blowing making the tree's sway. William was wearing a hat, scarf, and gloves. He was carrying a bouquet of flowers. In all of his years of controlling the family he had lost many dear friends, but this was the closest. He walked over to the plot escorted by his bodyguards. Then he motioned them with his hands to give him some privacy. They walked a distance away, but not too far. He was carrying the roses. He wanted to bend down and lay them on Clark's grave, but he did not have the strength. Instead. he just dropped them. The wind was blowing and the flowers rolled a little bit.

The police and the news reporters never gave up there relentless search on finding out the truth. One officer told William when they picked him up, "If your not going to cooperate with us, then we're going to hassle you to death. Every time you leave your house, we're going to pick you up." They did it for several weeks until William started calling his lawyer. The last time they pulled him over with his bodyguard he asked the officer.

"What are you harassing me for? Do you have any charges against me? I'm I under arrest?"

The officer replied. "No."

"Well then. I would appreciate it if you leave me alone."

The driver and bodyguard just pulled off leaving the cops standing in the streets alone.

The hardest thing about the war that the Johnson family was having was trying to pinpoint a target. It was easy to do a hit when every thing was at peace, and the enemy did not know he was an enemy or a target. But, now every one was on alert, so doing a hit was almost impossible. The crews had to hit the street and try to hunt it's target down. If this was the case, it took time. William had to stop all business so that the soldiers could go battle. But if you stopped all business, and went to war you were not making any money. The soldiers had to support themselves some how. But at least when you stopped business you could spend more time hunting down your prey. Mr. Johnson's men got in touch with Black threw a mutual friend. The ultimatum was his family was willing to give the peace as long as Black and his crew left them alone. The other part of the agreement was that Rose be turned over dead or alive. A couple of weeks passed, and William Johnson did not get a response, so he declared war.

Crazy Ed ran all kinds of rackets in the area he controlled in North Philadelphia. He street taxed all of the number runners, the people that ran gambling houses, every body. If he found out you committed a crime in North Philadelphia, and he did not get his share, you were going to have problems. He made a lot of money doing this but it also got him into a lot of trouble. His name was down at the police station so much that it was ridiculous. Most of the men he knew feared him, but they feared police and doing time a little more. He had killed a lot of snitches. If word got back to him that you might be a snitch then he would make it his personal business to have you killed, and that was how he got his name Crazy Ed. It was said that no one was safe around him.

Ed ran a small clothing store on the Avenue in North Philadelphia. The clothing that he sold was of poor quality. It was inexpensive and he made a lot of money selling clothing to the poor people who lived in the area. Mr. Johnson tried to convince him to invest in real-estate, but he did not. He loved having his millions hidden in his mothers house in North Philadelphia. He told Bill Will, "I don't care what anybody else got, I want to see my money. Fuck property." The only thing he did as far as spending money was invest in the store, and renovate his mother's house. He bought her a new car every single year, and anything she wanted he gave to her. He bought his wife a new car every single year. He would spend money on his family, but not really on anything else.

Crazy Ed and one of his workers from the store were loading his truck with goods he had purchased whole sale from some Koreans. They were out side stacking the clothing into the truck. He did not notice Raymond and a group of his soldiers cruise up the street in broad day light in a metallic van. As soon as they were besides Crazy Ed's Toyota 4Runner, the vans side doors slid open. Two soldiers carrying mac tens opened fire on Crazy Ed. They were standing so close to him that when they started shooting him they could see chunks of his flesh being torn from his skin. He was dead before his body even hit the ground. The van pulled off, at the same time that the soldiers started shooting, the soldiers ran up the crowded avenue threw a small crowd of people with their guns in their hands. They ran to the next corner where a blue get a way car was parked. They jumped into the car, and it pulled off.

The only reason they caught him off guard was because he never thought that someone would have enough heart to make an attempt on his life in broad day light. He was wrong.

EIGHTEEN

Nineteen Eighty-Eight

Crazy Ed's homicide made front page news. "YOUNG MOB LIEUTENANT DIES IN MOB WAR." Crazy Ed's homicide was in all of the local news papers, and some papers located in the surrounding area. Every time that one of the members of the family died the papers ran even larger articles. Big Will hated this. All of this attention scared him. Publicity was one of the worst things that could happen to a mob boss. All this, plus Big Will's falling health was taking a toll on him. Black had got in touch with the family threw Rose, and they were trying to arrange a meeting so that they could work out some kind of peace agreement. No side trusted the other. They needed to have an intermediate. The police were crawling all over the place. They kept picking Black up, questioning him about the hit made on Clark and Big Will. Crazy Ed's murder was a powerful blow for Big Will. his enemies underestimated his strength. They thought without the Italians he was weak, but he proved them wrong and he proved them wrong very quickly. Big Will's family had gotten together and decided to cut back on dealing with drugs. They could still make money financing drug dealers, running numbers, and some of the other rackets. Most of them were seriously considering retiring after the war was settled. Black was going to get what he wanted, but he was not getting a united family, and that could prove a weakness. He would never be able to reorganize the family like William did it. If he did do it, it would take years. Forming a organization had to happen naturally. Even if it was planned. Big William told the older lieutenants if they still wished to deal in narcotics they had his permission. They were allowed to deal with their own connections. The only thing he was concerned about was getting his cut of the profit. The lieutenants begged him to pick a new underboss and give the family some more control structure, but he declined. He told them he planned on retiring soon, and that his positions would have to be filled. He spent most of his time investing the money that he had accumulated into his real-estate business. The lieutenants were doing the same thing. All of them were getting charge by the casino control commission as being members of the black mafia. The commission was trying to band all of them from the casino. Will was thinking about opening some legal businesses in South Jersey, but this spoiled his plans.

Black owned several different kinds of businesses. But the one where he spent most of his time was at the pool hall he owned. It was the same pool hall where he got his start. A man name Red use to run a number spot out of the pool room in the early seventies. slack was a young hoodlum that use to run errands for Red. Eventually Red went to jail for running numbers. He was not a smart man. He had a heavy drinking problem plus he kept messing up Big Will's money in gambling houses. He had a serious gambling problem, as well. One year he disappeared for a week without telling the family anything. He had gone to Las Vegas and won a couple of hundred thousand dollars on the crap tables. Big Will took a hundred thousand dollars of it as punishment for him abandoning the business. Red's abandonment was Black's fortune. Black had met Mr. Johnson several times, but they had never conducted business. Big Will offered Black the chance to become a lieutenant. The only thing he had to do was remove Red. Black had never killed anybody before, but he knew his path, and he knew what kind of life he wanted to live. He wanted to be powerful, and one day run the black mafia with Big Will. Killing Red was harder than he thought. He had actually grown some kind of affection for Red. But life was life, and if you did not live it, you died. Black waited a couple of months. Later he admitted to himself he was hoping that Red would just disappear again, and go off to Las Vegas. But he never did, and Black's love turned into deep hatred. He started noticing how Red did not conduct business. He spent most of his time chasing his girlfriend around, or drinking. The other free time he spent gambling. Black was going to give him a couple of thousand dollars, and send him off to another city. Or just try to get Big Will to demote him, and operate business around him. One day Big Albert came to visit him. He picked him up in his Lincoln Continental. They took a long ride.

Big Albert asked him. "What's wrong? Why you ain't did it yet?"

"This might sound crazy, but I kind of feel bad for Red. He's a wino. He's got a drinking problem."

Albert looked at him seriously. "Look this is business. When the boss offers you a new position you don't refuse. He likes you. You think he's going to make you a lieutenant just because you killed somebody. Hell no. He thinks your the strongest soldier that Red's got. If you wait too long he's going to start thinking maybe Red knows, and you two are plotting against him."

Black was about to speak, and Albert pulled over. "Look, shit is falling apart up here. Will asked you to handle it. You better take care of it, and learn business. Fast." He reached over and opened his door. He was a couple of blocks away from the pool hall. He pushed his door open and Black got out. He got the message.

Most of the gambling houses in South Philadelphia had to pay Red a street tax which he split with Big Will. But after a while Red started gambling the money so Black was put in charged with collecting. Then he would take it to Albert or sometimes Big Will himself. One night Red was in the gambling house gambling. He paged Black, and asked to borrow a thousand dollars. He already owed a thousand from borrowing another time. This time when Black walked into the gambling spot, Red was sitting with a girl and some other gamblers at the table gambling. Black told some of his men to throw the girl out of the establishment. "Ruff her up a little bit." Were his commands. As soon as Black saw Red he smacked him. Red was a big man, but the smack shocked him.

Red stood up, but Black had a couple of men with him. "Red. Get your money we're leaving."

The guy that ran the spot came over. "Money. He owes money."

"Well I give it to you later. We're taking him home." He grabbed Black by his arm and helped lift him. He was not too drunk to walk. He brushed his clothes off, and started walking to the front door. Black grabbed his arm and pulled him back. "The car is parked in the back."

They walked to the back of the establishment, when they got to the back door Black pushed Red so hard he flew through the alley, he crashed against the wall. It took him a couple of seconds to shake it off, but before he could turn around Black had pulled out his gun and shot Red several times. The gun had a silencer on it. Red fell straight back. Black walked over to the car and popped the trunk. They lifted Red, and drove him all the way to Chester, Pennsylvania. A city that was located a couple of miles outside of Philadelphia.

Every morning one of Black's bodyguards picked him up from the house and drove him over to the pool-room. The war was still on so before he got to the pool room a small team of at least two bodyguards checked the area out first, and then he would come. A lot of times he drove with a group of bodyguards, and checked the area out himself. Things had been peaceful for a couple of weeks, and he was slowly getting his business together. His crack cocaine business was doing excellent. The only thing he was going to have to work on was organizing the other lieutenants. He really was not sure if he even wanted to do that, but he would need the strength of their unity. Big Will got in touch with him again, and gave him another proposition. "Andy Rose and a peace meeting." Were the messengers only words. Black felt bad about it because he was considering it. If the attempt on Big Will's life would have been successful things would have been a lot different. He heard from reliable sources that they were all actually ready to retire, but they were not going to retire until this war was settled.

Black came to work this morning with four bodyguards. He

just felt unsafe today. Things were getting a little too risky. He had decided he was going to change one of his rooms into a business office, and start conducting business from there until the war was over. Three times last week when he was making his morning security check he thought he spotted someone. He was getting just a little too paranoid in his own opinion. The only bad thing about conducting business from his house was that he would bring on a lot of police attention. He believed that feds had broke into his car, and placed a listening device inside. He was tired. When he first thought of asking Big Will to retire he was going to do it friendly, but his cohorts convinced him that if he asked Big Will to retire he was going to start a war. Instead of alerting him just make it easy, and take him out with the element of surprise. Sometimes Black would sit back and reflect on that. Maybe he should have just stuck with his original plan. Give Big Will a hell of retirement plan, and let him retire. Things were a little bit better before the war. It was hard forcing the younger lieutenants to pay a street tax to him. They were too greedy. Instead, they would give him a couple of thousand. If the war ended peacefully, the first thing he was going to do was kill one of them as a lesson to the others. Black opened the pool hall like always, twelve o' clock in the afternoon for business, and just like clock work the undercover officers assigned to follow him pulled up a couple of blocks away. The pool hall was suppose to be where all of the lieutenants that were under his command were suppose to come and meet with him if they wanted to discuss business. Instead, the only people that came by were the people that bought wholesale cocaine off of him. Today must have been an omen, he sat in the pool-room office just thinking. He had a small business office with a desk and a chair in it, and that was dangerous. If some gunmen burst threw the front entrance, the pool hall was so small that if he was in the office when they came he would be trapped. In one day he realized how foolish he was for still conducting business there. He just laughed to himself. Honestly, he was ready to retire. his bodyguards were sitting around the pool hall watching the door searching everybody that came in, and watching his back. They carried their guns out openly. This was South Philadelphia, and they were suppose to own it.

Black had been thinking like this so much that he walked out of the office into the pool hall. They had a television in the pool hall, and a stereo-system. They usually watched porno tapes on the V.C.R.

"Animal." Animal walked over.

"Yeah, what's up Black?"

"Tonight before you take me home make sure you remind me to get in touch with Big Drew." They did not call Andrew "Andy Rose." Because he told them he hated it. "Will probably made up that shit because he was jealous of me." Then they would burst into laughter.

"Plus, remind me I have to talk to Frog about something." Black had made up his mind. He was going to lay back, and let Frog handle almost everything. A guy named Archie Moore was going to take over Crazy Ed's crew. He was Crazy Ed's brother in-law. The day after Eddie died they had a meeting, and decided Archie was the one they could trust the most. Archie was making a list of anybody acting stupid because Black was going to have anybody that did not agree with his decision to make Archie a lieutenant, killed, Things had to get more stable and settled. Especially if they were going to really organize this thing.

"Yo, lets get out of here and go have something to eat. All of us. Where going to my house after lunch. No more meeting in the pool house. You guys will be guarding me at the house."

Black's mind was racing. He had some real-estate, but now it was time that he start really getting more real-estate. He just felt weird. He was realizing that it was time to grow, or he would die. He hated to admit it, but he should not have done the hit on Big Will. It was a wrong business move. When the family was united he was the most powerful lieutenant. Not financially, but physically. If he would have just waited for a couple of years he would have eventually became the most powerful lieutenant financially, and physically. It was not greed that made him make the moves against Big Will, it was just a young business executive wanting to be able to expand to his full potential, just like in the legitimate business world. Unfortunately, this was not the legal business world. In Black's world when a boss could not operate to the satisfaction of the rest of the company he died in a hail of bullets. In the legal world if his peers asked him to retire, unexpectedly, then he died of heart ache feeling betrayed, and unappreciated.

Black, Animal, and two bodyguards that he always used stepped out of the pool hall. The undercover police were sitting down the block. But this time Black noticed several other plain police cars. As soon as they stepped out of the pool hall, the police surrounded them.

"Shit." Black and all the other guys were carrying guns. Maybe it was just for questioning, and they would not get searched.

The cops jumped out of the car and started screaming. It was a form of subliminal intimidation. It did not work on experienced criminals. Black and his men started screaming back. The police picked Frog up in front of the crack house the family operated. They must have been following him all day.

Andrew and two of his bodyguards pulled up in front of his store in a brand new Cadillac De Ville. Andrew never kept an old car. If he liked it enough he would pay for it in cash, and trade it in after a couple of years or give the car to his wife. If he was not crazy about his new car then he would trade it in the next year for a newer model. Whatever the case, he never drove around in an out dated car. Another set of bodyguards lead them to the store. They were driving his Cadillac Fleetwood. They went to the store, parked, and jumped out. Then they waited for him to pull in. The bodyguards did that for security purposes. This way he could not be ambushed. Andy's store was located next to a bunch of other little stores in the neighborhood. Before, he did not even use bodyguards, there was no need, but this war changed everything. He had been to war before with other groups, but never people in his own family. It was worst when you were fighting your own family members because you did not know who you could absolutely trust. When the car that Andrew was driving in pulled up in front of the store, the police surrounded him. Almost every single cop out there that morning was a detective. When the bodyguards in the first car heard the cars skid they automatically reached for their guns. Andrew stepped out of the car, he waved his hands at his bodyguards and they lowered thier guns.

An older Afro-American detective walked over to him. "Mr. Stewart, we need to speak with you."

Andrew had been on the streets so long he knew the law. "Do you have a warrant?"

"No. But believe me it would be much easier on you if you come and answer some question for us. If not, the next time we come we might have a warrant with a charge. I don't want to make a scene on the street. It will only take a couple of minutes."

"I don't have nothing to say unless my lawyers present." They cuffed him and the others, then took them down town. They placed Andrew in the back seat of an undercover car in between two young rookies.

When they got down to the precinct, Black, Frog, and Andrew were placed in three separate rooms. All of the cops had authority. They were not your regular young rookie dick head, asshole cops. These were professionals. Maybe F.B.I.

"Do you know what your down here for?" Captain Daniel Banton asked Black.

"No. But I know nobody read me my rights, and I don't want you in my face until you speak with my lawyer." Black turned away from him in the chair.

"You're down here for the Clark murder, and I want to ask you a couple of questions."

"No you're not. Your not going to ask me shit. Where's my lawyer?"

The Captain was upset. "You're a stupid mother fucker. I'm just about to help you out."

"Fuck you... I don't need no fucking help from the police. I pay my lawyer entirely too much fucking money for that. I don't even want to look in your face."

The rookie cop that was standing against the wall could not keep his composure. He placed his hands around Black's neck and started choking him. "You stupid motherfucker. You pulled a gun out on an officer. That's attempted murder on a cop.

Let's see if your crack money can save you from that. We have some questions." He pushed Black over. He was handcuffed in a chair. The other officers grabbed him.

The Captain stopped them. "Get Spannoli outta here."

Black got a good look at his face. That was a rookey's problem. Most cops problem. They took work too personal. Every victory was their victory, and every lost was their loss.

The Captain walked over to the table and picked up some photo's. He walked over to Black and showed him the pictures.

"We have a witness that is willing to testify that she saw you in the bar shooting the night of this murder." The officer stood in front of him switching the picture. He saw the picture of Big Will. His face was covered with blood. He thought to himself, 'How did he survive them shots.' At the same time they were hitting Andrew and Frog with the same questions.

The Captain asked again. "Listen, you think we don't know you're at war with William Johnson. Well let me fill you in on a tid bid of information. You're dead. There about to kill your ass. This is your opportunity to work with us. But if not, fuck it... Were you there?"

Black had not really budged the entire meeting. Maybe those were the magic words. They must have gotten to him because the expression on his face changed.

"Listen. Black. I can help you. By law once we hear their going to kill you. We have to tell you in case anything happens, and you get hurt. If you get killed and we did not tell you, we're in trouble. We help people. Where you at that meeting? I know you're a tough guy. We grew up in the same neighborhood. You can trust me." Black smiled. "Since you know so much why are you asking me so many questions?" The cop walked out of the room mad.

He did not say another word after that. The police left them in a dark holding cell for a couple of hours without letting them use the telephone. When the cop returned he came back with a green sheet. Black was charged with possession of a firearm by a convicted felon.

Black learned something that day. He learned to trust his gut feeling. If he would have followed his gut feeling, then none of this would have happen. From now on he was going with his gut feelings like he use to.

After getting arrested Black decided to do what he had been planning on, and that was to call a meeting.

It took a couple of weeks to arrange the meeting because of safety precautions. A place where both parties had to feel safe, and a place where the police could not quickly set up surveillance.

Thomas McCants had lived in the suburbs of Philadelphia for years. His house was in a predominately black neighborhood. Most of the people that lived in the neighborhood did not even know that he was involved in crime, They thought he owned some kind of small business. He had a nice home, and he always had several nice cars. Sometimes more than one, but that was no indication that he was participating in anything illegal.

Thomas lived in a beautiful Tudor style house. He had already had an electrical gate placed around it so when the war started he just added some bodyguards. All these years he had fooled his neighbor's and his wife's family. They did not know anything until recently. When the papers ran articles they would show pictures of him, but they would always have the title of associate under it. The authorities did not know that he was the underboss in the family. But once Crazy Ed got killed the next series of articles identified him as a high ranking official in the family.

Black had Frog arranged the meeting with Big Will and the rest of the family. Usually when they had a meeting of this size nobody was allowed to bring weapons. That was the first thing that Black made clear. He was the enemy. He's not going to have a meeting in any public place, and he wanted to bring as many bodyguards as he wanted. "I assure you. Tell them I want peace. But this meeting is not going to be my death bed." It took them a week to respond, but the requirements were accepted.

McCant had his daughters decorate his dining-room. He had a business office, but it was too small. All these years his children had seen men that they thought were shady looking associating with their father, but once the papers came out, they knew. McCant did not seem like the criminal type. He did not whore around with a bunch of different women. Instead, he was quiet and humble. He was nice looking. He always did things. Shop all weekend with his wife, or they would take long walks. He would baby sit his grandchildren with his wife, all of those grandfather things. He never used a bodyguard. Only when he had to. On the week days he spent a lot of time at the office, and he did have a lot of money to have only owned a small business.

Black and his bodyguard came to the house. Black had just bought a black nineteen eighty-eight J30 Infiniti. One of the bodyguards with him was Archie Moore. He would have to come, and be introduced as the lieutenant that would be taking over Crazy Ed's spot. Frog came in a separate car with a bodyguard. Then Jeremiah from Jersey. He was still acting like he was loyal to Big Will, but he did most of his business with Slack. He would be able to set Big Will up if it was needed again. When Big Will came he drove his new nineteen eighty-eight 740i BMW. He got rid of the Bentley. They were too expensive to maintain, and it bought to much attention. He missed the enormous size, but he loved his knew car. He just wished it did not pick up so fast. He never really drove it anyway. Big Cliff's bodyguard always drove him around. He came with Cliff and two other bodyguards. He did not bring his wheel chair this time. Instead, he used a cane. He had to wait for them to help him out. Ray Guns came with a bodyguard, Big Albert, and Andrew Stewart.

As soon as they came in a group of bodyguards escorted them into the dining room. It was set up nice. A bowl of fruit in front of the table with a bowl of wine. Mr. McCant owned a couple of liquor stores in different neighborhoods. When he first started out he was working with the Italians, running numbers and gambling houses. They introduced him to William Johnson, and from that point on they became partners. McCant was stronger than Clark because McCant actually held street influence. Clark on the other hand was nothing but Mr. Johnson's right hand man. The man William trusted the most. That was why when the Italians gave him permission to organize he made Clark his counselor. It took them a couple of years, but they eventually expanded and took control of Philadelphia The Italians had helped him put everything together. For this they got a cut. It did not seem like much in the beginning, but if you added it all up it might have reached into the hundreds of millions of dollars. Those days were over now. The Philadelphia Italian Mafia was almost completely destroyed. Half of them were incarcerated. The ones that were left home, fighting to keep things organized. There was a new leader popping up every single day trying to take over and claim leadership.

"I want to thank you Tommy for arranging this meeting. We need it." Black raised his glass, and the other followed in motion.

Tommy made a quick reply. "For Peace." He returned to his seat.

"This might sound crazy and unique coming from me. But I see, gentlemen. The police they are going to take everything we got. It's to much too go to war, and have to watch the police. If we're not careful soon we'll be like the Riccobi's." That was the name of the organized crime family that controled Philadelphia.

"And I don't want to end up like the Riccobi's. I want the peace. If the police don't get us, we'll all end up dead in the street. I don't want to end up dead in the street. I have too many plans and things I want to do."

"How do we know you will keep your word. When I was coming up your word was good enough because if you did not keep your word, your own friends would kill you. We don't want insanity. If you come and say you want peace. A couple of years from now you can not start the war again, and try to get even. If you want peace. Make peace, and keep peace." McCant was leading the meeting.

He was still second in command Black thought.

"Yeah, you are young, Black." For some reason most of them were shocked when Big Will started to speak. He looked terrible compared to how he use to be. He use to be larger, but now his wounds and medication made him weak. "You have to learn if you want peace, keep peace. Because if you wait a couple of years and break the peace then there will be no more meetings, and I will personally make sure that the one who breaks the peace pays. We're not animals. We're businessmen. Genius. Look at us. Look what we have created. A billion dollar a year business. A multi-million dollar business. I'm tired. I'm not going to fight all of my life. I'm to old for it. I just don't have the energy. The next time somebody looks at me wrong, or spits near me. I will kill them out of frustration."

The others laughed. We still had our sense of humor

"The only thing I need is the guarantee. You keep your people peacefully away from mine, and I won't do anything to your men. Eventually when I retire, or one of you retire we will maybe try and bring the family back together. But the only way I can see that is if I have a guarantee of my safety."

Life was funny. Black was now speaking of his retirement. They had all done things in business that they knew created enemies, and things that would make your enemy want to get revenge once he got strong enough to retaliate.

"That is understandable. I hope you get to see retirement. I was going to wait to announce it, but the opportunity has presented it's self. After today I am officially retired. I make no more decisions for the family. The only thing I do is handle legal business. I have already picked the people who replace me, and that will be explained later in privacy. Black, we all make mistakes..... Atlantic City." He never really talked about it with the other guys, but he regretted killing Christopher. It caused his family too much confusion. It ended in a massacre. Michael, Big Aaron, and Little Aaron. Jeremiah was next. He had to make the peace.

"But the wisest thing that a leader can do is know when to make the peace, and when to retire. I'm telling you here as my last command, and I have already spoken with Thomas. Any decisions I make here must be carried over by the new leader. Black you have your peace."

Black looked over to Thomas. He looked back. "I swear to God you have the peace." Thomas was going to be the new boss. As expected.

Big Will reached his hands out to Black. Black stood up and walked over to him. It would be hard for William to stand. They embraced.

McCant stood up from his seat. "A toast." The other men jumped to their feet, Big Will raised his glass from his seat.

"To retirement, and to peace." The meeting was over. The peace was made that easily.

Big Will waited until they left, and then officially he retired for his family. Thomas McCant was made the boss. Raymond Guns was made his underboss, Big Albert was made counselor. It took them years of loyalty, but that loyalty paid off. Thomas let it be known he had no intentions of being boss for more than five years, and then he would go into legal retirement. They were all looking forward to retirement. Leroy Booth took over Big Alberts crew, and Earl Gilbertson took over Ray Gun's crew. They were young men in their late twenties. By the time they got to be in the upper echelon of the family, they would only be forty, or fifty. Everyone was learning to retire.

Black did not immediately find out, but he did a few weeks later. The other lieutenants had come together and asked William Johnson to retire. He had no choice but to agree with the single condition that they murder Black. With all in agreement, William Johnson arranged the meeting. It was a farce.

NINETEEN

Nineteen Eighty-Eight

Nobody knew, but the family had been under a federal investigation for at least eighteen months. Their telephones were taped, their automobiles had bugs in them, and they were under constant surveillance. The police and the FBI were watching every single move they made. Black had learned to stop worrying about things like that. He had to learn to concentrate on things at hand. Things like his case. It took a month for a grand jury to indict him, but they did. They indicted him and all the other members in his crew with possession of a concealed weapon by a convicted felon. Some of them had never been locked up before so they only got charge with possession of a weapon. The police were constantly arresting them, and harassing him. He had some police on his payroll so he knew when they were going to start harassing him, and that was an advantage. What really pissed him off was all the information that the police had. The gun charge was nothing. He found out that they were trying to get information everyday on the Clark murder. He had to do something about it. He had to concentrate. Veronica Dennison was really the only witness that the police had to the Clark murder. She was the waitress that served them their breakfast. The only time that she worked in the morning was on the weekends, because on the week days she attended city college. In a couple of years she would be able to switch and start attending Temple University, but as of now she did not have enough money. Black did not know how many witnesses the police had, but he knew Veronica had to be one of them because she was the waitress. The only thing he could think of was to offer her money and convince her to disappear. When she returned she could hire a lawyer, and then they could convince her to get amnesia. The officer in the department that was on the payroll told Black. "I don't know who the witness is, but the only evidence they really have is that she can identify you as being there."

Black sighed. That was a relief. "What else do you know? Did you hear anything?"

"I know the feds are watching you, but I don't really know how. "

"Cool, that's good. I'll make sure I'll send you some bonus money this week."

Philadelphia did not really have to many crooked cops, most of the cops that had been on the payroll were older, and they had been on the pay roll for years. Most of them were on the payroll when the family was only operating gambling houses, whore houses, running numbers and loan sharking. They stayed on the payroll, and when the family switched over to drugs they really had no other choice but to stay on. As long as they were not asked to assist in the dealing, they did not care.

Veronica was dating a track star that went to the same college that she went to. Every single night he would come past, and walk her home depending on how late it was. If it was not really late then she would come to his place and spend the night. At first her family did not approve, but they realized that she was going to do what she wanted whether they approved or not. She was grown now, and they were contemplating getting their own place anyway. Veronica got off from work around eight o'clock which was not late, but she had to cram for some serious testing so they decided it would be best if she went straight home until all the testing was over. She was doing excellent in school. Mark picked her up a half an hour before she got out of work. He worked on South street in one of the bars, and when he got off he would catch public transportation all the way to her job, and make sure she got home safe. The people at her job loved her so much that they would let Mark come in while she cleaned up her station. The restaurant did not close until ten, but it was usually slow after eight o'clock on weekdays unless some special event was happening.

Mark and Veronica walked down the street. There were a bunch of small stores lined up on the street next to the restaurant. They took the same path home everyday. It had been snowing a couple of days earlier so they had to stay on the side walk. The store owners cleaned the side walk off, and piled the snow on the edge of the curve. The area was kind of dangerous, but Veronica had grown up here, and most of the guys knew her, even the dealers. They were the ones that spent the most money in the restaurant, and they always requested her. That was the reason she did not want to testify, She knew dealers, and they were not as bad as the papers made them out to be. Plus it was none of her business if they killed themselves. She regretted even letting the officer know that she could identify the men at the table. Now all of the men she saw at the table kept appearing in the papers. They were not regular dealers. They were gangsters, and there was a difference. Gangsters were businessmen. They were united, and they were powerful. She had witness what drug money could do to a family. She had witness young men that lived in her neighborhood become rich. Exposing their wealth by purchasing expensive cars, houses, businesses. Everything.

Veronica and Mark were cuddled close together. The

winter chill and the snow prevented them from walking a part. Mark did not see the junkie run up behind them until he was right on them. The junkie grabbed Veronica's pocket book. He snatched it so hard that he knocked them both to the ground.

Mark's reflexes were excellent. Seconds after he was knocked to the ground he was back on his feet. He looked back at Veronica. "Are you okay?"

Before she could even answer he was running away chasing the robber.

"Mark, I have my money here." She patted her pockets, and was about to get on her feet when Archie walked up. She had just got her balance. He walked over to her, and shot her in the face five times. The gun hardly made any noise because it had a silencer on it.

The pocket book snatcher turned the corner. Threw the pocket book, and jumped into a car. The car sped a way. Mark saw the pocket book fly into the air, and chased it. It landed across the street near a bunch of trash cans. He picked the bag up. He was exhausted. "Stupid mother fuckers." He thought to himself. Why would somebody want to steal her pocket book? The most in it would be a hundred dollars. A hundred dollars would be a lot he guessed, on second thought if you really needed it. He opened the pocket book, and turned back around the corner. He saw Veronica lying on the ground yards away.

When Black first made the decision to pay Veronica off, Frog and the other family members agreed, but after thinking about it they realized that paying her off would not be worth the risk. It would be easier to take her life. They did not know how she felt. She might be one of the people that if they paid her off she would go straight to the police, and that would be more trouble. It was a hard decision. Because she was so young, and innocent. If she was involved in crime it would have been easier. She was just a victim of circumstance. Someone that had witnessed something she should not have. Black did not want to do it, but he had too. He was learning if you had problems and worries that you could handle. Then handle it. Plus, things were going too good. Business was getting stronger and stronger every single day. He knew the police were investigating him, but without him using the phone or traveling around, they were stuck.

Black's lawyer got his possession of a concealed weapon by a convicted felon charge dropped. The police could not prove to the jury that they had probable cause to even search Black, and his crew. To prevent a lengthy criminal trial that might cost the tax payers thousands of dollars they dropped all of the charges. With his gun charge out of the way Black could go about business like he wanted to.

The families arrest made it on all the major news channels. The female reporter was standing in front of federal building. She was there right after the vans dropped off the defendants.

"Today local police and federal agents made a pre-dawn sweep, and locked up what they called the largest Afro-American criminal organization in the Philadelphia and New Jersey area. Federal agents rounded up more than twenty-five members of what they believed to be a black organized crime family."

The FBI raided Black's house, they picked Frog up from a hotel, they picked Andrew up as he was leaving in the morning to his grocery store. They picked Big Will up at his house, Big Cliff up leaving his house to take William for his daily walk, Ray Guns up at his house, Albert outside of his house and Thomas McCant outside of his house. At the same time they were in New Jersey picking Corty, Martin, Corey, Lyn, Marc, Robert, and Henry up at their houses. The agents did not tear their houses apart because they knew that the family was to smart to keep anything in their houses. The did bring dogs in to search for money and guns. Some money and some guns were found.

News of the arrest made it to every single station. They were even showing clips of it in New York and other places. A lot of people did not know that Black Mafia exited, but it did.

The head of Philadelphia Organized Crime Task Force held a meeting in city hall. Their were press, and news reporters from all over the world. Some of the major magazines had even sent representatives. The head agent was sitting at a table behind a dozen or so microphones that had been taped together. He occasionally placed his hand over the microphones so that he could speak to his colleagues in private. He waited until the room was filled and then he opened the news conference. "Today I am proud to say that we have temporary dismantled, what we believe to be a organized crime family that has operated in the Philadelphia, and New Jersey since maybe as late as the late fifties. This organization had complete control over gambling, prostitution, numbers, loan sharking, and narcotics. It used murder and intimidation to protect it's interest. The organization was based in Philadelphia, but it had bases as far as Atlantic City, New Jersey. It worked under a chain of command very similar to the La Costra Nostra. It even had connections with the Lippitoni family of Philadelphia.

One of the reporters from a local paper was the first to speak up. "You mean to tell me. A criminal organization existed for more than twenty years, and your just putting a stop to it? What kind of charges are they facing? How many men have been arrested?"

"They have been charge with racketeering influence and Corruption act. Anytime a criminal organization uses violence to protect, or enhance their criminal empire we charge them with R.I.C.O."

"Was there any money, or narcotics found? How many people were arrested, and does Rico cover murder?" Another reporter asked.

"Yes it does cover murder. I don't have the details on how much money, or narcotics were confiscated. I do know several expensive automobiles were confiscated. I also know that the organization controlled the distribution of heroin, and cocaine in certain areas of Philadelphia, and South Jersey. Indirectly they had distribution points all over the east coast. If there are any more question, they will be answered later."

The media ate the arrest up. They ran articles on the organization in the front pages for weeks. Over night the defendants became celebrities. Their pictures were placed in the paper. The papers ran articles about their lives. How they lived. Where they lived. Their families. What they drove. They even had a genealogy chart in the paper stating what person held what position in the family. The next day the defendants were arraigned in court.

The arrest completely shook up the power structure of the organization in Philadelphia, and South Jersey. The feds did not lock up all the members in the family. Only the men with titles. The police did not know it but this was going to cause a war. Every single soldier on the street was going to try his best to take the position of lieutenant. Even Corty's family took a tremendous blow. They could never have been prepared for this in a million years. The feds kept all them separated so that they would not be able to conduct business while in jail. The only way they would be able to conduct business would be threw visits and that was risky because if a particular soldier kept coming to visit the police could get on to him. It would be a sticky situation trying to run the family from a jail cell, but it could be done. It would have to be done. Corty did not want to but he might have to use his lawyer too. His lawyer could come and see him at any reasonable time and would be allowed to speak with him in privacy. Lawyer/Client privilege.

News of the arrest reached Trinidad, and Colombia threw the family, and Sacha was upset. America was different from Colombia. Sacha did not understand how Corty and the rest of the family let the government just come and arrest them. They had to much wealth in Colombia for that. Sacha and his friends had vowed that would never ever happen. Not in Colombia. The government officials were too dirty for that. They would kill them first. Sacha had some American officials sitting with him in the living-room of one of his mansions. The officials were sent to the country from America to deter flow of narcotic traffic, but they realized it did not work, so instead of risking their lives for a country that did not appreciate their work, they made deals, and started quietly working for the Colombians. Mostly just by providing information for which they were paid millions of dollars a year.

Naptali walked in followed by his bodyguards. Everybody stood up to greet him except the Americans. The Americans did not associate with anyone but Sacha. Too many government officials were getting caught in corruption cases. So to avoid all of this commotion they never introduced themselves. They instead stayed in the background quietly. The Colombians and Trinidadians were treacherous people. But once they got incarcerated in America, and were facing two hundred and fifty years they began snitching too.

Sacha conducted a lot of business from his mansion in Mexico. The mansion was carved into a mountain. Sacha made most of his shipments from Mexico so he spent a lot of time there conducting business. Their government was like Colombia. It knew how to conduct business, and help the people that wanted to help it.

Naptali waited to speak. A lot of times he would have to sit threw several meetings that Sacha was having before they would be able to talk. They usually spoke in privacy. Just because someone was sitting with Sacha did not mean that he trusted them. He always told Naptali. "I don't trust everybody so when you have to speak to me. We speak in privacy."

Naptali only had to be told once, that was it. Naptali was born and raised in Trinidad. He had learned to speak in Spanish. His Spanish was not that clear, but he spoke in Spanish at times like this.

"Corty is gone."

Sacha already knew, but hearing the news was still a surprise. "So it's definite."

"I don't know the details. But it's serious. I will keep you informed. Tomorrow I'm going to fly over there and find out what is going on."

"Be careful you know how dirty those Americans are." Sacha had a sincere dislike for the police. He hated the macho act that came along with them. They arrested you, and tried their best to be macho when deep down inside they feared and respected you. The meeting was over. Naptali stood to his feet, and a couple of bodyguards escorted him out.

Sacha turned to one of his lieutenants. "I want you to send a couple of our lawyers over there, and find out what's going on. I can't handle anymore headaches." He already had several murder and terrorist charges against him. He was wanted by the

American government for all kinds of different charges. Every time there was an explosion in Colombia, he was blamed for it.

His lieutenant did not have to add it in, but he did. "If we lose Corty, we lost a lot of business."

Sacha was mad. He was tired of all these good men going to jail. It turned them into snitches. He picked up a wine bottle, and threw it across the room towards the fire place. The bottle exploded.

The government separated every single defendant on the case so the only way that they could really conduct their business was threw lawyers and visitors. But as time passed on they were allowed to start seeing each other on the compound. They even start letting them come out in the yard together. The only time they actually saw each other unmonitored was during visits. They asked their visitors to come around the same time. This way they could conduct business as much as possible which still was not enough time. Things got better as the trail started approaching.

Corty and Naptali were sitting in the visiting hall on visit. A thick glass partition separated them. All of the visitors had to get permission from a screening board, and then finally the visit had to be approved threw a judge.

"Hey, what's up, brother?" Naptali always called him brother. "Oh I'm hanging in there. What's up with you?" Corty asked.

"Waiting on you to come home. You mother fuckers crack me up. You know Gad will be home in a couple of years, and now your going. I hate it. Do you need anything?"

"I want you to visit me in a couple of weeks, and I going to give you the name of the people I want you to work with. Anybody else, forget them."

"You got any snitches you want me to handle from out here?"

Corty smiled. "I don't know yet. But I will let you know real soon. Okay?"

Louis "Kekell" Alderman took over Lyn's crew. Alexander Dunbar took over Marc's crew. Travis Hopkins took over Henry's crew, and Warren Pickerson took over Robert's crew. When ever a lieutenant got arrested the soldier that he trusted the most took his place. So the family had to know in advance who would take over in case of an emergency. Each soldier was powerful in their own right, but that power grew when they took over a crew. They were always the most trusted member of their crew. Once a person became a lieutenant he had to pick a soldier that would replace him just in case anything ever happen. That lieutenant would not become official until the family voted on it. No family could ever be prepared for the ruling body in their family to be removed. It was impossible. It just automatically messed things up. The four new lieutenants were having their first meeting since Corty and the rest of the family got locked up in the raid. Travis took over Henry's crew, and Henry had taken over Corty's crew which was the most powerful crew in the entire family. Travis got his commands from Henry, or directly from Corty himself, and that was what made him the most powerful lieutenant in the family.

"I spoke with Corty, and in a couple of days we're suppose to be having a meeting with Naptali so that we can resume business. So I want all of you to get all your money together so that we can start making our moves." Travis opened the meeting. All of the new lieutenants were actually equal. Some were more powerful then others, but they did not really know who was the most powerful. Since Trey was the closest to Corty he was considered the strongest. He was the only lieutenant visiting Corty. It was things like this that made him the most powerful. Even the meetings were held at his house, and for the first time in years there were no undercover cop cars parked outside. Travis lived in a condominium in Williams Town, New Jersey, but once the feds made the arrest he decided to purchase a house because if he was going to take over this family then he was going to have to have a place for the family to meet. He had a couple of small neighborhood grocery stores, but if the family was convicted in this case he was going to buy a small construction company so that he would be able to buy a lot of the property the family would be selling. Christopher was really a genius. The family's legal business when sold, made millions.

Even though Trey had just moved into the house, it was

completely furnished. He still had other apartments in the area, but they would not be safe places to hold the meetings in because he used most for his places for business. They held the meeting in Trey's den. It was the only place big enough to set up a dining room table.

"Why do we have to use our own money?" Alexander asked. "If they still want a piece of the pie?"

"Of course they want a piece of the pie. This is still their family, their business, and their operations. Don't you think they deserve a cut?"

"I think they deserve a cut, but when I went to jail two years ago wasn't nobody coming to visit me, and giving me a share while I was gone."

"Yeah, but you were just a soldier. I'm talking about our boss, counselor, underboss, and lieutenants. They hold permanent positions in the family."

"Permanent positions. What do you mean? If they get convicted do they expect us to still listen to them?" Alexander asked.

"I don't know. I haven't bothered them with that question yet."

"Well, you should. I mean, if we kept operating under them, we're going to get hot as hell. We won't be able to really make any money. In fact, we'll probably be in jail next year. I don't have no problem giving them a piece of the pie, but I don't know about taking commands. We could be taking commands from a snitch." Alexander was right. He did have a point there. Alexander had taken over Robert's and Corey's crew. He was the second most powerful lieutenant. His crew was probably the largest and most powerful, but it did not have connections to the boss like Trey's did and was really important.

"I know how you feel, and I feel the same way too. But this is a family with rules and regulations. They left us in charge for a reason, and that reason is because they thought that they could trust us with protecting what they left behind. It's all about loyalty."

It took the government's prosecutors three months before they were even prepared for trail. All of the defendants were presented with the evidence against them. Most of the evidence were wire taps. Corty and the Jersey faction looked good. They did not really have them conversing on the telephone like they had William Johnson, and a couple of his men. Trying their best to speak in code. The feds had made a couple of undercover drug deals from the lieutenants in Philadelphia, but they did not have many on the Jersey faction. The only way Corty and the rest of the crew would get convicted was if one of the men in Mr. Johnson's family agreed to testify against them, and the only ones that could really do that were Black, Jeremiah, and Mr. Johnson, and that would still put the rest of Corty's family in the clear unless all three of them were snitches, and wearing wires. So far the only person who was set to testify was a Italian capo from the Italian Mafia family and some Philadelphia associates. They were all facing life under the Rico stature if convicted. The first day they went to court the proceedings were postponed because the government received a new witness, and the defendants needed time to be presented with the new evidence that they were facing The new witness came to everyone as a big surprise. Big Albert had agreed to testify. William Johnson was shocked and hurt. The other lieutenants were horrified.

The next week when court resumed Albert was separated. He did not drive over in the same van with the defendants. Instead, he was moved to another facility and put in protective custody. If the government had it there way all of the defendants would spend the rest of their lives in jail, and they would never get the opportunity to see Albert or his family again. Albert agreed to take a plea agreement for one to fifteen years. The more information that he provided the government, the closer he would get to the one year. When they returned to court the defense lawyers requested another postponement because they needed more time to prepare a defense for this new evidence. The judge granted them another month. Every one was upset. This was the beginning signs of a lengthy trail.

The month seemed to pass very quickly, and when they finally returned to court this time they bought their new witness. The Italians testimony was put on hold. He would be used only if needed. He still was going to get his time in the Witness Protection extended. They brought the Italian to meet Albert, and he told him how he was doing the right thing.

"Albert you will probably be the only one to see the streets. I swear to God." He raised his hands above his heart like he was taking an oath. "And believe me you will not be the only one that is going to turn."

When they returned to court Albert was sitting near the prosecutors table. The defendants were not handcuffed. The were allowed to sit at the defense table free of chains. The only time they were handcuffed was when they were returning to prison.

The court room was jammed packed. The defendants family filled the entire room. There were a few spectators but the rest of the people were mainly press and they were there all day taking pictures, and trying their best to get interviews. The papers ran an article.

"MOB LIEUTENANT BECOMES GOVERNMENT WITNESS." It ran articles on Albert and his family. The press got new pictures of Big Will and the other lieutenants from Albert's family. The trail was getting more serious by the day.

The government had a prosecutor, an assistant prosecutor, and several different types of investigators that were helping them fight this case. The head prosecutors name was Jefferson Kennedy. He was no relation to the political Kennedys. He was no relation to the Kennedy's that he knew of but they were his dream of the ideal American family. He idolized them. Everything they stood for. He did not care about the rumors of Joseph Kennedy acquiring his wealth threw the moonshine business. He did not look at liquor as he looked at the other crimes people were committing at the time. Plus rumor had it that his grandparents had sold moonshine. He was not proud of it, but his family was poor, and that was excusable. He prayed that it did not come up later in his career like it haunted the Kennedys. Jeffery Kennedy grew up in North Pennsylvania with his parents and grandparents. He graduated from his high school with honors, and received a scholarship to the University of Pennsylvania where he graduated top of his class. As soon as Jeffery graduated from law school he went to work for the government of Pennsylvania. It took a couple of years before they recognized it, but he was an excellent prosecutor. He was sent to work in the government building prosecuting drug cases.

"Ladies and gentlemen of the jury. You are here as a small, but hopefully effective part of the American system that will assist in bringing the streets of Pennsylvania and New Jersey it's justice. You have been choosen because unlike these defendants you have choosen to make your living the honest way. These men on the other hand are the opposite. They choose to make their living off of society's misery. They are criminals, and to make it worst they are organized criminals. These are the men who sit and have meetings, who come together just for the sole purpose of committing crime. If you read then you will see that the Italian Mafia is almost completely destroyed. But these are the men that have the intention of taking it over. Fortunately because crime does not pay we have already caught them unlike the Italian Mafia which as secretly operated for years without the authorities even knowing they existed. Well ladies and gentlemen, you may not realize it, but what you judge on this case will change the course of crime in Philadelphia and New Jersey. You will make history, and this case will go down in history. You have the opportunity to stop a growing criminal empire. You will hear undisputable evidence. Wire taps. Witnesses and pictures. These men have built enormous wealth of the thing that is actually destroying the fabric of this country. Narcotics." The jurors were following Kennedy's every move. He spoke as elegant and sincere as a politician, and everybody told him. He continued. "Not only did these men make their livelihood off of crime. They are violent. Extremely violent. They murdered, and committed all kinds of atrocities in the name of protecting their empire. If the court permited, I would like to call my first witness. Albert Wagner."

Two men from the sheriff's department went to the back and pulled Albert from the back. When he came out he was wearing a suit and dark shades. He always dressed nice for his size. He looked rested. He was nervous. Extremely nervous. His hands were shaking.

Kennedy walked over to the stand. He could see Albert's nervousness. He wanted to break the ice so he said in a low voice. "Are you alright?"

Albert shook his head yes, but he was nervous as hell. He grabbed the collar on his shirt and loosened it up. Then he reached for the small cup of water on the stand, and took a drink. For one minute he felt free, and he started to relax a little. He was doing what he had to do to protect and save what was left of his life.

"Can you stand and please state your name?"

Albert stood up. Raised his right hand, and stated his name. "Albert Mason Wagner."

"Okay Mr. Wagner. Can you please tell the people in this court what you do for a living?"

"Yes. I own a restaurant in South Philadelphia called Albert's."

"Are you talking about the famous restaurant that all of the Afro-American celebrities dine at?"

"Yes."

"Oh, I ate there once, the food was delicious." The jurors, and the court room burst into laughter.

Albert relaxed a little bit. "Why thank you."

"Mr. Wagner do you know any of the defendants sitting across from you at the defense table."

Albert did not want to, but he had to look over.

"Yes I do."

"How well?"

"I know all of them. But I know some of them very well."

"Mr. Wagner besides the restaurant I see you own a small realty company, and some other interest. Is it true that you also belong to a criminal organization. A criminal organization that was headed by the defendant William Johnson? Is it true that the other men sitting at the defense table with Mr. Johnson are men who were apart of your organization?"

"Yes, that is true." Albert's words sent a unseen shock threw the defense table. It was one thing knowing that he agreed to testify, but witnessing him do it was shocking. It was sort of like walking down the street and seeing someone get murdered. Someone in the court room made a pig squealing sound very quickly.

William Johnson was in total disbelief. He could only shake his head.

"Mr. Wagner can you please tell the court what time you joined the organization? What position you played in the organization? Who was your boss, and what kind of criminal activities did the organization participate in?"

"I joined the organization sometime in the early sixties."

"How?" The prosecutor asked.

"Well I ran a gambling house in the fifties and sixties. Plus, I was running numbers, and all kinds of rackets with some partners of mine. We were getting rich. Making a fortune. Then come along this young man about the same age as me, his name was William Johnson. I was a gangster, and he was a gangster. He was getting famous in the streets of Pennsylvania though. He was about twenty-three, and people were saying he was already a millionaire. His father was a big time gangster. Well one day he starts gambling at one of my gambling houses, and he ask if he could have a meeting with me. He tells me he's backed by the Italian Mob and that he was forming his own organization with their help. At first I was a little hesitant, but he slowly and carefully explained his plans to me in detail. I could see them working, but I refused because I did not want to have to answer to no one. I had partners, and that was enough."

The prosecutor interrupted him. "So you never joined?"

"Yeah. Give me a minute. I'm not finished yet. Well any way, Will comes and starts his own gambling houses. He gets with all the other guys in my area making money, and some what organized them. So now it's me and my partners. Him and an army of unknowns. He comes to me again, and this time I knew if I did not take his proposition it would be war, and I would probably get killed."

"So you agreed to join?"

"Yes I did."

"Did you receive a title or anything?" The prosecutor

asked.

"Yes. He made me a lieutenant."

"A lieutenant. What did a lieutenant's responsibilities consist of?"

At first Albert was confused by the question, but it sank in after a couple of seconds. "Well as a lieutenant. He helped me get complete control over South Philly. I became his partner. We split everything down the middle. We stepped to all of the number runners, people running gambling houses, pimps, and dealers. There were not many dealers then. If you did a crime we wanted a cut of it."

"Did you gentlemen make any money?"

Albert broke into a smile. "Of course we made money. In the early sixties. I was collecting a street tax of fifty thousand dollars a week. Not counting the income my illegal activities were producing."

"How much were you making off of your rackets alone, profit wise?"

"Profit wise I was making about a hundred fifty thousand dollars a month."

"So your telling me that you were making a million point two a year in the mid sixties?"

"Yes." Albert was surprised that they were shocked. They were even more shocked when he told them in the conference room when he agreed to testify.

"So you're a millionaire I would assume."

"Yes. Many times over."

By this time Albert was relaxed. He reached over to the container and pour himself some water before he continued.

"Mr. Wagner, would it be a fact to say that you have been a part of this family, or gang since the mid sixties?"

"Yes that would be correct."

"So I can also say that you are close, or was close to the head of this organization."

"Objection your honor. What does the defendants closeness have to do with the case?"

The judge looked at the defense lawyer and threw his

glasses. "Objection overruled. The prosecutor is obviously trying to get a point across."

"Yes at one time we were close, He came to my house after he was shot."

Kennedy turned to the juror's. "The government would like to present exhibit 'A'." Kennedy walked over to the prosecutions desk and returned with a folder. He passed the folder to the jury. It was a bunch of surveillance pictures of Mr. Johnson and Mr. Wagner together. Some of the pictures were old pictures that Albert's family had provided for the court. The newer one's were pictures that the police had taken. Kennedy walked over and passed the defense lawyers the copies of the pictures, but they already had their own.

Kennedy asked a few more questions and then he presented "Exhibit B." It was a chart. The chart had every single family member on it. Some how they had inducted Corty, and his family on the chart. The entire time the defense team was sitting at their table taking down notes, and conversing amongst themselves.

Court was adjourned late in the afternoon. The papers loved it. They followed the proceedings, and printed everything they legally could. They made Albert a celebrity. "MOB LIEUTENANT STARTS TESTIMONY." Reports started calling Albert's house requesting interviews. A couple of literary agent's tried to get him to write his autobiography. Movie studio's called. This was the first time that America was really exposed to a Afro-American criminal organization.

TWENTY

The defense teams only form of protection was to file motions to oppose what the prosecution was trying to present, and this could take up a lot of time. Sometimes court proceedings could be tied up all day because of motions presented by the defense. For the family's coming to give support, and the prosecution this was the most boring part of the case, but it was these little motions that sometimes could win a case, or cause a mistrial. After Albert Wagner started giving his testimony the defense filed all kindS of motions. The first one was a suppression of evidence. This was when a defense team tried to restrict some form of evidence because it was illegally obtained, or could not legally be presented. The lawyers did not care. It did not matter how long the trail lasted. In fact, the longer it lasted the better. Most of them were getting paid by the hour which turned out to be extremely expensive. A lot of times when a lawyer agreed to a flat rate he would start messing up if the trail took long because eventually the length of the trail would cause him to stop working as hard on the case, especially if he has already been paid.

Albert Wagner was driving from protective custody every morning to the Federal Court Building. They had to wake him up hours before the trail was to start, ship him to the building and sometimes he would wait for hours isolated in a cell by himself. They let his family bring him nice clothing to wear to the trail, and he always dressed nice despite his large size. The prosecutor told him not to worry if they did not have any surprise defense motions. he would be able to take the stand. The prosecutors knew it pissed Albert off when he came all the way to the court building, sat in the cell isolated for hours and then be told he would not take the stand. The prosecutors knew that he was getting restless, but not as restless as if he got convicted, and had to sit in jail for the rest of his life. Albert was constantly feeling mixed emotions about the trail. It was hard to betray your friends. The people that had run the street with you. The people that at one time actually protected you. The government made them out to be monsters when in actuality they were only businessmen, trying to make a living. They did not kill innocent by-standers like the young kids selling drugs today. They only killed their own, and the ones that crossed them. Albert knew with the evidence the government had that they might be convicted, but when he thought of the street without any type of command over it, he felt sorry for Pennsylvania. The drug scene was about to become an animal house. He had only testified one time, but guilt was starting to come over him. These were the people he loved and respected at one time. He felt like he was betraying them.

The guards came to the cell and escorted him into the court room. When he came from the back to the stand he had to walk past the defense table. Sometimes, he could glance at the defendants and other times he could not even muster the strength to look at them. As soon as he took his seat Kennedy walked towards him. He was carrying a teacher's pointing stick. Prosecutor Kennedy walked over near the stand and set up a chart. He sat the chart next to the witness stand. This way the judge, jury, witness, defense table, prosecutors table, and the spectators in the court room could see the chart. Mainly the reporters and the family sitting in front seat. The people in the back had to look up at television monitors. They had cameras in the court room monitoring the trail. These same cameras were set up so that when the court room was over crowded the spectators in the back of the room could see up front with out standing up. Albert Wagner was sworn in, and the prosecutor walked over to him,

Kennedy walked over near the stand, and pointed his pointing stick at the chart. The pointer landed on a picture of William Johnson. The chart was set up like a genealogical chart. It had pictures of members of the family on it, including their titles.

"Mr. Wagner can you kindly for the court and the people of Pennsylvania identify this man, and tell me what position he held in your organization?"

It seemed like as soon as Kennedy came out Albert's fear and guilt for testifying disappeared. He looked at the picture the pointer was pointing to. He had already come this far, as far as testifying was concerned, but it seemed like every day he testified, the further and further apart he was pulling the family.

"His name is William Johnson and he was the head of our family." Under Mr. Johnson's picture the words boss and Big Will were printed.

"Was he the man that gave you your commands?"
"Yes."
"Has he ever commanded you to kill Mr. Wagner?"
"Yes."
"And did you?"

"Yes."

"How many times do you think you killed for him, or under his command?"

"Numerous times."

"Have you ever killed a man for your own personal reasons? Reasons that had nothing to do with the family?"

"Yes. I have, but not often. But every time I did I had to get permission from Mr. Johnson first."

Kennedy just smiled. He knew that when the jury heard information like this that it amazed them, and completely held their interest.

"Are you telling me every single man you killed you had to get permission first. Why?"

Albert was a little more relaxed now. Once he started talking, he realized he could not turn back, he might as well tell the authorities everything now because he would never be forgiven by the family. Ever.

"The reason we had to get permission was so that things could be kept in order. We did not want it where things got out of hand. Plus you never wanted to murder somebody that was connected to somebody. It might cause a war. If you were going to murder somebody connected to somebody you had to make sure it was done right so that you did not get repercussions."

"When you say somebody connected. Can you explain?"

"Yeah. When I say somebody connected I mean. There have been times when some young knuckle head is running around doing shit, and you want to knock him off, but you can't because maybe his uncle is family. Or maybe his people is tied to us some how, and we need them. If I did not check with the boss, and just knocked them off then it might be worst for the family in the long run. So to keep things cool. I had to get permission."

"So that means every single person your family had killed the boss knew about it."

"Probably."

"No. Most likely." Kennedy added in.

"Mr. Wagner you say that William Johnson was the boss to this family, and that you were a lieutenant. You say that you murdered for this man to protect your criminal interest, and his criminal interest. Besides murder what other illegal activities was your crime organization involved in?"

Albert paused for just a second. "The family was involved with different types of things. We ran numbers, gambling houses, drugs and sometimes prostitution, but not really that often."

"What illegal activities were your big money makers?"

"In the early sixties and seventies people were using and selling drugs, but not like they are now. I mean now people are making a fortune off of selling drugs, and that's the biggest illegal action, but when I first started out wasn't nobody really thinking about selling drugs. When I first met Big Will and joined the family the only thing we were doing was running gambling houses. In the sixties and even the fifties people were turning their stores into after hours gambling spots. People were running numbers and stuff like that. It was better then. A lot of people got rich running numbers. Whore houses made money, but I didn't bother. I just wanted to make my money running numbers, gambling spots, and a little loan sharking."

"What about extortion?"

Albert frowned. "We were into extortion, but there has never really been a lot of money in extorting legal business. That's one thing Will taught me, and I agreed with. Why extort a legal business when you could extort an illegal business and make more money? I would rather force an elderly gentlemen running a gambling house, or numbers in my neighborhood to pay me for protection then go to a legal business because they might turn around and inform the police."

"You would make the other dealers. Or should I say number runner's in your area pay you?"

"Yes. That's what we call a street tax."

"A street tax. Can you explain it to me?"

"Yeah, a street tax is when you force anybody doing anything illegal in your neighborhood to pay you for operating. Pay you for protection."

"Would they pay you?"

"Most of the time they would?"

"Why."

"Most of the time they paid us because they knew we were stronger, and if they did not pay us we would hurt them."

"Did you ever have to kill someone for not paying a street tax? "

"All the time, especially if they were big time. A lot of time the young guys would not want to pay because they thought that they could fight us. They did not realize that this is street business in Philadelphia. It has been that way for years, and I believe it always will be."

"Why didn't you just let the people that were running their own operations run them as long they were not bothering you?"

"The street business competition should never really exist. You do not want competition when it comes to illegal business. Even if they mind their business their taking your money. Keeping you from getting rich. You convince them to pay you, and you leave them alone, or you remove them. There's too many headache's on the street to let competition exist."

"So if you had the competition in your area paying you, you actually controlled the entire Philadelphia area directly, and indirectly."

"Almost. We did not make everybody pay. Only the ones that got large. Then we made them pay so we could keep a tab on them. We did not want them to become so strong that they would eventually want to challenge us. The street is a cut throat game. You want to have some form of control as long as your out there."

"You said you sold drugs. What kind of drugs?"

"I don't really know about the younger lieutenants, but the older lieutenants did not really want to get to involved in the drug business. Drugs did not really start getting big to me until maybe...... the mid seventies. Big Will had connections with the Lippontini, and he was buying heroin wholesale. He in turn sold it, or gave it to us on consignment. We made a lot of money, but the business was too risky. It wasn't like gambling houses, numbers, or loan sharking. If you were running dope houses you were bound to have run in with the police."

"So your organization stayed away from drugs?"

"No, not really, this is what we did. In the mid seventies their were really not a lot of drug houses. Most of the drugs that were sold were sold from bars. The business was good just a little to risky. I don't think the family got into drugs heavily until the casino's came to Atlantic City. Before that we were making a fortune off of numbers and gambling houses. But when the casino's came the gambling was damn near completely destroyed. I had already been a multimillionaire. I wish I would have retired, but I had an obligation to the family. I got involved in drugs. Mainly heroin. Sometime around seventy-five speed popped up. Then heroin with morphine base, and we lost a lot of business. We were cutting our heroin with some kind of cut, and it was not as good as the morphine base. I know I lost hundreds of thousands. Then the speed business started dying because cocaine popped up in eighty. By eighty-three you had crack popping up everywhere, and I had to step back. It was too risky."

"So you left the drug business alone?"

"No, I just stepped back. Instead of actually getting my hands dirty by trying to deal. I just started financing."

"Financing? What do you mean by financing? Can you explain?"

"Well, instead of purchasing and giving it to my soldiers, I would just let who ever in the neighborhood wanted to deal, sell as long as they became my partners. I would say, give them ten thousand dollars to start. Every week they would give me, let's say a thousand dollars. By the end of the year I would have made forty two thousand dollars. Some of the guys I gave more. So they would give me more. Then sometimes Big Will would get heroin, cocaine, and I would give it to them. But a little after eighty-three I really wouldn't touch nothing. It was easier for me to finance. The restaurant that my family owns was doing to good. I did not want to risk it."

"Your boss did not get mad?"

"The one thing I will give Will was he understood. He was a smart businessman. Before we started selling drug wasn't nobody going to jail. It was to good to be true. Once drugs came. Oh, we made millions, but we started getting in trouble one by one.

So when I laid back half of the other lieutenants laid back. They were to old for the risk too. That's why we had so many younger lieutenants. They were not use to making money the old way so to them selling was worth the risk. They looked at it like fuck it. If I get with the right people I can make a million in a year. Who gives the fuck if I go to jail."

The jury and the court room were silent. That meant they were interested in the case. Albert was turning out to be an excellent witness. Whenever a good witness took the stand in cases like this his testimony usually scared other defendants into cooperating. It seemed like every day the investigators that were working in the prosecutors office were calling the head prosecutor with more potential witnesses against the family. They were already in the process of charging Mr. Johnson with some other crimes they had just found out about. Indirectly William Johnson had almost complete control over organized crime in Philadelphia. Even the prosecutor was surprised at the power of this organization. They were not ordinary drug dealers. They were sophisticated businessmen. Drug dealers were the guys that stood on the street corners making a thousand dollars day. Not these men, they were making millions off of all kinds of rackets. They took the millions they made and invested in all different kinds of businesses. Most of them were so wealthy that they really did not have to commit another crime in their entire life.

Alexander Dunbar ran spots in Atlantic City, he ran a couple of spots in Bridgeton where he made more money. When he was made a lieutenant, and took over a crew. A lot of drug clientele came with that position. The family had customers from all over the east coast, and when Trey went to visit Corty he was ordered to divided the customers amongst the lieutenants. All of the new lieutenants were connected to old lieutenants, and all the old lieutenants customers went to the young ones whenever something like this happen. All of the lieutenants spent time at the spots they operated. Now that they were in position they made much more money, they would collect all the money they wanted to send to Trinidad where Naptali would sell them the cocaine for ten thousand dollars a kilo. It would have been six thousand, but guarantying the shipments to America cost more. The lieutenants would then transport the product back up North where it was sold. Then they would split their profits in half, and give them to Trevor. He would in turn divided the money and took it to the older lieutenants. Corty and the rest of his family were making hundreds of thousands of dollars a month sitting in jail. Another sign of Christopher and William Johnson's genius. Indirectly, Christopher and his family would have control over criminal activities for years. If not in action, definitely in name. Christopher had already become a street legend. Corty and his crew called themselves the Larkin Family. The reason the family had acquire so many customers was because of the quality and prices. They were the only people in the area selling kilo grams for fifteen to twenty thousand. Depending on how much you purchased. The only way you could get a better price than that was go to Florida, Texas, or California. If you went to New York you paid relatively the same price. So customers would rather deal with someone they knew than go to another city, and take the chance of getting robbed or killed over a business deal. The soldiers in the family had it the worst. They were the ones that had to deal with the small customers They were the ones at risk of getting arrested on a undercover investigation. The police had stopped trying to catch the upper echelon of the family. Instead they tapped their phones, and bugged their cars, or put up occasional twenty-four hour surveillance. It was easier to find one of their locations. Send some undercover officers in the spot, and get them to purchase drugs. Then they could arrest a soldier on a secret indictment. Once the soldier was arrested, they would try to convince them to become informants, but the soldiers would always refuse because they were making entirely too much money with the family. They never wanted for anything. They knew when the time came, they would move up to the upper levels of the family and they would be multimillionaires. Maybe the police would be able to break them if they could catch them with large quantities, but they never could because the family would not sell large amounts of drugs unless they knew the customers. If a customers wanted large quantities they had to be dealing with the family for years, or had to be highly recommended. This way if the person was a cop the family would be able to trace the snitch, and kill them.

All of the lieutenants had meetings. It was the way they conducted their business, and depended on each other. Trey beeped Alexander and told him he needed to speak with him when he got the chance, it was not important. Alexander, and Trey ran spots in Bridgeton, but now that they were lieutenants they tried to spend less time at the spots. The police knew that they belong to Corty's family, but they had no idea of the power structure. They were getting an idea because the feds had passed information to the South Jersey police department, that Trevor was constantly visiting different defendants. Once they got word of this threw some people they knew in the police department. Trevor cut his visits to only visiting Corty. The other lieutenants were allowed to make visits to the head lieutenant but kept it at a minimal. Trevor drove a fully loaded gray eighty-nine Acura Legend Sedan LS. He always moved around with at least one bodyguard. Things were at peace so their was no need for him to move around with a bunch of bodyguards. When he pulled up to the small apartment complex in Bridgeton, Durbar's Nissan pathfinder, and his 740i BMW's were parked outside. Trevor was trying to encourage him to lease his cars, it was wiser. When you got arrested the authorities could not confiscate the car. When the feds locked Corty and the rest of the family up they could not confiscate the cars because most of them were leased or put in family members names. Which was smart. When Trey and his bodyguard pulled up their were a couple of guys standing in the hallway of the building looking through the window. That was the look out system that Christopher had seen in New York and brought down to the bar years ago, and it still worked. If the police came to raid, the soldiers would run to the apartments and destroy the product. Some of the residents complained about drug activity, and the police had raided several times, but they never found anything. Once they caught a couple soldiers with guns, but that was in Atlantic City, and the cops that made the arrest were undercover cops posing as customers. That was another system they used. The apartment they did the transactions in was not the apartment they kept the drugs in. The police got so frustrated they were willing to start spending large amounts of money to buy large quantities, but the department could not afford to fund it. The department figured, a small arrest was just as good as a large one, and that eventually they would get lucky.

When Trey and his bodyguard pulled up in front of the building the look out's for the operation noticed them, and informed Big Al that they had arrived. Almost every member of the family knew what was going on. The family members had to be strong and confirm their strength on the streets. They did not want anybody challenging their authority. Without the leaders, enemies might assume that they were no longer powerful, and of course there would be the natural power struggles that comes within an organization when something like this happens. All of the new lieutenants were powerful within their own rights, but first they would have to get the loyalty of their soldiers, and build on that. They all needed the connections that the family had. Without those connections they were like any other group that sold drugs. These connections gave Corty's family it's strength. By the time that Trey got to the door Alexander and one of his bodyguards were walking out. When they approached Trey, his bodyguard and the two lieutenants embraced. They were both in their twenty's, and both on their way to becoming multi-millionaires. Plus they were extremely powerful.

As big as Alexander was he was quiet. When Trey looked at him he realized why they called him big. He was tall and he was handsome. He was suppose to go to college when he finished high school on a scholarship to play ball, but he was not quite good enough. He never got a scholarship so instead of going to college he stayed in the area and continued dealing drugs. When he first started out he was selling marijuana for his cousin. His cousin went to jail and he started doing business with the family. He knew how to get money, but he really started making money when he started selling cocaine. Alexander never looked back since Alexander came up under Lyn, and that was no good because they had the same kind of personalities. They were violent. Trey had heard of Alexander hurting people over the smallest things. He had a reputation for being a nut. Alexander would not even have gottten the chance to be a lieutenant, but the guy that he was close to got locked up trying to sell a hundred grams to an undercover cop. The police blew the case out of proportion. The soldier that did it, Jake Pea got twenty years with a ten year stipulation. He eventually went to court on appeal, and the family lawyer got his sentence reduced to twenty years with a five year stipulation.

Trey and Alexander decided to walk threw the neighborhood because it would be safer. They did not know it, but the police had their telephones tapped. Their cars bugged, and all different kind of things. They were not sure if their phones were tapped, but they could never be too safe. It would be safer to just take a walk down the block and get some fresh air anyway. It was not that cold outside. Their bodyguards followed them to make sure they were safe, and that nothing happened to them. Alexander was the first to open conversation. "What's up with the case? How does it look?"

"They got their discoveries, but their not really sure yet. Did you ever go to that fancy restaurant in Philly?"

"Yeah. I think I've been there a couple of times."

"Well the guy that runs that is in Big Will's family, and he's snitching, but Corty said that dude don't know none of their personal business. The only thing they got besides him is wire tapes and bugs. He told me to be careful. No speaking on the phone. You got it?"

"Hell yeah. I knew that the phones were taboo so if that's all they got, shit is looking good."

"Yeah shit is looking pretty good so far. Are your ready yet?"

"No, I' m not ready yet, but I will be in a couple of days."

Trey smiled. "That's good."

Alexander reached into his jacket pocket and pulled out two envelopes. He discreetly passed them to Trey.

Trey grabbed them and put them in his pocket. "How much is in here?"

"Fifty thousand."

"How did you fit fifty grand in two envelopes?"

"I told you what I do. I might take a couple of thousand every day, throw it on the crap table. They give me chips, and I might play say twenty-five dollars. Then I take those chips to the cage cashier, cash them in and she will give me hundreds. What do you think is going to happen to them?" That was a hard question. Was Alexander trying to test him. You could never lose with the truth. That was not true in this business. The truth could get you killed sometimes. "I've been following the trail, but right now I can't honestly say whether or not their going to lose. Corty says the lawyers think so far they might win, but you never know with a federal trial. The longer the case, the more snitches. The more snitches, the more information."

"What if they lose and get life? What are we going to do as far as they're concerned?"

"If they lose and get life then they're automatically retired. We won't have to give them money, anything. But until that happens the only thing Corty wants us to do is remain loyal and then if he's convicted he'll turn everything over to us. He'll introduce us to the Colombians, and everything."

"What do you think he would do to us if we were not loyal? He's in jail. He can't control anything."

This put a smile on Trey's face. He was surprised. Alexander underestimated the family's power. "If we were not loyal Corty still has the power to start a war. Especially if he gets the other lieutenants support. We don't know what the other two lieutenant would do if commanded. They might fight us if he gives the word. Together we could beat them. But we really don't know how strong they are. None of us can afford a war. To much fucking heat."

"Listen..... I didn't mean anything by it. I was just curious about what you thought he might do."

"Look at it like this. Even though they're in jail. They still have loyalty. Look at me. If they give me a command. I do it. You have to show loyalty now. I mean I don't say it, but they might get convicted. So why go to war and fight now when I can wait, and they'll have to pass everything over to us?"

"What if he don't pass everything over? What if he picks

somebody else, and still tries to run the family?"

"Then he can kiss my ass." They both started laughing.

"But he can't be that foolish can he? I mean if they don't get convicted the feds will be so far up his ass he will never make another dollar again. If they do convict him I'm not taking any orders from somebody in jail so they can fucking tie me up in some bullshit. I love Corty, and believe me. Nobody has loyalty like me. But this is business. He say's if we remain loyal. He will give us the connections, and those connections are billion dollar connections. You can't put a price on having a strong Colombian connection. Plus he's willing to sell us his real-estate. You can't beat it. Of course they will want some kind of cake." That was a slang word for money. "But believe me it's worth it."

"Well I'm with you, I don't give a fuck. What ever. Whatever. I got some cousins in New York with connections. I don't know if they're strong, or not. But we won't starve."

"Well you can almost forget that because nobody is going to beat ten thousand a key here, and five in Trinidad. That's how the family got all of it's out of town clientele. If we lose the connections we got now, we will lose our out of town clientele, and that's millions of dollars. You know they sell that crack shit in New York, D.C., and any where South of Virginia, and that's where we make our money." Cooked up cocaine, or crack did not really sell in South Jersey. The area was too small, and the police concentrated on it entirely to much.

"All we have to do is remain loyal because if you break off they're gonna make me come against you, and go to war. I do not want to do that. Now if they tell those other fools, then they will do it. Just lay low, and remain loyal so when they get convicted we can do our own thing. After that if anybody does not agree, or acts funny. They're history."

They had talked so much they made it to the park and back.

"I'm going have another hundred thousand tomorrow. Who's going to pick it up?"

"I don't know." Trey added. "I'll let you know tomorrow when you call me."

Albert Wagner walked out of the back holding cell wearing a brand new suit. The press was still printing articles about the trial on the front page. Albert Wagner's testimony was really making it bad on Mr. Johnson. The state was in the process of charging him with some old murders that he had ordered Albert to do. Plus they were charging him with conspiracy for some murders that Albert had committed, and told the authorities William had knowledge of, the police had locked up several of Albert's soldiers that had done murders for him, and tried to convince them to testify against Mr. Johnson.

"Look. Your boss is going to testify against you, and your going to be convicted of murder. If you testify, and make this easily on yourself you will be fine." Some of them agreed. Some of them spit in the prosecutors face.

Mr. Johnson did not let anybody know, but all of these new charges were slowly destroying him. His health was already failing, and now he was facing four more homicide charges. The only person that he would even let see him worry was his lawyer.

His lawyer was honest, and kept it straight with him. "Listen, this case. It doesn't look too good. I really don't think we'll be able to beat it. If you plead guilty, and start cooperating with the authorities you won't get an asshole full of time. They'll let you get the witness protection program for risking your life, but not if you don't do it soon.

"Why won't they give me the witness protection program?"

His lawyer gave it to him straight. "The only way you'll get the witness protection program is if you tell them something they don't know. Some really good shit. If you can't tell them something new they might say fuck you because they don't need you now, they already have a snitch. Why kiss you ass when they know they already have a snitch. Why kiss your ass when they got Wagner up there telling every fucking thing?"

"Why can't I just plead guilty?"

"Sometimes they get so pissed off that you're not cooperating they refuse to accept a plea agreement."

"I thought that was against the law."

"Against the law. That's the problem. They are the law."

When Albert took the stand this time he walked out, and look directly in the defendants face. Today was one of the days that he had heart.

Black raised his hand like a gun when he walked past and fired it as soon as he came within ear shot. This broke Albert's confidence a little bit. Both families were using inside and outside people to find out where they had Albert detained. They even had some of the snitches in protective custody trying to find out. But thus far nobody was coming up with any information. They could not let the people in protective custody know too much because they were snitches themselves.

As soon as Albert got comfortable on the stand the prosecutor approached him carrying the teacher's pointer stick. The evidence chart was still up. The prosecutor walked over to it and pointed to the second picture. It was the picture of Clark, the counselor of the family.

"Mr. Wagner for the records can you please identify this man, and what position he held in your family?"

"Yes, his name is Clark. I think his first name is James or Gerald. We never really used it. We called him Clark."

"What position did Mr. Clark hold in your organization?"

"He was the counselor."

"He was the counselor. What's the counselor's job?" The prosecutor asked the question. He looked towards the jury. When they saw him look their way they usually started paying attention if they were not.

"Clark was Mr. Johnson's right hand man. A lot of times when Big Will gave a command, and it was too small to call a meeting he sent Clark to give the lieutenant the command. What ever commands the boss ordered Clark presented them to the lieutenants, and enforced them. He was also the one that if anything happen to the boss he would take over."

The prosecutor studied him, and shook his head as Mr. Wagner talked. He wanted to show the jury that he was truly interested in the evidence.

"Is Mr. Clark in this court room right now?" This question

got the attention of everyone, and some of them started looking around.

Black bent closer to Corty to whisper in his ear, but the words came out where every one at the defense table could hear him. "If Clark comes out of here to testify. I'm pleading guilty." Every single defendant burst into laughter, even Mr. Johnson, the homicide was personal for him. Later when he thought about it he felt a little ashamed.

"He's dead." The words seemed like they echoed threw the court room. The entire court room fell silent.

Black felt a sting of nervousness shoot threw his chest. This case was going to turn serious.

"How did he die?" The prosecutor asked.

"He was shot in the head during a business meeting."

"A business meeting? what kind of business meeting?"

"He was having a business meeting with Black, Frog, Andrew, and Mr. Johnson when a man wearing a waiter's suit came up and shot him and Mr. Johnson in the face."

"Why did the waiter try to kill him and Mr. Johnson?"

"He tried to kill them over a disagreement they were having with Black and Andrew."

"Can you please identify the two men you are talking about on the chart, and in the court room if you see them." The prosecutor walked over to Mr. Wagner and passed him the pointer stick.

Albert stood up from the stand and walked over to the chart. He pointed to the pictures of Black and Andrew.

"Let the records show that the witness pointed to Theodore Quinn. Also known as Black and Andre Stewart. Also known as Rose, and Big Drew."

"What positions did these men hold in the family?"

"They were lieutenants."

"Was anybody else hurt at the meeting?"

"Big Will was shot in the head, but he did not die."

"So the waiter shot William Johnson and Harry Clark. Why would the lieutenants try to kill their boss?"

"They made an attempt on their lives because they were

having disagreements."

"Black and Andrew were unsatisfied on how Mr. Johnson was running the family."

"That brings up to exhibit 'C.'" The prosecutor walked over to the table and picked up a stack of pictures. He walked over to the other side of the court room where there was a projector. He turned the projector towards a screen that they had set up, and turned it on. The pictures that the homicide detectives took of Clark. Clark's wife, daughters, and other immediate family were in the court room. When the pictures flashed across the screen, his wife jumped up and ran out of the court room in tears. The pictures of Clark showed the shots in his back, and the shot in the back of his head. One of the pictures was a close up of the shot in the back of Clark's head. It was terrible. You could see the hole, and brains splattered. Even some of the jurors shuddered in horror at seeing the pictures."

"Black was the lieutenant that controlled South Philadelphia, and Andre controlled North Philadelphia."
"Did any of these men arrange the meeting?"

"I'm not sure. I don't really know the details."

The defense attorney's seemed to start jotting down things on their pads simultaneously. This would be one of their strong defense points.

"The only thing I know about the meeting is what Mr. Johnson told me. I know that Rose was suppose to handle security. He guaranteed Mr. Johnson's security."

"I don't think Mr. Stewart is very good security." The juror's, and some of the people in the court room burst into laughter.

"Objection, your Honor. Prosecution is intimidating the defense."

"Objection granted. Mr. Kennedy you must stop the jokes."
"Sorry your honor."

"Mr. Wagner did Mr. Johnson tell you how he survived the attack?"

"Yes, the doctors told him the bullet entered his head, and then for some reason immediately curved and exited the top of his scull."

"So you're telling me that Mr. Stewart and Quinn ordered the murders because of disagreements. What kind of disagreements?"

"Well, they thought that Mr. Johnson was losing his grip on the organization. He had no contact with the streets, and the younger lieutenant are involved in selling drugs. They were catching cases left and right. Big Will was sitting back getting rich from collecting a street tax. I guess Black and the other lieutenants got tired of it. If I'm not mistaken they wanted him to retire. Will had been promising to retire for years. When he didn't they made a move against him."

The prosecutor turned to the jurors. He wanted to see their faces. He knew like himself most people were fascinated by organize crime. Albert was turning out to be the best witness a prosecutor could ask for. Even the press loved the case. They were constantly running articles on the front page. The news reporters always rushed Kennedy and his colleagues when they exited the court house. Kennedy loved it. He was becoming a celebrity. The reporters called his house, followed him, put him on the front page, and he loved it. He would go home and cut the newspaper clippings. He put them in a photo album, and saved the clippings. What he really loved was how all of the prosecutors that worked in the building started looking up to him. They were interested and fascinated by the case. He knew that some of them were jealous that he was chosen to represent the case for the government..

TWENTY-ONE

After the federal raids Animal started laying low. The raids had come as a surprise to everyone, just like Albert Wagner's testimony. Even though Animal was not as powerful as the other members in the family he was still getting information off of the streets. He had did a lot of things for the Johnson family, and he was afraid that eventually his name might pop up, and they come to get him with a federal warrant. It was already bad enough that he did not have any money, or the means to make any. The streets of Philadelphia were constantly changing now. New dealers were coming up replacing the Johnson's family dealers, but they were never united so they never lasted long. Even if they lasted they were not capable of operating on the level that the Johnson family did. The only way a person, or a group could make money like the Johnson family did was if it organized.

Animal was doing terrible. He let his hair grow, and his hair line had receded making him look about ten years older. He grew a beard, and he never kept it managed. He had gotten word from a couple of his buddies that the police were looking for him for all different types of stuff. He was wanted in almost every section of Philadelphia. He had done a string of arm robberies in this area and was wanted. Someone had informed the police he had something to do with a homicide in South Philadelphia, so the authorities there wanted him. All of this pressure was wearing him down. When he was doing good he had met a lot of women, and now all of that traveling and meeting different women came in handy. A lot of times if he stayed in a certain area, and thought that the police were on to him, he would just pack his things which were usually nothing more than a couple of shirts, jeans, sneakers, and maybe a pair of shoes. After collecting his things he would go to another section in Philly, and shack up with another girl. It worked for a little while, but eventually they got tired of him, and tried to put him out. Which never worked because he would beat the shit out of them, and they knew it. Most of the women he convinced to let him stay would never call the police on him. They were to terrified of him. Animal was abusive.

Black had a couple of soldiers that remained loyal to him while he was incarcerated and it was these men that he had to depend on. He had made money while he was on the streets, and that money was still a form of influence. Corty had showed him how to hide his money in the island's banks, but he did not put all of his money there. Most of his money was hidden at his in-laws house. It was safe there. His in-laws were not rich, but they were not crazy either. They would protect his money just like he was home. His wife always went to the house to check on the money, and sometimes count it. She did not know that sometimes her father was going into the money and sneaking down to Atlantic City to gamble with one of his girlfriends. Black and one of his soldiers were sitting in the visiting room. He let every soldier that was loyal to him visit him. He wished that he could trust his soldiers more, then he would just make one a leader to let the other deal with him. But trust in his business was a hard thing to come by. The soldiers that remained loyal to him were the ones that still owed him money. He allowed them to conduct business what ever way they wanted to as long as they gave his wife a couple of thousand dollars a week, and so far everything was smooth. Black had connected his soldiers with Corty's people so that he could still have some type of influence over them. Corty and Black were talking about forming some kind of official alliance if they made it out of this trail. Deep in his heart Black doubted that they would ever make it. It seemed like every day they were getting weaker. The only bright light was that the cross examination had not started yet. His lawyer kept speaking positive.

"I'm not going to lie to you." He would say. "You got a fifty-fifty chance."

Gregory came to visit Black every weekend. Black gave him a list of people to watch out for. People that he could trust, and people that he could not trust. Black gave him a mental list of people he should try to connect with, and do business with, and people he should definitely stay away from. He had a couple of cops that were on the payroll, and maybe they could still be trusted. One of the new things he should ask them was who was snitching, and who was not.

Out of all of his soldier on the street Gregory was the one that Black trusted the most. He had done business with him for years, and Black had taught Gregory everything he knew. They grew up together in the same neighborhood, but Gregory was much younger than he was. Gregory was only twenty years old. He was a nice looking guy that came from a hard working family. His father had skipped town on them when he was young, and his mother supported their family with two jobs. At first Gregory started out dealing drugs on the street corner like the rest of the young boys in Black's area, but eventually Gregory showed promise. Unlike the other guys he was not satisfied with petty dealings. He saved his money and started branching out on his own. Black immediately recognized his potential. He knew when somebody had potential, and it's a thing people in any business share. Legal, or illegal. Ambition is ambition. Whether it's on a street corner of Philadelphia, or a executive board meeting in one of the casino suites.

The more the trial proceeded the more Albert's confidence increased. He had come to the realization that there was no turning back, and after realizing this, he knew that he should not hold anything back. This was his life now, and he must live it. Live it, and live it to the fullest. He was no longer afraid to look his former colleagues in the eye. When he came out of the holding cell he would look them directly in the eye. He was sorry inside, but he could not see doing life in prison knowing that he would be sixty-five in a couple of years.

The defense team was hungry for cross examination. This trial was getting enormous recognition, and it was going to make them famous. If a case brought you fame and recognition, you would never have to worry about working again, period. Some attorney's would practice for years, and never receive this type of recognition. The only thing that could top this type of recognition was beating the case. Then your asking figure would probably double.

Albert Wagner took the stand again. The defense team kept coming to the prosecution with plea agreements, but the prosecution would always reject them.

"Unless your client is willing to testify. I don't even want to hear a plea agreement. Forget it! I'll see them in court." Kennedy was letting his job go to his head. He was playing with people's lives. The lawyers immediately filed motions to speak with the judge.

When Albert Wagner took the stand this time he was nicely dressed. His family must have bought all of his clothing. In fact, they must have purchased new clothing because none of them remembered him dressing this nicely.

"Will you please state your name for the record?"

"Yes. My name is Albert Wagner."

"In the future Mr. Wagner would you please speak into the microphone. It will allow everyone to hear you more clearly."

The prosecutor walked over to the chart and pointed to the picture of Thomas McCant. It had the words underboss printed under it.

"Mr. Wagner. Will you please identify this man for the record please, and tell the ladies and gentlemen of the jury his duties and responsibility in your organization?"

"Yes. His name is Thomas McCant, and he's the underboss in our organization."

"As underboss what were his duties in the organization?"

"If Clark was Mr. Johnson's right hand man, then Tommy was his left. He did everything Clark did. Give out small orders. Handled details of business with the lieutenants. He was third command in the family. If anything ever happen to the boss or counselor, he was expected to take over."

"How did you meet him?" Kennedy asked.

"When I joined the family he was introduce to me by William Johnson."

"You said earlier in your testimony that you had soldiers. Men who worked directly under you. Some were initiated into the family, and other were not. Is that correct?"

"Yes, that is correct."

"Your soldier carried out the orders that you gave them? Is that correct?"

"Yes, it is."

"And you made money, but taking a cut of their profits is that correct?"

"Yes."

"So how did Mr. Johnson, Clark, and McCant get paid?"

"Every single lieutenant was expected to split their profits evenly with Mr. Johnson. Mr. Johnson in turn split what the lieutenants gave him with Clark and McCant."

"Mr. Wagner you told me in testimony that there were some weeks that you made as much as a quarter million dollars a week off of your rackets. Is that true?"

"Yes, on a good week."

"Did you know that is one million dollars a month, and about twelve millions dollars a year? If you split that in half you gave Mr. Johnson about six million dollars a year. Is that correct?"

"Yes, but sometimes the figures were lower, and sometimes I did not split the profit evenly. Sometimes I would make a hundred thousand and say I made fifty. But he still made millions."

The prosecutor walked back to the chart. "Mr. Wagner can you please identify this man for the records, and tell us what position he held?"

Albert bent forward and looked at the chart. "Oh that's Aaron. Aaron Gaston. He was a lieutenant in the family. He controlled South Jersey for the family."

"Do you know how far his territory expanded?" The prosecutor asked.

"He controlled the Atlantic City area, and what ever other cities are in that area."

"So you're telling me that the Johnson family actually had influence over crime as far as Atlantic City, New Jersey?"

"Yes."

"How did the family get connections in Atlantic City?"

"See that's the problem with the police. You guy's think you know things, but you don't know shit."

The judge slammed the mallet down on the bench. "Mr. Wagner you will have to refrain from using such language. Please."

"I'm sorry. The Johnson family's power in Atlantic City extends as far back as the late twenties. If I'm not mistaken, Aaron's father and William's father use to run moonshine together. They became millionaires off of that which was rare for blacks back then. Once liquor was made legal again they became partners in numbers, and the other rackets. From my understanding they were very close. When their children got involved in crime they raised them together. Initially they started working together because the Italians introduced their fathers, and they carried their business relation over from that."

"So they were both connected with the Italian Mafia?"

"The Italians really started it, but Mr. Johnson was the one that thought of organizing and starting our own family. He patterned it off of the Italians, and he got permission from the Italians to operate."

"What kind of activities did Aaron Gaston do for the family?"

"At first like everybody else he ran numbers. Gambling. Maybe a little bit of prostitution. Then the early seventies rolled around, and everybody gets into selling heroin and speed. I know he made a lot of money selling drugs in the seventies and early eighties."

"Is Aaron Gaston here in this court room?"

Why Albert looked around nobody knew. "No. He's deceased."

"Do you know how he was killed, and why he was killed?" The prosecutor asked.

"He was killed over a war that the family was having with another group." Before Albert became an informant the authorities did not know how, or why Aaron was killed.

"He died in a car explosion, and his son died on the same day in a bar or something. I don't really know the details."

"Do you know why your family was at war with the other group, and what the other groups name?"

"I believe that the other family was called the Larkin Family, and we were going to war because we killed a guy name Christopher Larkin because he started his own family."

"So he died because he started his own family?"

"He died because he started his own family, and he was making so much money selling drugs that Big Will ordered him killed. Another reason we had him killed was because we offered him a position in our family, and he refused. Mr. Johnson had him killed because he was a threat."

"Is Mr. Larkin, or Aaron Gaston's son in the court room?"

"No. They are both deceased." The prosecutor walked over to Albert and passed him the pointer stick. "Can you please point to these gentlemen on the chart."

Albert stood up from the stand. Walked around to the chart and pointed to the picture of Christopher and Little Aaron.

"Let the records state that the witness pointed to the picture of Christopher Larking, and Aaron Gaston Jr. That brings us to exhibit "D and E"."

The prosecutor went over to the prosecution table, and returned to the screen with several photos. He placed the photos on the screen and they were pictures of Christopher when he got murdered and Aaron Gaston Jr. When he showed the pictures of Aaron senior it was only the picture of a car blown to pieces. The pictures had powerful impact on the jurors.

Animal would not spend more than a month in a certain area. He would usually fight with the girl he was staying with so much that he got tired, and decided to find himself another place to stay.

This time he went to South Philadelphia to stay with his baby's mother, Patrice. She had a little boy for him. They use to be close, but she was tired of his ways. She had started doing good. She was not in school or anything, but she was sticking to herself, and that was doing good for her. When she was not dealing with a man, she had peace in her life. When Animal returned this time he had changed a little bit. He seemed to be acting better. She did not know he was scared, and sticking to house because he could feel things closing in on him. The only time Animal came out was to do a robbery or some other business he had to do to get a little money.

Animal was walking up the street carrying grocery bags. His girl had been in the house all day cleaning so he decided to go to the grocery store and buy something for them to eat. Animal was really contemplating sticking with Patrice this time. She was starting to get herself together. Now all Animal had to do was stop getting high. In fact, since he had been back with Patrice he started doing better. He had sold his car to get high, but he was doing good off of robberies. He wanted to start selling drugs and buy himself a new car. The day before he went to North Philadelphia with a couple of his friends, and robbed a dealer for five thousand in cash, and three thousand dollars in cocaine bottles. It was three of them, and they split the money down the middle. Then they went to his house and got high. After they got high, and left Animal spent the rest of the day with his girl. He gave her some money, and paid all of the bills. He was doing better. Animal was walking back home with the groceries when he noticed the police car coming up the street. He had been on the run so much that this did not even scare him. Something must of happen in the area, and the cop was checking the street. Once the cop noticed the groceries he would probably just keep riding past. Animal kept his cool. The car was approaching slowly. Then it stopped. He was about to start running, but he decided against it. He still had time. He was wrong. He did not see the other cars that were trying to surround him. Once they start skidding to a halt he knew he was the target. A bunch of the officers jump out of the car. They had their guns drawn, and they were screaming for him to freeze. Animal kept walking as if he was dumb. One of the officers walked around the parked cars that protected Animal on the sidewalk. As soon as he got in hitting range Animal threw the grocery bags at him and started running, but he did not get far because the other cops were already out of their cars and on him as soon as he started running. The police caught him a couple of yards away, and detained him.

Albert was sitting on the witness stand again. The defendants thought that after a couple of months the public would be tired of reading articles of the court case, but they were not. The papers kept running articles and the defendants kept getting new charges. The only good thing about when someone informed on you, the authorities gave you new charges. They could only charge you with state charges. The state prosecutors were sometimes crooked, and could be paid off. Or a lot of times the family's attorneys were too advanced for them.

The prosecutor returned to the chart. He was carrying the pointer. The defense had jokingly started calling him coach, or teach.

Albert was sworn in, and he stated his name for the records.

"Mr. Wagner. You previously testified that the Johnson

family, and a independent group from Atlantic City area were at war. Who headed this group, or family?"

"The Johnson family was at war with the Larkin family."

"Who was the head of the Larkin family?"

"Christopher Larkin headed it. First he violated by refusing to join our family. Second because he formed his own family, and third he refused to pay a street tax."

"Why would he have to pay a street tax anyway?"

"Christopher Larkin used to work for Aaron Gaston, but he started breaking off."

"Was he an initiated member to your family?"

"No. I don't think so because if he was we would have known."

"Do you know who runs that group now?"

"I believe that Cortney Taylor does."

"Is that the same Corty Taylor of Taylor Construction and Realty company?"

"Yes. I believe he does own a construction company." Albert did not know hardly any of this before the trail, but the prosecutor filled him in with the little details he needed to know. They were playing dirty, and almost willing to do anything to win this case.

Corty knew that his name was going to be brought up in the case, but when he heard it himself it sent shivers down his spine. Something had to be done. He knew once information like this was presented in court, the casino control commission was going to try and prevent his construction company from doing any business with the casino's. His company was going to eventually make millions from the casino industry, but once it was affiliated with organized crime, the casino control commission would ban it from doing any business what so ever with the casinos.

"If Corty Taylor is not a lieutenant in your family, then who represents the Johnson family in the South Jersey area?"

"Miah Lewis."

"Excuse me." The prosecutor asked.

"Jeremiah Lewis."

"Thank you sir. Let the records show that the witness

identified Mr. Jeremiah Lewis, one of the defendants as a member that handles the Johnson family's South Jersey business interest. Mr. Wagner do you know who actually killed Christopher Larkin?"

"I believe that Black, Frog, Jeremiah, and a young boy named Animal did it?"

"Are these gentlemen in the court room today?"

Albert looked around before he answered the question. "Yes they are. Everyone, but Animal."

"Do you know this Animal's government name?"

Every one in the court room burst into laughter. "And was he a member in your family?"

"I think he was one of Black's soldier, but I'm not really sure. He might have been a freelance."

"Why do you think that the gentlemen you named participated in the murder of Christopher Larkin?"

"I think they did because all of the lieutenants had a meeting in Philly a couple of weeks before the hit, and everyone decided that Black would be more capable because of his age. We used the younger lieutenants to do hits a lot because most of us are fat and sloppy. I weigh a little under three hundred pounds. I can't run around and gun fight with these young boys. My targets have to be sitting in a car or something." Some of the spectators and juror's laughed.

The prosecutor walked to his table. " I would like to present Exhibit D, and show the jurors another casualty of this war." He pulled out the pictures the homicide detectives took of Michael.

"Mr. Wagner to your knowledge who are the other men on this chart?"

"Soldiers and lieutenants in the Larkin family."

"So, the organization from South Jersey is known as the Larkin family?"

"Yes to the best of my knowledge."

"Is that the same family that runs and controls Larkin Construction which is also a business associate on several projects, and development in South Jersey with Taylor construction?"

"Yes it is. I believe."

"Objection your honor. Neither Larkin Construction or the Larkin family is on trial here."

The judge smiled. "Okay defense I agree. Omit that from the records."

TWENTY-TWO

Popayan, Colombia

Sacha and members of his organization owned millions of dollars in real estate all over Colombia. They would go to a poor neighborhoods build apartment complexes for virtually nothing, and then rent the apartments at extremely affordable prices. By doing this alone his organization had acquired many friends. Any neighborhood that Sacha traveled threw he was treated like a king. He was a modern day robin hood. The people of Colombia admired and respected him. Many times he was approached, and asked why he would not run for political offices. People believed in him so much they thought that he should run the country. That was only in the area he grew up in.

Sacha knew with his power as a drug lord he was one hundred times more powerful than any politician in Colombia. He always told his men. "You do not have to wear a general's suit to be considered a powerful man. Power is strength, and you can see strength threw a command."

Most of the property that Sacha owned was used for one reason or another. Most of his property was used for business purposes, and some were used for pleasure. In the early seventies all of the kingpins in Colombia started working together instead of fighting against each other, and business almost completely changed. The kingpins realized they were each others worst enemy, and if they changed they could come together and conduct some serious business. They went from making kilo-grams of cocaine in apartment kitchens, to investing together to open under ground, and over ground facility's just to produce high grade cocaine. They went from flying two and three hundred kilo shipments to Florida, to sending two and three thousand kilo shipments to several major city's in the United States.

Anytime something important happen the cartel would all get together and have meetings. They did not always agree or even really trust each other, but all of them were intelligent enough to know that if they did not work together then they would eventually destroy each other. If that did not happen then their weakness would allow the American government to come and completely destroy them all. A lot of times when they came together they were able to share important information, and sometimes that information was almost as powerful as the cocaine it's self.

Even though most of the Colombian government was very lenient to the kingpins whenever they held meetings they were extremely cautious. The only time they held business meetings together was when it was absolutely necessary because sometimes the American government would conduct investigations that the Colombian government had no knowledge of, and raid a compound. All of them feared the American government because unlike the Colombians they could not be bribed. If the Americans got one of the kingpins they would give them a thousand years just to make examples out of them. All of them were facing federal charges in America and some of them had been taken to court in absentee and then found guilty.

When the kingpins got together and held a meeting they called it La Compania. It was the Spanish word for The Company. They decided to hold the meeting at one of Sacha's mansions near a mountain in Colombia called Purace Volcano. Sacha's mansion was beautiful. It sat near the base of the mountain just in case a couple of year down the line the mountain decided to erupt. The mansion was located in dense forest, Sacha had built a under ground cocaine facility there. They were constantly building new facilities because the American forces in Colombia were constantly trying to raid them, but the government was so corrupt that a lot of times days before the Americans even raided, the kingpins would get the word and disappear. A lot of times the same Colombian generals that were on television raiding the cocaine factories were the same one's that had called the kingpins and informed the kingpins about the raid. That was why Sacha loved his country. He knew that as long as he had money, he was safe here.

All of the kingpins that meet at the house flew in by helicopter. Sacha had a under ground cocaine facility built next to his house. It seemed like yesterday that they started building the facilities. The facilities allowed them to stop making hundreds of kilo-grams a week in kitchens to producing tons a week in factories. The factories were also storage houses. Even with the new factories the demand for cocaine could not be met. There was a new European market that was constantly growing. Sacha had several different types of trucks at the base of his mansion. Even though his house was at the base of the mountain it was still built on a upward slope, and once you flew the helicopter to the base you would have to drive one of the trucks up to the house. Sacha had a helicopter landing on the mansion, but it was only room for about three helicopters. After that the kingpins had to leave their helicopters at the base of the house. Sacha had a Chevrolet Blazer, Ford Explorer, GMC Jimmy, Honda Passport, Nissan Pathfinder, Isuzu Rodeo, Jeep Grand Cherokee, Land Cruiser, Mitsubisi Montero, and a Toyota 4Runner. Once the trucks got to the estate they had to pass security. The visiting Kingpins flew their helicopters to the base of Sacha's house, and then a truck drove them to the actual mansion. The mansion was surrounded by security.

Sacha had a business office in the mansion, but he decided to hold the meeting in the living room. It was more spacious and much more personal. Plus the living room gave a view of the mountain and his enormous Olympic size swimming pool.

Henrique Valencia a top ranking Colombian official was the one that called the meeting. He was wearing his military outfit because he was suppose to be at work.

"I was asked to call this meeting because things have got to change. The American government is pissed. They're tired of your guys running around blowing shit up and bragging about it. The communiques will have to stop." Every time they came together and had to settle a disagreement with the government, they blew something up. "Pretty soon they're going to start sending troops here thinking that we need help, and believe me that it not what you want."

"Who runs this country?" Calo asked. He was one of the most powerful kingpins in Colombian, and definitely one of the most respected. The only problem was that he had a lot of political views, and he like to express those opinions threw violence. "The President of Colombia or America. Fuck America. Colombia has her own money. We don't need her anymore. If we want he can have Cuba." Some of them laughed, but he was dead serious. They all knew that Calo had political views and his vision was blinded by them. But not blinding enough to stop him from becoming a billionaire after only a couple of years in the cocaine business. He hated the American government.

"Things are changing." Henrique added in. "The Americans are really getting tired, and their pressuring the President to do something about it."

"Something like what?" Calo asked.

"They want some arrest, and all of you are on it."

"So what did the President say?" It Was the first time that Sacha had spoken. He was more rational than Calo who took every thing personal. Sacha wondered how Calo had gotten this far, it would be impossible for him to last.

"The American government is approaching other countries, and trying to pressure us into passing a bill that would allow them to come and hunt the kingpins down. If we do not come to an agreement now, the President's hands will be tied."

All of them were upset, but Calo was the first to speak out. "All of those millions I donated to his campaign fund, and all those pay off brides. What are we paying them for? You dirty fuckers are robbing us. Before I would let someone extradite me to America I would blow up the Presidential palace. I swear on the Holy Mother Mary." He kissed his own hand and raised it towards the sky to swear before God.

"What can we do to prevent this?" Sacha asked.

"Antonio. I have sat with the Presidents for days and we

have tried our best to come up with a resolution. The only thing we can suggest is that you turn yourself in here and we'll give you light sentences. You'll have complete freedom, and you will be out in a couple of years. If not, the Americans will eventually send troops over here and arrest you. It may not be today. It might be five years. But they will come. Turn yourself in and then we'll have a reason to reject extradition. We can tell the Americans to go fuck themselves."

Nino spoke, the Americans wanted him badly. "Fuck that, I will move to Spain and live the rest of my days in my Castilla. I can run my business from there."

"America needs a scapegoat. If you go to Spain, you will eventually get arrested, and extradited to America. If you stay here you will hardly do any time. Just enough to satisfy the American's foolish idea of justice."

"The only way I go to jail here is, if the President lets me build my own jail. I want to go to one of those jails like they got in America for the politicians. Swimming pool and everything."

"Can you talk to the President and see what he says?" Sacha asked. "If the President will agree to let us build our own prison, and negotiate our own plea agreements with the Colombian government then we will think about turning ourselves in. But even before we do this we must have time to straighten out our business, and no extradition. That must be guaranteed."

"How does this sound? In a couple of months the President will announce Colombia's tactical war on drugs. We will bring in some Americans and go on a national man hunt. A couple of months after that we'll negotiate the surrender of the cartel members, and you can come to jail. We'll guarantee with your surrender that you will not be extradited, and I will personally guarantee light jail sentences."

"That sounds good to me. But what if the American government does not agree?"

Calo answered for Henrique. "Then we must make them agree. We must make things for them here so bad that any kind of surrender or arrest will make them happy." They all knew what that meant. More bombings.

Six months after the meeting the Colombian government released a press issue that they would start a national man hunt for the Colombian kingpins. If the kingpins turned them selves in then they would not be extradited to America for crimes they did not commit. One week after the press release a small Colombian court house was blown up that showed favoritism to extradition. The entire time, the President of Colombia and the American government were trying their best to think of ways to stop the violence.

Surprisingly, nothing had really interrupted the trail. All of the defendants were getting prepared for their lawyers to present cross examination when another blow came. Andrew had agreed to turn states, and testify against the others.

When court resumed, and Albert came out his confidence was at an all time high. He had just found out that Andrew Stewart had agreed to turn states. All of the other defendants were trying to get plea agreements, but the prosecution kept denying them. The only way anyone was going to get a deal was if they agreed to testify, and present a homicide that has not been presented in the case.

The defendants came into the court room and took seats. Everyone was there except Andrew. The court room was filled every single day. There was never a place to sit. Black and Gregory were sitting in the visiting hall. They never really talked about the trial to much because Gregory thought when he brought it up he depressed Black, and he did not want to do that. He knew that Andrew had decided to turn states, and testify against the others so Black was kind of depressed. The only thing Black did while he was incarcerated was lift weights and read books.

Sometimes it would take the officers hours before they would let Black receive a visit. He knew that they were calling the authorities and having the person checked out, or that they were sending an undercover in the visiting hall to ease drop on their conversation. A lot of times they were probably trying to set up a tap on the telephone that he was using.

Black asked Gregory. "Did you read the paper?"

Gregory held the paper up in his hand. The news lines

read. "ANOTHER BLACK MAFIA LIEUTENANT TURNS STATE" The only thing that Gregory could do was shake his head.

"What's wrong?" Gregory hated to see Black looking like this.

"I don't know man. I'm just tired. This shit is starting to get to me."

"Is there anything I can do?"

"The only thing I can really think of is Andrew telling who did that restaurant thing. I want you to get in touch with Animal and his brothers. Tell them to lay low because the police are going to be looking for them. If you have any money try to help them get out of town. That's the only thing that can hurt us." Black did not want to say that much over a prison telephone, but he had no other choice. This message had to be conveyed. "If the police catch up with those boys they might flip, and I can't afford that. After Big Drew's testimony you never know who might flip."

"Yo bro don't worry about it, I'll handle it, I'll personally make sure they get the money, and chill. You know Animal's out here getting high and robbing people?"

"I know. He is wild, but you have to convenience him to split. If he won't leave keep him close to you, and make sure he hides out. In fact, let him help you run the business, and make some money. How much money should I give them to split?"

Black paused for a second, he had to think. "Give them something like ten thousand a piece, and promise them another ten thousand in a couple of months. By that time the trial will be over, and you won't have to give them shit. I doubt after this trial if the government tries a retrial. It's costing entirely too much money."

"Is there anything else you need?"

"My lawyer."

Gregory interrupted him before he could finish speaking. "I gave him fifty thousand, and if he needs more give me a date.

Black smiled. Gregory had earned his love and respect just by being loyal. He was coming through on everything that Black asked him to do. It was times like this Black wished he would have never started the war and divided the family. If the family was still untied he would still have his entire crews loyalty, and he would still be able to conduct business properly. Gregory had really impressed him. He was doing good, and coming threw.

TWENTY-THREE

Animal had been incarcerated for a month on a fifty thousand dollar cash bail. His mother was to old to raise the money for bail, and he did not have any friends on the streets. The guys that use to rob and steal with him were junkies, or petty dealers. There was no way in the world that they would be able to come up with fifty thousand dollars in cash. Once there was a time he had fifty thousand dollars, and if he did not he had the friends that would come together and raise it. If he was not getting high he could have done a lot of things. He knew the Johnson family still had members out on the streets. He could have been initiated by now or maybe even a leader. But that would never happen as long as he continued to get high. As long as he got high no matter how much money he made on the streets he was still a junkie, so when a lawyer came to visit him in jail and told him that Gregory Reynolds had hired him to defend him. He was surprise.

The first thing the lawyer did was put one thousand dollars on his books. This would allow him to purchase all of the necessities he would need while he was in jail. Then the lawyer arranged a bail hearing. Animal's lawyer went in front of a judge and tried to convince him that his client should be let out on bail. The judge raised Animal's bail to two hundred and fifty thousand with a ten percent option. That was twenty five thousand dollars cash.

Animal had his bail hearing a week after the attorney came to visit him. He purchased all of his necessities. He knew that the only reason that they were trying to help him was because they did not want him to start snitching, he was reading the papers. The feds were looking for the men that participated in the Clark murder. They would never have to worry about him. He did not have telling in his blood. Animal sent his girlfriend and children one hundred dollars. The only reason he even thought of sending that much was because she always came to visit him. Which could be some what of an embarrassment. Patrice never took good care of herself. She would come and visit him. Her hair would be a mess, and her clothing would be ridiculous. Other guys' girls would come up looking good, and his girl would come up and look like shit. If she brought the kids, they looked like shit. Their clothes would be filthy, and they never really looked clean. Patrice would ruin the visit with her appearance alone. A lot of times they would get into fights just because of her appearance. But she still came to visit. When Animal met her she was beautiful and young. They hit it off. She was young and naive. He was old, slick, and stupid. He got her pregnant and she kept in touch. At first he never did anything for his son, but once he got in trouble and went on the run he looked her up.

The day after the bail hearing Animal had been released. When he heard the guard calling his name he was sitting around a table bragging about his past and his people. The young dealers in prison idolized Mr. Johnson and the family members. A lot of them had heard of the family, but seeing them in the papers made them automatic legends. The other guys in jail had heard of his lawyer. Animal went to the reception hall and collected his things. The only things that he had at the reception hall were the dirty clothing he was arrested wearing. Once he went to the reception hall he was a little embarrassed.

When Animal came from the back of the reception the lawyer, Gregory, two bodyguards, and a woman were standing in the hallway of the county jail waiting for him. Animal gave all of them hugs, like he knew them, but he did not. He knew Gregory from Black. Gregory must be one of the members that was planning on taking over the family. They all embraced him, even the lawyer. When he embraced the men he could feel that they were carrying guns.

The lawyer got straight to business. "Brandon I talked to the prosecutor, and she said she would drop the attempted murder on your robbery victims if you plead guilty to two and a half years. On a couple of the robberies the state got in touch with the victims, and not only did all of them identify you, they're willing to testify." Animal dropped his head to the ground."I don't want to take a plea agreement until I review the cases. I'll let you know what cases we can beat and what cases we have to plead guilty too. Just make sure you come by my office first thing Monday morning." He extended his hand, and they shook hands. "Gregory did you forget my tickets."

"Hell no. I told you. I'll get your tickets." Gregory reached into his pocket and pulled out an envelope. It had two tickets in it. Tickets for the fights in Atlantic City.

Animal, Greg, the bodyguards, and the girl walked out of the building. They had their cars double parked in the front of the building.

Animal stepped out of the building, and the fresh air hit him. He felt a little dizzy which was usual after being incarcerated then freed.

Gregory, Animal, and one of the bodyguards walked to Gregory's Infiniti Q-45. It was pearl white, fully loaded with shell white leather interior. The other bodyguard and the girl walked over to an ES 300 Lexus. It was black with black leather interior and fully loaded. Both of the cars had factory rims. Just seeing this made Animal want to get himself together.

Gregory did not start talking until they pulled off. Animal looked in the back window, and the other car was not following them.

"Mitch, this is Animal. Animal, this is Mitch." They both looked at each other and shook their heads in greeting. "Mitch is going to take you to get some clothes. Your going to stay in the apartment we got in North Philly, but you have to find your own place soon because that apartment has to be vacated within two weeks. Do you have any money?"

Animal was about to lie, but it had only been a week since they came to the prison and put a thousand dollars on his book.

"Yeah, I got a couple of dollars left."

"Okay." Gregory reached into his pockets and pulled out a wad of money. Animal did not count the money until he got home. It was five thousand dollars, Animal just smiled. It was a little over a year ago that he was running around with a pocket full of money doing hits for Black, and driving a brand new car. This time he was going to keep things together. Invest his money, and get his own business.

"Mitch are we still getting our hair cuts tonight?"

"It depends. I don't know if Mike is going to be home or not. You know how he is on the weekend. He's probably somewhere partying."

"Well, call him and see what's up. I got two tickets for you for the fight in Atlantic City. If you can't get a girl let me know, and I'll get my girlfriend to get one of her friends." Gregory reached inside of his breast pocket and pulled out another envelope. It had two tickets for the fight. "Do you have a girl you can bring?"

Animal paused for a couple of seconds. "Naw, I ain't got no girl I can bring." Animal glanced over to the bodyguard, and he was snickering. Animal was embarrassed. He got a little pissed off, but he tried not to let it show. These young ass mother fuckers must not know who he was. They were pretty boys. He was a killer. A real live killer. They killed to protect their businesses. He killed because he did not give a fuck, and for business, That meant whether it was business or not he was not afraid to kill.

The bodyguard drove threw the city trying to waste time, and give Gregory and Animal a chance to talk. "Animal. There is a lot of money out here in Philadelphia, and nobody is really getting it. The young guys out here they know how to get money, but they don't know what to do with it. The only thing they know is buying cars, and fucking as many pretty girls as possible. I'm all about money. I'm all about getting money, and I have a loyal team down with me, and I want you to join me, our new family. Black taught me everything, and now it's my time to pay him back. He told me to get with you because you can help me. But you can't be running around getting high. I'm going to be making a lot of moves, and I'm going to need you. If you want to join the family then your going to be my personal bodyguard. Hit man. Whatever I need, but you can't be running around here getting high. By this time next year you'll be a millionaire. I'm not bull shitting. Just stick with me because I know you can help me, and I need you."

Mikell Davis

Frederick Edward Windsor the head of the Federal Bureau of Investigation in Philadelphia was sitting in Louis Casazitto's office waiting for him to finish whatever duties, his secretary lied and said he was busy doing. Frederick Windsor was the same way. He was always busy, but if his secretary said he was busy then it was true. Mr. Windsor had been with the Federal Bureau of Investigation for twenty years and he loved his job. He would be able to retire before he turned sixty, but he had no intention. He would rather die while serving. Not necessarily in action, but at least while he was still employed. Mr. Windsor believed in his job. He actually believed he was one of the main reason's that the streets of Philadelphia were half way safe. Mr. Windsor loved his job more than he loved his wife and family. That was why he lost them both. It did not even phase him. He just kept on working. It was the only thing in life that really gave him satisfaction. His superiors were constantly offering him better positions, but he would refused them. He like having his office and his small staff. He never wanted to be one of the agents that sat in there offices, had meetings in Washington, and missed all of the action.

Agent Windsor was sitting in Casazitto's office waiting for twenty minutes, he did not mind. The longer the warden took the more time he would have to pry into his personal business. Agent Windsor closed the door of the office and looked on the wardens desk. There were pictures of the Wardens family. His grandchildren and a couple of pictures of some average looking children that must have been his kids when they were younger. The wardens telephone kept ringing and he could hear the wardens secretary in the other room answering the calls. Agent Windsor was starting to get a little restless. He walked over to the wardens desk and plopped down in his chair.

The warden burst threw the door. He must have obviously been told by the secretary that he had a visitor. Windsor was surprised. The warden seemed to look reasonable. his sleeves were rolled up on his shirt. A sign of hard work, and he was wearing thick glasses. His hair was oily and his skin was a thick reddish. He was obviously not from the Philadelphia area originally unless he was one of those people that refused to let go of the fifties. He looked like one of the police officers that would play in a movie about an officer from the south.

"May I help you sir?" His voice was heavy with a Southern accent.

Agent Windsor looked away, and replaced Caszitto's picture on the desk. "Where in the fuck have you been? I've been waiting in your office for thirty minutes."

"Well I'm sorry Mr....." The warden extended his hand.

"Agent Frederick Windsor, but my friends call me Freddy."

"Well Mr. Freddy. I didn't mean to take too long. It's just that this is a prison, and prisons take time to run. Sorry to keep you waiting. What can I do for you?"

"I have a warrant for an inmate here by the name of Brandon Wallis. He's wanted on federal charges for attempted murder. He is a potential witness. I want him moved out of population, and immediately prepared for shipment."

The warden pressed his intercom. "I need the file on an inmate by the name of Brandon Wallis. Get in touch with one of the supervising sergeants, and have the inmate processed for shipment immediately."

The warden waited for a couple of minutess, and then she returned on the intercom. "Mr. Caszitto. The prisoner that you named has recently been processed for bail and released. I can draw up his information and a sergeant is on the way with the necessary paper work."

Agent Windsor was pissed. "Can you please check and find out who bailed him out?" He was thinking quickly. "I'm also going to need some pictures of the inmate to release on the news." A few seconds later he thought about that. He better not let the news know until it was absolutely necessary.

Gregory, Animal, and the bodyguard drove over to the apartment that Gregory had set up, it was nice. It had everything. A stereo system. A television. A completely furnished bedroom.

"Don't mess up these sheets! This is my wife's brand new bedroom set and I don't want nobody fucking in it. If your going to fuck, there are hotels all over here. I mean, you can entertain in here, but please don't use that bed. You got to hurry up and get ready to get your hair cut." Gregory walked over to the kitchen and dug in the kitchen draw. He pulled out a piece of paper and a pen to write his numbers down. After he did he told him. "Hurry up and get dressed. When you beep me we're coming right back to get you." Gregory reached in his waist band and pulled out a gun. "Here." He passed Animal the gun. It was a nice looking .380. It was the perfect size for carrying around.

"You know what I gave you that for right?" Animal would have answered, but Gregory did not let him. "I gave you that because that's our protection. You're my bodyguard now. Anybody I don't introduce to you as family from here on, you can watch them like an enemy. You got it?" He gave Animal a light smack across the face. Put a little money in your pockets tonight because if nothing happens we're going to the club."

Gregory looked over to the bodyguard. "After you drop me off. I want you to come right back here and take him shopping because he can't go to the club looking like this." Gregory grabbed Animal's shirt and lifted it. They exited the apartment.

Gregory and the bodyguards did not call the house until later that night. When Greg called he told Animal they were going to the club and for him to get dress. Animal was not there, so he left the message on the answering service. By the time that Animal came home from shopping he got the message went on ahead and got dressed. He beeped Gregory and told him he needed a hair cut. The apartment that Animal was staying in was located in a very nice area. Gregory had told him that his fiancé and his children had lived here with him for years. Now he purchased a house, and they had moved in. The only thing that they were waiting for was for a moving company to come to the apartment, and move his bedroom set to the house. They were suppose to do it over the weekend. Gregory told him he would be able to stay until the beginning of the month, and then he would have to find an apartment of his own.

It was not until twelve o'clock at night when the telephone in the apartment rang. Gregory was down stairs on the intercom. Animal was pissed off. He was upstairs waiting on them for hours.

He did not want to leave because he did not want to miss Gregory's call. But if he knew Greg was going to take this long, he could gotten some pussy. Animal walked down stairs, Greg was standing in front of a Black Eighty-Nine Infiniti 530. The car was pretty. It was nice and clean. It had plain quiet rims, and a wing on the back. The windows were tinted. Animal liked Gregory's style. The car looked like it belonged to a lawyer or a doctor. Not a major drug dealer. To his surprise Gregory was driving. Animal automatically thought some women were in the car. Gregory opened the back door for him. They jumped in the car, and sped away.

"Where are the girls at?"

"At the house waiting for us. Mitchell you're gonna have to get your car. We can't all sit in this car." Gregory picked up his cellular telephone, and made a call.

"Hello. Is Amirah there?" Some one must have said yes, and went to get her because Greg was silent on the phone for a couple of minutes, "Hello. Amirah. Yeah. What's up? I got my man here. He's ready to meet her. Yeah, he's nice looking. You know I hang with all pretty boys. Well, first we're going to head to the barber shop. Mikell is there waiting for us. Yeah he's open. He's waiting for me, I'm his partner. Okay. I call you when we leave there. Mitchell. Nah, Mitchell will not be late. He's right here with me. Okay. Okay." Gregory hung up the telephone. "Animal did you bring your pistol?"

"Yeah." Animal lifted his shirt to display his pistol. Gregory looked threw the rear view mirror. "Good. Never leave home with out it."

It took them a little under a half an hour to get to Mikell's barber shop. The craziest thing in the world was that Animal remembered Black bringing him here, he was part owner. The young boy that owned it with him did a little dealing, but now he mainly ran the shop. He had been in trouble a couple of times, but now he was doing good. They pulled up in front of the barber shop, and the lights were not even on. Gregory picked up his cellular phone and dialed the barber shop number. There was no answer, "Shit. Mikell is not even here yet. Let's just chill."

"Fuck that. My cars right up the block from here. Call Amirah and them. Tell them that I'm coming to pick them up. I'll go get them, and then meet you and Animal back here at the barber shop by that time Mikell will be here."

"Okay, what street then?"

"Broad and Passyunk." Gregory sped off. They drove to Mitchell's car. It was parked. Gregory pulled up directly behind it. He lifted the gun that was lying on the middle of the floor on the front seat. He raised the gun. Animal was looking at him, but what was going on did not get his attention until it was to late. Gregory pulled the trigger, and the bullet caught Animal directly in the face. Animals brains splattered on the back of the wind shield. The only thing that protected them from being detected was that the window's were tinted.

Mitchell looked back. "I'll hit him again. He's shaking."

By this time Gregory had turned the car off. He opened his door, stood out, and bent back into the car. He hit Animal three more times in the chest. He locked the car doors and carried the gun in the open. Mitchell had jumped in the other car. Gregory had tapped the trunk of the car. Mitchell got the hint and popped the trunk. Gregory dropped the gun in the trunk, walked around to the passengers side and they pulled off.

"Are we going to Amirah's?"

"Hell no. We're going to park the car. I going home to wash up. I want you to go and throw the gun away immediately. Throw the gun in the river. You got it?"

"I got it. What do I tell the girls when they beep me?"

"Tell Amirah to get her ass over here to my house. We'll go partying next weekend. We party every fuckin weekend. We can miss one weekend."

The feds put out a massive manhunt for Animal. They passed his picture around to every single station. They waited for a day then they put it in the local news. It made headlines.

"BLACK MAFIA HIT MAN ON THE RUN." The papers ran front page articles in the news papers, and the local news ran a cover story on all of the channels. Agent Windsor did not want to do it, but he felt if he did not, Animal might be in trouble. They immediately started getting calls.

The girl that bailed Animal out was named Amirah Claudia Clayton, and she lived in a condominium on the outskirts of Rittenhouse section of Philadelphia. It only took the FBI a day to catch up with her. All of the bail information was in the computer. When she pulled up in her parking lot the first thing she noticed was all of the undercover cars parked in her parking lot. She was driving a eighty-nine M30 white with a black rag top. As soon as she entered the parking lot the agents cornered her in.

"Hello Ms. Clayton. I'm agent Burns. May I please have a couple of words with you?"

"Yes, you may." She tried to remain cool, but he could see the fright on her face. The agents walked her upstairs to her apartment. She watched silently as her neighbors peeped threw the Venetian blinds. When she walked into her apartment there were at least twelve officers in her apartment. It looked like the scene from T.V. She had never seen this many officers in one place at one time.

"The officer that introduced himself asked her. "Do you want any coffee because I need to ask you a couple of questions?"

"No, I'm fine, but I'm definitely not going to answer any questions without my lawyer present."

Agent Burns laughed. "This is not as serious as it looks. If you want, we can wait a couple of hours for your lawyer to come. Because first I would have to take you down town, or you can answer a couple of questions now for five minutes and I'm outta your hair. Cool?"

"Cool." Agent Burns immediately liked her, she had balls.

"Do you know a man by the name of Brandon Wallis?"

"Yes, that's suppose to be my boyfriend, and?"

"Well, you're smart, you work in a bank, haven't you read the papers? He's wanted for murder."

"Well, I bailed him out a couple of days ago and I have not seen him since."

"He's your boyfriend, and you have not seen him in a couple of days. Of course you know where he is?"

"I swear to God. I have not seen him since."

"How much was his bail?"

"Twenty-five thousand dollars."

"Did you bail him out? Where did you get money like that?"

"I don't have money like that. It was Animals. He left it with me." The police would have been shocked to have known the first, and only time that Amirah ever met Animal was the day he got bailed.

"Did you know we found fifty thousand dollars in your bedroom?"

"No. "

"Well, we did, and who's money is it?"

"It's Animal's."

"So he should be coming back here."

"Not if you only found fifty thousand dollars back there." "Why do you say that?"

"Because he had to have at least a million dollars in those draws back there, and if it's not there. Either your men stole it or he's gone."

"I need you to come down to the station and fill out these papers for me."

"I'm sorry officer. You have to wait until I get in touch with my lawyer, I need to use the telephone so that I can call my lawyer. I answered all your questions. Can you get your goons and please leave cause I don't have nothing more to say."

The same time that the agents were in Amirah's house they were down at the lawyers office that had represented Animal at his bail hearing."

Animal's lawyer jumped out of his seat. "Fuck you. Get the fuck out of my office."

"Listen Mr. Hoyt, we can make it hard for you."

"Fuck you. Get the fuck out of my office." The attorney walked over to the intercom, "Elisabeth call the fucking police."

The attorney looked at the agents. "If you ever come into my office again without the proper papers, I will sue the shit out of you." The agents got the message. They just got up and left. Lawyers never cooperate. They knew the law.

TWENTY-FOUR

The defense team was made up of several prestigious lawyers. Every lawyer was highly respected in his field, and each of them came from different ethnic back grounds. The defense had hired at least ten lawyers, and they were all getting at least a quarter million dollars for representation, not counting court cost. Out of the ten lawyers the top four were the ones that directed the defense. Each of them had an entire firm behind them.

Lennard Lehman was an Jewish attorney that represented Black, Mr. Johnson, and another defendant. He had been practicing law for at least twenty-five years and was a legend in Philadelphia court rooms. He had become so wealthy from practicing law that he would often turn down cases. The only cases that he represented were the cases he personally found interesting, and if he did not he would send the clients to one of his partners in his law firm. He belonged to the law firm of Lehman, Joyce, and Lieberman, but he could have easily practiced law himself, and became just as powerful and rich.

Corty and the rest of the family had hired a man named Daniel Craft. He had not been practicing law for as long as the other attorneys, but he was good and highly respected. Corty loved him because he was intelligent, and he played dirty. When a witness turned states and agreed to testify against the defendants, Craft would tell Corty. "Man if that cocksucker makes it home you better put two bullets in his head."

Daniel Craft would try to bribe other lawyers, judges, politicians.... anybody. He looked at law as a business. There was one time that he believed and respected the law, but after seeing how prejudice the system was, and how an Afro-American would never be able to properly rise in the judicial system without being an Uncle Tom puppet. Whether people wanted to recognize it or not, even the judicial system had prejudice.

The other attorneys were Arnold Dooley and Charlie Nespoli. They were both respected lawyers in Philadelphia that had started their own firm recently. They knew that an Afro-

American attorney and an Italian attorney working together would present a picture of racial harmony, and create a lot of business. They were correct.

Each of the attorney's came from lawyer firms, and each of them had at one time or another their entire firm helping them with the case. The defense team had come up with some unethical tactics, but the defendants had no other choice but to agree.

Lennard Lehman was going to do most of the defense cross examination. He was the attorney that had been in practice the longest, and the other attorneys agreed that he should be the one to lead the defense team. Even if he was not the most intelligent he was definitely the most respected. Lehman and the other defense attorneys sat at the table conducting what would look to any spectator like an important meeting. There were a lot of small outburst coming from their table, and laughter. The prosecutors would look over at them occasionally wondering what they were doing.

Albert Wagner was escorted from the back of the waiting cell right after the judge came out. Albert was sworn in, and the cross examination began. Lennard Lehman jumped from his seat, walked over to the chart and picked up the pointer stick. He might use the chart, or he might not. That remained to be seen.

"Good morning Mr. Wagner, how are you doing?"

"Fine."

"That's good, I'm very glad to hear that. Mr. Wagner you have testified in this court room that you were a lieutenant in a criminal organization that controlled a large majority of the crime in the Philadelphia, and South Jersey area. Is that true?"

"Yes it is."

"You have also testified that you have murdered for this organization. Sold drugs, ran numbers, and other illegal business ventures for this organization. You have testified about meetings that you did not attend. Is this true?"

Albert had to pause for a couple of seconds to think about the questions.

Since he took so long to answer, Lehman continued. "Did

you attend the so called quote, unquote mafia summit that night of March, the third, nineteen eighty-seven?"

"No."

"Isn't it true that the reason you did not attend the meeting was because you were the actual gun man that shot William Johnson, and Harry Clark in the face? Is that true? Is it also true that you only came to testify because federal agents offered you a deal because they had you on numerous murder charges? Isn't it true that you're here testifying, but you have not told the FBI about every single homicide you did? Only the ones that they already knew about?!" Lehman was kind of screaming.

The prosecutor jumped to his feet. "Objection your Honor. Complete hearsay."

Albert was about to jump to his feet. "No, that's bullshit. Will knows who tried to have him killed. If he would have bought me, I would have protected his life."

"Okay then. If you did not kill him with one of your associates then who did the actual killings?"

"A guy named Animal."

"A guy named Animal. Is that an actual fact. How do you know this?"

"I heard it on the streets."

"So you're sitting here in court telling me that the only reason you think a guy named Animal did the actual killing was because you heard it on the streets."

"I heard it from Big Will's mouth himself."

"So you're saying you don't have any concrete proof who did the actual shooting. You're just going by what you claim one of the defendants told you on the streets. Is that correct?" Albert paused. He had to think for a second.

"Yes, that is correct."

"Why did you sit right here in this court room, and testify without knowing the facts? Like you actually knew first hand who planned the murders, and witness the actual shooting. "Were you with the people that planned the murder?"

"Were you at the meeting when the attempt took place?"

"No."

"So every single thing you know is heresay. Is that true?"

"You can say that."

"A yes or a no is sufficient! Did you get the information you're testifying about first hand by witnessing the events or attending the events?"

"No, I was not at the restaurant when the hit was made on William, or Harry Clark."

"Okay then. All I want to hear is the facts. Nothing that someone else told you."

Animal's mother lived in a small row house in West Philadelphia. This was the same neighborhood that she grew up in, the same neighborhood that she worked in most of her life. This was the neighborhood she met and married her husband in. To her, West Philadelphia was heaven. It was here that she found solace, and it where she wanted to be when she died. She lived alone. Her only means of support was her husband's social security, and the pension that she received from working at the toilet tissue factory. It was not a large income, but it was enough due to the fact that she lived humbly.

Four federal agents pulled up in separate cars outside of her house. There was a small corner store near her house where all the locals sold their drugs. As soon as they saw all those undercover cops pull up they left the area.

It had only been a couple of days since they started looking for Animal and his little brother. This time for their little hunt they decided to use Afro-American officers. They tend to get more information out of their people.

Agent Cornell Blackwell knocked on the door. It took a couple of minutes before Animal's mother answered the door, and when she opened it Officer Blackwell was surprised at how old his mother was. As soon as he saw her his intimidation tactics disappeared, and he put a smile on his face.

"Hi, how are you doing?"

She was standing behind the screen door and she would not move. "I'm fine and you?"

"My name is Agent Cornell Blackwell, may I come in and speak with you for a minute?" He reached in his pocket and pulled his federal identification out.

She did not say a word. She unlatched the screen door and stepped out of his way.

Blackwell grabbed the door and walked in. He looked back at his partner that was standing on the steps and waved him to stay outside. When he walked into the house the television was on in the living room, and a pot of coffee was brewing on the stove in the kitchen. This did not look like the environment that a criminal would live in. The house looked like the average elderly Afro-American house. Most of the furniture was old, but in excellent condition. The house had the old mill dew smell to it. The same smell that was in a house when the furniture and other things have not been replaced. The house smelled like mill dew because it needed to be dusted properly. It was clean, just old. The house reminded him of his great grandmother's house. Most of the pictures that were sitting in various places were old black and white pictures. It was not possible that she had anything to do with the criminal way of life that Animal chose. Her face showed signs of working hard and seriously struggling to raise a family honestly. Agent Blackwell knew immediately she was good people.

When she walked through the living-room she told him. "You may have a seat."

There were two chairs that sat near the television. A mother and a father chair was what he called them when he was a child. When he sat in the chair he looked into the kitchen and saw all the food sitting on the stove in pots wrapped in aluminum foil. Agent Blackwell wondered why elderly women cooked full course meals, and lived alone. He guessed it was just tradition. A tradition that comes along with raising a family.

"Mrs. Wallis have you seen your sons?"

Animal's mother came out of the back of the kitchen. She was carrying two small china cups with saucers. She sat them on the small tables that sat next to each grandfather chair. "No. The only time I see my son is in the newspapers. He is foolish. He does not understand I am all he's got. I will not be here for long." She smiled and Blackwell thought what would one of his partners have done if they were here. They would have interrogated her, and that would be disrespectful to him, and her. Blackwell had been on the force for entirely to long. He knew that she was telling the truth. She did not know anything.

"What about Harvey?"

"Oh Harvey is not my son. He's my husbands nephew. He's Brandon's cousin."

"Do you have an address for him?"

"No not really, but he stops by once in a while to give me money. He's doing good you know. Owns some kind of business. He's alright isn't he?"

"Yes Ma'am, he's fine, but I need to get in touch with him. It's important. Tell him when he gets the opportunity to definitely get in touch with me." Officer Blackwell reached in his pocket and pulled his card out. He passed it to Mrs. Wallis.

Since the family was on trial, court was held every single working day. Sometimes court might be canceled for little things, and sometimes it was not.

Over the weekends the defense attorneys would come together and try to formulate a strategic plan. It took a lot debating, but the defense decided to call William Johnson to the witness stand. When the defense attorney called Mr. Johnson to the stand prosecution was a little surprised. It could be good for the defense, but if the prosecution could destroy him on cross examination it could be positive. He was sworn in and got comfortable in his chair.

If there was such a description of a Black Mafia leader, Mr. Johnson was it. It was tall and dark with the prettiest teeth. He still had all of his hair which was salt and pepper. He always kept it cut. He had smooth chocolate skin, and medium size lips. He was just plain handsome, and the way he kept himself displayed his wealth. He looked like a doctor or a lawyer, but his charm was too smooth for that. He commanded more power than that. He looked like a powerful businessman.

The defenses main attorney jumped to his feet, and introduced himself.

"Good morning, Mr. Johnson. Can you please state your name for the records."

The Secret Society

"Yes. My name is William Marshall Johnson the third."

"Mr. Johnson can you please tell the ladies and gentlemen of this jury how long you have been friends with Albert Wagner?"

It took him a couple of seconds to answer because he was thinking, but he got it. "About twenty, twenty-five years."

"Mr. Wagner is claiming that you head a criminal organization and that you were it's leader. Is that true?"

"Absolutely not."

"Have you ever been involved in any type of criminal activity with Mr. Wagner at all?"

"In the late fifties, sixties, and seventies we use to run numbers together and things like that, but not the crimes he sat up here, and said we were doing. I mean when the feds came and picked me up I was willing to plead guilty to the crimes I committed, but I'm not pleading guilty to anything I did not do. That's ridiculous."

"Have you ever killed anybody in your life?"

"Of course not. I have never ever killed anyone in my life, or ordered anyone killed, and I pray to God that I never have to."

"What would cause you to kill somebody Mr. Johnson."

William paused for a couple of seconds. "The only way that I could ever kill somebody is if they tried to kill me. I will never hurt anybody. It's not in my nature."

"Mr. Johnson can you please explain what happen on the night that you, Harry Clark, Theodore"Black"Quinn and Andrew Stewart were sitting having breakfast and a gun man ran into the restaurant and shot you in the head and Mr. Clark in the face?"

"Well. I was having a business meeting with Mr. Quinn regarding our construction business, and Mr. Clark informed me that he borrowed a million dollars from Mr. Stewart and Albert Wagner. We were waiting for Mr. Wagner to show up for the meeting, but he never did, so we went ahead and ordered breakfast. A few minutes after the meeting Mr. Wagner pops up with a man dressed in a waiter suit, and the man in the waiter suit pulls out a gun. I tried to jump up and move out of the way, but he hit me. I don't know if the attempt was definitely on my life or not. Clark was hit and killed."

"So are you saying that you believe that Albert Wagner and Andrew Stewart might have tried to have you killed? Why would they try to have you killed when you were not in debt?"

"Well a couple of weeks before the meeting they told me that they had intentions of killing Harry Clark, and I begged for his life. They told me if Harry stopped ducking them. Sat down and had a meeting they would leave him alone plus give him time to pay off his debt."

"So did he agree?"

"Yes he did."

"Mr. Johnson why would two semi-successful business-men try to have an associate killed over a gambling debt?"

"Mr. Lehman. A million dollars is a million dollars."

It was a hard decision, but the defense had to do it. Mr. Wagner and Mr. Stewart's testimony could probably be broken down easily, but it would be wiser to make some kind of counter attack. Number one, it would plant doubt in the juror's mind. All of the defendants had agreed to plead guilty on some of the crimes, in turn they could reverse and testify against Albert Wagner. This way everyone would go to jail, but hopefully not for a long period of time.

"Mr. Johnson if all the things that Mr. Wagner is saying is not true why would he come to court and tell lies under oath?"

"I don't know. The only thing I can think of is that when they agreed to plead guilty the government came to them with a bunch of stories. I don't know if the stories were true or not because half of the stories I knew nothing about. I told them what I knew. I also told them I could not tell them about the things that I had no knowledge of. They told me if I would say what they wanted to hear, I could take my plea and stick it up my ass."

"Objection, your honor. The defendant in blatantly telling lies. I demand an objection."

"Objection over ruled. Defendant may continue."

Mr. Lehman walked over to the chart that the prosecution had set up.

"Mr. Johnson can you tell me anything about the allege war that your family had with the New Jersey family in South Jersey."

283

"First of all I never controlled an organization, and number two, I never was in any kind of war with anyone."

"Did you know Aaron Gaston and his son Junior?"

"Yes I knew them. They were very good friends of mine. They owned real-estate, and some other businesses. We were partners in some business ventures."

"Do you know who killed them and why? Do you know a man name Christopher Larkin?"

"I really did not know him by name, but once I saw his face on a chart. I remember him."

"Did you ever have a disagreement with him?"

"I knew Christopher Larkin from Aaron Gaston, and I never had a disagreement with him in my life. We knew each other threw mutual friends. Besides that I know nothing of this man. Nothing at all."

William Johnson was sitting on the stand blatantly lying, but the jurors did not know that and his testimony was starting to make them wonder. You could see it on their faces.

"Mr. Johnson how do you know Theodore"Black"Quinn?"

"He's a business associate."

"Are you enemies?"

"If were enemies. I didn't know it."

"Thank you, that will be it for now."

Kennedy jumped to his feet. "Prosecution plans cross examination."

After court adjourned Kennedy picked up his paper work and placed it in a brief case. When ever he exited he left threw the same door that the other attorneys left threw. A lot of times they would walk threw the same corridor, but they never spoke to each other. It was a prosecutor and defendant type thing. A lot of times after a court room session he would sit at his table for a couple of minutes and talk with the other prosecutors. This time Mr. Johnson's testimony upset him so much that he walked over to the exit and left. The exit lead to the main corridor of the building. As soon as he walked out a bunch of reporters attacked him with questions.

"Excuse me, Mr. Kennedy, does today's cross

examination mean that you're losing the case?"

Even if he was thinking about answering it another reporter shoved a portable tape recorder in his face. "Mr. Kennedy what does prosecution have planned for cross examination? Does the prosecution have any more witnesses?"

"I am not at liberty to answer any questions."

He walked towards the bathroom. It was a tactic to make the reporters leave him alone, and it always worked.

F. Edward Windsor, the agent that headed the investigation against the defendants followed Kennedy into the bathroom.

Kennedy went into the urinal and urinated. When he finished he walked over to the sink and washed his hands.

"How's the case looking?" Agent Windsor was always questioning Kennedy about the case as if somebody assigned him to interrogate him.

Kennedy was already upset over the fact that William Johnson got on the stand, and was blatantly lying. "What do you mean how does the case look? Your sitting in the same courtroom with me everyday, can't you tell?"

"It looks to me like your fucking up." Kennedy was surprised by his words. How could a man in a position like Agent Windsor's be so ignorant. "I told you not to bring the fucking Jersey boys to court yet. You should have just brought the guys we got from Pennsylvania, and handled them first. Then you would of had enough snitches to bring the Jersey boys down."

Kennedy was about to walk away, but he decided not to, he was upset. "You got a problem with me or something?" Kennedy was tired of all of the nonsense that Windsor had put him threw.

Windsor just snapped. He grabbed Kennedy by the neck, and rushed him against the wall. His hands were so tight around his neck that Kennedy started gasping for air. Once Windsor saw that Kennedy was almost breathless he pushed him towards the other wall.

"Yeah I got a problem. If it wasn't for you rushing we would have these mother fuckers. You rushed this shit!"

"Look don't ever put your fucking hands on me again. I'll have department charges placed against you, and have your fucking ass locked up!"

Windsor balled his fist up and did a fake swing.

Kennedy jumped.

"That's why I grabbed you. Cause your a fucking punk. You think you know everything. The next time we suggest something you better listen."

Windsor walked out of the bathroom smiling. Mr. Johnson had only testified for a couple of days, and the entire prosecution could see the case swaying in the defendants favor.

Kennedy asked for a one week recess. He had to get with the prosecution and plan the prosecutions next move. Kennedy, his prosecution assistants and some federal agents that had been working on the case. The agents that investigated the defendants could be called to the stand as potential witnesses. "Do you think Johnson's testimony destroyed Wagner's?"

Kennedy smiled. "Honestly I really don't know. I mean I know his testimony was powerful, and it has definitely had to have some kind of effect on the juror's."

"What can we do now?" Kennedy looked at Agent Windsor. It felt insane conversing with him now after just fighting with him the other day. Kennedy tried his best to understand. Sometimes trying a case could be very stressful.

"The only thing we have to really rely on is this cross examination of Andrew Stewart, and if we can find these brothers. Cousins what ever they are. I know we can get some convictions, but I don't know if everybody will get convicted. Lehman is a genius. I see what they're doing. Wagner was such an excellent witness that instead of opposing his testimony they're making Johnson somewhat agree with it. Now, once he does not deny some of the charges, the jurors start to believe him and if he says he did not do all of them, they believe him still and Wagner becomes a liar. It doesn't matter who's lying as long as doubt reaches the jurors. Get it. Who would you believe. The child that is telling on himself, or the child that telling on all the other children?" Kennedy took a sip of his coffee. "Did you find out who bailed out this Animal character?"

"Yeah, we found her." The agent looked at his notes. "Amirah Claudia Clayton. Comes from a wealthy family, and does not deny her associate with the wanted. She comes from a family with money and she has a high priced lawyer. We were harassing her, but that high priced lawyer filed a complaint. It's not against the law to bail somebody out of jail. Especially when the bail is only twenty-five thousand dollars in cash."

Kennedy just smiled. "These people are more powerful then we thought. Well, we should at least set up some kind of surveillance on this girl. It might lead us to Animal, or his brother."

Windsor interrupted. "I sent a agent to his house. His brother is his cousin. We think. His mother is very cooperative."

"What about Parole?" Kennedy asked.

"You know we checked with them. Nothing. But we're going to find those mother fuckers. I don't care if we have to put them on America's most wanted." They all broke into laughter.

Later that evening when Kennedy was alone in his office Windsor came in, and gave what seemed like a sincere apology.

The police officer walked up to the car that Animal's body was lying in. The windows were tinted so he knocked on the window. He did not even have to do that. The cars license plates came up as stolen. The license plates on the car did not even belong on this car. The license plates were registered to a man named Paul Gregory Davis. The license plates were registered to a eighty-eight Plymouth Horizon.

The officer looked down at the car and noticed the blood leaking on the ground. He told the neighbor who had called the police. "Step back. Janasky we got blood on the ground call back up!"

He pulled his gun out as soon as he saw the blood. The cops sniffed into the air. "I should have known it. You smell it? We got a dead body."

Janasky walked over to the car. He was carrying a small device that looked like a miniature crow bar. They had to open it here. It might be a crime scene.

It only took a couple of minutes, and a crowd had formed.

Even the neighbor that made the call returned, and now they were surrounding the car.

The other cop disappeared. He called back up. He returned to the crowd. "We're going to need everybody to step back because this may be a crime scene." As he was speaking other officers were arriving.

Janasky popped the door with the device. A small cloud of smoke came out of the car. When the smoke cleared Animal was lying in the seat with his eyes wide open, and a bird sticking half way out of his mouth.

The smell alone made the crowd and the officers turn away.

"Phew. I'm leaving this shit to forensics. Okay I need every one to step back. This is a crime scene." The smell drove some of them away, and the other noisy one's walked over to the sidewalk.

When forensic arrived, they were wearing latex gloves and they had the medicine under their noses that blotted nauseous smells. They opened the door, viewed the body, and started taking pictures. Another officer came and placed the yellow tape around the crime scene.

Kennedy was sitting in his living-room watching the eleven o'clock news. Watching the news was a pleasure he allowed himself when he was handling a case. He made sure he made time for current events such as the news. It was important that he knew what was going on in the outside world. His telephone rang.

He picked it up. "Hello Kennedy residence."

"Hello this is F. Edward Windsor." Hearing his name sounded like a joke. "We got Animal."

Kennedy jumped out of his seat. "Were!"

"The morgue. He's got a couple of bullets in his head, and a bird stuck in his mouth, and a bag of shit in his pants."

Windsor could not resist adding the joke. The next question surprised Kennedy.

"So how do you think this is going to affect the case?"

Damn and they thought he were obsessed with the case. "I don't know. I do know we have to find this clowns brother and put him in protective custody. Obviously his life is in danger."

"I thought these guys were a bunch of bums. These guys are serious."

"We better keep those telephones taped, and beef up surveillance."

"I got some good news too. Animal's brother works in a grocery store in East Philly or something."

"Good, jump on that immediately,"

"All we need is a couple of days."

Just as they were speaking the news reporter came on the air. She was a brown skin Afro-American and extremely nice looking.

"Today police discovered a man s body in an exclusive area of Philadelphia. The man is apparently a victim of a mob hit. He was shot in the face several times and a small canary stuck in his mouth, but he has yet to be identified. Police speculate he is the victim of the black mafia wars that are going on now in the streets of Philadelphia. Our news sources are trying to check and find out if the victim has anything what so ever to do with the Black Mafia trials that are presently being presented in the federal judicial system. Now we go live to the scene."

The camera flashed to the crime scene. "Thank you Mary." The reporter on the scene was a white male. "This evening sometime around six or seven o'clock police discovered what they believe to be a victim of a black mafia hit. The victim."

The reporter turned around and pointed his finger to the crime scene. It was the parked car. The doors were open and Animal was lying inside, but he had a sheet thrown over him. The reporters would not have even got that much, but they had arrived immediately.

"Was apparently shot in the face several times and a canary, or some kind of bird was found in his mouth. Which is believed to be a sign from the mob to authorities, cronies, and enemies that betrayal in the mob is still not accepted.

Agent Windsor must have been sitting home watching the same thing because he was silent on the phone too.

TWENTY-FIVE

The prosecution took a one week recess just so that they could prepare for their cross examination. William Johnson's testimony not only shocked them, but Kennedy knew that his testimony had put a great amount of doubt in the juror's mind.

Here was a defendant that was easily getting on the stand admitting to his guilt in some crimes, and willing to accept punishment. But then there was the government refusing his guilty plea because he would not fully cooperate. The case was not that simple, but that was how the defense made it appear to the jurors. Kennedy had been in too many trials not to know when the tides of victory were swaying.

The entire mood of the court room changed. The defendants sat at their table laughing and joking all day while court proceedings were under way. The judge had to stop the proceedings sometimes just to quiet the court room.

Corty, William, and Black realized this might be the only shot at freedom that they might have so they started conducting business in the court room while the proceedings were in process. It was in this court room that they came together and convinced Big Will to take the stand and incriminate himself. As long as he admitted to the minor crimes then when he denied the larger ones the jurors would have doubt. It sounded crazy, but it worked. It was working.

All of the defendants sat at one table with their lawyers, and it was from this table that they started making their business decisions. In return for Mr. Johnson agreeing to testify and clear them. He would receive a million dollars in cash. If Black did not make it out. Corty, and his family guaranteed it. All of his real estate property would be purchased by the families real-estate companies. His wife and children would make millions of dollars. The only thing that he would have to do is keep his mouth shut. The attorneys had plans of making Andrew Stewart and Albert Wagner liars. Pathological liars. If the defendants were found guilty they could come back to court on appeals and the lawyers were promising that their time would be cut in half.

William Johnson never thought that he could do it. It was brave, but he had to do what he had to do. Plus he agreed with them. If he could somehow reverse everything and make most of it seem like a bunch of lies then that would be better for his appeal. Yeah, he might have to do a couple of years, but at least he would be able to return home and live in peace. Opposed to losing everything legally, moving into the witness protection program, and starting from scratch. He just had the confidence that his case was not strong against him. There were people that had beat federal cases, and if they did not beat them at least put enough doubt in the juror's minds to get light sentences.

Returning to court was a joyous day for the defense. Black was carrying a news paper. On the front page was a color photo of Animal lying in a parked car with a sheet over his body. The only time that the defendants got the chance to talk was when they came to court.

Black passed Corty the paper with a smile. "That's Animal."

Corty grabbed the paper and quietly read the article. Mr. Johnson was being sworn in on the stand. A smile crossed Corty's face.

"Now all we got to do is get those other people we were talking about."

Black just smiled. "Oh were going to get them."

Kennedy, the head prosecutor, walked over to the stand. He did not really want to cross examine William Johnson, but he had to, just to get it out of the way.

"Mr. Johnson would you please state your name for the records."

"Yes. William Johnson the third."

"Mr. Johnson." Kennedy walked over towards the chart that was set up on the table. "Is this a picture of you Mr. Johnson?"

"Yes."

"Do you know any of the men on this chart?"

"Yes."

"You know them because they worked for you, is that

correct?"

"Yes some of them do work for me or have at least worked for me in the past. I own several different businesses with my wife family." Almost every single business that William Johnson owned was under his wife's family name. Legally she was really the one with all the millions.

"No. Legally none of them really worked for you. You had them listed as working for you so that they could have proof of legal income, but in all actuality none of these guys in this court probably ever did any legal work a day in their life. Is that true?"

"I don't know, you would have to ask them." The court room burst into laughter.

"Mr. Johnson were you ever involved in any illegal activity?"

Big Will paused, and it seem liked the question threw him off, but it did not. He was just pausing to collect his thoughts.

"Yes."

"And did those illegal activities included, prostitution, illegal gambling, narcotics, loan sharking, extortion? Anything illegal that makes money?"

"Yes and no."

"Yes and no." Kennedy laughed. "No. Yes, and true."

"No. I never sold drugs a day in my life and I never ran whore houses. My wife's in here, have a little respect."

"So you are admitting to illegal gambling?"

"Yes. I use to run gambling houses, and I use to loanshark, but I never hurt anybody. Or never been involved with any drugs."

"What about in the mid fifties when you approached Albert Wagner with running numbers and everything. Is that true?"

"Yes. We were partners in running numbers in the fifties, sixties, seventies. Almost to the present, but I never threaten him or any of that nonsense, and we were never an organization like he said. I never killed anybody. He might have, but he never told me. I know he bragged about it. But I mind my business, and I never asked him who, or if he really ever killed anybody."

"So how long have you and Albert been friends?"

"We have been friends for years, but not anymore. He's a liar and a coward."

"A coward. Why is he a coward?"

"He's a coward for sending all of these innocent people to jail, or trying to at least with a bunch of nonsense lies. If he's guilty of the crimes that he's charge with, then he should live up to them not make up things and try to bring people down with them."

Kennedy was making a big prosecution mistake. He was letting the defendant speak too much.

"Mr. Johnson. I believe Mr. Wagner and Stewart. I also believe that you did everything they said, and that you're the one sitting up here lying, trying to clear your self."

"Mr, Kennedy. I'm not a liar, I controlled gambling operations. I did illegal things. But your not going to get me in court and make me say I did things that I never really did. That's untrue, and I refuse."

Kennedy raised his hands. "That's enough thank-you."

"No. You government guys done came up with some crazy stuff. Organization. There was never no organization. Never no drug war. That man over there is one of my best friends." He pointed over to Black. "And that man. I never really knew until this court session, yet you got me in here on a chart saying I control him. I never even step foot in the man's house. Or honestly recall ever really meeting him. If this is what prosecutors with political ambitions do for future popularity and vote. Then I'm going to make sure when I'm free I'll never vote again in my life!"

"Objection your Honor. I would like to have those statements removed from the records."

"Objection granted. Mr. Johnson, when the prosecution says that it is finished with you, that means it's finished. You can not continue to comment about things that were not even asked of you, or your opinion. We only want to know the facts of this case. Not your political views."

Mr. Johnson's lawyer jumped to his feet. "We apologize your Honor. The trial is taking a toll on these men. Especially after wanting to enter a guilty plea, but being refused."

The judge just shook his head, and stopped Kennedy before he could object. "Mr. Lehman. I'm going to want to see defense and the prosecution in my chambers after this session."

"No problem your Honor. Thank you."

TWENTY-SIX

Defense and the prosecution requested a seven day recess after William Johnson's testimony. Every single court date a group of news reporters, and television crews were outside of the court house trying to get interviews with anyone associated with the trial. The trial was still getting national coverage.

Andrew Stewart walked out of the back of the federal holding cell looking like the FBI had taken him to a training camp, and just let him rest. They let his family bring him a decent looking suit, and they cut his hair. When he walked into the court room he was wearing a hat. One of the defendants burst out into laughter. Why was he wearing a hat to match his outfit when he could not have been outside of the compound unless it was in the prison yard for exercise and play.

Andrew had followed the trial, and he knew that the case was fifty-fifty now. The prosecution had a chance of winning or losing. When Andrew walked out he was too ashamed to look over at the defense table. his old lawyer was removed from the defense team because they knew that at one time or another he had secretly worked out some kind of deal with the government for Andrew Stewart without them knowing.

The trIAl was finally coming to a close. What ever points the prosecution got across this time would count the most, and Kennedy wanted to make sure that Andrew Stewart remained an excellent witness. Kennedy had the chart pulled out. Andrew Stewart was escorted to the witness stand. He could be sitting in that seat for months, or he could be sitting for a couple of weeks only. Everyone was praying for weeks only. Kennedy walked over to the witness stand and asked him. "Please state your name for the records?"

"Yes, my name is Andrew Stewart."

"Mr. Stewart for the record, will you identify this man right here?" Kennedy took the pointer stick, and pointed to the picture of William Johnson on the chart.

"Yes, his name is William Johnson."

"Is this the man that you testified controlled an criminal organization that control Philadelphia and South Jersey?"

Andrew paused. "I'm not exactly sure how old the organization was, but yes he is the head of a criminal organization that controls the underworld of Philadelphia."

"Did you hold the position of lieutenant in this organization? Did you have an illegal relationship with the defendant Mr. William Johnson?"

"Yes. I was one of Mr. Johnson's lieutenants."

"As a lieutenant in Mr. Johnson's organization what were you responsibilities?"

"To control Mr. Johnson's illegal interest in North Philadelphia."

"And can you please tell the ladies and gentlemen of the jury what some of these illegal business interests were?"

"Yes. I over saw such things as gambling houses. Numbers, loan sharking operations, and narcotics. We were involved in all kinds of crimes."

"Who introduced you to Mr. Johnson?"

"I grew up with William as a child, and then my family moved to a house in North Philadelphia. Once we got older we separated, and I did not see him until several years later. When I saw him again he was a young man getting a reputation on the street for making money. I had heard about the things he was doing so when I ran into him again at a college football games in the early fifties I told him I was running numbers, and making money doing other things. He told me he had a crew, and that he wanted me to get in touch with him because he could help me get rich. He was only about twenty something years old then, and he was already a millionaire. If I'm not mistaken his father had become a millionaire from selling liquor during prohibition. His father was black mafia, associated with the mafia, and when Will came of age he introduced him to the business. Will did not even grow up in the neighborhood that I met him in. His father use to have a small business office there. Will played with the other children in the neighborhood while his father conducted business."

"Mr. Stewart have you ever murdered anyone under the direct command of Mr. Johnson?"

"Yes I have. Numerous times."

William's wife was sitting in the court room. She could not help but cry when she heard all of the terrible things about her husband. She knew that he had made his fortune off of illegal activities, and now hearing all the things that came along with it made her ashamed. She had sent her children and grandchildren to better lives with this money. Now she was to ashamed to even have one time felt proud that her husband had done what ever he had to do to make ends meet. That saying was a lie. William had money as a young man. The last thing he had to do was continue doing illegal things.

"Mr. Stewart did you ever sell drugs?"

"Yes."

"Did you buy your drugs from Mr. Johnson?"

"Sometimes yes, and sometimes no."

"If you were a lieutenant in his family, he allowed you to buy narcotics from other people?"

"No not really. This is how we did it. By the time that the drug business started getting big in the mid seventies we were already millionaires. It wasn't worth it for us to actually physically sell drugs. It was too risky. So instead we would do finance people. I had soldiers that worked under me. I would maybe loan them say twenty thousand dollars. They could take the twenty thousand dollars and buy a package. I would tell them I want two thousand dollars a week. That's about one hundred thousand dollars a year. I would split every single dollar they gave me with Mr. Johnson. That's just one soldier. I had about twenty five soldiers, and some of them made more money then that. Some of them I would purchase heroin and cocaine for. Then what ever profit they made we would split. Then I would split the money they gave me with Big Will. That's not counting the dealers that I extorted by making them pay me a street tax, or the other little rackets we had going on."

"Mr. Stewart please explain the street tax?"

"The street tax was when someone in your area was doing something illegal, and you made them pay you a part of their profit so that they could continue operating hassle free."

"Were all the criminals in your area paying you?"

"Yes, all of the ones that were making any real money. We wouldn't fuck with the little ones because they might go to the police, and it wasn't worth the hassle. But the bigger criminals actually depended on their criminal income, and they would pay. The younger generation that was coming up was giving us hell. It's hard to make them pay, but we did."

"How did you make them pay?"

"We showed them that we were extremely serious. Hurt them, or kill one of them if we had to."

"Was there ever a time that you actually got narcotics from William Johnson to sell?"

"Yes."

The court room was completely silent. The witness had the attention of the jurors.

"Do you know where William Johnson got his narcotics from?"

"He told me from the Lippitoni family, but I'm not actually sure."

"What kind of narcotics did your organization deal in?"

"We sold anything. Heroin. Cocaine. Crack. We made a fortune in the mid seventies off of speed. I know I made millions selling narcotics, and financing narcotics, and every single penny I made since I've been in the business I split it with Will. He got millions from my crew, and probably millions from the other lieutenants too."

"Are there any other men that participated in your organization? Lieutenants, soldiers. Any one?"

"Yes. That entire defense table."

"If William Johnson would have asked you to murder for him, would you have done it?"

"Of course I would have. I have already killed for him. A lot of times if a lieutenant in the family was having a beef with somebody in his territory, Will would order a lieutenant from another area to handle it with his crew. This way the enemy didn't even know who was hitting him. It was business warfare genius, and it worked. None of my soldier have ever been locked up for murder because when I needed somebody taken care of I told Big Will, and he let another lieutenant from a different area handle it. It worked every single time."

"Mr. Stewart were you present the night the attempt was made on William Johnson's life at Gloria's restaurant in North Philadelphia?"

"Yes I was. Mr. Johnson asked me to be security.."

"Why did he ask you to be his security?"

"He asked me to be his security because he was having a meeting with Black and Frog, and he did not trust them."

"Are you talking about Theodore Quinn, also known as Black and Percy Hall also known as Frog?"

"Yes."

"Isn't Quinn a lieutenant, and Percy a soldier?"

"Yes."

"So why would he need you to be security against his own men?"

"Well, Mr. Johnson was having disagreements with Black, and they were suppose to be getting together and settling their differences. He knew that they were cool with me so he asked me to set the meeting up. He did not know that I had already been doing business with Black, and that we had come together and decided to kill him."

"Who?" Kennedy asked.

"Mr. Johnson."

"Why?"

"Well, the younger lieutenants were displeased with him because he had made millions, and was always talking about retiring, but he didn't. They started to feel cheated because they were repeatedly getting arrested, and Will was just sitting back reaping benefit's."

"Did you have the support of the other lieutenants?"

"No."

"Why would you even consider setting William Johnson

up knowing how powerful he was?"

"Well, I looked at it like this. In a lot of ways. I agreed with Black. Now that I think back on it, I would not have done it. We were figuring if we killed Big Will that the other lieutenants might want to retire also. Then we would have the freedom to do as we pleased. I guess that was my greed. I got a little blinded by greed."

"Who were the gunmen that had killed Harry Clark, and shot William Johnson in the head?"

"Honestly I'm not sure. The only thing my men were instructed to do with to sit tight, and act like security. I told them if anybody shot me they were to shoot Black and Frog."

He looked over towards Black, and Black was smiling. It was funny. Now it was official. Stewart was a snitch and he really did not have to snitch. He could have reversed his testimony, or refused to testify, but he did not. Now he would never in his life be able to return to Philadelphia safely, and Black was going to see to that.

"Mr. Stewart you did not fear Mr. Johnson enough to inform him against Theodore Quinn?"

"Well at the time, I was not thinking because if I was I would have just knocked Black off, and I probably wouldn't be here right now as we speak. Now that I look at it we underestimated Big Will. We thought that he had lost his touch, but we were wrong. When he survived and a war started he came back hitting hard."

"Did any body die?"

"A couple of soldiers died, and I could really feel them getting closer to getting one of us. Me or Black."

"Did you and Black discuss the homicide after it happen?"

"Yeah, we left in the same getaway car. We thought that both of them were dead, and we decided to get in touch with the other lieutenants and try to convince them to make the peace. Right after the hit I could sense trouble. When I thought about it, I knew that the other lieutenants were not going to go for sitting tight. They were going to go to war."

"Did Theodore Quinn tell you who did the hit?"

"He said he used a guy named Animal, and one of his brothers. I think."

Kennedy walked back over to the prosecution table, and picked up two pictures. He placed them on a large screen. It was pictures of Animal, and his cousin.

He walked over with the pointer, and pointed to the picture of Animal. "We found this one in a parked car with a bird stuffed in his mouth, and a couple of bullets in his face. Obviously the result of someone in this rooms anger."

Lehman jumped up. "Objection your Honor, prosecution is presenting complete hearsay. He's trying to send messages to the jurors."

"Objection granted. Stricken the last part of that statement off of the records."

The papers went crazy with the new articles. "ANOTHER MOBSTER TURN WITNESS."

Corty, Black, and Mr. Johnson were paying attention to the trial, but they had other important business to attend to. They had to try and organize things on the streets just in case they did not make it home. That took priority right next to the importance of the trial. With their attorney's reviewing the case they had time to conduct their illegal business from the court room threw verbal commands.

Harvey Wallis pulled up to the curb in his brand new 300 Mercedes Bent. It was four door mid-night blue with tinted windows. He was contemplating removing the tint on the windows because sometimes the police would harass him on the pretense that tinted windows were illegal, but then congress passed a bill threw legislation that now they were legal, so now the police in the area he lived in would have to figure another excuse to pull him over.

Harvey was engaged to a Spanish girl that lived in West Philadelphia. Her father owned a small bodega in the area. When Harvey first started messing with her they had to hide it from her father. Her father had made a lot of money from dealing cocaine and heroin. He wanted her to mess with one of the young men that did business with him, but she did not want to so he always figured that she would find another Latino. Maybe even a guy that was in school studying law, or medicinee or maybe even a cop. That would be good if he had a cop in his family. Maybe he would receive inside information that he would be able to sell. But she did not. Instead she met this young black guy that lived somewhere in West Philly, and she hid it from him until she got pregnant. Once it was definite that she was pregnant she told her mother and her mother did not tell her told her father. She had to, if she did not she would be disrespecting him. Surprisingly her father was not as mad as she thought he would be. He went pass the apartment she shared with a cousin and the cousin told him that she did not stay there anymore. He told the cousin to have her get in touch with him immediately.

When Maria got the message that her father knew, at first she was terrified. She decided to call Harvey and tell him immediately. They decided it had been too long since they had started hiding their relationship. It was time that everyone knew. They got together later that night when he came home from dealing, and they went to her families house. Surprisingly her father embraced them, and told her in front of Harvey that she had disrespected him by not introducing him to her boyfriend.

"You are my angel. You think I do not want to meet who is courting you. That is crazy. Of course I wish that he was Latino and Catholic, but if my angel loves him then that is enough for me."

The introduction was as simple as that. After that day Maria's father would invite Harvey over for all kinds of celebrations. He told Harvey about his past, and Harvey told him about his past. Maria's father told him he had connections and maybe he could help him, and he did.

He connected him with his cocaine connections, and everything. He helped Harvey buy a grocery store. A Spanish grocery store, and the store did excellent. Harvey employed all of Maria's relatives, and her family fell in love with him. They called him the Black Puerto Rican.

Harvey was sitting in his car talking on his cellular telephone. He had just finished talking with his mother on the cellular phone about Animal's funeral. She told him federal agents were their asking the entire family questions about him. Things were falling apart. The agents had a federal warrant for him on the

Clark homicide.

'Shit.' He thought. 'As soon as shit was going right I had to get fucked up in the game.'

Now he was definitely going to have to rush his wedding date. They might come and find him any day now. He was going to have to get a high price lawyer and turn himself in. He did not really have anyone he could trust enough to turn his illegal business over too. So it would be best if he just took his quarter million dollars and split it in half between his mother and his wife. His wife was expecting a little boy, and he knew that it was his. They spent entirely too much time together for her to had been sneaking around doing something. Any money he left with his mother would be safe until he came home, then he would at least have a small income to start his life over with. The only bad thing was this case was a federal case and the feds did not play. If he refuse to cooperate then they might try to send him away for life. If it was a state case and he had a good lawyer, he would only be facing about ten years. He would be home in a little over five, and that would not be bad, but the Feds were different.

Harvey had been sitting at the curb for about fifteen minutes. When he called his mother's house he would use an alias, and once his mother picked up on his voice she would speak to him in code.

He would call the house and say things like. "Hello. Mrs. Wallis, may I speak to Harvey."

And she would reply. "Who's this, Charlie?"

"Yes. Ma'am."

"He's not hear Charlie, but if you see him please tell him to turn himself in or get in touch with me because they found his cousin Animal dead, and the FBI want him for questioning on a homicide. They were at his cousins funeral looking for him. "

Then Harvey would reply. "Okay. I'll tell him. I love you, Ms. Wallis."

"I love you too Charlie. Be safe out there."

Harvey's mother in no form or shape condoned his life style, and she would never assist him in anything illegal, but she had to protect him from the police until she could convince him to turn himself in. That was the only illegal thing she would ever do. Protect her child.

Harvey sat in the car. The Mercedes was in his girlfriends name. Legally, there were not too many things the FBI could actually connect him to. Right now he was safe. Some of his friends told him his picture was on the local advertisement channel. The channel that displayed advertisements, weather, and the time. Once in the blue, the state would have a show, and that show displayed all the people that were wanted on federal and state warrants.

Harvey pulled up to the front of the bodega that he owned. The entire area was Spanish. Everybody knew him here. Even the police. Once they saw his warrant he was as good as incarcerated. He was going to have to marry Maria this weekend. He might not be free when the baby arrived, but at least he would be able to have married his fiancé. That would make his son legitimate, and his wife's family would be extremely happy.

Harvey pulled up to the store about fifteen minutes before closing. He called the store phone on his cellular from the car. He was sitting in the car with the music blasting. He had to turn it down so that she would be able to hear him. The days of putting enormous systems in cars started to die out. The factories were putting loud factory systems in the customers cars because they knew that people had started wanting to have systems that they could play loudly.

Harvey's car had a CD player and a tape cassette deck player in it. If he turned the knob up to ten it was loud. Loud enough to jam to.

It was not a hard decision, and family had made the decision while they were sitting at the defense table in court one day. Animal and his cousin had to die. They could not afford to have somebody else come and testify against them.

Every single lieutenant was told if they had any loyal people that a contract was put out on Animal, his brother, and some other people. Animal and his brother... cousin, whatever he was, had to be done immediately. They were on top of the list.

It was Ray Guns soldiers that did the work. He still had a

lot of influence over the soldiers that were in the West Philadelphia area. They remained loyal to him because he treated each and everyone of them like sons. He promised if he did not make it out they still would all be straight.

Ray's soldiers had been watching Harvey's bodega for a couple of days now, and they picked up his pattern. He picked his wife up faithfully at nine o'clock on the dot every single night.

The car that the hit men were driving was moving slowly up the block. There was a driver and three hit men. Two were carrying machine guns, and the others one had a hand gun with a silencer on it.

The two men in the back jumped out of the car half way up the block. It was dark, but if someone looked at them they would see that they were carrying machine guns out in the open like it was legal.

Harvey was sitting in the car on the cellular telephone. The driver pulled the car next to Harvey's Mercedes. He rolled the passengers window down, and the last gun man stuck his hand out of the window and fired into the Mercedes Bent. He shot threw the window five times. He did not know how many times he hit Harvey, and it did not matter by the time they pulled off. The two gun men that were carrying the machine guns were at the back of the car firing into it from the back side. The bullets from the machine guns destroyed the car. After their clips were empty the gunmen ran up to the other end of the block and jumped into an awaiting get away car.

Maria ran out of the bodega after she heard the firing stop. Her stomach was so big it did not look like she should be working. She slowly walked towards the car in a daze. It was filled with smoke. Harvey's hand was sticking out of the drivers window. She walked to the car and saw his body. It was filled with bullet holes. She fainted.

The next morning the news papers showed the crime scene on the front page, and ran a full page article. "NO MORE INFORMERS, BLACK MOB KILLS POTENTIAL WITNESS." The article explained how the police obviously underestimated them, but the Afro-American mafia was just as strong as any other criminal organization.

Kennedy was right. They should have never made the federal warrants public a week after the homicide. Animal's mother, Harvey's mother, father, and fiancé were put in temporary protective custody. They would not have to stay there, the agents just wanted them hidden for a little while. At least until they had an idea as to who might have done it or ordered it. They were really getting frustrated because they did not have a clue as to who might be carrying out the hits. They had an idea as to who might be ordering them.

F. Edward Windsor was the agent that initiated the surveillance. "I don't give a fuck how many people or lawyer's they got. I want you to make a list of the people visiting, and I want them investigated. If you find something on them then you better get with me, and we'll pick them up immediately. If you have to, harass them."

What he did not know was that the family was thinking a couple of steps in front of him, and after the hits most of the soldiers took brief vacations.

Windsor got in touch with all of the papers, and they stared running articles. "WHO WILL TAKE OVER THE BLACK MAFIA?" The article ran a series of pictures and comments on some of the soldiers that might take over the organization. Gregory Reynold was on top of the list.

The hits changed the entire atmosphere of the case. Security was beefed up, and the judge was asked to pass a motion to have court room security tighten. Now everyone was searched when they came into the court room. Produce identification, and sign their names on a court listing.

Andrew and Albert were constantly being moved from protective custody housing in one prison to another.

Gregory's life completely changed after the hit. The news papers started running articles, and calling his house requesting interviews. There were other soldiers and new lieutenants that were being harassed. The papers were not really sure who was going to take over the Black mob, but they knew that he was a member and that was enough. The last thing that Gregory needed was a federal investigation. He started noticing the agents following him every where he went. News reporters followed him almost as much as the federal agents did.

The homicides were bringing the case national attention. Things seemed like they were getting out of hand. So the district attorney of Pennsylvania. The judge, that was directly under the governor, called a meeting with Kennedy, his staff, Agent Windsor, and his staff.

The district attorney's name was Elliot Thonsen. He was one of those men that believed in the judicial system, and he consider anyone fighting against it a spy, or a national defense risk. He had graduated from Duke Magna Cum Laude with honors, and he came from an extremely rich hard working family.

Kennedy was in awe of him. He highly respected him because Thonsen was a legend in the field of law. Kennedy felt he was surrounded by his future peer when he was in a room with this man. A man of equal intelligence. Thonsen had even been in the military. Something he obviously did not have to do.

Mr. Thonsen's office was like one of the those offices you would see in the white house or at a prestigious law firm. All of the furniture was quality wood stained oak. He had books and plaques of over the wall. Then there were pictures of other district attorneys on the wall. A small bar at to the end for any one that wanted to have a drink. You could not even set foot in this office if you were not highly respected in the judicial system. If you made it into this office you were considered on the government of Pennsylvania's side.

Thonsen was the next man running for Governor. Forget Mayor. That was for children.

"Have we put the witnesses families in protective custody yet?" The head district attorney asked.

"I did not do it yet. First I was going to talk to the witnesses and see if they feel their families need to be put in protective custody."

"You must be joking with me. Get in touch with the witnesses families immediately, and offer them protective custody. Then I want you to set up some kind of surveillance. We have to pressure the guys that might be doing this."

Agent Windsor was never impressed with all that title bullshit. He spoke up. "Your Honor." He did not know what to call him.

"We have been investigating them constantly now. We compiled a visiting list of people that visit the defendants, and where starting there."

"Well how are you going to pressure them?"

"As soon as we find out who they are we are going to start harassing them. We have it all planned out already."

"Good. "

TWENTY-SEVEN

The prosecution continued their cross examination on Monday. The weekend only gave them a breather so that they could continue to prepare their case.

Harvey Wallis' homicide change things, but not really for the worst. The only thing that the prosecution lost was a potential witness.

All of the defendants were sitting at the defense table. As soon as they came into the court room and took their seats they started conducting business.

"Did you read the paper?" Black asked.

"No." Corty replied.

"We got him. But I don't know who did it." They were whispering.

Ray Guns looked towards them. "My people did it." He broke into a broad smile. He felt honored that he could do something to help the family.

Kennedy waited for Stewart to be sworn in, and then he walked over to the stand. This was going to be his last day for cross examination.

Kennedy walked over to the chart that he had set up in the court room. He pointed to the picture of Thomas McCant.

"Can you kindly identify this man, for the record?"

"Yes, his name is Tommy Cans."

"Let the record state that the witness identified a Mr. Thomas McCant for the records. What position did he hold in your organization?"

"He was the underboss."

"Was Harry Clark the underboss also?"

"No, Harry was the conselor, but when he died Thomas McCant was made the counselor. Then, if Mr. Johnson would have retired like he was planning, McCant would become boss."

The prosecution had evidence pictures of Thomas McCant, but during the entire trial his name was rarely mentioned. When he was identified by Stewart he just bowed his head a little bit. The police did not really know too many things about him.

Then Kennedy returned to the chart. "Can you please identify this man?"

It was a picture of Big Cliff.

"I don't know his full name, but we called him Big Cliff. He was Mr. Johnson's bodyguard."

"Was he present the night of the Clark homicide?"

"No. Mr. Johnson kept him home."

"This man right here. Who is he?"

"His name is Big Aaron."

"Let the records state that the witness pointed to Aaron Gaston senior. What role did he play in your organization?"

"He was a lieutenant that controlled the South Jersey area."

"And this man."

"Crazy Moe."

"Oh he was Aaron Gaston's bodyguard. Right hand man or something."

"This man."

"That's Jeremiah."

"Let the records state that the witness identified Jeremiah Lewis. What position did he hold in your organization?"

"He was the lieutenant that took over South Jersey when Aaron Gaston and his son got killed,"

"Would you please identify this man for the record?"

"Frog."

"Let the record show that the witness identified Kenneth Campbell. What position did he play in the organization?"

"He was Black's bodyguard, a soldier in the family."

"This man." He pointed to the picture of Theodore Quinn.

"What position did Theodore Quinn play in the organization?"

"He was a lieutenant."

"Can you identify this man?"

"Who? Crazy Ed?"

"Let the records show that the witness identified Edward Reiss. Who is now deceased. Do you know how, or why Mr. Reiss got killed?"

"He was one of the lieutenants that sided with us in the war against Big Will."

"This man."

"Ray Guns."

Small laughter came threw the court room.

"Let the records state the defendant identified Raymond Pierson. What position did he hold in the organization?"

"He was a lieutenant."

"This man." It was a picture of Albert Wagner.

"He was a lieutenant."

"This man."

"Archie Moore. He was the lieutenant that took over North Philly when Crazy Eddie got killed."

"This man."

"Big Roy."

"Let the records state that the witness identified Leroy Booth. He took over West Philly for Ray Guns."

"And. "

"Earl Gilbertson. He took over South Philly for Albert Wagner."

The government did not have too much evidence against Archie Moore or Leroy Booth. It did have evidence against Earl Gilbertson because Albert Wagner testified and told the authorities every thing he knew about the soldier that took over his area. Earl thought that they were closer than that, but they were not. He was hit with so many state charges after Albert Wagner testimony that he was contemplating becoming an informant. Then the family promised all of them a million dollars if they kept their mouths shut.

"This man."

"Corty. "

"Let the records state that the witness identified Corty Larkin. What position did he hold in the organization."

"He's the boss of the New Jersey faction."

"This man."

"Big Marty."

"Let the records show that the defendant pointed to Martin Callahan."

"What position did he play in the conspiracy?"

"He's Corty's underboss."

"Thank you Mr. Stewart, that will be all."

Lehman, the head attorney for the defense, jumped to his feet. "Defense would like a one week recess to prepare for cross examination."

Andrew Stewart's eldest daughter Janine was sitting outside of her condominium garage washing her truck. Her mother had co-signed for her to get a Nissan Pathfinder truck. She had been doing good, and her mother always wanted to help the children. Especially on the little things like co-signing for automobiles.

Janine's father on the other hand was a little different. He was mad at her because instead of finishing college at Temple University for Afro-American studies she dropped out and moved into a condominium with this white guy she worked with. They might have had a pretty good relationship, but Andrew did not care, and did not want to know any thing about it. It was not that he was prejudice he just did not want any of his children marrying white men. Especially after the things his parents told him they experienced living in the South. He really did not understand how his wife accepted it because she was born and raised in the South. Southern blacks are usually against interracial marriage.

Andrew wanted his children to marry professional blacks. They did not have to be doctors or lawyers. He just wanted them to be educated, or at least trying to open their own businesses. Something he could be proud of. His children really did not need for money because he was wealthy. He owned hundreds of thousands of dollars in real-estate properties. Mr. Johnson Sr. got him into the real-estate business in the late sixties when he first started running numbers for them.

Janine's Pathfinder truck was her pride and joy. She had gone to the local discount store and purchased washing mittens. They were the Terri-cloth gloves that she dipped in a bucket and scrubbed her car with. The condominiums that she lived in were made like town houses.

If these same house were in a low income area they would be called row houses. The area was nice though. It had low crime, and the streets were clean, plus her town house was spacious. She had her own private garage out front of the town house.

Janine had pulled the truck out of the garage and started washing it. This was the way that she started her weekends. She would wake up every Saturday morning and slip her small short shorts on, and a tight fitting shirt. All of the guys that lived in the neighborhood would peep threw their windows trying to get a glimpse. Her boyfriend did not mind. He got a kick out of her showing off her sexiness.

Janine and her father were really getting close again. Andrew knew that Janine was helping her mother handle his legal affairs, and that strengthen the weakening bond that they had. She was a part of his life again, and he finally realized that he missed her. She was over seeing most of the rental properties, and that was a blessing because his wife was not stupid, but she was not cut out to operate any kind of decent size business.

Janine was outside working on the wheels. She really enjoyed washing the car. It was one of the rare times that she could be alone by herself and it gave her time to think. All of these events had messed her head up a little bit. The trial had turned every single defendant, and witness into a instant celebrity.

The news papers haunted her family. The government

offered her mother protective custody, but she refuse it because if she went into protective custody then they would have to rush and sell their property. So instead she opt to having police protection. They assigned two cops to sit outside of her house twenty-four hours a day. Then she would have to tell them her schedule for the day, and they would try to get an additional undercover officer to escort her every where she went. This protection extended to immediate family only. If Janine and them got any kind of threat then they could receive protection, but only after a threat.

Janine did not see the commercial van pull up behind her town house until it came to a halt. A black man jumped out of the truck, and was carrying a weapon in broad day light. When the scene came into focus with her she started to run, and the man started running behind her. He raised the gun and pulled the trigger. The bullet hit her in the back and she fell to the ground. He walked over top of her. She was screaming. He shot her in both of her elbows, and since she was on her stomach, the back of her legs and then her back. She was still screaming, but the screams did not come out with a sound. The gunmen could have killed her, but he did not. Instead he walked back over to the van, got inside, and it pulled off.

Albert Wagner's wife opened the restaurant every single morning like clock work. Then a shift of waiters, waitresses, bus people, and chef's would come to the restaurant to prepare for lunch. It did not have to open for lunch because it never made money during the lunch hours. It made all it's money dinner time.

Mrs. Wagner usually let one of her grandson drive her to the restaurant. Occasionally one of them had to attend a college class, and she would drive over to the restaurant by herself. When she pulled up to the restaurant she noticed the two commercial vans pull up behind her, but that was not unusual. It could be delivery vans, or anything.

She parked her car and stepped out. Three men jumped out of each van. They were all carrying bats, and they walked directly over to her.

She turned around to question them, and one of them

swung a bat hitting her directly in the mouth. A large amount of blood burst out of her mouth after the bat hit her. She fell to the ground, and the man hit her in her head twice. Then he pulled out a gun and shot her in her face. The impact from the bullet made her appear to jump and raise her hands in a grabbing motion. The gunman jumped back into the vans and pulled away.

Mrs Wagner and Mrs. Stewart had both refused protective custody because they did not want to see their husbands businesses go down the drain, and they did not want to leave the area's they had spent most of their lives in.

The shootings would not hit the news until twelve o'clock, but the news got to the witnesses, the defendants and the authorities. This was the most serious message that the defendants could have sent the witnesses. Anyone who betrayed the family from this point on was going to have to pay.

Kennedy was sitting in his office buried in his work. His door flew open, and his secretary marched in. She was followed by Agent Windsor and a couple of his men. Kennedy could tell by his expression something terrible was wrong.

"Did you hear about the two shootings this morning yet?" Agent Windsor asked.

"No." Kennedy replied.

"Stewart's daughter and Wagner's wife were both shot this morning at about the same time."

"I thought we had them under guarded protection?"

"We did. Twenty-four hour house protection. If they went to work someone escorted them to work, and then left. We assumed they were pretty much safe. Your witnesses said they never made a move against a snitch's family before."

"Yeah, but there's always a first time for everything. What's their medical conditions?"

"Stewart daughter's in critical condition, and Wagner's wife is in critical condition, but she went to the hospital brain dead. She's living off of life support system, and as soon as they take her off of it. She's history."

"I want you to get Stewart and Wagner's family, and put them both in protective custody."

The Secret Society

"Too late. I already did it. I even looked in the phone book, and put every fucking body with the last name of Stewart and Wagner in protective custody. If I saw a bum on the street I asked him his name, and if he said Wagner or Stewart. Get his ass protective custody." Windsor was famous for telling a joke, but it always seemed like the wrong time.

Kennedy's secretary burst back threw the door. "Excuse me, sir, but you have several news agency on the line requesting interviews."

"Tell them no fucking interviews until after the trial."

Kennedy must have been upset his secretary thought because this was the first time that she had heard him use a curse word.

"You got that list of everybody that's been visiting these assholes?" Agent Windsor asked.

"Yeah ."

"Well give it here because I'm going to pick these dirty mother fuckers up."

At one point during the case Albert had laughed at the defendants for being so stupid not to flip over and agree to testify. But once he got the news on his wife the feelings that he had buried deep inside came out. Why was he so foolish and stupid. He called to his daughter's house, and she hung up on him crying. She called him a coward. The only thing that the agents told him was that his wife was in critical condition, but he had a feeling she was worst off than that.

Andrew Stewart and half a dozen federal officers were sitting in the prison reception hall. It was the same place that lawyers would come and visit their clients. Andrew had been sitting in a private room watching television when he saw the news. It took him a little while to figure it out, but he did. He was sitting in the hall in his pajamas smoking cigarettes, one of the luxuries of having money while you were incarcerated. Being incarcerated did not bother him. What bothered him was the fact that they were trying to give him life. He was sixty years old, and he could not see spending the rest of his life rotting away in jail. But after finding out that somebody pumped all those holes in his little girl, and that Big Al's wife might be dead his concept changed. He was a coward to switching on his friends. He even laughed while he was destroying them. Now they had paid him back. But the payback that they were giving him was a million times worst.

"Listen, I'm not testifying. I want my lawyer back, and I want to retract every single statement that I made. You guys don't have to give me shit. I can handle this shit. Just leave me the fuck alone."

Andrew was sitting around smoking on cigarettes. He had made up his mind as soon as he heard that his daughter was in critical condition.

"Look I was going to work with ya'll, but ya'll can't even fucking protect my family. I'm not going to jeopardize my family for freedom. Fuck that, I knew what I was doing when I was out there, and I'm willing to accept the consequences. My kids ain't never done anything to anybody. In fact you can take me back to my cell at e-pod." E-Pod was the holding cell that he was in before he decided to become a witness and help the government. If they sent him back there then somebody would kill him.

Agent Windsor never really got to speak with him much. Only when he was being interviewed, and then Kennedy, or one of the prosecution team would handle that.

"Look man. Those men don't give a fuck about you. The same mother fuckers you're refusing to testify against are the same people that tried to put a bullet in your daughters head. They don't give a flying fuck about you, or your family. You call this shit honor. This shit is not honor. They're pieces of shit, and if they could, they would kill you."

The words were powerful, but instead of having the affect on Andrew that Windsor thought they would have, they had the opposite. He really felt like a traitor now. He was a coward. The family had stuck together. But he thought he was doing the wise thing. To save his own life he looked at their lives like one big joke, and they reminded him that they were as frighten as he was, and that life was not a big joke. Especially, the life of a gangster. A real gangster that lived and breathed the life.

"It don't matter. I ain't really got anything more to say."

Kennedy walked over and bend down. He placed his hands on Stewart's knee's. "You have a cross examination. We don't want you going around switching testimony. You have come to far for this."

"You know what Kennedy. You mother fuckers really used me like a whore. I wonder how it would feel if you went home today, and something was wrong with your little girl. I don't want you mother fuckers up in my face no more. Protect my family, or I'll switch this shit so much that the juror's will have to acquit."

Agent Windsor was about to comment, and Kennedy jumped up and stopped him. Kennedy placed his finger to the agents mouth.

"Please later."

Judge Erminio Sikora was sitting in his chambers. He was a handsome looking man of Greek descent. He had smooth skin, but the brown spots of age had slowly started covering it. He had long thin hair, but it was not thin enough to look funny or anything. He parted it, and wore it long on the side. He had beautiful teeth, and he took excellent care of himself. His mind was over worked, but not his body. The signs of wealth. He had small spectacles he used strictly for reading documents pertaining to cases, and trials.

Kennedy, the assistant prosecutor, Lehman, and Craft the defense attorney's were sitting in the judge's room. The shooting had disrupted the case, and the prosecution requested a conference.

"Your Honor, I don't think that the witnesses will be able to finish the trial. He's acting like the shootings have prejudice his testimony, or intimidated him a little bit."

Lehman interrupted him. "Excuse me, your Honor, and I mean no disrespect, but why is the witness acting so erratically when it's defenses time from cross examination? This is ridiculously absurd. If we recess for too long. My clients constitutional rights of a speedy trial have been violated. This trial is reaching a year. Every body involved has lost something because of it."

"So what do you suggest?" The judge asked.

"Your Honor, we can not hold the trial up for nothing. I

suggest that the defense interview the witness in front of a judge, and then prosecution can interview. It does not matter who goes first as long as he's interviewed. His daughter may never get better. What are we going to do wait for recovery?"

The judge was listening intently. "Okay. I can agree with that. Let's set up an interview, and see if he's ready for cross examination. If not, we recess for a week, but no longer. I will grant the witness another interview after that, but that's it, and if he's not suitable then we recess for two days and resume trial."

They all stood, and one by one thanked the judge. "Thank you, your Honor."

TWENTY-EIGHT

First, the prosecution interviewed Andrew Stewart and then a psychiatrist paid for by the state. Then the defense interviewed him, and had a private psychiatrist interview him. All of this was done in front of a judge. Every side came to the conclusion that he was more than able to continue testimony.

Court resumed on the first working day. Andrew Stewart walked out of the back of the holding cell dress in a even better suit. He looked rested despite the fact that his daughter was sitting in a hospital somewhere with a bunch of bullets hole in her. He did not get the correct news until he was allowed to see his wife. The feds had let him talk to her several times, but this was the first time that they let her come, and have a contact visit.

Stewart and his wife were sitting in a room surrounded by a bunch of federal agents.

"How is she?"

"Andrew she's fine." His wife was the only one that called him by his full name. "The doctors said who ever shot her was not trying to kill her. Maybe cripple her for life. The worst injuries were the two shots in the back of the knee caps. The doctors said the shooters were trying to give a message."

"Louise I made a lot of mistakes. I should have not testified against these men. I don't know what I'm going to do now, but just stay strong and tell everyone that I love them."

They talked, hugged, and caressed for the last couple hours of the visit. All that time being away from his family was finally catching up with him.

When Andrew walked to the witness stand he avoided eye contact with the defendants. He took his seat, and the sheriffs swore him in.

Lehman the head attorney for the defense was going to lead cross examination. He was the attorney receiving all of the glory. His face was in the papers. his former cases were in the paper. The ones that were won, and the ones that were lost. The defense team became like one big family. This case had consumed their lives. Private and personal. They even started visiting each other's homes during recess.

Lehman had almost been paid a million dollars already for his representation. Lehman walked over to the chart and picked up the pointer stick.

"Mr. Andrew Stewart you say that you belong to an organization. An organization that the defendant William Johnson claimed did not exist. Did the prosecutors read federal laws to you that explain in detail what they consider a organization? Do you in your own mind considered these men part of an organization?"

Andrew sucked all the words in. "No, I said we were an organization because we were."

"Mr Stewart have you ever conducted illegal business with Thomas McCant?"

"Yes, he has given me orders from Mr. Johnson."

"How do you know that the order was from Mr. Johnson?"

"Because he told me so."

"Well that's hearsay."

"Objection, your Honor. Defense is leading the witness."

"Objection over ruled. Defense may continue but with more direct questions."

Kennedy smiled. "Thank you, your Honor."

"Mr. Stewart have you ever done business with Aaron Gaston, his son, or Crazy Moe."

"No."

"What about Jeremiah Lewis, Ray Guns, or Kenneth Campbell? Have you ever committed a crime with them?"

"No. But I have committed crimes for them under the command of William Johnson."

"Who gave you those commands?" Lehman asked.

"Big Will, Harry, or Tommy Can."

"So if you got your orders from these men how are you testifying about homicides that you did not participate in? Did William Johnson ever come to you, and tell you I had this person killed today, and so and so did it?"

"No."

"Then it would be fair to say that you have testified about crimes you did not commit. The only information that you had was hearsay. The words of other men." He continued.

"Mr. Stewart do you think that it's possible that you might have killed someone that lived in North Philadelphia, and the killing not be for Crazy Ed, the lieutenant that this chart claims controlled the other half of North Philadelphia?"

"Yes, that could be possible."

"Mr. Stewart have you ever met Corty Taylor, or Martin Callahan?"

"I met them a couple of times when I went to Atlantic City to gamble."

"Did you ever conduct business with them?"

"No."

"Do you know them personally?"

"Did the police give you information that you did not know, but added into your testimony?"

"Yes."

"Mr. Stewart you testified that Theodore Quinn ordered the hit on William Johnson and Harry Clark. Who were the gunmen?"

"I can't honestly remember who Black said did it. I don't know."

Kennedy was upset. Andrew was changing his testimony just enough to put doubt in the juror's mind.

"Mr. Stewart, describe your business relationship with Theodore Quinn."

"We really did not have a long relationship. He ran numbers for me, and sold some drugs for me. I can't remember a lot."

Kennedy was so upset he was about to cry.

"Mr. Stewart I believe you have testified about crimes you did not commit, or had no first hand knowledge of. Is that true?"

"You can say that."

"Thank you, defense rests it's case, unless prosecution has more witnesses. Thank you."

Cross examination was that simple and quick.

The judge spoke. "Court will be in recess for a week so that defense and the prosecution may present their closing arguments."

TWENTY-NINE

Corty Taylor's lawyer Daniel Craft arranged the meeting. He came with Louis Alderman, Alexander Dunbar, Travis Hopkins, and Warren Pickerson. He got them into the lawyer client room of the federal facility by saying that Louis was his assistant attorney, Alexander was his secretary, Travis was his para-legal, and Warren was his assistant para-legal. If the authorities found out he lied they could arrest him for adding a criminal organization. They would never really find out though. Especially with the fake identification. The family paid him fifty thousand dollars to arranged the visit.

It took a little over an hour for Corty to come down to the visit because when they came to visit it was dinner time. He had to finish his food then come to his visit.

Corty came down, and whenever he came down he came shackled in handcuffs. The guards sat him in a chair, and then they left.

"Danny could you move your chair over there. I have to speak to these men in private."

"You better whisper because this room might be bugged."

Corty was sitting across from them at the table. He did not

really know them like he knew the lieutenants that were under him. It felt a little strange giving them commands, when he knew that because they did not know him personally that they resented him giving them commands.

"I don't know what the verdicts going to be, and I have no idea, but I have talked with the other people." He was talking about the lieutenants incarcerated with him. "And all of you have our blessing to operate the family in our name. If we get convicted them, we have a lot of legal opportunities that we can offer you. If we don't get convicted, then were expecting to come home to the same positions that we held previously. But if we are convicted then we will officially retire. Every single one of us no matter how small the time. If we retire the only thing will be expected to do is handle the family legal businesses. If were not convicted when we come home, and resume our old positions every single one of you will get something special, and we'll iron out all of the ruff edges in a business meeting at one of our houses."

Alexander was not going to say anything, but he had too. "We've been thinking about it, and if you guys don't make it home we were going to all break up and do our own thing."

Corty smiled his famous smile. It felt good conducting business. He knew in his heart it might be his last time. "I don't know. That will have to be something that you guys handle when the time comes. I think it would be better if you guys did stick together,"

"The longer we stick together the easier it will be for the police to catch us,"

"Not if you conduct business right. You just have to lay low."

"On behalf of the entire family. We truly appreciate your loyalty, and if something happens to us will make sure you have all of the connections you need."

The meeting was over.

Alexander Dunbar, Louis Alderman, Travis Hopkins, and Warren Pickerson were sitting in a restaurant in Center City Philadelphia. They had driven up in separate cars. They knew that it was not safe to talk in the car especially when the feds were breaking into them bugging them.

"This is no disrespect. This is only business. When they come home if you think that we're going to make it we're going to have to bump Corty off, and force the other lieutenants to retire. Corty's worth millions that greedy bastard. If they get acquitted the feds are going to be on us so bad we won't be able to take a shit without them knowing. But I'm not going to fight them if we don't stick together. I don't want to move under these mother fuckers, and get one hundred years for nothing."

Travis just sighed he was caught between a rock and a hard place.

"I don't know. I would have to think about it."

"Well, you better hurry the fuck up, because these mother fuckers could be coming home right after the verdicts read, and I'm not waiting a couple of months to knock one of them off after he comes home. We give them a month, and they'll have a loyalty base. If we knock them off as soon as they come home, they're weak."

"What about the feds?"

"Fuck them. Will just bury the bodies. That's it."

"Where going to get hot if they disappear." Warren added in.

"Your right, but where going to jail if we don't." The waitress came and delivered their food the meeting was over.

Court resumed the next day. The prosecution were going to have to present their closing arguments first, Kennedy was upset, but the decision was at the discretion of the judge. They flipped a coin, and Kennedy lost. When ever the prosecution had to present the closing argument, first it could mean bad luck. Especially when you had a defense team like the one the defendants had. By him presenting his closing arguments first the defense had the opportunity to base their entire closing arguments on opposing his, and what was planted in the juror's head last was extremely important.

Kennedy walked directly in front the jury's box. "Ladies, and gentlemen of the jury. Please do not let the trickery that the defense has bought into this case confuse you." Prosecution and defense loved closing arguments because they could not be interrupted. "These men sitting in this court room are the very reason that American society is being destroyed. They have flooded the streets of Pennsylvania, and New Jersey with narcotics. They have murdered to protect their business interest. They kill children. They kill witnesses. They are ruthless, and for several years they have hidden their identity behind successful businesses. The only reason their businesses even flourish is because of the evilness they commit on the streets. When you leave here, read the papers. Watch the news, and you will see that you have help change America for the better. This is the future of organize crime. No longer will it be numbers running. Gambling and loan sharking. Now it's drugs, drugs and more drugs. Death, violence, and more death. Ladies, and gentlemen of the jury, if you stop these men right here today you will be saving a lot of innocent peoples lives. It has not been proven yet, but it will be. These men still commit murders. They still cause hell on the streets of Philadelphia, and New Jersey without even being there, and it is up to us to stop them. If you do not stop them for me. Stop them for the crack addict mothers that need help with stopping there addiction. Stop them for the homeless children that are homeless because their parents refuse to stop abusing drugs. Please. Stop this madness."

Before Kennedy could even take a seat. Lehman was on his feet.

"Ladies and gentlemen of the jury, I know that you are tired. You have been sitting here for a couple of days short of a year, and a lot has changed in a year. The state of Pennsylvania has charged the defendants with crimes that they did not commit. They've been looking for another group of people to charge with the R.I.C.O stature every since they arrested the Italian Mafia, but believe me ladies and gentlemen. This is not an organization. Some of these men have committed crimes, and they have actually admitted it. But not all of the crimes that the government has accused them of. They have presented witnesses that do nothing but contradict themselves. They present you with witnesses that openly admit that they know nothing about half of the charges. The group that is suppose to control New Jersey for this organization is not even connected to it. That comes out of the mouth of every single witness. This case is a travesty of justice. You must acquit. There have been thousands of people that have falsely been accused of crimes they did not commit. Please don't let the government convince you into sending innocent people to jail."

Both of their closing arguments were short, but very effective. Short, but to the point.

The jury went into deliberations. After they could not come up with a verdict within a decent amount of time. The judge recessed the case until the next morning.

THIRTY

Travis Hopkins purchased a house in Vineland, New Jersey. He liked the area because it was quiet and still undeveloped. He could not live in the city. It would be to easy for the police to surveillance him. Instead he moved to an exclusive area in Vineland. He Purchased a quarter million dollar house, and built an office on his property for his real-estate company.

Happy Realty and Construction Company. He had to placed a large security fence around his house just in case someone wanted to harm him and his family. The area was so spread out that by the time the police would have gotten to his house he would have been dead.

Travis woke up at six o'clock in the morning. He made the necessary phone calls. Then he woke his wife, and she made him breakfast. The first person to come over was his bodyguards.

Today was the big day. They had to go to the court room and see if Corty, and the rest of the lieutenants would be acquitted or not.

Travis's wife finished cooking breakfast then she, and the kids left. They were headed to her mother's house.

Alexander and one of his bodyguards pulled up to the security gate. The bodyguard that was covering the gate let them in. Alexander was driving a brand new metallic gray Lexus GS 300. He had just bought recently off of a show room floor. It was one of his many cars.

The next person to pull up was Louis Alderman. He drove a 740i BMW Gray fully loaded with white leather interior. When he pulled up the bodyguard opened the security gate for him, and told him.

"The boss wants you to park your cars in the garage so that Warren can fit his car in the gate.

Warren pulled up a couple of minutes later. He was driving a white Q45. He jumped out of the car with his bodyguard, and they ran into the house threw the front door. When they got to the entrance they were greeted by a bodyguard. The bodyguard frisked them for weapons, and they were surprised. The same thing happen to Louie when he came threw the garage.

The bodyguard led them all to the kitchen. Travis was sitting there playing cards with one of the bodyguards. As soon as the others entered the kitchen, the bodyguard got up and left.

"I did not mean any harm when I had you frisked at the door. It's only a safely precaution. It took me a little while to make my decision, but I did. Were going to get rid of Corty and the others. Now I don't need any help, everything has already been arranged. The only thing I need is for you guys to lay low. If you do not agree with what I'm doing, when you leave my house, jump in your car, and never come back. If you do agree meet me at my house after our court appearance."

All of them except Alexander Dunbar were shocked.

"Louis what's your answer going to be?"

"Trey I'm with what ever you want to do. Your the boss."

Everyone looked over towards Warren. "Trey you know I'm down with the family all you have to do is give the word, and it's done."

"Good, that's all I want to hear. That I have your support."

One of the bodyguards knocked on the kitchen frame. There was no door there. Just the entrance to the kitchen.

"Excuse me, boss, but you said let you know when it's eight o'clock. It's eight o'clock."

Travis looked at his watch. "Okay we have to get the hell out of here and pick those pussies up. Later tonight after the party we'll have another meeting."

They all got up and went into the garage to start their cars up.

Travis drove a black exterior, black leather interior LS 400 Lexus sedan. He went into the garage, and his car was parked.

"Dunbar. I'm going to drive with you. James. Take my car, and follow us."

The bodyguard got in car and warmed it up. Dunbar, and Travis jumped in the back. One of Travis bodyguards burst threw the garage door. The door that lead to the house.

"Trey, telephone. It's Mike from the court house."

"Shit." Travis jumped out the back seat, and ran in the house to use the phone. After he finished using the phone he returned.

He walked up to Durbar's Lexus. He had rolled the back window down when he got out of the car. He stuck his hand threw the window. He was carrying his gun with the silencer. He pulled the trigger, and the first bullet caught Dunbar in the face. His body started shaking he needed another hit. Not yet. Travis turned the gun on the bodyguard who had just realized what was going on. Travis shot him in the back of the head. his blood painted the front window. Then Travis turned back to Dunbar, and emptied the clip in his face. Now, Corty and the rest of the family could come home safely it they were released.

THIRTY-ONE

Travis, Louis, and Warren arrived at the court room at nine thirty, and by the time that they got there, there was standing room only.

The honorable Judge Erminio Sikora came out, and the entire court room stood. Then the jury came out and took their seats.

A bailiff came out walked over to the jury, and the jury

handed him a piece of paper. The judge took the piece of paper. He placed his glasses on. After he finished reading it he looked at the head juror, and told her. "Mrs. Riddick I'm going to read the list of names of the defendants in the order that you have received them. I need you know whether the juror finds that particular defendant guilty or not."

"The defendant William Johnson,"

"Guilty." The court room was so quiet that it seemed like the words echo. As soon as she heard the verdict William's wife burst out in tears. She started crying hysterically and had to be escorted out of the court room.

"Jeremiah Lewis."

" Guilty."

"Clifford Jones."

"Guilty."

"Theodore Quinn."

"Guilty."

"Percy Hall."

"Guilty."

"Kenneth Campbell."

"Guilty."

"Archie Moore."

"Guilty."

"Thomas McCant."

"Guilty."

"Leroy Booth."

"Guilty."

"Earl Gilbertson."

"Guilty."

The court room was still silent. There were a couple people talking. Mainly the defendants family members who were attending the trial, and surprised over the verdict.

"Martin Callahan."

"Not guilty."

"Cortney Taylor."

"Not guilty."

"Corey Crammer."

"Not Guilty."

"Leonard Rilley."

"Not guilty."

"Marcellus Jordon."

"Not guilty."

"Robert Stuart."

"Not guilty."

"Henry Williams."

"Not guilty."

The crowd in the court room burst into cheers. The cheers were so loud that the judge had to hit the mallet to quiet the court room.

Corty stood up embracing Black and William Johnson. He had every intention of keeping his promises.

Everyone found innocent was immediately released.

Corty still had property left in his cell. He just left it there. He could buy what ever he needed. He was free.

When Corty and the defendants that were found not guilty were released they were let out the front of the building like all of the other people that attended the trial, and a group of reporters attacked them.

Travis and several soldiers were Corty's personal bodyguard. They shielded him from the reporters as he walked to the car. All of the other defendants had bodyguards to protect them. They were attacked by the reporters, as well.

It was only an hour ride from Philadelphia to Atlantic City. First the defendants went to a small restaurant to have lunch and discuss a little business. After the late lunch they drove home to Atlantic City.

Corty's house was located in Pomona, New Jersey. It was a city located about fifteen miles outside of Atlantic City.

When the bodyguard pulled up to the house they were met by bodyguards. Their were about twenty cars parked in the area. Even Corty's neighbors came to his coming home party. When Corty and the rest of the defendants walked threw his door. They were greeted by a surprise party.

Travis was following him every where he went. He turned

back to him. "Get the lieutenants, we might as well have the meeting first. Get it over with. I don't want to be disturb after I start celebrating with my family."

"Are you safe?"

Corty smiled. "I don't think that anybody is going to hurt me in my house in front of all these people. If I'm not safe here I'm not safe anywhere. Relax you did good."

Corty patted Travis on his shoulders.

"Where are you going to hold the meeting?"

"In the business office. Did you have it swept for bugs?"

"Of course." Travis walked away.

Corty walked into his business office, moved over to the bar, and then he took a seat. A few minutes later Martin, Corey, Lyn, Marc, Robert, Henry, Louis, Warren, Travis, Gregory walked in with three other men. They were lieutenants still loyal to the Philadelphia organization.

"First thing I want to offer is my congratulations." There was a tray filled with glasses of champagne.

"A toast. To the family." They raised their glasses.

Repeated the words, and clashed them together.

"I hate to come home and go straight to business, but that is this life. Certain things must be handled immediately. A lot of things we will have to go over at another time."

"Gregory. Thank you for everything. If there is anything you and your family need. Anything. You come to me personally, if I can offer assistance. Anything. I know I don't have to mention you're more than welcome to join my family."

Gregory was touched. He stood up. Walked over and embraced Corty. The men in the room clapped.

"We'll talk about it later."

"You see the things that happen in these months, and you see the things that happen to the ones that snitch. It's official. Once a person snitches he is considered a traitor, and a enemy. His family is to be dealt with accordingly."

Deep down inside Corty did not agree with that, but after being on trial and seeing his life in jeopardy he agreed with hurting a snitches family.

"There is too much business to cover at a time like this. Martin will get with each one of you personally and arrange a personal business meeting. That's it. I'm going out there to join my family."

Without a word being said, and before he could stand they all surrounded him. Martin walked over to him, grabbed his hand and kissed it.

"I pledge undying loyalty."

Every single one of them line up and followed suit.

Corty did not leave the house until it was time to attend Alexander Durbar's funeral. He sat in his house the night he came home and watched all of the television special the news papers were running on his organization.

He was also straightening out family business on the streets, and preparing to defend his construction company against the charges it faced at the Casino Control Commission. When he thought about it none of it mattered. He was almost a billionaire. If they would not have locked him up he would have been one.

After he handled his business here he was going to fly to Trinidad. Gad came home the year he was on trial, and Naptali his younger brother got caught up in a federal case in New York.

Things were changing again. Alexander Durbar's funeral was at twelve o' clock in the afternoon. Corty would be riding with two bodyguards.

He attended the funeral, and all of the lieutenants were there. Even Travis the knew lieutenant. Then after the funeral they drove over to the grave site. The same grave site that Big Aaron, Little Aaron, and Christopher were buried in. It felt strange thinking about Christopher. It seemed like he had been dead for centuries. Corty felt a little sad when he arrived. He was thinking that maybe Christopher was cold and sad in the grave.

Corty had four half a dozen rose bouquets in his hand. While the Reverend was saying the last words over Alexander Dunbar's grave he walked over to Big Aaron, and little Aaron's grave. He sat the roses on their graves.

Then he walked to Christopher's grave. The wind was

blowing strongly. So strongly he pulled his coat together.

He bent closer to his grave. "Rest in peace, my brother, rest in peace." The two bodyguards that he was with followed him everywhere he went. Corty looked up and he saw the under covers parked in the unmarked car taking pictures. It looked like the officer that Corey use to pay. The department must have promoted him.